In Praise of Robert Carr

Advance Praise for A Question of Return:

"In *A Question of Return*, Robert Carr interweaves the dark forces of Stalinist Russia with the light of contemporary Canada. Naturally, the two narratives meet as they should and must, the former casting its long shadow over the latter. But these histories are personal too. When Russian émigré Art Laukhin falls for the incurably western Audrey Millay, the darkness of their own lives and memories casts a pall over what might have been a great romance. *A Question of Return* is a profound, rich, layered and compelling story, a must read."

> – Joseph Kertes, award-winning author of
> *Gratitude* and *The Afterlife of Stars*

"[It's] been my pleasure reading and re-reading it over the past months ... A terrific, compelling story ... No matter where you end up you never really escape Russia ... Not a mystery novel per se, but it manages to carry a sense of mystery over more than a hundred thousand words, and that is called Art."

> – Ken Alexander, freelance editor and
> former editor of *The Walrus*

Praise for Robert Carr's debut novel Continuums:

"In ten opening pages of concise and subtly suspenseful exposition, Robert Carr's debut novel pulls us deeply into the world of a Jewish woman in communist Romania....A closing chapter, even a closing sentence, can make or break a book, dissipating its promise or gathering its themes into a knockout punch. Robert Carr's uncompromising final punch fully honours the dilemmas of his characters, their deep regrets, their fragile hopes."

> – Jim Bartley, *Globe & Mail*

"From my perspective, this book deserves a lot of credit for presenting such a realistic and undiluted representation of the world of research mathematics. More importantly, from a literary perspective, it does a fantastic job of setting up a scenario in which the reader can explore some deep philosophical questions about the human condition."

– Alex Kasman, Department of Mathematics,
College of Charleston in Mathematical Fiction blog

"In this remarkable first novel, Robert Carr asks age-old questions about the heart in conflict with itself: how do we choose between our life's work and the needs of loved ones? Carr manages ddeftly to draw us into his characters' lives, such that by turns, we agonize and rejoice with them, particularly with Aroso, the outgoing genius, and Alexandra, the incoming one. An extraordinary debut! One can only wonder why Carr didn't come to this art sooner. It's where he belongs."

- Joseph Kertes

A Question
of Return

Library and Archives Canada Cataloguing in Publication

Carr, Robert, 1945-, author
    A question of return / Robert Carr.

Issued in print and electronic formats.

ISBN 978-1-77161-147-3 (paperback).--ISBN 978-1-77161-148-0 (html).--
ISBN 978-1-77161-149-7 (pdf)

    I. Title.

PS8605.A773Q83 2015   C813'.6   C2015-906897-5
                                                   C2015-906898-3

Pubished by Mosaic Press, Oakville, Ontario, Canada, 2015.
Distributed in the United States by Bookmasters (www.bookmasters.com).
Distributed in the U.K. by Roundhouse Group (https://www.roundhousegroup.co.uk).

MOSAIC PRESS, Publishers
Copyright © 2015 Robert Carr

Printed and Bound in Canada.
Design and layout by Eric Normann
Cover art by Andelid © 2015

We acknowledge the Ontario Media Development Corporation for their support of
our publishing program

We acknowledge the Ontario Arts Council for their support of our publishing program

ONTARIO ARTS COUNCIL
CONSEIL DES ARTS DE L'ONTARIO
an Ontario government agency
un organisme du gouvernement de l'Ontario

We acknowledge the financial support   Nous reconnaissons l'aide financière du
of the Government of Canada through   gouvernement du Canada par l'entrem-
the Canada Book Fund (CBF) for   ise du Fonds du livre du Canada (FLC)
this project.   pour ce projet.

 Canadian   Patrimoine   Canadä
                     Heritage   canadien

MOSAIC PRESS
1252 Speers Road, Units 1 & 2
Oakville, Ontario L6L 5N9
phone: (905) 825-2130

info@mosaic-press.com

www.mosaic-press.com

A Question of Return

ROBERT CARR

mosaicPRESS

Other Works By Robert Carr:

Books
    Continuums (Mosaic Press, 2008)

Anthologies
    TOK Volume 1: Writing the New Toronto (Zephyr Press, 2006)

"Granny, this small room fills me with fear. All
I realy want is to fall on your shoulder and
cry with you. Remember: there is only murder in this world.
Suicide has no existence here."

> – Yevgeny Yevtushenko
> From the poem "Yelabuga Nail,"
> translated by Elaine Feinstein

1

"*H*ere I am unnecessary. *There* I am impossible." In Paris at the time, and apprehensive about a return to the Soviet Union, Tsevtayeva wrote these words in a letter to one of her friends. She fretted and delayed, but she did return in 1939. Within two years, she was dead.

Laukhin was picked up last, and in the short drive to the Bakers' house Tsvetayeva's pithy prophecy came back to him. It was in his mind when he awoke that morning, and it stayed with him throughout the day. True, on Friday Laukhin had seen Ben with a collection of her letters under his arm, yet why these two sentences? And why now? Seven years earlier, almost four decades after Tsvetayeva's, he'd made the opposite—westward—journey. Although he had become impossible *there*, in the Soviet Union (he had that in common with the poetess), he was not unnecessary *here*. Not because of his poetry, no, there had been too many dry years already, but because of what he'd promised the day he learned of his father's sentence. He'd gone along with him, of course, and remembered the cold November wind and his father's worried face. Statistically, his father was told in the poorly lit whitewashed room, he had three more years to live, and the last one would be difficult. The doctor was a tall thin Jew who, Laukhin learned later, had been imprisoned and tortured just before

Stalin's death. In a neutral voice, he granted a small likelihood of more than three years, even of a miraculous remission. He talked with an otherworldly detachment, as if he were already in the realm beyond and was offering his father several conceivable timetables that would possibly get him there. He went into details about chemotherapy, radiation, and surgery, which he didn't advise because of the location (assumed, they weren't entirely sure) of the brain tumor. On the metro ride back his father tried to appear cheerful. "I'm growing fond of statistics," he said. "With luck I could hope for five more years. Or ten, at lottery odds." When they climbed back to the ground level he told him about the journal he'd kept for so many years. Laukhin was stunned—how could he hide it from them for so long? Near their building, leaning pale and unshaven on his arm, his father began to swear. "Fuck Oleg, Tyoma, fuck Oleg Vinograd. The million and a half words I wrote about him are not worth one page of my journal. You must publish the journal, Tyoma, you must see to it. Promise me. Fuck Oleg Vinograd, Tyoma, fuck him."

He heard Helen say she'd park in the street. It was an evening in support of Soviet dissident poets and writers, or something like that, and Laukhin had brought along his students to lessen the pain. The fancy envelope had arrived through the dean's office, but the card inside had not been very clear, and he forgot about it until the dean reminded him that he could turn down any invitation except those from the Bakers. Most of Laukhin's chair—at least three of its legs, the dean liked a laugh—was their endowment.

The column-fronted house on Bridle Path was huge—a scaled-down, scrubbed, floodlit Union Station. The entrance hall was vast and circular, and its several statues, patterned marble floor and cloakroom gave it the look of an antiquated theatre foyer recently renovated. At the donation desk, strategically placed near the cloakroom, two young women beamed at Laukhin's small group as he removed an envelope from his breast pocket and dropped it in the large glass bowl. Ben and Paul watched him with smirks on their faces. He shrugged and said, "Back to where it came from."

Briefly blocked by a devotee who seemed to have met him before, he caught up with the others in time to hear Helen cry, "Merciful God, who are these people?"

"I think they are *zeks*," Ben said.

"*Zeks? Zeks* serving canapés?"

"An order is an order."

Grunting, a *zek* thrust a large tray at them.

Paul speared a glistening slice. "Yes, I'll have some herring."

"I don't know. What's this?" asked Helen.

"It's *seeniye*," Laukhin said. "Caviar for the working class. Try it. It's made of eggplant."

"And this?"

"Veal tongue and pickles. I think."

"Oh, I'm not sure ... Did you say tongue?"

"Now this, friends, is the real thing. Buckwheat *blinis* and caviar. Mmmm..."

"These little things?"

"Is this what they serve at the camp commander's soirées?" Paul asked.

"*Zeks* wear grey cotton-padded jackets, that's the Gulag fashion. These fellows are in nightgowns, burlap nightgowns."

"Look, stitched numbers, and buzz cuts too. All very *zek*-ish."

Laukhin said, "Ben, Paul, stop playing stupid. Now, where are the drinks?"

"I can see the bar. Artyom Pavlovich, follow me."

Artyom Pavlovich. Well, if it made them happy. It had been at least a year since his students began to use his patronymic—he couldn't remember who first addressed him that way—but he still cringed whenever he heard it. Colson Emslie was certain it was the pronunciation that offended him. "Get over it, Art," he said. "What do you want them to call you? It shows their affection and respect. I wish I had a patronymic."

They were late. Smiling broadly, Galya Baker approached them dressed in glinting black. Laukhin wondered if people smiled more with the onset of middle age. Women on this continent certainly did, and Galya did a fair imitation of a jovial North American. Her round face and spiky blonde hair made her look like a child's joyful sun. She hugged him, and began to speak quickly and with a harsh Russian accent. They were delighted he could make it. Art Laukhin's name and support meant so much to them and their cause. Could they count on a few words from him? Or, even better, one of his wonderful poems, a brief one, of course. A few stanzas? Perhaps from *Sunless Seasons*. Would he? Splendid. She'd tell her husband—Ian had insisted on being the

3

MC—that the famous poet had arrived. Perhaps after Solzhenitsyn's letter, in about half-an-hour, while everybody was still sober.

She turned to his companions. "These must be your students. Helen Jeffreys? Dear Helen, it's you. I didn't … You look splendid. Oh, let me hug you too. I had no idea you were Art's pupil. Your husband must be very proud of you. I never know how to pronounce his name."

"Nobody knows, Galya. My mother-in-law doesn't either."

"Is he here?"

"He isn't. I came as a student. And a driver."

"I hope you don't mind I brought my students with me," Laukhin said. "These two are Ben Paskow and Paul Karman."

Sweeping Ben and Paul with her eyes, Galya Baker said, "Galyna Shukin-Baker. Galya, please. I'm so glad you could come." She laughed and moved away.

The crowd was confined to two large rooms connected by wall-to-wall folding, mullioned doors. Halls would be more appropriate, he thought looking above him at the high, *bleu-ciel* curved ceilings sparsely flecked with golden stars and conches. Paintings, some with heavy, gilded frames, were artfully positioned on walls which were a slightly darker shade of blue than the ceiling. Clusters of armchairs and sofas were paired with coffee tables and bulky pots of tropical plants. At the back of the farthest room a few wide steps rose to a marble-tiled platform that ended at a row of French windows. A simple lectern stood near the top of the stairs, a bit to the left.

The bar was in front of a gigantic fireplace, and the scowling, hirsute bartender, in white jacket and bow tie, looked like a civilized cave-dweller topping up his income. The crowd near the bar was dense.

Laukhin said, to no one in particular, "Did you hear? A letter from Solzhenitsyn will be read. A long sermon, no doubt. It should give me time to have a drink or two. I wonder if other versifiers are unpacking their hearts for the cause tonight."

An elderly woman in a dark blue dress, leaning on the arm of a teenager, pointed a bony forefinger at Laukhin's chest and said, in Russian, "Seven years you've been here, in Toronto. How much longer, young man? When will your father's journal finally be in bookstores?"

Had he met her before? He used to boast that he never forgot a face, but he wasn't that certain anymore. "Before the end of the year," he said. "The first volume only, of course. This time I promise."

4

"I knew your father, you know. I want to read it before I croak. Years of promises, that's all we've had from you."

She began to swear and the teenager pulled her away, horrified.

* * *

His third drink in hand, Laukhin hid behind the foliage of a potted plant. He needed to collect himself before the ordeal. He was at best an indifferent renderer of his own poetry, and rarely agreed now to read or recite. When he did, he often rushed, and then, suddenly aware of it, he would slow down, never quite achieving the right rhythm. It was always this jarring alternation between fast and slow, like traffic on a crowded highway. His heart wasn't in it and had not been for a long time. He didn't believe in poetry readings despite the great tradition they had back home. He had grown up with them, and had read his own poems aloud many times as a young man, but now thought such displays had no merit at all, unless the act itself was the message. That had been the only reason he'd recited his own poems in Mayakovsky Square, and under Pushkin's statue, and in Moscow's crowded clubs and apartments. He was young then, and animated by the sheer exhibitionism of it, by the excited eyes and (mostly) young faces staring at him in awe, and by the adrenalin that comes from courting danger. He had lost all that years ago.

Oh well, he had promised. He took another sip from his glass. He'd recite the four stanzas from *Sunless Seasons* in which he implores Mandelstam, Babel, Pilniak and Tsvetayeva to come back from wherever they were, however briefly, to tell everyone what happened to them. It wasn't the main work he was known for in the West, but Galya Baker had once told him, "I simply adore *Sunless Seasons*, Artyom Pavlovich. The grey reflection of life, the maddening lack of answers." He'd humour her. One should humour one's patrons. These stanzas at the beginning of the collection were the easiest to follow, anyway. He wondered how many at the Bakers' gathering spoke Russian. Judging by the crowd at the bar probably quite a few.

Most of the poems in *Sunless Seasons* were written before he turned twenty-six. He recalled doing the rounds of Moscow's literary magazines and publishing houses, manuscript under arm. No one wanted to or dared touch the collection. Not even *Novy Mir*. At the time,

Tvardovsky was both its chief and poetry editor. He remembered the big man, surrounded by cigarette smoke, staring at him with his blue bloodshot eyes, dismissing the beginning stanzas in a long tirade. "Tell us what? What do you expect those four to tell us besides what we already know? Two of them were shot, one died of a weak heart in a transit camp, the other hanged herself. There, the truth is known. What's with this need for gruesome, grisly details? Why brood on the past and the mistakes that were made. It's done, finished, enough. Don't help our enemies. Our fight is not easy, and you're adding grist to their mills. Yes, we had our storms, but it's time for some fair weather. The people are thirsty for it. You are a poet, focus on and paint the future." Laukhin couldn't believe his ears. Was this the publisher of *Ivan Denisovich* and *Matryona's Place*? As Laukhin stood up from the oval table to gather his manuscript, a young man said, "Trifonich, we might take another look. Maybe we could publish one or two less pessimistic poems." Had the overly familiar tone made Tvardovsky turn violet? He waved the young man off without even looking.

He left the manuscript with *Novy Mir*, but after hearing nothing from them for two months he took it back. The editor of *Moskva* published a few stanzas under the title *On the Riverboat*, and a few short poems were published elsewhere over the next couple of years, with no introduction or commentary, buried in the back pages. And so *Sunless Seasons* had an undignified, slow, official death. It had a good life in *samizdat*, though, and he recited its poems in smoky halls and apartments, and under statues, where he was never sure anyone could hear him. And it had a new birth in the West, starting with one poem in *Grani*, followed by the publication of the full collection by the YMCA Press in Paris. Tvardovsky had called it an "untidy heap of grimness" that day in his large office, with the editorial board around the oval table. Perhaps he was right, it was a heap—a jumble of untitled poems and lonely stanzas that evoked the eponymous feeling of cold, of grey rivers and skies, of lives without warmth being slowly squeezed away. But that was it, wasn't it, that was the way he'd begun to see his surroundings and the life in it. Maybe Tvardovsky was just being cautious, or reserving his strength and standing for what were, undoubtedly in his mind, more important battles. Yet, as he left the board meeting, Laukhin remembered Pasternak's words to his father. "Tvardovsky likes no living poet other than himself."

His father had briefly hoped that *Novy Mir*, by far his best prospect, would publish his journal. A censored version of it, of course, heavily pruned by himself to start with. But after a long evening with Ehrenburg during which he asked, obliquely, many questions, he realized that hardly anything would remain of it if he were to do what Eherenburg did in order to see his memoirs in print.

* * *

Somebody began to read Solzhenitsyn's letter and Laukhin knew that he was next. He stepped out from behind the potted plant. Everybody had moved closer to the platform to hear better. Not far from him Galya Baker was whispering in the ear of a particularly attractive woman. Mid thirties? Alluring. How had he missed her? A black pantsuit hugged her waist and hips. If this was a female tux, he was all for it. Without thinking, he took a few steps toward the two women. She had dark brown hair pulled back in a chignon. A strand fell delicately in front of her ear, and he wondered whether it had escaped or had been carefully placed there. Earrings that seemed vaguely Egyptian, not unlike her profile. Endless eyelashes. Her mouth half open.

He stepped back. He'd soon be asked to say his bit. Anyway, no more follies with young women at his age. Fifty! Well, not really, not even forty-nine yet. He shouldn't think of himself as being fifty, especially not while admiring younger women. Besides, she wasn't as young as mad Erika Belov-Wang who was probably still in her twenties. Good God, such recklessness. He should have sniffed something was up when she suggested that for the second day of his interview for the *Paris Review* they move to his office at Alumni Hall, so that she could better understand his working environment. He didn't get it even when she asked him, after they'd talked for two hours and as he was about to suggest a lunch break, to shut the door to his office because of the noise. It's true that he had ogled Erika Belov-Wang's legs, long and in long boots, and had speculated what lay farther up, but he didn't realize he'd have an answer so soon. By the time he shut the door and turned back, her boots and skirt were off, and her panties too, if she had been wearing any. He found himself looking at a skimpy, lacy garter-belt, stockings, and a small puff of pubic hair. She said she needed help undoing her belt. He lost it, and he shouldn't have. He couldn't lock the door because he had misplaced his key the previous week and had forgotten to ask for another. He pointed to the door and said, "The door isn't locked." But she had already turned away and was stepping past his desk. She was a thin young woman. Tightly fit just under her small waist, the black garter rode two unsettling white buttocks. A familiar witches brew. When he reached her, she pulled him down with her on the small carpet and whispered, "Even better."

Somebody came into the room while they were going at it. He heard a gasp of a sufficiently high pitch that it could have been a woman, although it was more likely a man. He had not heard the door open, but he heard it shut. That was a month ago and he hoped, even prayed, that the intruder had been Colson, whose office was next to his. Colson Emslie often came in without knocking.

He heard Ian Baker mention his name, there was clapping, and he made his way through the crowd to the platform.

* * *

In time the soirée lost its colour, and people's faces grew out of focus. The Bakers moved through the crowd with practiced ease. He was introduced to a genuine Russian prince—very old and wrinkled, barely breathing. A woman who seemed as ancient as the prince looked around and remarked, "Not enough frivolity and frippery here." Then, having forgotten who he was, she asked, "Are you with the KGB? No?" He had a long conversation with the very proud architect of the house and got a whole lecture about symmetry and the hierarchy of spaces. A welcome distraction from the polite nonsense about poetry and literature, but it was hard to get away from him.

Kate Emslie slid her arm under his and leaned on him. She had gained weight.

"A bit squiffy, Kate?" Laukhin asked.

"Squiffy?"

"Squiffy, squiffed. Happy with drink."

"Joan Geraldine taught you nothing worthwhile. Yes, squiffed I am. I better stop, I've got to drive Colson home."

Colson was talking to Ben. Ian Baker, separated from his wife, approached them with the woman Laukhin had admired earlier. He

8

had followed her with his eyes after he'd finished his reading. From her body language he surmised that she knew hardly anybody that evening and wondered how she had ended up there. He discerned, or thought he discerned, a flirtatious side to her, the way she moved, the way she tossed her head back with laughter, the way she touched her hair. He felt melancholic and offended—his youth had passed.

"Take your eyes off that shapely young woman," Kate said.

"It's that body-molding tux."

"Art, it's not a tux."

"Let's join them."

He pulled Kate along. Ian made the introductions. Her name was Audrey Millay. Laukhin asked her if she had known the Bakers for a long time.

"Not until today," she said. "It's an accident I'm here, an accident I'm in Toronto. Well, temporarily here. I'll go back to England in a few months."

"A vacation?" Kate asked.

"I thought I'd take some time off."

"From?"

"Oh, I don't know…mainly from married life. A sabbatical, in a way."

Audrey Millay sipped from her champagne flute. A droplet left hanging from her lower lip was unhurriedly reclaimed by her tongue. A beautiful woman, the body of a fashion model, but not the toothpick variety so common in the West.

Ben said, "And a good thing it is. More women—what am I saying?—all women should consider it. A sabbatical from married life. Brilliant. The mind fogs up in marriage. Have a few affairs for a year and then, refreshed, duly return to your hubby. Civilized and practical. I wager it will lower divorce rates. My sister is toying with the idea, although she might have a permanent sabbatical in mind."

Ben was squiffed too. Everybody was, except Audrey Millay.

"Is she here?" Audrey asked.

"My sister? No, she's probably in Corby Falls."

"Corby Falls?"

Galya Baker joined them. "Audrey, my dear, you must meet some good friends of ours from England. Colson, please join us. He claims he was in school with you." She hesitated, and then told her husband to come too. She smiled at the rest of them, took Audrey's arm, and walked away with her. Colson and Ian followed her.

Jean Lezzard, older and shorter than he remembered him, was chatting with Paul on the platform, although his student was mainly listening and shaking his head. It wasn't easy to keep Paul quiet, and Laukhin surmised Lezzard was practicing the quaint, before-the-revolution Russian he'd acquired from his émigré parents. He'd seen the gallery owner earlier near the bar and delayed replenishing his drink until Lezzard moved away. Paul began to look around as if trying to get away, and then pointed to where he and Kate and Ben were. Lezzard waved his hand in their direction and began making his way toward them.

"Shit, here he comes," Laukhin said. "I've been trying to avoid him all evening."

"Who?" Kate Emslie asked.

"Jean Lezzard. He'll ask again to see my father's journal, won't take no for an answer. Change the subject, Kate."

"He looks like a desiccated beetle."

From the way he approached them, Laukhin guessed Lezzard also had many drinks that evening.

"Artyom Pavlovich," Lezzard said, "a beautiful poem, and so well recited. It brought tears to my eyes." He repeated Kate's name after Laukhin introduced her and kissed her hand. Returning to Laukhin, he added, "You haven't dropped by my shop in a long while."

As he had feared, Lezzard began without pausing, always the same words or almost. A great admirer of Laukhin's poetry, and fully aware of his many years of toil on his father's journal, Lezzard, couldn't wait to read it. He had always been intrigued by the artistic life in Russia during Stalin's years. Alas, he was old. He certainly wouldn't live long enough to see all the volumes of Pavel Laukhin's journals published. In fact, he wasn't sure he'd even see the first volume. Yes, he knew he had made this request many times already, but why not let him see the journals? Why not make an old man happy? He was ready to make a significant contribution to Laukhin's department—within his means, of course.

He spoke a mixture of English and Russian, both with a French accent. Sighing, Laukhin repeated what he'd always told Lezzard—that his father's notebooks were not at all readable, that they were now being deciphered and transcribed, but that the first volume of the journal meant for the public would be out soon. Listening to the abominable English accent of his own words, he thought that he and Lezzard were like two destitute vaudevillians who, desperately or inadvertently, had strayed into another country.

"I'll be long dead and buried by the time it's all out," Lezzard said. "What about the draft of the first volume? Humour an old man. What do you have to lose?"

"Art is a stubborn mule," Kate Emslie said. "Better tell us about the gallery, Mr. Lezzard. What's new and—"

Lezzard ignored her. "The galley proofs?"

"An advance copy, that's the best I can do, and only if I have enough of them."

"When will that be?"

"The advance copy? End of the summer."

Kate excused herself.

Lezzard turned his back on Ben in an attempt to get Laukhin's full attention. "I stumbled on some old letters belonging to my mother. Letters sent to her during the late twenties and the thirties. We were in France then, in Paris, as you know, and my father was already dead. Some of the letters are of literary interest."

"In what way?" Laukhin asked.

"They are from artists, well, mainly writers. I don't know how it happened, we were fairly young then, my brother and I. She had literary friends, my mother. You know, the intelligentsia, the cultured old layabouts, do-nothings all of them, but lovers of the arts. I think there are letters to her from Pilniak, and Mayakovsky, and also Babel."

Ben appeared from behind Lezzard. "Sorry, who sent these letters to your mother? Did you say Babel? Isaac Babel?"

Kate was right—Lezzard did look like a beetle, an annoyed beetle. He was short, bald, with a pointed nose, skinny limbs, and a protruding belly.

Lezzard half-turned to Ben. He said he didn't remember all of the names, but, yes, Babel was one of them. His mother had left an extensive correspondence, and he'd gone through half of it a year or so ago, when he had been close to moving house and had thought of getting rid of things. He had changed his mind, but the letters were still there. He was reminded of them tonight seeing Professor Laukhin. He'd have to go back and look at them again.

Laukhin moved a couple of steps away. Lezzard talked too much, and he was blocking his sight line.

Helen reappeared and said, "It's time to go, Artyom Pavlovich. The bus is leaving."

"One more drink," Laukhin said.

Helen frowned. "I am tired. Help me here, Ben, you seem ready to go too. Where is Paul? I saw him ten minutes ago and he seemed wasted."

All right, they'd leave. It was one way to flee Lezzard.

"Let me know if you're interested in the letters," Lezzard said to him.

"Of course he's interested," Ben said, "very interested."

Lezzard stared at Ben, nodded and, moving carefully, left them.

"He's had much more to drink than I have," Laukhin said. "Admirable at his age."

Paul joined them, and he had had his fill too. A fine scholarly group they were, Laukhin reflected, the professor and his students, all squiffy. Well pregnant Helen wasn't, sober as a nun. He said, "If you want a ride back, boys, get ready."

As they lined up to get their coats, he asked for a couple of minutes. He walked around the emptying rooms but did not see Audrey Millay. She was gone, and he knew nothing about her. He was an old, certifiable idiot. This would never have happened to him in the past. When he got back to the other three, Helen looked crossly at her watch. Paul said it was snowing outside.

"Snowing?" Helen scowled. "I thought we were done with it for this year. When will it end? I can't walk in the snow with these shoes."

The car was parked up the street. Laukhin couldn't see the neighbouring houses, only trees and the white road. The snow was heavy. It was quiet, with only the muffled sounds of slammed doors. The cars passing them seemed to have their engines off, as if being pulled along by invisible ropes.

Ben sidled up to him. "Do you believe the old man? I mean, about the letters of literary interest?"

"You heard him. Letters from Russian and Soviet writers, never published, never seen by anybody. Letters written to his mother. The mother lode. Bad joke? But a mother lode, nonetheless, if it's true. I have my doubts, but we should check them out. From what I understand he's willing to give them to me. He was half-drunk, mind you."

2

Laukhin was in his office on St. Joseph Street, holding his regular Monday morning hour with Ben, a rather quiet, low-key session because he was nursing a hangover. He described his mood for Ben's benefit—both exasperated and elated. Exasperated with his constitution, upset nowadays after an evening of only moderate drinking. Elated because the first volume of his father's journal was almost ready—true, three years later than the date stipulated in his contract—only a few months away from the printing press. The 1936–40 volume, the first one chronologically, and the one Ben had mostly been working on.

"The worst is over, Ben, I'm certain. I always believed the first volume would be the most difficult."

There was another cause for his elation. On Friday he had rung Bart, his agent, in New York and convinced him that there was much to be gained from the extensive introduction he had been working on. As he was about to hang up, Bart told him he just learned that the *New Yorker* had agreed on Marina Tsvetayeva as the subject of the next bundle. The journal excerpts on Tsvetayeva, Laukhin relayed to Ben, were needed by the end of August, at the latest, and would appear in an October issue.

A brilliant idea, the bundles—each one a collection of entries from the journal related to one writer or poet—he had to give it to Bart. The agent had explained the bundled excerpts were a way to keep the public's interest in Pavel Laukhin's long overdue journal, and had promised the *New Yorker* material that was gripping, poignant, novel, and self-contained. The Tsvetayeva bundle would be the second one. The previous year, with his students' help, he had linked many of the Fadeyev-related entries into a coherent narrative. The Fadeyev bundle turned out to be, judging from the letters to the editor, extremely successful. Long dead, Fadeyev may have been largely forgotten in the West, but his wild drinking, hard-line Stalinist positions, bouts of unexpected kindness, bitter last letter to the Politburo, and his suicide, provided ample drama. Whatever the reasons, it had been a pleasant surprise for everybody, and now there was pressure to prepare another bundle, one to come out just before the first volume of the journal. Pasternak had been considered, but such a bundle would have been impractically large. He was also too well known. Laukhin had proposed Marina Tsvetayeva and now they had the green light.

He and Ben talked about Tsvetayeva as they went through the first of the excerpts in Pavel Laukhin's journal involving the poet. Tsvetayeva had been a tug of war between them—a reverse kind, of pushing instead of pulling—and Laukhin felt he was slowly winning. Finally.

Ben had been dithering for a long time over the exact topic of his thesis, although he knew it would be the Russian literature of the thirties. His best student was fascinated by the first reactions to the 1932 decree "On the Reconstruction of Literary and Art Organizations" (unveiled by Stalin himself at a meeting with Soviet writers held in the grand house of a vain, callous and declining Gorky), the slow loss of an already restricted freedom of expression and the gradual imposition of the rigid aesthetic rules of Socialist Realism, the paralyzing terror following the assassination of Sergey Kirov, and the arrest and execution of many writers. Yet Ben wasn't sure whether to keep his thesis general or focus on one or two writers. He had Isaac Babel in mind, but Babel had written little in the thirties, or at least little that had surfaced or was known. Babel had even turned his deficient literary output into a bitter joke at the 1934 First Congress of Socialist Writers when he said, "I have invented a new genre—the genre of silence." To Ben's disappointment, there was hardly any mention of Babel in Pavel Laukhin's journal beyond trite notes like "Babel was sitting two rows in front of me, alone, chin down as if asleep," and "Babel came late, had a quick drink, exchanged a few words with Fadeyev, and left." Laukhin was pushing Tsvetayeva on Ben, convinced it was in his student's interest. He felt Tsvetayeva had been the best of that remarkable generation of Russian poets first heard at the dawn of the revolution. He argued that as she was not well known in the West—less than Akhmatova or Pasternak or even Mandelstam—Ben could make a name for himself in academia with a thesis on her; and that there were excerpts on Tsvetayeva in his father's journal that contained new and scholarly material. He badgered Ben relentlessly about her and her poetry, and told him to translate and research all of Pavel Laukhin's entries that mentioned her.

Laukhin's arguments made sense to Ben, or at least that was what his student would say. But in the next sentence he'd add that he didn't trust his critical appreciation of poetry, that he belonged, resolutely, in the prose camp. And yet, Tsvetayeva's life had all the drama a scholar could wish for, and he was beginning to lean toward her as well. But he couldn't decide. "Procrastinator," Laukhin had sneered at Ben in the fall. "You're dragging your feet, like a Soviet bureaucrat, afraid of consequences. Don't worry. Whatever you decide, I won't put a bullet in your neck at dawn."

Toward the end of their session the discussion drifted to Ehrenburg, whose name appeared frequently in the journal's early entries. In the spring of 1938 he, Artyom, was almost two years old, the Laukhins were living in two tiny rooms on Merzlyakovsky Lane, and his father's sister was dying of cancer in one of them. The bathroom and kitchen were shared with another family. His father had nowhere to write except at night, in the ill-lit, cluttered kitchen, the overpowering smell of unwashed dishes left in the sink. His distress was obvious in the many sarcastic remarks about family life that he jotted down. Ehrenburg was in Moscow at the time, hoping to be posted back abroad as a correspondent for *Izvestia*. For Ehrenburg the wait was long and unnerving, his fears and frustrations expressed in somber monologues. A couple of times he carried on about the last meeting he had had with Tsvetayeva in Paris. Ben knew that Laukhin had Ehrenburg's memoirs and asked for them to do some crosschecking.

"Don't spend too much time on Ehrenburg," Laukhin said, taking the books from his shelves.

"Your father seemed quite fond of him, if the journal is any indication."

"Ehrenburg brought medication for my aunt from abroad. Pain killers."

"He was unusually tongue-free with your father."

Paul appeared in the doorway for his session. "Should I come back later?" he asked.

Laukhin glanced at his watch and the image of Ehrenburg and his watch suddenly came to him. Ehrenburg had surprised them with a visit three months before Laukhin's father died. Pavel Laukhin could barely speak by then, and what he did say made little sense. No one knew how much he understood. Ehrenburg had stepped into the stuffy bedroom, looked at Pavel Laukhin's swollen face, and, breathing heavily, complained the elevator again wasn't working. He then sat down on the sick man's bed and began to talk. He went on for some ten minutes, mainly about what a relief it was to him to see his memoirs in print, and how much more he knew and had wanted to say but couldn't. He wiped his face with a white hand-kerchief while he talked. "A little truth is better than none at all, Pavel Nikolayevich, and for too long we've had none at all," he said. Laukhin couldn't believe his ears, and, briefly, he wondered whether his father had told Ehrenburg about his notebooks. As Ehrenburg stood up, Pavel Laukhin grabbed his arm and for an embarrass-ing minute wouldn't let go, his gaze fixed on Ehrenburg's large wristwatch. It was as if his mind was preoccupied with the only thing that made sense in the moment—the flow of time. Neither Ehrenburg nor Laukhin knew what to do or say, and then his father said *"polnoch,"* midnight, in a clear, powerful voice, and let go of Ehrenburg's arm.

Ehrenburg came to the cemetery too, leaning on his daughter, small, frail, aloof, shrewd, the ultimate survivor. He was, once again, at the centre of attention, with his memoirs being serialized in *Novy Mir*, and his letter in *Literaturnaya Gazeta* defending Yevtushenko's poem "Babi Yar."

"Come in," Laukhin said to Paul. "We're done, or just about."

As he was leaving Laukhin's office, Ben turned around. "What about this new fellow, Gorbachev. Will he be any different?"

The incurable naïveté of westerners. "Why would he be any different? Gorbachev has been a protégé of Andropov, the KGB chief for many, many years. They're all the same: spies, murderers, crooks." He saw a faint smile on Paul's face. He knew that smile, that look on his students' faces—oh, there he goes again, Artyom Pavlovich and his hyperboles. Was there any point? Exasperated, he told them about the money Chernyenko had stashed away. When Gorbachev, his successor, had opened Chernyenko's personal safe after his death, he found it filled with bundles of money. More bundles were found stuffed in the drawers of his desk.

"How do you know such things?" Ben asked. "He died only a month ago, in March."

Laukhin switched to Russian. "How do I know, how do I know? What kind of question is that? I keep my ears open, that's how. Gossip needs no carriage."

Ben was halfway out the door when Laukhin called him back. "Don't go, not yet. I knew there was something else I wanted to ask you, and you just reminded me. I heard the Chernyenko story last night, from Galya Shukin-Baker. This brought Jean Lezzard to mind. You met him at the Bakers a week ago, not long before we left—short, shriveled, cranky. He owns an art gallery—Gallery Kerguelen-Lezzard—not far from here, on Hazelton Avenue. Remember what he said about the letters to his mother? I'd like you to go to the gallery and talk to him and, if these letters do indeed exist, get them."

He wrote down the address of the gallery and gave it to Ben. Then, looking at his two students, he said, "Today is an unusual day for me. It's twenty-four years since my father died. And it's exactly seven years ago that I got out. Seven years since I embarked on this. So many years. Who'd have thought?"

* * *

Monday was dedicated to his students and to his teaching duties. Helen's hour with him was in the afternoon, just before his weekly lecture. He stayed late in his office afterward, wanting to have another go at the first Tsvetayeva excerpt in the bundle.

He had sent it to the *New Yorker* as a sample. Via Bart, the editor asked him to prune it of excess names and variations of the same name, and to replace initials or abbreviations. He said that their readers would quickly lose themselves within the sea of names, and lose interest. One couldn't expect the American reader to grasp, for example, that Yevgenya, Zhenya, Zhenka, Yevgenya Fyodorovna, Volkova, Y, and YF, were one and the same person. Laukhin would need, as well, to cull the number of characters. Tsvetayeva needed to emerge more clearly; right now she was drowning in a sea of other people.

That morning, with Ben, they decided to drop all abbreviations, although they opted to keep some of the variations of the same name. "It's part of being Russian," Laukhin said, "all these Pavels, and Pashas, and Pavlushas, and Pavel Nikolayeviches." They'd go along with the requested culling of characters too, and drop names and lesser incidents, and they'd use descriptors—Yevgenya's husband, for example. They might even fuse two characters into one, if they were minor but the incidents in which they were involved were worth keeping. "It's true, Ben," Laukhin said, "the editor is right. For once. Too many names, too confusing to the readers. We don't want to discourage them. It's one thing when the journal comes out; the readers know what they're dealing with, and they'll have encountered some of the names earlier. But we don't want unwary *New Yorker* subscribers turned off by an excess of names. We want to hook them, slowly reel them in."

"But dropping names changes the texture and feel of the journal."

"Just for the bundle, Ben."

* * *

Tyomka was himself, of course, the three-year old Artyom Laukhin. Not that his parents had ever stopped calling him by that diminutive.

Varya, the name his father had used most often in the journal for his mother, didn't make Laukhin think of her. His father had called her Varenka most of the time. Varya's parents had lived some distance away, on the road to Leningrad, and she often took her little Tyomka to spend the night there.

The Volkovs were a highly placed couple. Through Yevgenya Volkova, they were related to the Molotovs. There was a lot about the Volkovs early in the journal. His father had been disturbed by his addiction to the Volkovs—that's what he had called it, an addiction. Yevgenya Volkova held a salon—if the term could be applied to Moscow's society in the thirties—where artists, writers, academics, and more mysterious and mundane comrades, gathered and tried to relax. No doubt, his father had been in love with Yevgenya Volkova. Love or lust. She had both beauty and wit, and was generous with both gifts. Stalin liked to flirt, and Yevgenya Volkova thought she had some influence on him. The Volkovs were shot after the war, in 1949, she first, he a few months later. There were rumours that she had been raped before she was killed. Either that, or she had tried to find a way to stay alive. A gory version of their end was that one of Volkova's breasts had been cut off and presented to her husband to make him more cooperative with his interrogators. "Stone-arse" Molotov did not put up much of a fight. He had not fought for his own wife either.

Tsvetayeva was Marina Ivanovna Tsevtayeva, the not yet famous poet who, reluctantly following in the steps of her husband and daughter, had just returned to Russia from the West with her son Georgy.

Aleksandr (Sasha) Cornilov was his first cousin and a young poet of some promise. The son of his mother's much older sister. The difference in age meant they had little to do with each other, but there was more to it; his father never got along with Sasha Cornilov.

Fadeyev was the well-known novelist and for many years the first secretary of the Writers' Union. A favourite of Stalin.

Shnaideman was an old friend of Pavel Laukhin. An obscure poet and critic.

Pavliuk was an enigma. Laukhin remembered him as a large man with a laughing face. He might be wrong, though—to a child most adults are large. And Pavliuk's novel *Steel Tracks* didn't ring a bell at all. He had asked Colson and a few others in the department, but no one heard of it. How could a successful novel sink without a trace?

He jotted down his thoughts on the needed changes. Ben should have another go at it, and then he'd have a final one. The excerpt had immediacy and drama. There was always drama around his countrymen, no need to strive for it. He still wasn't sure how to connect the Tsvetayeva excerpts, and he wondered whether to leave out a few. He needed another chat with the editor the *New Yorker* had assigned to him. The space was limited, that he knew, but he also knew that it would be changing almost every week, and he was inclined to prepare several versions, each of a different length, in order to be ready for all eventualities.

Wednesday, 25 October, 1939

I saw Tsvetayeva tonight at the Volkovs.

I'm jumping ahead. An exhausting day. Exhausting and wasted. I have not written a word, and it's tomorrow already.

Can't get Tsvetayeva out of my mind; been thinking about her since I left the Volkovs, two hours ago. That image of her, wandering about, lost, bewildered, grey, drained; the hush and void that moved with her.

I'm drunk—always am when I get back from the Volkovs—that's why I keep jumping ahead. Here we go, from the end of yesterday.

In the morning I went to see Shnaideman, who had taken refuge at his stepfather's dacha in Barvikha for a couple of weeks. It was a windy day, cold but sunny. It had rained the night before and the roads were heavy. We walked and talked for much too long. Shnaideman can be a pain some-times, and he likes to show off and to lecture, but he's often amusing. Got back to Moscow tired, hungry, and with a nagging ache in the toes of my left foot. Could it be gout? Couldn't be, too young. More likely bad boots.

Varya had left a note on the bed. She had taken Tyomka to her parents and they'd stay there overnight if it got too late.

I lay in bed for a while and I might have fallen asleep when, through the thin wall, I heard the Marchuks at it again. Drunk, shouting, the usual drama. You'd think their newborn would keep them busy and they'd for-get to quarrel for a while. No such luck. I dragged myself into the kitchen for a glass of water. The sink was full of dirty dishes. Pigs!

Washed, changed and went out.

What is it about this urge, this addiction, this need to be and to be seen at the Volkovs? What's the attraction? Obviously, the large, well-lit, comfort-able apartment, warm even on the coldest day. The delicious food and the drinks, of course, the latter in endless supply, often in bottles with exotic shapes and labels. The people too, amusing, intelligent, informed, lethal. Learning about this and that, spicy gossip, and hearing news intended for only a select few and best not repeated. A sliver of danger, a gentle frisson of terror—always just a touch, though enough to keep you on your toes and buzzing. Like being in love without knowing what the object of your love has in store for you. The Volkovs, so free with their words, so critical and cynical, and yet so closely connected to the elite of the elite. Connected to the court, some say, delighted by their own audacity in the face of the threat that everything you say might be reported. And I keep going there, wishing to be daring and witty, in spite of Varya's warnings and unhappiness. Like a moth to a flame, Varya told me, a form of Russian roulette. Could those words see me taken away in the middle of the night? Could this joke bring the Black Marusya to our door? The worst part is that after a few glasses you start to let down your guard, and who has only a few glasses at the Volkovs? Is being drunk a defence? Can't be, or nobody would be convicted in our blessed country.

Of course, in my case, Yevgenya Volkova is the added attraction. The other night I dreamed of her again. We were in bed together, with Varya watching from not far away. I was aware of Varya's presence, although I wasn't sure where she was or of how things would unfold. I was begging Yevgenya to change sides. She was mocking me—that's all you're interested in? She straddled me, and her breasts, her magnificent breasts, glimpsed and often fully imagined, were suddenly there in front of me. I stretched out my arms but my hands went through them, touching nothing but air, and I woke up.

Yevgenya hardly looked at me tonight as we crossed paths in her large rooms, and yet she made sure that her hip brushed me slightly as she floated past. She was playing, quite aware of the effect she was having on me. On most men, actually, but she always picked just a few for her cruel teasing. I was one of them. Pavliuk said this was only the prelude, the acceptance into the antechamber from where I'd be beckoned to her bedroom. If only.

Tsvetayeva was already at the Volkovs when I arrived. It was there that I saw her the first time, maybe a month ago, when Pasternak brought her and Sergey Efron, her husband, along. Pasternak had hoped to find Fadeyev there, and he didn't stay long as Fadeyev had sent word that he wasn't coming. Her husband had wanted to leave too, but Tsvetayeva insisted on staying. Efron went by a different name, "Andreyev" I believe, but everybody quickly learned who they were. Yevgenya's husband became quite upset when, getting home late, he saw them there, in his house. Yevgenya, who had been gracious to Tsvetayeva throughout the evening, shouted at him to stop being an ass. Pavliuk witnessed the scene and reported it to me with a drunken grin. Pavliuk had pointed out the odd couple, whispering that they probably shouldn't be there; not good for them, not good for the Volkovs. Later he introduced me to Tsvetayeva, who told me that she and her husband had come back to Moscow to see if anybody knew about the fate of their daughter. That's why Tsvetayeva insisted on staying, hoping against hope that somebody would have heard something, and that this something, however vague and doubtful, would be whispered to her.

This time she came without her husband, and I knew why. Her hair—grey, rat-like—was parted on one side. She moved like a rat too, a trapped rat, with hurried, jerky motions and then, suddenly, standing ramrod straight and staring. She is not an attractive woman, and she was the worst dressed. I wondered about the stories of her many affairs, how true could they be? Everything is grey about her, like the smoke from her unending cigarettes. It is impossible to figure out the colour of her eyes, even when she is close by, talking to you. Blue, green, grey? A light shade in any event, dissolved, as if their initial strength had been washed away by many sorrows. Poverty is not kind to eyes either.

We talked. She said she didn't know where to turn. Her husband had been taken away a few days earlier and she had not slept since. She was losing her mind. First, her daughter, and now, two months later, her husband. Would she be next? Or her fourteen-year-old son? She had returned to Russia because her daughter and husband had returned, and now they were both gone. She was beginning to think that she was the cause of their imprisonment. Why else would they both be arrested so soon after her return? She stopped and looked around her, as if hoping for an answer, and then went on. Her return to Russia had been a terrible mistake. But her daughter chose to return, as did her husband, he with very little notice. For two years she had agonized over whether she should follow them here. For two years she was unable to decide. Two years obsessed by the question of her return.

She said she wasn't sure why she was telling me all this, she barely knew me, but she had lost all sense of what was reasonable or appropriate, and she didn't know where and to whom to turn. She was exhausted, with little hope of making a living from her poetry. She had gone to see an old friend from her Koktebel days whose job had something to do with movies, thinking that he could find some translation work for her. Not that she had much hope about what he could or would do. Only his wife had been at home, and she had shut the door in her face, shouting that they wanted nothing to do with her. If they'd let her teach at least—again, not a chance. She asked me if there would be any work for her at the Union— lowest clerk, anything. There was desperation in her eyes. Desperation and tears. I told her I'd see what I could do. I mentioned Fadeyev. She said she had already appealed to him, and that he had talked about some possible translation work. Georgian poets, some Baudelaire if she was lucky. I told her I'd talk to him myself—and to others too—about her situation. (I have no influence, and although I intend to do it, I know that I won't be able to help her.)

She smoked one cigarette after another, the smoke as she exhaled giving the impression that her thin body, covered by that dreadful grey dress, was slowly sublimating under my eyes into a grey gas.

It was hard to listen to her. The last thing she said before I pulled away was that she had no place to call her own. She moved from one place to another, with her son, Georgy. She didn't need much, but her son often yelled at her, blamed her for everything.

Georgy was there with her. I'd heard he's not quite right and that he's nasty to his mother. He seemed together to me, and was polite, when I exchanged a few words with him. He ate the entire evening and kept away from his mother. Big for his age—somebody said he was fourteen.

The odd war in the West, with its lack of battles or movement, was a main topic of conversation. Sneers too. The German-Soviet treaty, which had stunned everyone only two months ago, was now being talked about, and the *vozhd*'s wisdom was on everyone's lips. Such foresight. The only one who realized you could talk to Hitler. We were not threatened anymore, and it was not our war. Let the capitalists destroy each other.

Perhaps. "And the people?" I asked a younger man, who had been ogling Yevgenya while holding forth along these lines. "Which people?" "People like you and I. Those in Poland, for example." He shrugged. "They didn't want our friendship. They're always troublemakers, the Poles. Why talk about Poland?"

There. Poland was no longer of interest.

There was a buzz about Finland, and someone said the Baltic states would soon agree to Soviet garrisons.

Pavliuk, who arrived much earlier and was already drunk, whispered to me that Molotov's wife was in trouble. Likely nonsense, since Yevgenya seemed as relaxed and cheerful as ever. She looked ravishing, glowing—she must have a new lover. Who could it be? Would her eyes ever fall on me? Not likely—a scribbler of silly spy stories.

After looking around to make sure we couldn't be overheard, Pavliuk said that we'll soon attack Finland. Not to be repeated—an army source. Pavliuk was in a very good mood because he'd just heard that *Steel Tracks*, his endless novel about a tractor and tank factory near the Urals, had been well received and would have a huge print run. Yes, the waiting gamble had paid off. The book's conflict centered on increasing the production of either tanks or tractors. Cynical Pavliuk had prepared two endings. He had held back, uncertain, during the crisis with Czechoslovakia, but this September he bit the bullet and sent the manuscript in with the faction in favour of increasing tank production winning the argument. Cynical and without illusions. He had a lot to drink last night, and toward the end I heard the story all over again. He was loud, hanging onto my neck, and I had to drag him into a corner. What he wanted, he said, all he wanted, was to survive and to be surrounded by good food and laughter. He'd write anything that would increase his comfort and chances of survival. We lived in times of absolute madness. There were no sides to take, and the only thing we could do is take cover and try to survive. Rabid times like ours came every three hundred years; the one before was the Thirty Years War.

I ate and drank my fill, mingled and talked, but I couldn't help following Tsvetayeva with my eyes. I watched her the whole evening. Most of the crowd avoided her, the returned White Russian émigré, at least that was my impression. She looked older than fifty, but couldn't be. Thin, exhausted, grey, intense. It was the greyness that got to me. She also seemed slightly unhinged. Who wouldn't be?

Before I left I took her aside and whispered that her daughter's fiancé was not to be trusted. She said, "He's no worse than anybody else. Maybe better." She looked at me as she said it (looked through me? People who suffer a lot seem to be able to look through matter, as if pain gives them X-ray vision) and shook her head. Then she walked away. Afterward I wondered why I'd told her about her daughter's lover. It's not likely that it would save her. I should leave such mercies out of my life right now—with Tyomka, and another one on the way. I had learned about the fiancé being with the NKVD from Pavliuk, of course.

Young Sasha Cornilov was at the Volkovs as well. Big, tall, charming, dangerous Cornilov. How old is he? Twenty-two? Twenty-three? Varya would know. A star poet already at nineteen, fêted by all, watched by all. He had kept bad company—black marketeers, prostitutes—and disappeared for a while, almost two years. Then he suddenly came back, somber, darker. And with that scar, which started on the left side of his forehead and wound down to the middle of his cheek. He claimed he got it while in the army—that's where he said he had been. Training with some special forces. He still writes poetry, and his poetry is darker too. Darkness within the limits we are allowed, of course.

(I must tell Varya to keep away from Cornilov. Easy for me to say it, but how will she keep away from a nephew she likes very much—and whom I used to like too—and is very proud of, and who, furthermore, seems to be very fond of her? He brings her presents, foreign things that women die for—soap, perfume, silk stockings. Where does he get them?)

Cornilov watched me the whole time I talked to Tsvetayeva. Watched us. Or rather he circled us, like a vulture. I checked the colour of his scar. Still white, maybe a tinge of pink. We had a joke about it—was it Pavliuk who said it first? If Cornilov's scar turned red, he was drunk enough that you could say anything around him. Otherwise, beware.

3

He was like a dull adolescent walking to his first date. To think that he had even shaved off his moustache that morning. It wasn't much of a moustache, as he had only recently decided to let it grow again, but he felt ridiculous. Could this really be happening to him, closing in on half a century? They talked of trees like this, in terms of centuries. He had seen her once, only once, a month or so ago, but she had stayed in his mind—the memory persistence of beautiful women. And then, on Thursday afternoon, after the seminar, Ben told him he had gone to Gallery Kerguelen-Lezzard to inquire about the letters of literary interest.

"I saw her, Artyom Pavlovich."

"You saw who?"

"That woman."

"Get on with it, Ben. Did you get the letters from Lezzard?"

"He wouldn't tell me anything. Would only talk to you. No intermediary, no underlings, he said. But I saw her, I did, the one who, at the Bakers' soirée, said she was on sabbatical from married life. Audrey something. She works at Lezzard's gallery."

"Audrey Millay?"

"Yes, I think so. Well, I'm not that sure about the name." Ben smiled and, slyly, added, "I thought you might be interested. She did seem to make an impression on you that Sunday."

"Sit down, Ben. Sit, for God's sake. Take a deep breath and start over, properly this time. Details, I want details. You went to see if Lezzard had any of the promised letters. Go on."

"I got there just before noon. There was an open crate in the middle of a large room, and paintings were lined up against the walls. Two men were moving them around as if trying to fit a puzzle. I asked for Mr. Lezzard and was directed to a smaller room behind folding doors. There was a large, ornate desk in the centre of the room. Lezzard was standing with his back to me by a small, simple desk set at a right angle to the larger one. He was holding some papers in his hand and dictating names and numbers to a woman, typing, whose face I couldn't see at first. But when he turned around I could—the beautiful woman we'd met at the Bakers. Aphrodite at the typewriter."

* * *

Gallery Kerguelen-Lezzard was in an ugly townhouse on the west side of Hazelton Avenue. Under an arch, brick stairs led to the gallery, half a storey above the street. Laukhin had been there many times in the past. He couldn't remember how he had met Lezzard, but he had liked the art dealer at first—his stories, his cynicism, his nasty tongue, his fondness for serious drinking, his old-fashioned usage of Russian. Not lately, though, not since Lezzard began pestering him about his father's journal.

Audrey Millay was talking with a man in work boots and overalls, and pointing up at some wires protruding from a wall. She didn't notice him at first. Laukhin took a few steps and glanced into the smaller room. Empty. No sight of Lezzard, just as he had hoped. Lezzard had leisurely daily lunches at a French restaurant on Yorkville Avenue. Laukhin had been his guest there a few times.

He looked around the large room. The paintings were patches of colours—not to his taste. The man in overalls said he'd return in a couple of hours. Audrey walked over, wondering whether she could be of help. Her eyes were green with specks of brown. He hadn't noticed this at the Bakers. Beautiful, beguiling Audrey Millay, apprentice to

Jean Lezzard in the commerce of art. Laukhin's heart pounded, but she didn't seem to recognize him.

"Art Laukhin. We met at the Bakers last month. A Sunday do in support of Soviet dissidents. I mumbled some of my verses that evening. No? I must have made quite an impression. My turn came after Solzhenitsyn's letter."

Her face lit up with recognition—probably his accent. "Professor Laukhin, the famous poet, of course. Sorry. I see so many new faces every day."

"Art, please."

They were silent for a while.

"Jean is not here," she said eventually.

"Ah."

"He'll be back in, oh, half an hour or so. You must have come for the letters."

"I'll wait for him."

She gestured toward the back of the large room, where a sofa and two armchairs surrounded a low table loaded with flyers and books. They sat down.

"It's intriguing, isn't it?" she said. "I mean, the letters."

"We'll see." He had anticipated being alone with her, in close proximity, yet now, facing her, he was a tongue-tied poet. Unpoetlike conduct. She was the one more at ease, keeping the conversation going. But then, that was what she did all day long, chat up new visitors.

"The young man who was here yesterday, your student, seemed very excited."

"Ben is much taken with Isaac Babel, and gets emotional about it. There's very little left of Babel's life or work that has not been churned to exhaustion. The merest scrap of paper that even mentions him nowadays gets students of literature agitated."

"But you're not convinced. You seem to doubt that Jean—"

"It's not that. I'm sure some letters exist. Will they have any literary interest, though? I mean, why did Lezzard mention this to me only now? No, he probably remembered, vaguely, that his mother knew some writers, Russians, in Paris during the late twenties and early thirties. He had a few drinks at the Bakers, and blurted it out. I may be wrong, of course. I hope I am, for Ben's sake."

"How long have you known Jean?"

"Several years. I was—"

Three people walked into the gallery, two men and a woman. One of the men, short and rotund, waved hello at Audrey, guided the other two toward a large painting and began talking rapidly in front of it. Audrey stood up. "Sorry," she said. "I might be needed over there." Laukhin watched her join the newcomers. She shook the hand of the tall, elderly man, who bowed to her. The woman said something that made them all laugh, and then the short man put his arm through Audrey's in an affectionate way and took over again with a long speech that involved pointing his finger at various parts of the painting.

Laukhin got up and meandered over to the small room. He might as well wait in what Lezzard called his "Chemakoff Shrine." He was again startled by the art dealer's huge desk. Was it Pasternak who told him that Stalin had an immense desk? Small men need large desks, it seemed. He looked around. It was almost a year since he'd last been in the gallery. He remembered mainly Chemakoff prints from his past visits, and one or two oil paintings, but now there were four oils. He wasn't doing badly, Jean Lezzard, if he could afford four Chemakoff oils, although they may not all be his.

He moved slowly from painting to painting, lost in the melancholy brought on by scenes of older times and lands he'd likely never see again. Elongated women, with diffident, narrow heads, and heavy thighs. Their lovers, fat, lecherous merchants, doddering generals of the empire, governors of provinces where nothing happened. Foolish youth with wanton looks and unfettered passions. Calculating Nastasia Filipovnas staring at him with mocking eyes, as if inviting him to the cooler and dangerous air of St. Petersburg. He bowed to the men of greed and power, and to the elegant ladies with their long necks and liquid eyes. One of them resembled Audrey.

The elderly Lezzard had surrounded himself with Russia—the Russia his parents lost. Laukhin felt his eyes tear up. Rather silly. Another sign of age encroaching on him.

He stopped in front of a small ink and watercolour called *Strong Symmetries, No. 2*. On the legs of the two figures, half mannequins, half birds, words he could hardly make out were written vertically in minuscule Cyrillic letters. He hadn't seen it before. The heads, all bright blues and greens, were smoothly round and with short pointed beaks. An arm—he wasn't sure to which mannequin bird it belonged—seemed to widen towards its tip, suggesting a wing. Yet another arm ended with a hand with clearly drawn fingers. The wing-like arm was a thin plank, and so was one of the legs. The body of the larger mannequin was cleanly saw-sectioned at the back and hollow. In places, the colouring implied a wooden texture, and many of the ink lines were rule-straight. It was all very clever. They were a male and a female, he gathered, the smaller one, obviously the female, leaning backwards on the larger one. They were looking up at something beyond the frame. Maybe the strong symmetries—the secret recipe of happy living and loving, or the mysterious building blocks of the universe—had suddenly appeared in the sky. Beautiful. He should ask Audrey about the price. The year under Chemakoff's signature was 1957. It was quite small and he might be able to afford it, although an original and prior to the painter's Paris period.

An early Chemakoff oil painting had hung in the sitting room in the Lavrushinsky Lane apartment. His father had bought it in the mid fifties, and it was now with Tanya and Vadim. Laukhin had been very fond of it, and so had been Tanya. It depicted a soirée of the empire's ruling class—or it would were it not for the incongruities scattered by the painter here and there. A woman in a ball gown with a leather jacket thrown over her shoulders. A Soviet *militsya* man, in full uniform, wearing an officer's cap and cockade. A privy councillor with a chest-full of imperial medals and a huge hammer and sickle insignia pinned to his trousers. These absurd, whimsical insertions were signs of Chemakoff's evolution as a painter. They were very subtle at first—a Lenin medal barely noticeable on a chest covered by imperial decorations. However ambiguous and timid, there was a political message there, and it was that that got Chemakoff into trouble—more trouble—with the Soviet authorities. That, and his earlier reluctance to depict the new world being built around him.

"Did you know him?" Audrey asked, walking into the smaller room.

"Chemakoff? I met him a few times, but I didn't *know* him. Different generation, different art, different city. He lived in Leningrad. I didn't find him very articulate, or particularly warm. A quiet man. Perhaps a cautious man, in some way, although quite stubborn artistically. In 1961 he was allowed to exhibit in Paris after the French made a big fuss about his work. The Soviet authorities half-expected him not to return."

"Is that why they approved his trip?"

"Probably. I don't think Chemakoff had planned to stay in the West. The police raided his apartment in Leningrad when they heard he was coming back. They confiscated his paintings, papers, letters, everything. They did it to ensure he'd never return. The French loved him. They discovered him, and they loved him. But he was not happy in Paris. Made a lot of money, of course. Printed indecently large series of lithographs. When he died, he was a bitter man."

"I think Jean is back."

* * *

He'd loiter in sight of the gallery, watch and wait, and soon after Lezzard left for lunch he'd park himself in a chair near Audrey's desk. She didn't seem to mind his company. When Lezzard returned, Laukhin would mutter he had dropped by to remind him of the promised letters and he'd be off. Lezzard would shout after him, "Hey, what's the hurry? When do I get my advance copy?"

On his fourth visit he lost his head. On his way to the gallery he thought of asking Audrey out on a proper date. Dinner somewhere, possibly with the Emslies if she seemed hesitant. But at the gallery, while sitting near Audrey because he had inched his chair closer to hers while she talked to a customer, her perfume reached him and he experienced a precipitous and laughable yearning. He felt ridiculous, but he was a poet, and a foreigner to boot, and he shouldn't be expected to show common sense. He likely reddened, touched his chest and said, "This heart is all yours, Audrey. It's here, on your desk, and you can do whatever you want with it." Appalling for a poet, outright silly in fact.

She opened her eyes wide. "Who says things like this nowadays?"

"I can't help it. I'm in love, and I need to shout it."

"Don't. I hear Lezzard's voice in the other room."

"Any second I am not thinking of you is wasted."

"Here we go again. Original?"

"Probably not."

"You have your father's journal to think about. You don't need love games right now—you can't possibly delay the journal any longer."

"I feel capable of anything. Your mere presence in my life has this effect."

"I'm not in your life, Art."

Audrey's "sabbatical from matrimony" bewildered Laukhin. He tried to learn more, somewhat fearful of what he might find out. But all he gathered from her figurative and brief account was that she was at a personal impasse in her married life, a stretch of muddy waters, and that she needed time to navigate it. She completed the metaphor by saying that Toronto was only a brief stopover for her to unload and clear the deck. She intended to return to London in the near future. "Unload and clear the deck" sounded hopeful, but when Laukhin asked her whether that meant divorce, Audrey shook her head and said, "We have problems. We're living apart for a while. It was my decision more than his. I don't want to talk about it, Art."

If Laukhin persisted, Audrey would switch subjects. She'd talk about Lezzard, odd customers, or Caniche, a dog beauty salon a few doors away where she'd sometimes take refuge from Lezzard's caustic tongue. She talked about her mother, Martha, who lived all over the world, but mainly in Montreal, and with whom she was constantly at war. She talked about London, the city where she had lived her entire life, and how much she missed it. And she talked about her half-sister, Mary, three years older than she. A very young Martha was briefly married before meeting Audrey's father, and Mary had been the result. Mary was brought up by Martha's parents. "The truth is I'm not certain Martha was ever married to Mary's father," Audrey said. "I mean, really married. I'll probably never know for sure. Mary thinks it was a fib spread by our grandparents."

"I gather the father didn't stick around."

"He didn't. But it wasn't because he was a bad sort. No. It was Martha who told him to disappear. He got on her nerves."

"What does she say?"

"Martha?"

"She'd know whether or not she was married."

"I asked her once. She laughed. She said, 'Whatever makes a better story.'"

"You English are shocking. All this makes my Moscovite parents seem eminently virtuous. Although I think my father had affairs. One passion in particular consumed him for years."

"Reciprocated?"

"To some extent."

"What does that mean?"

"Her affections were shared."

"What happened?"

"She was shot after the war. Her husband too."

"Good God. That wasn't what I meant. Why were they shot?"

He sighed. Why—as if there was always a reason. How did one explain the unexplainable? "I don't know. They fell out of favour. It was a murky period—people disappeared and were shot without much reason."

She hesitated, as if searching for the right words, and then said, staring straight at him, "I hear you had affairs too. Many affairs. Runs in the family, it seems."

That came out of nowhere, a blindside blow that stunned him. Well, it had been all over the press at the time he defected, and she was bound to learn about it sooner or later.

"Not that many," he said.

"You left your wife in Moscow. And when you arrived in Toronto a few months later, there was a young woman with you."

"Did Lezzard tell you this?" he asked.

"Yes."

"Lezzard is a fool. My wife and I had our problems. It was a bit more complicated than it appears."

"Was it?"

"She divorced me, you know. Tanya, my former wife, filed for divorce two months after I left."

"She likely learned you wouldn't return."

She was still looking at him intensely, as if trying to read his rotten soul. He laughed. "I didn't say I was virtuous—I said my parents were."

"I'm sorry," she said. "It's not my business."

* * *

It was a pleasant May with hardly any rain. Thinking of Audrey and waiting up the street for Lezzard to leave the gallery made Laukhin feel young again. The euphoria of anxious expectations. He recalled the days he'd fallen in love with Tanya, long ago, also during a warm spring. On Tuesday and Friday evenings he'd take the red line to the Kamovniky district, get off at Frunzenskaya, walk through the park to the Sechenov Medical Institute, and wait across the street from the side exit until Tanya came out. They had developed a game or ritual of it, because he had once told her that he didn't mind at all—quite the contrary—watching her chat with her colleagues and friends and waiting for her to say goodbye to them. When she left the building, she'd look across the street for him, smile happily and then talk with her friends for ten or fifteen minutes. His sister, Larissa, would often be with her—Tanya was her colleague, and it was through Larissa that he'd met her—and often, when there were only the two of them, they'd carry on with the ritual, and they'd point at him and laugh in a pantomime of exaggerated gestures and noises.

He knew he was ridiculous, absurd, just as fifty years were waving encouragingly at him. Mockingly too. He heard himself whispering Pushkin:

It ill-becomes me; I get older...
Time, time to be more sensible!

He had vowed to visit the gallery no more than once a week, but he rarely kept to it. He'd wait for Lezzard to leave, and if that didn't happen he'd walk back to Alumni Hall. Once, after a couple of days when Lezzard didn't leave for lunch at his usual hour, Laukhin walked in. A middle-aged woman in a dark green turtleneck was sitting at Audrey's desk and showing Lezzard something in a large, thick book. Laukhin had met her before in the gallery, and he vaguely remembered a French first name. He asked where Audrey was. Was she sick?

Lezzard laughed. "She's in London. Went to talk to her husband."

"I thought they were separated."

The woman looked at him with amusement. A huge triangular pendant pointed to the rise of very generous breasts.

"When will she be back?" Laukhin asked.

Lezzard laughed again. "That's the thing about Audrey and her trips. It's hard to know. Spontaneous departures, surprise returns. Part of her charm."

After he left the gallery Laukhin remembered that the woman's name was Mrs. Grunwald, Josiane Grunwald. She'd worked for Lezzard for many years. He knew from Audrey she'd been ill with some mysterious malady and was slowly recovering. "It's something tropical," Audrey had explained. "She went to Kenya on a safari. Time seems to be the best treatment, but she's had relapses, many of them. There are days when

35

she can't get out of bed." The Osterhoudts—Martha and her husband—had bought many paintings from Lezzard, and when Martha asked him if he could temporarily employ her daughter he couldn't refuse. It turned out to be fortuitous too, because of Josiane's shaky health.

* * *

Nicholas Millay, Audrey's husband, was a bureaucrat at the Foreign Office. He began his career under his future father-in-law, and that's how he met Audrey. Her father had been an economist who had been assigned to the Foreign Office during the war and never left it until he retired. Although there was a real earl in his family—a great-uncle on his father's side—he had no money, and that was one of the reasons beautiful Martha, Audrey's mother, had left Gerald and Audrey. It happened when Audrey was quite young, five or six years old. In her fifties now, Martha was still striking. Her latest husband was a Dutch-Canadian who had made a fortune in drugstores. He moved with Martha—often without her—from house to house, and from continent to continent.

Laukhin learned all this from Lezzard the day he asked about Audrey's whereabouts. When he left, Lezzard followed him to the door and went down a few steps with him. "Audrey's life is there, in London, together with her father whom she adores, and all her friends, and she had—has—many. She flies back whenever she can, almost every week. If you ask me, I don't know why she's still here. She'll patch up with her husband, I'm sure. I have no idea what went wrong there, she won't say. All I got is that it took a while for it to become a crisis, or for her to make up her mind and cross the ocean. Her husband desperately wants her back. All right, you're a poet, a famous poet, and your education provides you with a veneer of social polish. Barely. But it's the money, Art, or power. The means. That's what attracts women in the West. They don't go weak near a poet, like in the old country. A poet has no weight here. What are you offering her? A few *bons mots* from your literary friends before they get drunk and bemoan their poverty and how the world ignores them?"

He seemed to delight in describing the chasm between Laukhin and Audrey. Irritated, Laukhin asked about the promised letters.

Lezzard said that he'd had no time to look for them. He grabbed Laukhin's elbow. "Get me a copy of your father's notebooks. It's the one incentive that'll make me keen to look again through the trunk of papers Mother left me."

"Can't do it."

"Can't or won't? I thought we were friends."

"Jean, friends get that *no* is an answer too."

"What's the big deal? Where is the crime? What could happen if an old man reads your father's journal ahead of the other readers? Who would know, anyway?"

"We've been through this many times. The notebooks are not readable."

"Surely you have most of them transcribed by now."

"I told you I may have an advance copy of the first volume for you at the end of the summer."

"But you have the galleys by now, so close to publication, don't you?"

"I do."

"When does it end?"

"The first volume? The end of 1940."

"Let me have a copy of the galleys."

Laukhin sighed. "All right, but only the half I've gone through already. I had to stop in the middle in order to do something else, and it's taking me much longer than I expected. I'll make a copy of it and send it to you."

"If you'd spend less time in this gallery..." Lezzard mumbled. "How far does it go, the available half."

"The end of 1938."

Lezzard swore.

"That's the best I can do, Jean."

* * *

"Stop. Why are you telling me this?"

"You asked me why I'd fallen behind."

"I don't want to know about your heartaches, Ben."

"It's the reason why, Artyom Pavlovich."

"Nothing else?"

"Nothing else."

He didn't understand his students. He was fond of them, but they were a mystery to him. He'd never have attempted such a confession to any of his professors. It wasn't just the cultural and political difference, it was generational too. He was almost twice their age.

He sighed. "All right, tell me."

"Her name is Marion, and she's—"

"No, no, I don't need details."

"How else can I explain?"

Should he slap Ben, or take him out for a drink? Duty upended by pangs of love. Christ.

He gestured Ben to carry on, hoping that his face showed both his perplexity and displeasure. He'd have to put up with it, since Ben had been his main help for the first volume and was now for the Tsvetayeva bundle.

* * *

Audrey talked at length about her parents after she got back from one of her many trips to London. She was worried about her father's health. She was sitting at her small desk, addressing invitations to the opening of the gallery's next show. A boring and mindless task, she said, and asked Laukhin to keep her company. Watching her profile as she wrote, he experienced, as he did when he first confessed his love for her, a perplexing anguish. He recalled the lines of the love-mad Moor, "... *so lovely fair and smell'st so sweet, That the sense aches at thee.*" His senses, visual and olfactory, ached for Audrey. Her lips were silently shaping the names of the invitees. He longed for a similarly mute but clear signal: come and hold me, come and kiss these lips. But nothing. Only silent invitations to Mr. and Mrs. David Mortimer, Mrs. Lieberman, Ms. Rockwell. The folly of his love became more apparent with each silent summons. Dr. Ruart, Mr. Wells, Mr. and Mrs. Benjamin Elkin.

After his lunch, Lezzard came in noisily, parked himself at his desk, released a discreet belch, and asked Audrey whether she could concentrate with the professor inanely twaddling in the background.

"It's the belching that disturbs Audrey," Laukhin said.

Lezzard got up and stepped out of the small room, clearly irritated.

"How old was your father when he died?" Audrey asked after a few more invitations.

"Sixty-one."

"Very young."

Lezzard shouted from the other room, "I need those invitations sent today."

Audrey made a face, and Laukhin said, without moving, "I should go."

"I'm worried about my father," Audrey said. "He's seventy and he has a weak heart."

He wasn't sure what she wanted to say.

"Of course, I knew about his condition," she went on, "but I didn't realize how bad it was until I went back to my old home after I left Nicholas. My father has trouble breathing and his legs are swollen. A nurse comes once a week to check on him, and a woman is there two other days to do the housekeeping and keep an eye on him. She's fine, but she gets on his nerves. He looks forward to weekends simply because he'll be alone." She smiled. "He has all the time in the world for me. For me and my foolishness. He and Martha never hit it off."

"Have you always called her Martha? I've never heard you say *my mother*."

"I stopped calling her Mother when I was five years old. I had waited, with an increasingly irate Mrs. Bloom circling around me that Saturday, at the end of what turned out to be my last drawing lesson, the other pupils having long gone home with their parents. My father finally answered the last of Mrs. Bloom's desperate ringing attempts, and rushed over to get me. He was flustered and was apologizing profusely when Martha arrived, only a minute or two later. She'd been two hours late, an eternity for a child. It was then that I, all of five years old, addressed my mother for the first time by her name. I asked, angrily, 'Where have you been, Martha?' She's been Martha to me ever since."

"You're not fond of her, I gather," Laukhin said.

"Martha is smart, determined, and glamorous. Witty too—yes, she is. She's fifty-seven years old, and she can still turn heads. I look dull in her presence."

Nonsense.

"She's a very rich woman now. The MacNeil and, especially, the Osterhoudt marriages have seen to it. When she was forty-three and still beautiful, Martha married Diederik Osterhoudt, who everyone calls Dirk. He's nineteen years her senior. This time she did exceedingly well financially, and she settled down. I mean, she didn't divorce again and remarry. To her credit, she's been very generous with her new money—Dirk's money. She likes to give. I can ask anything of her, as long as it can be purchased. It's her apartment that I'm in right now. It's usually empty."

Monday, 11 December, 1939

I went to the Writers' Union this morning. Word reached me that I'd done something wrong on my application form for the Volinsky Retreat and that I should drop in and fix it. The fat boss of Progress Publishing was just leaving as I arrived, and he had good news. *The Iced Waterfall* had been selling well, much better than my first book, and they were talking about another printing, quite a large one. He seemed to be dancing around me. I was delighted by the news, of course, but also surprised to hear about the hefty reprint, given the shortage of paper. As I looked at him manoeuvring his large body into the waiting car, I wondered what bureaucratic bungle had caused my good fortune. I soon learned that it was no mistake.

But I went to the Writers' Union mainly for drink and palaver. I had both, and a good laugh, with Shnaideman and Pavliuk. Shnaideman, officially divorced now, is still living with his wife in the same room, which has led to some embarrassing situations. He's a good mimic, and his stories were side-splitting. He laughs loudly at his own jokes, and his huge torso sways like a mountain of gelatin. Shnaideman's brother was supposed to have been transferred to Gorky, and Shnaideman was counting on getting his room when he decided to leave his wife. But his brother is not moving to Gorky anymore, hence the mess he is in.

Bedrosyan saw me as I was leaving and asked me to step into his office. "You must, Pavel Nikolayevich," he added. "It's important. Good news, don't worry, very good news."

I assumed it was the "good news" I just heard from the boss of Progress Publishing, but I followed him. His office smelled of un-emptied ashtrays and fear. Bedrosyan's face, unshaven for a few days, had the colour of the ash that was always perched on the tip of his cigarette. A couple of months ago his brother-in-law was taken away and then, two weeks later, the wife, Bedrosyan's sister, disappeared. A blessing that they had no children.

Bedrosyan was afraid that they would come for him and his family too. Or that he'd lose his sinecure.

He was smoking, of course. Whiff of an early drink? His long face was wrinkled by a forced smile, his teeth as bad as ever. He patted me on the shoulder and we shook hands as he let me in. "Good to see you, Pavel Nikolayevich," he said.

What caused this sudden pleasure at my presence, this unexpected surge of affection? I had no weight that warranted more than an indifferent nod.

He offered me a cigarette. "Yes, good news," he went on, "excellent ones, in fact. It warms one's heart to be the bearer of such news."

It was indeed way beyond good news. We got the apartment! The union had allocated a four-room apartment to us, in the writers' building on Lavrushinsky Lane, the one across from Tretiakov Gallery. A prestigious building and location. An apartment of our own, with four rooms! One room would be my study. A room of my own!

We applied for an apartment when Tyomka was born, and we renewed the application when Varya got pregnant again, but in my mind we had at least two more years to wait and even then it would be a matter of luck, and of finding or buying some favour.

"It wasn't easy," Bedrosyan said, shaking his head and alluding to his efforts on my behalf. "Such scarcity, Pavel Nikolayevich, but you fully deserve it, especially now, as the family is growing, and you need privacy to write your wonderful books. How is the new novel coming? People are eagerly awaiting it, important people."

I didn't know what he meant at first, and was too jubilant to take in the grave inflexion in his tone. He took two glasses out of a drawer and a bottle of vodka. We clinked and drank; I could have kissed his ashen cheeks.

"When? When can we move in?" I asked.

"Give us a couple of weeks, the papers, you know. It's like new, almost new. Four rooms—two of them quite large. A bathroom, of course, and a spacious kitchen. I went to have a look at it myself. The apartment has been empty for a couple of months." He lowered his voice. "It belonged to Fredkin... Well, it doesn't matter now."

The name Fredkin was somewhat familiar—a theater director or a critic. Both? Pavliuk told me about him in a whisper, several weeks ago, at the Volkovs. They came to take Fredkin away—but that was not the core of Pavliuk's story. While they searched the premises, Fredkin snuck into the bathroom and cut his wrists. When he didn't come out, they broke down the door and found him, alive, of course, and as they bandaged him, they pummelled his face for trying to kill himself. How did he dare? How were they going to explain his wounds? They'd have to admit that they'd left the prisoner alone for a while. Were these the thanks they deserved for being nice to him? Fredkin's wife fainted, the children, young twins—he had an older daughter too, but she was away—were woken by the noise and began screaming. They came back for his wife a week later. Aware that she might be detained as well, she took the children to her sister in Kiev. They were waiting for her when she returned.

I was too elated to give it further thought.

(How easy it was not to dwell on such matters. Even now, the simple imperative "I will not think about it!" works. It stops the imagination from taking over, and with it, the horror. And then, there are the easy justifications, "What good would it do?" or "By taking the apartment, you yourself haven't done anything wrong, anything vile or abhorrent.")

Bedrosyan refilled our glasses as we were standing near his desk. He looked at me with curiosity and deference. "You see, Pavel Nikolayevich, people in high places have taken an interest in you. They like you. Well, I don't know if they like you personally, ha, ha, but they like your books. Somebody very high up took a liking to Boris Vinograd."

"Oleg," I said. "Oleg Vinograd."

"Yes, precisely, do you know who likes the hero of *The Iced Waterfall*? Think high, very high."

I shook my head—I had no inkling whatsoever. I was tempted to say Bedrosyan, but decided not to offend the messenger.

"The highest of all! Comrade Stalin himself! Yes, he's read your book. Imagine, Pavel Nikolayevich, Comrade Stalin read *The Iced Waterfall*! He's tireless, Comrade Stalin. Hardly ever sleeps. He read your book and liked it so much that he ordered a movie to be made of it. He was delighted with the way Vinograd made mincemeat of the English spies. I was told that he was laughing and telling the story to all those around him the other night in Kuntsevo. He said the English were the worst, the worst of our enemies, and this author—that's what he said, referring to you, Pavel Nikolayevich—had captured it all: their intrigues, and their boasting and perfidy. He inquired about you, and Comrade Zhdanov instructed me to collect information about you. I don't know who gave the book to Comrade Stalin, but you must have more than one admirer up there. Comrade Zhdanov read your book too,

43

and many more around Comrade Stalin are reading it as we speak, believe me. That's how it all happened, that's how they found out about your application for an apartment. An order from high up. Very high up."

Then, half-serious, half-ironical, he said, "If I were you, I'd apply for a dacha as well. Appetite comes during a meal, as the saying goes."

I didn't know what to say, so I kept shaking my head incredulously.

Bedrosyan went on, "He's quite a reader, Comrade Stalin. Sharp, critical eye too. He asked about what you were working on nowadays, and when he found out that you had just forwarded the manuscript of your new Oleg Vinograd novel to Progress Publishing, he ordered a copy for himself. In no time, he read it. Yes, he just finished reading *Under the Acacia Trees*. He's not that fond of the title. It's not punchy enough, not congruous with the pace and the vigour of the action. He has marked down a few title suggestions—well, you'll see for yourself. He made other observations too and sent his annotated copy back for you. With his own handwriting! Our dear Comrade Stalin's own pencilled notes on how to improve the novel, how to make it more powerful, more pertinent. I have it here with me. You should take a careful look at it, see if you agree with what he's suggesting. Between you and me," he winked, "a cat always knows whose meat it eats."

He walked to his desk to refill his glass and gestured at mine. I lifted my hand to signal I was fine.

"I was told that Comrade Stalin appreciates Oleg's personal troubles," Bedrosyan continued, "the difficulties he has with his wife, their inability to have another child, which seems to be at the root of their marital discord. That's life, real life, that's what he said. I agree, Pavel Nikolayevich. Oh, yes, I've read *The Iced Waterfall* too. When I became aware of the interest in such high places, I decided to read it myself. It's a very good read, transcends the genre."

Transcends the genre! He was mocking me, of course, but did I care? I practically floated out of his office.

I phoned Varya and told her to meet me in front of the Tretyakov Gallery. Right away, I insisted. I said I had a wonderful surprise for her and left it at that. Of course, she was very curious and wanted to know what it was all about, but I held firm. She said it would take her at least an hour, maybe more. She needed to find somebody to mind Tyomka. She also reminded me that, given her condition, she was rather slow getting anywhere.

It was still snowing, but it wasn't too cold. I walked slowly along Povarskaya (I can't think of that street as Vorovsky, no one can) toward

Arbatskaya Square. Slowly because I liked the quiet, old street under new snow, but also to still my beating heart. How suddenly things were changing for us! It had been about a month since I first heard about the sudden popularity of *The Iced Waterfall*. I knew it meant money would be less tight, but it was more, much more, than that now.

I was overwhelmed with joy, and thought of the books I would write in my quiet study, with Varya happy in a tidy and clean kitchen, the quarreling Marchuks a mere memory. And yet, I felt a curious uneasiness and anxiety. Was I wary of being noticed by the mighty gods? Was I worried of being unable to stop thinking about the Fredkins?

I took the bus for a few stations. It was crowded, but mine was probably the only smiling face in it. Two women were whispering to each other, and I heard something about Finland and a dead cousin. One of them asked, "Finland? Do you understand, Lyusha, do you? Why Finland?" I did not catch Lyusha's answer. I got out and, feeling impatient, walked the rest of the way. It had stopped snowing and the sky was clearing. On Kamenny Bridge I stopped for a few minutes and looked at the Kremlin, wondering about the frail, pockmarked creature who could change the lives of so many people between two puffs of his pipe.

I knew the building on Lavrushinsky Lane, but wanted to have another look at it before meeting Varya. Its grey stone façade looked massive, solid, indestructible. We'd be all right, more than all right, in this building. Imagine, Stalin liked Oleg Vinograd's adventures, and before you could blink an apartment was found. And not just any apartment, but one in a new building in the heart of the city.

I wondered which were the windows of the Pasternaks' apartment. I knew from Kolya Klyuchev that he had a large one on the top floor. Was he home, pacing, weighing the next line, now and then looking down on this mild December day as I was looking up? Paustovsky lived there too, and Vsevolod Ivanov, and others. A building for literary figures. Ehrenburg's daughter, Irina, lived there with her husband. She and Varya had been best friends for many years, and they'd both be delighted by how close they'd be now.

I had joined the literary elite. An apartment in that building conferred that status —or its outward appearance, the peacock plumage. Its kernel, its real strength, came from the little man in the Kremlin, and from his zealous servants.

It was still too early for Varya to show up and so I strolled in a loop, along the embankment at first, then Pyatnitskaya Street, and back along

Klimentovsky Lane. Near the metro station I saw Tsvetayeva, smoking and talking with another woman. Suddenly my joy disappeared—some of my joy, anyway. That woman carried grief with her like the plague and spread it to those around her. I turned back and crossed the street, hoping not to be seen. Walking along the other side of the street, I saw Sasha Cornilov in an animated discussion with another man. He didn't notice me and I didn't stop. I wondered what Tsvetayeva was doing there, so close to Lavrushinsky Lane. Had she been to see Pasternak? Was she on her way there?

Varya was in front of the Tretyakov Gallery when I got back. I told her about the apartment and we walked across the street to the building, and then back and forth in front of it, hugging and laughing. Varya couldn't stop babbling. "Pavlusha, is it true? Stalin liked *The Iced Waterfall*? Stalin himself? How does he find the time? Four rooms, Pavlusha, four rooms! Is it true? Tell me again. It's not a silly joke, is it? No, it would be too cruel. Pavel Nikolayevich, you are a genius, and I love you. And Irina, Pavlusha, Irochka, so close. What floor, do you know what floor? Not that it matters much. You didn't ask? How could you not ask? Oh, well, I'll find out from Irina—she'll know which apartment is empty. Who lived there, Pavlusha, do you know, which famous writer?"

I thought of hiding what happened to the Fredkins from her. But I knew she'd find out from Irina. Better she learned now—easier to put them out of her mind while her joy and delight was so fresh. So I told her, not in all the details I had from Bedrosyan, only that they'd been taken away.

Then I saw Tsvetayeva again, coming toward us, and there was no avoiding her this time. I introduced Varya. We were still smiling, couldn't stop. Tsvetayeva said she hoped we had good reason for our cheerfulness. I felt uncomfortable, almost embarrassed, but luckily Varya told Tsvetayeva that her poetry, the little she could get her hands on, had touched her like no one else's. She said, "God bless you, Marina Ivanovna." Tsvetayeva took Varya's hand and said, "It's rare that I hear nice words these days. Thank you. News about my family would do me more good, though. Or a place to call my own, however small." She told us that she and her son were now camping out in the few square meters of her sister-in-law's apartment. She had some hopes for a place in Golitsyno, thanks to a vague promise from Fadeyev, but she wasn't holding her breath. "I wish I had my own place to sleep, to call home, but it does not seem possible," she said and she walked away.

It was hard to believe. It was almost as if she knew about our new apartment.

"There walks a killjoy," I said looking after her.

"Tragedy," Varya said softly. "Marina Ivanovna is tragedy."

And then I saw Cornilov again, walking in the same direction as Tsvetayeva. He passed us, turned back and hugged his "dear aunt Varya, always beautiful, quite sublimely pregnant," and gave me a mocking salute. He took off quickly, pointing at his watch as if he were late.

We didn't talk on our way home. I began to wonder whether seeing Cornilov was accidental. Varya kept her thoughts to herself. Clearly talking to Tsvetayeva had upset her. Inside, Varya made tea. We drank quietly, and then Varya said, "What did poor Fredkin do?"

It was not a real question, and we both knew that. I sighed. "Let's not think about it, Varenka. Especially you, in your situation ..."

She asked, "What's happening, Pavlusha? What's happening with us, with our lives? How did we become what we've become?"

I didn't say anything. What was there to say? I took her hands in mine. It was almost as if we felt ashamed of our luck, of our new apartment. Like everyone else, we were now fearfully elbowing at the trough. I forced myself to think of Tyomka, and of the new one, for now still swaddled in the safety of Varya's womb, and of the fact that we needed a decent place to live, and I needed a room to write in.

Bedrosyan's words keep coming back to me, "The apartment has been empty for a couple of months. It belonged to Fredkin. Well, it doesn't matter now." Who knows where Fredkin is now, if he is still alive. He doesn't matter anymore. Fredkin has ceased to matter. How apt Bedrosyan's words were.

In a better world, a world inhabited and governed by good, decent people, Fredkin wouldn't be rotting in some cell, or freezing to death in a camp. And Tsvetayeva and her son would get a good, decent place to live (and her daughter and husband would not be in prison either). Or, the creator of Oleg Vinograd would invite Tsvetayeva to stay with him and his family in his new apartment. After all, we'll soon have four rooms. Above all, he'd extend this invitation unafraid, without a doubt in his mind. And not only for a few days, but for as long as she needed shelter.

4

It was unusually hot for June, and Laukhin, who dealt poorly with the heat, suggested they walk to the gallery a bit later. They sat in his office and went through the second Tsvetayeva excerpt.

"What happened to the Fredkins?" Ben asked.

"I don't know."

"Your father never found out?"

He shrugged. "I don't know. A few years ago I tried to track them myself, so that I could add a scholarly note, saying, oh, I don't know, 'Fredkin died in nineteen-something in Camp X, or Fredkin spent Y years in Camp Z and was freed in nineteen fifty-something. His wife, et cetera, and his daughter, et cetera.' I got nowhere. Being here, of course, didn't help. I asked my friend Kyril to see if he could dig something up, but so far nothing."

"How could no one know anything?"

"It happened forty-five years ago, Ben, forty-five years, and in the Soviet Union. A scorching war ago too."

"People can't just disappear without a trace. A whole family."

He glared at Ben. "I don't want to hear daft things from my students."

"You never heard your parents talk about the Fredkins?"

"The first time I learned about the Fredkins was when I read the journal."

"You didn't ask your father if he knew anything about them?"

"No. He was already quite ill."

"In the journal he seems quite worked up by what happened to them."

"He was upset by how easily he accepted it—being 'at the trough', as he put it. He was upset for being no better than Bedrosyan, whom he despised, and because he ultimately agreed with Bedrosyan that Fredkin, or the Fredkins, didn't matter anymore."

Laukhin looked at his watch. "It should be cooler now," he said. "Let's go."

"He tried to bribe me," Ben said.

"What?"

"Lezzard tried to bribe me."

"When? How?"

"I wanted to see the famous Chemakoffs and I went two weeks ago. Took Marion with me."

"Who?"

"Marion, you know."

"Ah. Is this relevant, the fact that Marion was with you?"

"No."

"Tell me about it on the way there."

* * *

Lezzard was busy with a group of tourists in the main room, and, as no one else was in the back room, they admired the Chemakoffs undisturbed. They were about to leave when Lezzard found them. Ignoring Marion, he planted his short body in front of Ben. "Get me a copy of Pavel Laukhin's notebooks. I want to read them."

"Sorry?"

"You heard me. I want to read the notebooks."

"No, I can't do that. Talk to Professor Laukhin."

"There's money in it for you."

Ben was stunned. "What do you mean? What money?"

"I'll make it worthwhile for you. I'm not stupid."

"Out of the question, Mr. Lezzard."

"Think what you could do with money, the things you could offer your girlfriend." He glanced at Marion for a second, then went on. "I'm talking about serious money, not a paltry amount. It's Ben, isn't it? I have no family, Ben. What am I going to do with my money?"

"Mr. Lezzard, I couldn't do it, even if I wanted to. It's impossible for me to make a copy of the notebooks."

"Why?"

"They are kept in a safe at the university. We have limited access to some copies, all closely monitored."

Lezzard shook his head, incredulous.

"Anyway, I wouldn't do it, Mr. Lezzard."

Lezzard looked at him with something between pity and disgust. "What about the first volume? Come on, you can easily get a copy."

"Of the draft?"

"Surely some draft exists already. The same financial offer stands."

"Laukhin has it. He's the one who is putting it together."

"Tell him you need to have a look at it for some reason."

"I thought Professor Laukhin already gave you the first half of the galley proofs."

"I want the other half too, and I can't get it. Your professor says that he hasn't gone through it yet. He's working on something else, I don't know what."

"There's nothing I can do, Mr. Lezzard, and I don't want to talk about it any more."

"You are a mulish, stupid young man."

* * *

The walk wasn't long, but the air was still oppressively hot and humid. They climbed the brick stairs to the gallery behind a middle-aged couple who moved with the uncertain steps of tourists. The woman wore a short yellow skirt and had powerful calves.

It was an oasis of cool and quiet inside. At the back of the room Lezzard was snoozing in one of the armchairs, his head fallen back, mouth open.

The couple began a clockwise tour. Laukhin and Ben went the opposite way, admiring the works of Dorbao-Uitlan, a painter—according to a loose sheet Laukhin picked up near the door—of the "dark heart of Brazil." Thick, luscious strokes of oil. On the other side of the room the couple was making appreciative noises. Back from his nap, Lezzard stood up and walked toward them.

"Ah, unique, mysterious, yes? A mystery that makes demands on us, requires us to pause longer, to fathom the soul of the work. Dorbao-Uitlan, a robust, vital, hypnotic painter, *n'est-ce pas?* You sweat when you look at these paintings. You get the odor, the decay, the poisonous hazards of the Amazon forest. He was born there, Dorbao-Uitlan, a savage with a brush. Astonishing colours, wouldn't you say? Luminous. Some of the pigments he uses are his own, extracted from plants he learned about while growing up. Real painter, not one of the piss-ass modernists of today who are proud of keeping the same colour inside a rectangle. *Mais difficile, celui-la, très difficile.* But then, all great artists are. Which one do you like?"

The woman seemed on the verge of saying something, but changed her mind after her companion whispered a few words in her ear. Lezzard's eyes were darting between the two of them, unable to choose which one to concentrate on. He noticed Ben, who was closer to him, and then Laukhin. "Ah, good, the master is here," Lezzard said. "Don't go away, give me a moment."

He turned back to the couple. They were from Michigan, from a small town that might have been a suburb of Detroit. They liked all of the Dorbao-Uitlan's paintings, but they wanted to know if they were affordable. Lezzard told them the price of one of the smaller paintings. The Michigan couple had to think about it. They'd come back, though. They had a daughter studying in the city, and were in Toronto for several days.

Lezzard drew back, realizing he had wasted his time. With timid steps, the couple retreated into the smaller room.

"Is Audrey around?" Laukhin asked.

"She's away."

"Will she be in today?"

"I don't know."

"Where is she?"

Suddenly the man from Michigan appeared next to Lezzard, "Would you take a few post-dated cheques?" His wife had stopped near the folding doors.

There was another abrupt change in Lezzard's demeanour. He got up and walked toward the wife, smiling and pushing her husband along. "Of course, of course. If you are thinking of buying the small Chemakoff ink and watercolour, make sure you set it away from strong colors. It's a very delicate piece, *très fragile*, one of my favourites. I was thinking of keeping it for myself, but..."

Audrey walked in, struggling with a large travel bag and complaining about the heat. She looked drained. Lezzard introduced her to the Michigan couple, and the four of them filed into the smaller room.

Laukhin went back to Dorbao's paintings. Groups of South-American natives, green-brown rivers, exotic plants and birds, monkeys. In one large painting, marked by a red dot as already sold, three natives with impassive faces sat in imposed, artificial attitudes, perhaps a metaphor of their fate since civilization reached them. One was a very old woman, with teats like wide ribbons. Bits of the conversation reached him from the smaller room.

He was looking at his watch when Audrey and Lezzard emerged with their new customers and walked them to the door. More chatter and smiles, and Laukhin did another round, before the couple left.

Audrey approached him and, touching his arm, whispered, "I didn't notice you when I came in."

"A drink, let's have a drink for the sold Dorbao," Lezzard said. "It calls for celebration. Can't let an old man drink by himself. And the letters, we must celebrate the letters from Babel too."

Audrey said, "Oh, you found them." She tried to smile. "I should be pleased, I know, but I've spent three hours on the tarmac." She didn't say where, and Laukhin didn't ask.

Lezzard walked to the small room and returned quickly with a large white envelope, which he handed to Laukhin. "Don't look now," he said.

They followed Lezzard out of the gallery and onto Yorkville Avenue. The heat had subsided a bit. They settled under the shade of a Cinzano umbrella, in a courtyard with a few round tables. He and Lezzard agreed on red wine, Ben ordered a beer, Audrey asked for soda with a slice of lime. She wore a white sleeveless blouse, and as she lifted an arm to arrange her hair, Laukhin noticed a patch of perspiration below the armhole. She looked tired, but lovely. He reflected that a certain amount of disorder in a woman's attire and make-up revealed unexpected beauty. He couldn't take his eyes off her.

Audrey and Lezzard talked about Dorbao-Uitlan for a while. From what Laukhin could understand, Dorbao was trying to get out of the agreement he had with the gallery. Lezzard ordered a second drink for himself and for the men. Raising his hands, he said he didn't want to spoil a very good day talking about Dorbao. He persuaded Audrey to have a "serious" drink—white wine she decided—and asked for a plate of cheese. His face had become red and mischievous. "Are you in love with Audrey?" he asked Laukhin, enjoying himself tremendously.

"Jean, stop this nonsense," Audrey protested.

"I'm bewitched," Laukhin confessed.

"Lovely. Get married, have children, be happy. I was married once, briefly. Never been good at it myself. Even had a daughter. Have, I guess."

"When did you find the letters from Babel, Jean?" Laukhin asked.

Lezzard shrugged, annoyed, "Oh, two or three days ago. The day I called you."

"Were there many letters?"

"I didn't get through even half of them. Most were from people unknown to me. Some names sounded familiar, but I couldn't put a face to them. A couple of letters written during the war were in German. Imagine! God, she kept everything, and I have too, carried them around for too long. I should throw away the lot."

"No, no," Ben said, horrified, "you mustn't throw away any of your mother's letters, however insignificant they may seem. Give them to us. They might contain, almost certainly do contain, allusions and names that would be of great interest to researchers, invaluable to those interested in the Russian émigré community between the wars."

"Would they, now," Lezzard said. "*Un peu tard.* Too bad they weren't interested in that community then, when it could have helped a few. Ha. Well, here is a story for you, a story typical of the Russian émigré community between the wars. My mother's story. Yes, let me tell you about her, an interesting woman she was."

It was a rambling monologue peppered with French words, a disconcerting mixture of melancholy and anger. Laukhin had heard parts of it before. At the death of his father in 1925, Lezzard's mother found herself penniless in Paris, with two young sons. They had emigrated a few years earlier from Soviet Russia. The family fortune, or whatever they'd salvaged of it in cash and jewelry, had been frittered away while they took refuge in Piatigorsk, a town in southern Russia. They had gone there hoping that the revolutionary storm would blow over and they could return to their former life in St. Petersburg. There had been a family estate, but Lezzard had been too young to remember it. When his father died, a resentful and discouraged man, Lezzard was nine years old and his brother twelve.

"Mother remarried briefly—we all became Lezzard then—but it didn't work out. She became a *modele*. You know, posing naked for aspiring artists. That's what she told us. She had an arresting face and a good figure. In time, my brother and I figured out that there was more going on than posing naked. But then, what else could she do to feed us?"

"A bottle," Lezzard said waving his empty glass. "Let's get a bottle of wine."

"Count me out," Ben said quickly. "I'd like to be sober when I read the letters."

"It would be a waste, Jean," Audrey said. "Have another glass instead."

"Oh, let's go for it," Laukhin said.

Lezzard signaled the waiter and ordered the bottle. "She died after the war, soon after she learned of my brother's death," he went on, "although, by that time, she had given up all hope of seeing him again. My brother had the stupid idea of fighting the Bolsheviks on the German side. Mother had a heart attack in the *metro*. Thirty joyless years would do it to anybody. She died instantly, underground, changing trains at the Châtelet. I was with her."

Ben said, "Maybe I will have another beer."

"When we got older, Mother used to joke that she had been an immigrant by profession. Not a prostitute. Prostitution was her second job. Like delivering pizzas after a day at the office. I do the same, following in her footsteps, a professional immigrant and prostitute."

He swept the air with his hand. "All this is due to dear Mother. After her death, I found about a dozen unframed paintings in one of her suitcases. Among them, three Matisses and a Vlaminck. Well, that was a shock, *n'est-ce pas*? A real dilemma for a son. Did mother get the paintings for services rendered or did she steal them from customers sleeping off the effects of too much wine and *amour*? How many rendezvous was a Matisse worth in those difficult days? In which rich bourgeois homes in the Marais or in the *huitième* had these paintings once hung? Come on, young people, another sip to the memory of the dear lady. Whatever her choices in life, she had excellent taste and was a brave heart."

Lezzard eyes were bloodshot. He stood up with some difficulty and went inside. They watched him, moving slowly and deliberately.

"How many times have you heard this story?" Laukhin asked Audrey.

She shrugged. "I don't think he's lying, if that's what you are asking. He may be overdramatizing it a bit, but then most people do that with their own lives."

"Why does he say he's a prostitute?" Ben asked.

"It's about art that sells well but, in his opinion, is bad, worthless. He says he has sold a lot of worthless art with great success. I don't know if it's an act, or he's really troubled by it."

They were quiet until Lezzard returned. "Hard to find the *pissoir* in this place. Couldn't remember where it was. I'll finish the story, quickly, then put me in a cab.

"Even then," he carried on, "those paintings were worth quite a lot of money. Especially for me, drifting from job to job, with hardly any prospects. I took everything I'd found and went to America, to New York. I told myself that's where the money was. Besides, I felt it risky to try to sell Mother's treasure in France. Who knew how she had acquired them? In the early years of the war, you know, I'd seen her with German officers. She stopped after a while, and that's probably what saved her. That, and the anonymity of Paris. My fear was that if they were shown in France after the war, somebody could claim ownership of any one of the paintings, and I would not be able to explain their provenance.

"There you are. That's why I left, in 1947, after Mother's death. With the paintings I brought over I became half owner of a gallery. It had a good run. For many years, my partner and I had a very successful business. I was young, energetic. I even got married, a disaster that ended shortly thereafter in a nasty divorce. American women should be kept in caves and brought out at intervals for reproductive services. I have no idea where my former wife is, even if she's still alive. I have a daughter in Denver, or nearby. She sends me Christmas cards, but she doesn't tell me her whereabouts—probably afraid I'd visit her. I would, you know, if she'd only half-invite me. I seem to have many grandchildren, because the list of names signing the card is always increasing. Either that or she's living in an ever-growing commune..."

Lezzard closed his eyes and nodded off. They watched him for a while, asleep in his chair, his head tossed back, mouth half open, a defiant and pained man.

Audrey got up. "I'm sorry, but I'm very tired. Do you mind? He's a docile drunk."

"I know," Laukhin said.

"Make sure he gets into a cab all right."

Laukhin followed her for a few steps. "It's going to be over thirty degrees this weekend," he said. "Why don't we run off together to Corby Falls. Ben is from Corby Falls. He shares a cabin there with a friend of his, on the south shore of Clara's Lake, only a mile or two from the town. I'll get the key from him. It's a bit rustic—there's no electricity—but if you call it a dacha it acquires a romantic glow. I've been there once. There's nothing near it except a pasture at the back and a few cows that won't be interested in us. In the morning the water is fresh and undisturbed. We could jump in as the birds begin their morning chorus. In the evening, we'd eat canned dinners and drink wine by the light of the smelly oil lamp, and we'd go to bed early and tipsy."

"Did you say, smelly oil lamp?"

"Basic, yes, but deliberate simplicity. Minimalist—we Russians started it. Total communion with nature. It's where we are at our best."

She smiled. "I'll think it over."

"Think it over?"

"Give me some time, Art."

Time. That was what he didn't have, closing in on fifty. She should have said, "Have patience, Art." Trees have patience.

He went back to the table. After a while, they woke Lezzard, who had a hard time finding his credit card and cash for the cab. As they walked to Avenue Road to hail a taxi, they had to hold him steady.

* * *

Ben and he looked at Babel's letters the next day in Laukhin's office. He cleared half of his desk, and Ben carefully laid the three letters on the freed surface. The ink had faded, and the paper, tearing at the folds, had yellowed. Ben kept realigning the letters, and Laukhin believed he saw the beginning of tears in his eyes. The earliest letter, dated October 1928, was short and disappointing.

Mashenka,

I came by yesterday, but you were out. I left the money with your older son who didn't recognize me and was reluctant at first to take the envelope.

I'm going back home in a week's time. I'd like to see you again before I leave. I'll be free for a couple of hours this coming Wednesday, at two o'clock in the afternoon. The usual place? I'll wait for you. Please come.

The signature was illegible, but they could make out an 'I. Babel.'

The second letter, from 1932, was more promising, although of indirect literary interest. It was long, full of anguish about what the future held in store for him, and contained details about friends and acquaintances. There was an entire page about his daughter, whom he had never seen before. Seeing his three-year old daughter, he wrote, had filled him with unimaginable joy, but "it's a tortured joy, a joy unable to find rest or a future." It must have been a slow and dark time for Babel to write a letter that long.

The third letter had Ben's heart pounding—that's what he told Laukhin afterward—by the time they finished reading it.

Dear Masha,

I am rushing to respond to you. Please tell your friend that I'm very keen to meet Marina Ivanovna while I'm here in Paris—any-time, anywhere. I'm motivated not just by the desire to meet a true, untainted poet—few are left—but also because it would help me with XX.

I worry that XX is becoming too long. I must constantly be on guard against this Russian sickness. But it's so much easier to let your pen just go, floating over the paper like a sailboat blown by recollections. The first part—about the boy's child-hood in Odessa, in a Jewish family at the turn of the century, a family in which tradition and the pull of change clash under ominous signs and revolutionary hysteria—keeps getting lon-ger and longer, and I keep cutting, and then writing more, and cutting again.

Familiar? I could write about this forever. I seem to have written about this forever. At first, I tried to stay away from obvious autobiographical details, so I changed many things from my own childhood. In time, I relented somewhat. I don't have a vivid imagination so I'm better off sticking to what I know. Although my hero also starts in Odessa, I changed facts here and there. What I can't change, what I don't want to change, is what I take most delight in writing about: the smells, shouts, and cruelty; the nuttiness, the vanishing of a way of life and a certain innocence. So, without question, this is an autobiographical book in the sense that it draws heavily on my life (who said that we have only one book in us?) except, of course, in the last part.

I'm quite happy with the middle part too. Love, literary ambitions, revolution, civil war, Moscow, marriage and family, first literary success, fame.

And then (can you hear me sighing?) the hero's many doubts, inability to write, family problems, distress, unexplained anguish, thoughts of emigrating. It's here where I have the greatest difficulties, and where meeting and talking with Marina Ivanovna would help. My hero's final choice is different, of course, but even with him taking the "correct path" I'm beginning to think I don't have much of a chance of ever seeing my novel on bookshelves. Well, we'll see.

It would be best if the meeting were not advertised. The fewer people who know about it the better. I'm free tomorrow the whole day. Sunday would do too, although with more difficulty, and not in the evening. As for next week, Monday and Wednesday are fine, but I prefer Monday so that we do not leave it to the very last moment. I'm leaving on Thursday.

They read the letter several times, passing it back and forth between them. Laukhin warned Ben that all that glittered was not gold.

Ben disagreed. "It's gold, Artyom Pavlovich, pure gold, twenty-four karat. The Marina Ivanovna in the letter has to be Tsvetayeva. And, yes, I am almost afraid to believe it, but...Babel was talking here about a longer narrative work that was taking him many years, a novel, this *XX*. That's what he did during those barren years. *XX* is the reason for Babel's mysterious silence."

They spent more than an hour speculating about Babel's novel. They wondered whether *XX* was a tentative title alluding to the century the hero's life overlaps or just a placeholder; whether *XX* was definitely lost or still in some archive of the secret police. Likely it was lost, but there was no way of knowing. Laukhin said that he had heard rumours of a novel by Babel, autobiographical in spirit. "I remember my father talking with Pasternak about it."

"There's nothing in the journal about it, is there?" Ben asked.

"No."

"Odd, isn't it?"

Laukhin shook his head. "My father was unduly influenced by his great hero, and Pasternak disliked Babel. Couldn't stand him."

He told Ben the story of the long awkward train trip the two writers had taken together. They travelled to Paris in 1935, to the Congress of Writers in Defence of Culture—only communists could dream up such insipid names—just the two of them. They had not been part of the initial Soviet delegation, but, at Malraux's insistence, they were added by the Soviet authorities and sent together on the same train bound for the West. During their trip Babel was dismissive, mocking, sometimes even rude to Boris Leonidovich. Pasternak had not been in good health, and he was known to be a hypochondriac, a complainer, a man used to having one or several women around him, looking after his smallest needs. Pasternak's constant whine about his health and his complicated family life probably drove Babel crazy, and he might have been testy with him. From that trip onward, Pasternak's talk about Babel was always tinged by dislike.

"I never heard Pasternak say one good word about Babel," Laukhin said. "Never. And he dismissed all rumours of a Babel novel by saying it would not have amounted to anything. He saw Babel as a jeweller, a craftsman of miniatures, a man who never had what it took to write a great novel. Babel was a small time conjurer, a magician with two or three good tricks."

Turning back to the letters he was holding, Laukhin told Ben he was particularly pleased about the connection with Tsvetayeva. The simple mention of a potential meeting between Babel and her, which, as far as he knew, never took place, was yet another reason for Ben to include Tsvetayeva in his thesis, and he made it clear that he expected Ben to fall into line. It didn't matter to Laukhin whether the thesis focused on Babel or on Tsvetayeva. He understood that Ben preferred the former, but—he said, wagging his finger at him—with the Tsvetayeva material from his father's journal being so extensive, she should certainly take up more room in the thesis. "The rest," he concluded, "is a matter of how much academic weight you can give something that is pure conjecture."

Ben protested. "The letter is not a conjecture. Nor the fact that Babel worked on a novel during his years of silence."

"Yes, of course, but we don't have the novel."

Last night we had Kolya Klyuchev for dinner—the first dinner with guests in our new apartment. Two days ago, before noon, Kolya and I dismantled the Volkovs' dining room table, loaded it in a truck together with its six chairs, and moved it to Lavrushinsky Lane. The table is a bit too long. We'll see. We'll take the middle leaf out most days, and move two chairs against the wall. It was Pavliuk who found the truck, through his brother. The driver was very happy with the money I gave him, a young, cheerful lad just released from the army. He loved the elevator. He helped us put the table back together and afterward, as he left, asked, "What kind of a room is this, with no bed in it?"

Yevgenya said that their new dining table would be twice as big as the one they sold us—maybe more than twice. Ignoring Kolya, she steered me into a corner, pressed her body against mine, and said, "I hear your books are becoming a must read. Who'd have thought? *The Iced Waterfall* is on my night table right now. There must be more to you... But, you know, I always sensed that. Well, well, we must find out." I said, "I could read to you from my book, Yevgenya, before you fall asleep."

Since Kolya had helped with the new table and chairs, we thought we'd have him as our first dinner guest. Not that we had much choice, as cousin Kolya had been practically living in our place since his actress wife ran off the morning of the new year. A third and recent wife, he had not seen it coming. He wouldn't say whether there was another man, or she had a swift change of mind. Often tearful, he told us he couldn't bear to be in his empty apartment, and that he was grateful for our understanding. With Kolya lingering around many evenings, Varya would catch me in the kitchen and whisper, "Why is he still here?" I'd try to placate her, "Varenka, it's for a while only..." "I dreamt all my life for some privacy, Pavlusha, just us, a bathroom to share only with my family. I finally get it and it comes with Kolya." Most times, chased away by Varya's words or hostile silence, Kolya would retreat to sleep in his own place, only a few metro stations away, but now and then he'd leave us only to climb upstairs to the Pasternaks.

Varya's mother had sent us a black-market chicken, and Varya cooked a delicious stew with onions, peppers, potatoes and cauliflower. She put aside the neck, the back, and the wing tips for a soup later this week, and the gizzards for Tyomka. I bought fresh bread in the afternoon and Kolya brought two bottles of vodka. Quite a feast. Kolya also brought along his new girlfriend—she's more than twenty years younger than he, a child—and he couldn't keep his hands off her. He told us at the last moment he'd bring someone, and Varya commented, "Hallelujah, we might see less of him in the future."

We told Kolya's new friend about our luck with the apartment and our awkward meeting with Tsvetayeva. And it turned out that we talked about Tsvetayeva the entire evening—in truth, Kolya told stories and we listened. He was in very good form. The tears, the sighs and the bitter words for his treacherous wife were forgotten. The young woman was working miracles on him—that evening at least—and he entertained us with gossip about Tsvetayeva's affairs before and during her marriage. And yet she had loved her husband, Kolya insisted. After all, she had followed him when he left Russia, and then, fifteen years later, followed him back here. Was he worthy of such devotion?

The lives some people have!

Three months after she returned to the Soviet Union, both her daughter and her husband were in jail. She has not heard a word about them since, and she has no idea if they're still alive.

During the civil war, alone in Moscow with her two daughters and with nothing to eat, Tsvetayeva placed her younger daughter, Irina, in an orphanage, thinking that the child would have a better chance of surviving. Little Irina, not even three years old, died there of hunger.

The lives some people have!

It's as if they constantly make the worst possible choices. And so the anguish goes on and on. Varya is right, Tsvetayeva is tragedy. Her end is near; it's unavoidable, already decided by our modern gods. I can hear the choir chanting about the inevitable, praising the Party's huge steamrollers that crush anybody different. I rarely have these kinds of premonitions, but I do about her. Is it because she seems so helpless, so impractical, so ineffective, so lost, so alone?

Toward the end of the evening, Kolya's new girlfriend ran to the bathroom and threw up. As they staggered out of the apartment, Kolya was calling her Grushenka, Little Pear, and she was very pale and shivering.

After they left, Varya wondered how my cousin knew so much about Tsvetayeva. Or appeared to know. I told her he must have heard many stories about Tsvetayeva from Pasternak. Almost ten years older than me, Kolya had been a good friend of Boris Pasternak since their days together at Moscow University. Kolya had written poetry in his early days (and, he recently whispered to me between sobs, that he was writing again) and it was this common interest that led to their friendship. They remained good friends after Kolya gave up the idea of writing poetry as a permanent occupation and—to his parents' delight—turned to medicine. I told Varya too that Kolya might have met Tsvetayeva before she left Russia. Pasternak and Tsvetayeva knew each other before she went abroad to join her husband, and they sporadically corresponded during the many years Tsvetayeva was away. They admired each other as poets, but—as he said during dinner—Kolya felt that there must have been more to it than that. It was hard to keep their friendship going through letters, though, even if they were both poets. They saw each other the one time Pasternak traveled briefly to Paris. Tsvetayeva may have expected more on her return, but Pasternak had married again and had his own life and worries.

What a luxury it is to have your own room, and to be able to write undisturbed!

I slept poorly last night. Too much booze, of course, but my mind was restless. I thought of Tsvetayeva, then of the Fredkins, and there I got stuck, couldn't get them out of my mind. Kolya's girlfriend, Little Pear, had said soon after she walked in last evening that she knew our apartment quite well, but then she clammed up. Later, much later, not long before she threw up, she said that she had been a good friend of the Fredkins' oldest daughter.

Had been? I shouldn't have shown my distress and astonishment, yet I did. Worse, it came out with a hint of blame.

Little Pear said she didn't know where the daughter was. Maybe she had been taken away too, or had slipped quietly away somewhere—if that were possible—hoping to be forgotten.

"You didn't ask around, didn't ask anybody? I mean, other friends of hers?"

Little Pear looked pale and unsettled. "I did, for a few days, but then, you know..." She stammered and looked beseechingly at us. She had realized, or had been told, that it would be safer not to try to find out what had happened to her friend.

I felt terrible. What right had I, now living in the former Fredkins' apartment, to ask her such questions.

It was then that Little Pear rushed to the bathroom and threw up. Kolya rushed after her, but not before he threw me a reproachful look. Varya stared after him and said, "Christ, he could be her grandfather."

Could it be that the Fredkins were entirely innocent? Well, of course they were, but could they have been so hideously unlucky that they were fingered simply because they lived in the apartment that the Kremlin master thought would do well for the author of the Oleg Vinograd stories? I could imagine it:

"Did, what's his name, that writer of spy stories, Laukhin, yes, did Laukhin get an apartment?"

"Not yet, Comrade Stalin."

"Make it happen. Immediately."

"We don't have anything available right now, Comrade Stalin. Unless, of course, we move a bit faster."

A thoughtful puff of the pipe, followed by a weak exhalation of blue smoke. "Who do you have in mind?"

"I brought with me a list, just in case. Here it is."

Fate, in the form of a tobacco-stained finger, moved down the paper slowly, methodically. "There, Fredkin. Never liked him much—I think."

"Will do it. Tonight, Comrade Stalin, tonight."

What if the apartment was the one freed up by the disappearance of Bedrosyan's sister and brother-in-law? Would Bedrosyan have talked about the party's gift to me with the same enthusiasm? Would he have asked somebody else to tell me, somebody less conflicted? It didn't seem to affect him much. He talked about the Fredkins as if they are no longer in this city of ours. No longer even in our world. And he was right, they aren't. What did Bedrosyan say? "It belonged to Fredkin. Well, it doesn't matter now." Did he say that on purpose or was it a slip-up? Probably on purpose, to let me know that I am not better than him, not better than all the others with their snouts deep in or waiting their turn. It's not that I didn't feel sorry for the Fredkins. I did, for a few seconds, after Bedrosyan mentioned their names. A few seconds, and then I succumbed to the thrill of being at the trough at long last.

5

Ben was outside Alumni Hall, checking the grey sky. Laukhin pointed his umbrella at him. "Is it going to rain?"

Ben shrugged.

"How far have you got with the trip?" He had asked Ben to do a first translation of the trip to Yelabuga for the Tsvetayeva bundle.

"I've translated the first entry," Ben said. "Their routine on the boat, the cold weather and the brief forays on the deck, steward Arkhip, Captain Korotkov's table. It's still in rough shape." He hastened to add, "And I typed in the excerpt about Tsvetayeva and her son staying for a few nights in your parents' new apartment. Do you remember her at all?"

He shook his head. "I remember Georgy, her son. He seemed huge to me."

"Such fear, stifled, smoldering, unable to find an outlet. Your mother must have been out of her wits. I've gone through it at least a dozen times by now, and it's still gut-wrenching. It tugs at one's heart, Artyom Pavlovich. That cousin of yours, Sasha Cornilov, he was a nasty piece. Did you know him well?"

Laukhin thought for a while. "You could say I didn't know him at all. I was still a child when he stopped coming to our home. He and my father, as you've already discovered, didn't exactly get along. Mother would sometimes see him at her sister's place. She took me along a few times, but my father was not happy about it and so she stopped taking me with her. I completely lost touch with him. A poet too, ha. He was—maybe still is, he was very much alive when I left—like that fictional poet cop, Adam Dalgliesh, who caught murderers and wrote poetry in his spare time. Although Cornilov's job wasn't to catch murderers. He wrote most of his poetry—not that bad, I read some of it out of curiosity—in his youth. Perhaps he never stopped writing."

"What exactly did he do?"

"He worked for the KGB, quite high up, but I never knew exactly what his title or role were. My father wanted nothing to do with him. I knew from my mother that his first wife died relatively young, leaving him with a twelve-year-old son, and that he was a good, devoted father. He remarried a younger woman, but only after his son left home."

"For somebody who didn't know him, whose family avoided him, you seem well informed about him."

Laukhin smiled. "I knew his daughter."

"How so?"

"She liked my poems."

"A groupie, a *poklonnitsa*."

"She wrote poetry too."

"And you helped her."

"Not much. It was just before I left the Soviet Union."

"Ah, you did help her. How well did you know her?"

A few drops of rain fell on Laukhin. He looked up at the low clouds and said, "It's starting."

"You didn't answer me. How well did you know her?"

"We had an affair. A brief one."

"With Miss Cornilov? With your first cousin—well, once removed?"

"We weren't related at all. She was Cornilov's stepdaughter. His second wife, a widow, came with a daughter. Not Miss Cornilov, though, because she kept her father's last name—Lyutov."

"Lyutov? You're making this up."

"I'm not. Miss Lyutov, indeed."

"How did you meet her? I thought you had no contact with Cornilov."

"At a poetry reading several months before I left. She came and talked to me afterward. She told me we were related, kind of, and she smiled. It had the right effect on me. It was a hot summer evening, and I was tired and irritated with all the fawning words, and the small apartment was crowded and stuffy. Yes, I was also keen to know what had happened to my cousin. And Anna was young—a young beautiful woman, who tempted this older poet."

"What happened?" Ben asked. "Tell me about it."

"There isn't much to tell. We had a banal—how should I describe it— romantic episode. The usual story: famous, middle-aged poet, youthful admirer. She was a ripe piece of fruit dangling from a low branch. An easy pick, like many others, and so I picked and tasted. It's not that she didn't know what she was getting into. She had her eyes wide open, despite her youth. It might even have led to a book of poetry—about a departed lover, about waiting and betrayal. I heard she'd published a slim volume of verses a few years after I left. I tried to get a copy—vanity, Ben, vanity—but couldn't. Maybe it was just a silly rumour, nothing more. Who'd publish such drivel in the Soviet Union, anyway?"

* * *

Anna Lyutova. The first image that came to his mind was of her small, perfect breasts, a touch asymmetric and that made them all the more beguiling. It was the early afternoon, the second time they had made love, and a spot of sunlight was dancing on her cheek. She had straddled him, and he touched her breasts softly, hesitantly, as if he were blind—the diffidence of a lecherous older man not believing his luck.

"Hypocrite," Anna laughed when he said he felt guilty to have her in his bed. "I'm twenty years old. Anyway, *I* was the one who seduced you, remember?"

"I'm too old for you—twenty-two years older."

"So?"

"We have no future together."

"No one has a future in this country of ours."

"Still."

"I don't want a future with you. I want a *now*. I want to know what makes a poet."

"You know that already. You are a poet yourself."

Later he moved to an armchair to get a better view of her. He held, prudishly, a pillow on his lap, and began peppering her with questions about her family. She was guarded and somewhat puzzled about her stepfather, but talked about her mother, Natalya, with much irritation. She didn't understand why her mother had married Sasha Cornilov. Well, perhaps she did, but for a long time she had refused to accept it.

"What did you think—what do you think—of your stepfather?" Laukhin asked.

It took her a while to answer. She'd been a typical, boring, exasperating teenager when her mother remarried. She didn't think much in those days—she had boys and poetry on her mind. She appreciated the material comforts Cornilov brought them, but otherwise she kept her distance from him. As he did from her. She was now thinking of moving to Leningrad and hoped he'd help her, because this way she'd be out of his hair and he could give free rein to his love for Natalya. A complicated man, undoubtedly, probably ruthless if provoked. But he'd been kind to her, protective, in a detached, wary way.

It struck Laukhin that she talked not like a twenty-year-old, but like somebody much older, or as if this was not her first lifetime. Had she asked, startled and distressed, "Dear God (Lord Vishnu?), why the Soviet Union this time?"

"Is he still a Chekist?" he asked.

"Yes."

She thought her stepfather's career had faltered as he approached retirement. Cornilov became soft, talked imprudently about trying to understand those who went astray, and was seen in a church crossing himself, tears in his eyes. Marrying Natalya Lyutova had been a bad decision, and a surprising one. Not only because his new bride was sixteen years younger than him, but also because her former husband had had skirmishes with the NKVD.

"How old were you when they got married?" Laukhin asked.

"Sixteen."

Cornilov towered over her mother. They were an odd pair because of the difference in age and size, but he worshipped her. He looked at her and after her with the fervour and devotion of a dog, always trying to anticipate her smallest need or whim. His talk became peculiar, annoying to their friends. Whenever he'd say something he'd immediately turn to her and ask, "Isn't that so? Isn't that so, Natushka?" He wanted her approval for everything—his opinions, the books he read, the shoes he wore, even his choice of shoelaces. It was embarrassing to witness. "Am I right, Natushka?" or "Do you like it, Natushka? Tell me if you don't, and I'll..."

He began writing poetry again. His superiors frowned upon it—somebody who wrote poetry was not likely to posses the single-mindedness and concentration required by their work. He had not published anything in the fifties and the sixties, but later a few poems appeared in two literary magazines and a slim volume of selected verse was printed. Had his position opened doors to editors and publishers? Of course. But he was not a bad poet. His verses were dark—always had been—although, lately, this was less of an issue provided due balance and respect was paid to the regime.

"And your father?"

"What about him?"

"How old were you when he died?"

"Nine."

She was lying on her side on the large bed, facing him, her head cradled in her hand, a pillow under her elbow, naked, a corner of the sheet covering her ankles and feet.

"What kind of man was he?"

She didn't have a clear picture of her father, she'd been too young. She remembered him shouting. No, her father had not treated Natalya with the same reverence Cornilov did later. Far from it. Disappointments had turned him to drink, and, a couple of times, he had knocked her about. Maybe more than a couple of times. He was often depressed, and he killed himself in 1967. Afterward, her mother had slowly succumbed to Cornilov's adoration. Adoration, worship, and a comfortable existence. A much easier life. Cornilov adored her mother, and she liked it.

Anna smiled, but her face reflected disappointment. "One day, two months ago, I got home at an earlier hour than expected. I found my step-father in the kitchen, sitting on a low stool, shining my mother's shoes and boots, unfolded *Izvestias* carefully spread on the floor. Footwear, all Mother's, a dozen pairs—a dozen, imagine it! Mother was in the living room, reading. She said, embarrassed, 'He won't let me do it.'"

And yet, in a way, her mother was afraid of Cornilov. It sounded odd, of course— afraid of a husband who worshipped her. But with Cornilov's worship came constraints and reproaches. Natalya was untidy, wasteful, couldn't give proper directions to the woman who came to clean their large apartment. She couldn't look after her own health. Because she had high blood pressure and some vitamin deficiency, Natalya was supposed to take pills every day, some brought from abroad at great expense and difficulty, but she was casual about taking them. It drove Cornilov to a cold, cutting rage that her mother found frightening. Anna had never witnessed any of his rages, and her mother had never complained to her, but she did to her own mother, once. Only once. Worried, her grandmother told Anna about it.

Anna delicately scratched her pubic hair with a finger. An hour earlier his head had been there, and he'd heard her whisper something he didn't get, probably because her thighs had closed over his ears. She turned onto her back and pulled the sheet up.

"He knows about us," she said.

"Cornilov?"

"He does."

She didn't know how, but Cornilov had known about their dalliance from the very beginning, almost before it started. He hadn't told her mother about it, but he'd taken Anna aside and warned her that Art Laukhin had had many affairs, and that she would get hurt. He knew it because Art Laukhin was his cousin on his mother's side. He'd kept a distant eye on him.

"It was the only time I had a tête-à-tête with my stepfather."

* * *

It began to rain as he turned onto Hazelton Avenue. A luxury minibus, tall and yellow, was parked illegally outside the gallery, its lights flashing. Inside, a group of loud German tourists had taken over. They had a lot to say to each other, their need for cultured communication kindled by irritating spirals of glistening colours. Not the typical quiet Tuesday, as Laukhin had hoped. Audrey saw him and raised her eyebrows in resignation. He approached her and said he'd wait in the small room. She whispered, "The things I learn from Jean Lezzard. We had three buses last week."

He understood Audrey's remark only afterwards—the dealer must have bribed a couple of tour operators to drop their loads of tourists in front of his gallery.

The new oil painting was right across from Lezzard's desk. He'd never seen such a large Chemakoff before. The small ink and water-colour he liked so much—what was it, *Strong Symmetries?*—had disappeared. A couple of late Chemakoffs were gone too. Lezzard must have removed them to make space for his new acquisition. He walked over for a closer look. It was striking, and he began to understand Lezzard's enthusiasm. When he had called the gallery a week earlier from out of town, Audrey told him that Lezzard had been beyond himself with excitement over his new Chemakoff paint-ing. Audrey and the man who carried the canvas inside had helped Lezzard hang it so that he could look at it by just lifting his eyes. Afterward Lezzard sat down at his desk, leaned back with his hands behind his head, sighed, and said he wished he didn't have to sell it. Audrey said, "Don't sell it, then." Lezzard shook his head. "I have to. I run a gallery, not a museum."

In composition, the new painting was similar to the Chemakoff that had hung in his Lavrushinsky Lane apartment—a soirée of the empire's grandees, with a smattering of absurd presences—only much larger. He didn't quite get the significance of some of the interlopers, but he recog-nized a welder, a *zek* with a number on his torn jacket, a trim SS officer wearing a red armband with a swastika, a knife grinder bent over an archaic, foot activated wheel but dressed in a modern three-piece suit, and a skeletal man wearing a miner's hat complete with oil lamp.

Two men came into the small room just as Laukhin sat down again at Lezzard's desk. The younger one looked briefly at him, said something that might have been construed as a greeting, and led the shorter, elderly man to the new Chemakoff. Laukhin thought of leav-ing but he heard them speak Russian and decided to linger. Linger, eavesdrop, snoop. He'd have a story for Audrey later.

The younger man seemed anxious. "Well, what do you think? Wonderful, isn't it? Didn't I tell you? Isn't it his best?"

He was swirling around the elderly man, in a curious choreography of impatience and respect, like a boy showing his father a toy he coveted. The elderly man took his time, cleaned his glasses, put his nose close to the canvas a couple of times, nodded and mumbled something to him-self. His brown trousers, belted way above his waist, exposed grey socks. At last, he said, "It is beautiful, no doubt. One of the best. I remember it."

"Didn't I tell you?"

"It's odd though."

"Odd? What's odd?"

"The date, what's the date? I can't see it that well. Is it nineteen-sixty?"

"Yes, nineteen-sixty."

"It was there, in his apartment."

"What was?"

"This painting. It was there, in Chemakoff's apartment when they barged in and took everything away."

"They took this painting?"

"This, and several others too. He had many paintings in his apartment. He had no place to store them, and he couldn't sell any of them in the last few years. They took away all of them."

"Are you sure?"

"Of course I'm sure. I remember this one very well. I remember when he painted it. I was the one who suggested he include the Donbass miner. It is Chemakoff's only painting that has a miner. It took him quite a while to find a thirties miner's hat. And I know where he kept this painting—in his bedroom."

The young man said something that Laukhin didn't catch.

"Yes, yes, I was there," the older one went on.

"How come?"

"I was fighting with my wife in those days and I needed a break. Chemakoff had given me the key to his apartment. He told me to make use of it while he was away in Paris for his show."

"You mean, they came in, searched the place, and took his paintings while you were there watching them?"

"They told me to disappear. They were quite startled to find me there and weren't sure at first what to do. But they made a phone call and then they told me to get lost. I went back several days later. All of his paintings were gone, and his books and papers had been ransacked."

They paused, still looking at the painting. Then the young man asked, "But how, then?"

The old man nodded. "Exactly."

Laukhin was keen to hear more—although the two men were almost whispering by now—but just then Audrey came into the small room and dropped exhausted into her chair. "Oh, good, I'm glad you're still here. Let's kill that idiot."

"The spiral artist?" Laukhin asked. "I'm in."

"The plumber."

"You have a plumber here?"

"Since this morning."

"You can't kill plumbers, Audrey. Not in Canada, it's not that simple. Perhaps you can in England, but not here. You can kill painters, though. It's legal. That's why they stick together in groups. But plumbers, no. We have laws, procedures."

"He keeps telling me I don't understand the building code."

"What's he done?"

"Nothing, apart from tearing down a wall in the basement, and the water is still leaking. Art, would you go down and take a look? I can't get hold of Jean."

"I'll go. I know plumbing. I'm unique, Audrey—plumber and poet. Most women wouldn't hesitate."

She noticed the two men near the new Chemakoff's painting. "Oh, Mr. Karpov," she said to the younger one, "you're back. So soon."

Karpov turned to her. "Yes, yes, I said I'd be. Let me introduce a friend of mine, Ms. Millay. Mr. Gratch, a friend of Chemakoff too. Mr. Gratch and Chemakoff knew each other back in Leningrad. Best of friends they'd been, long before my time."

Mr. Gratch advanced toward Audrey. "How did you get this painting?" he asked.

Audrey seemed nonplussed. "Sorry? Which one?"

Mr. Gratch pointed at the new Chemakoff oil. "That one, of course."

"Oh, I couldn't tell you. Sorry, I didn't ask."

"You don't know?"

"I'm sure Mr. Lezzard will be able to tell you. The owner of the gallery, you'll have to ask him. He doesn't come on Tuesdays, but he'll be here tomorrow. Are you interested in that painting?"

The two of them looked at each other, and then Mr. Gratch said, "You can say that. Very interested. Do you know where he got it from?"

"Well, I presume from his usual sources. He knows a lot of dealers in Europe. I don't know the details, but I'm sure Mr. Lezzard will be delighted to give you all the particulars of the painting's provenance tomorrow. He'll part with this painting only reluctantly, Mr. Gratch. He loves it. Do you have a card? A phone number we can reach you at tomorrow?"

Gratch waved his hands, annoyed by Audrey's questions. "No, no. Not necessary. I'll be back tomorrow."

They watched the two men leave, Gratch shaking his head at Audrey's ignorance. Audrey groaned. "What a crazy day. And now these two. I saw the young one, Karpov, this morning. He wouldn't leave this room—another admirer of Chemakoff. He said he didn't know our gallery had a special room for Chemakoffs. What on earth was the old man going on about? He didn't look like someone who'd buy such an expensive painting, and seemed rather upset."

"I think I know why," Laukhin said.

He told her what he heard. She didn't seem to grasp the implication immediately, so he added, "How did this painting get here?"

"On this continent?"

"Anywhere outside the Soviet Union. The road this painting took to Lezzard's gallery is rather suspicious."

"You mean, because it was confiscated by the Soviet police?"

"Surely, how it got into Lezzard's hands is a legitimate question."

She thought for a while. "There might have been an auction."

"With confiscated art? Open to western art dealers?"

"Maybe the Soviet authorities have a side agreement with some western dealers. A quiet understanding, something nobody talks about, but to everybody's profit. Hush-hush, you know, after Chemakoff's death. A way of getting some western currency. I'm sure there's an explanation. You said the French loved Chemakoff."

He nodded, but his doubts must have been clear on his face.

"You don't think Lezzard…Do you?" she asked.

"I don't know what to think."

She clapped. "This is very exciting. We have unearthed an illicit art network run by the KGB. I love this. Who says Toronto is boring? I can dine out on this story, shadowy Russian art thieves."

"There's probably an explanation."

"No, no, don't say that. Something stinks. Martha almost bought a painting like this one in the fall of 1982. I was visiting her at the time and she and Dirk talked about it. The deal fell through when Lezzard, for reasons he never explained properly, demanded cash, quite a lot of it, too. Dirk said no, and that was that. Martha wasn't that keen on Chemakoff, anyway. Lezzard then suggested a painting from Chemakoff's Paris years, very different, but Martha didn't like it at all, although they could have gotten it for much cheaper and paid for it by cheque."

Laukhin said, "I'll check on that plumber now, set him straight."

* * *

"Did one of the two Russians buy it?" Laukhin asked Audrey the following Tuesday as soon as he noticed that the large Chemakoff oil was no longer in the small room, or anywhere in the gallery.

She shook her head, impatient and animated – she had quite a story for Laukhin. She told Lezzard first thing on Wednesday morning about the interest two Russian visitors had shown in the new Chemakoff oil the day before, and about what Laukhin had heard while eavesdropping on them. She told him that one of the men, the older one, had recognized the painting from his days in Moscow, and that they'd likely return to the gallery. But she had told Lezzard a censored version of the events; she had skipped over the dramatic circumstances – the KGB raid in Chemakoff's Leningrad apartment, the older man's accidental presence there, his question of how the painting ended up in Lezzard's gallery. She couldn't, didn't know how else to tell Lezzard about the two Russians. There was an implied accusation in what Laukhin had heard, that Lezzard was involved with, well, she wasn't sure, the KGB or some unsavoury Soviet organization making money from confiscated art. She had not known how to put all that to Lezzard.

"What did Lezzard say?"

Not much. He hadn't looked pleased, but she might have been imagining things. He hadn't looked overly concerned either. But he wrote down the names of the two Russians, and he asked her to describe them.

There was more. The older one, Mr. Gratch returned Thursday morning. He spoke Russian to Lezzard. They didn't seem to have met before, but she couldn't be sure. She didn't think they had a good time with each other. No smiles. She had watched them closely and heard the name Chemakoff a few times. Mr. Gratch kept pointing to the smaller room, and then Lezzard pushed him in there and slid the folding doors across. She still heard them, and by the sound of it they were not talking prices. Mr. Gratch left first, without looking around him. Lezzard remained in the small room for about half an hour afterward, most of the time talking on the phone in Russian.

She scrutinized Lezzard when he finally left the small room, but he didn't seem more upset than usual. Hard to know – he was always upset. She asked Lezzard what the visitor had been after. A penniless Russian fool, was Lezard's reply. Not exactly answering her question.

That evening she'd flown back to London for a short visit and she'd been away Friday and Saturday. When she came back to the gallery on Sunday, the Chemakoff oil was gone. Lezzard said he'd sold it to an old client from his New York days, a Chemakoff collector. He used that irritated, dismissive tone of his, which meant he didn't want to talk about it any further.

She was flushed with excitement, Audrey, and she went on. She had checked the main book, the gallery book that kept the status of all the paintings that were going or had gone through the gallery: arrived, on exhibit, on loan, sold, returned, whatever. She was really curious to see whether the large Chemakoff oil had indeed been sold. No trace of it – wasn't even listed in as arrived in the gallery. Still more to it. She was the one who usually kept the main book up to date. The odd thing was that when Lezzard first brought that painting in, he'd told her he'd enter it in the main book himself. True, he'd do it, now and then, not that often. But after she checked whether the painting had indeed been sold, she played the naïve but straight assistant, and told Lezzard he'd forgotten to list the Chemakoff just sold, and offered to do it herself. He answered angrily that he'd already done it somewhere else. No doubt about it, Lezzard kept two sets of books.

There was a gap where the large Chemakoff oil had been. Audrey said that one of her tasks that Tuesday was to rearrange the art on the wall so that balance was restored.

"Back to the way it was," Laukhin said.

"More or less."

"I'll help you."

Saturday, 31 August 1940

Another draining evening and sleepless night. It began with a tense, early dinner. Varya sighed throughout, without saying a word. Tsvetayeva was quiet too, except to scold Georgy for his manners. She was probably sensing Varya's fright and mounting hostility. Georgy scowled at his mother. Tyomka and I tried to lift the gloom.

After dinner Tyomka was sent to bed. He's temporarily sleeping in the small room I use for writing on a narrow blue mattress, which Varya borrowed from one of the neighbours. As he had for the past few evenings, he was yelling and squealing, still thrilled by the novelty. I was tempted to walk in there and box his ears, but I refrained because he was excited, and Georgy was there with him. Georgy is only fifteen, but looks older. Big, a bit chubby. He plays with Tyomka for half an hour every evening with the air of an adult who understands he has a duty, and is willing to do it, but won't admit he's enjoying the task. He's an odd boy, clever I think, who's trying to understand his abnormal family, his unusual mother, their vagabond existence, his father and sister's imprisonments. Because he cannot, he often seems cruel to his mother. Yet they need each other. Clearly she needs him more than he needs her. He believes she's at the root of their troubles and the reason they are being treated like untouchables. Yesterday, as he and I were clearing the table after dinner, he said he wished his mother were in prison instead of his father. Luckily Tsvetayeva was not within earshot. I told Georgy that surely he wished that neither of his parents was in prison, and he shrugged, as if saying, you know very well what I meant. His mother annoys him. She either mollycoddles him or is unexpectedly harsh; there is no in-between.

By ten o'clock we were all in our bedrooms. Tsvetayeva had retired to the children's room—hers and Georgy's for now—and was probably writing. Not poetry, though. She confirmed that much this morning, when I mentioned to her that she'd have a few hours by herself in the house, except for little Larissa, who'd be sleeping most of the time. Tsvetayeva shrugged and said she had not written one verse since she had returned. "I'm like a squeezed slice of lemon, Pavel Nikolayevich. Dipped in boiling tea too. There is nothing left in me, nothing. No molecule of the poet, no atom of the woman or of the wife I once was. And I fear that motherhood is seeping out of me as well."

We had moved little Larissa's cot to our bedroom, and she was already asleep, oblivious that her mother was unhappy and crying. Varya was in bed. Her sobs were subdued, the sound muffled somehow. I was grateful that she hadn't made a scene in front of our temporary live-ins. They're leaving the day after tomorrow, and with any luck she'll not have a melt-down in front of them. I wonder if they hear her crying every night—our arguments, and my begging her to keep her sobs and voice down. The children's room is only one wall away.

Varya was in her nightgown, lying on her back, and as I switched on the night lamp I looked at her red face and eyes. Her neck was red too, as if more was needed to enhance Varia's overall expression of distress. I undressed quietly, slipped into bed and picked up a book, although I knew very well that I wouldn't be allowed to read for long.

She began to talk, and for a while I didn't pay attention, knowing what she was on about—Agranova, the neighbour from who we had borrowed the mattress. I had heard it all earlier, after lunch, while Tsvetayeva and Georgy were out. Agranova had been very angry that morning. She told Varya that letting Tsvetayeva stay with us was dangerous and stupid. She feared it would affect everybody in the building. Had she known what the mattress was for, she would not have lent it, and now she wanted it back. Not telling her who our guests were had been an abuse of her trust and friendship. How could we shelter the wife and child of an enemy of the people—a former White Russian, an émigré now imprisoned for treason?

I was tempted to say that Agranova was a stupid woman who had no idea—nobody knew—why Efron and Alya had been taken away, but I didn't.

I'd heard something similar on Thursday, from Bedrosyan, at the Writer's Union. He summoned me to his office and could barely restrain himself. "I was told you have Tsvetayeva in your apartment. Are you insane or just stupid? Do you really believe that this is the reason the Party has given you that beautiful, large apartment—to shelter enemies of the

Soviet Union? My God, you've lost your mind. Don't you think ahead? Don't you ever think of the consequences? Don't you think of your family? Don't you love them?"

He was smoking, as usual, and walking rapidly around me as if trying to spot evidence of my madness. Then he stopped and, pointing a stained finger at me, said, "Pavel Nikolayevich, get rid of them. Get rid of your guests. That's an order."

I didn't have the courage to punch him in the face, but how I wished I had. Instead, I looked through the window at the empty courtyard and, beyond it, the leafy lane, and waited for my anger and panic to lose their sting.

After a while, I turned to Bedrosyan and said, "They are moving out on Monday, Anastas Koryunovich. They've got a small room on Perzliakovsky Lane, more of a cupboard than a room from what I hear, but the people in there now have not moved out yet. So you see, it's only for a few days, until the room on Perzliakovsky becomes available."

He shouted, "Not one day! Not one hour!"

"A few days. You wouldn't put dogs in the street like that, would you?"

"Let's keep dogs out of this. We have to think about ourselves, about our families."

He put out his cigarette and straightened his back, readying himself to deliver the official line. "Comrade Laukhin, what you are doing could be viewed as collusion with foreign agents. There is a special meeting on Tuesday to discuss attitudes toward returned White émigrés. I sent you a letter early this morning, by the way, expressing in writing my displeasure and views. This is not just *my* message, Pavel Nikolayevich. I was called too—never mind, someone close to Comrade Zhdanov—late last night. The order is loud and clear: get rid of your guests. There was also a special message for you, sort of a personal message. That you shouldn't abuse your luck. People in high places may like your books, but even their considerable patience and benevolence has limits."

He was afraid he would be punished too.

That morning, as I was leaving home, I told Tsvetayeva that I'd be passing by the Writers' Union. She said, "I used to live not far from there, on Borisoglebsky Lane, for eight or nine years, until I left Moscow. I can't imagine any more what it means to live for so long in one place. My study was in the attic. The Civil War and the famine kept me there. I starved and wrote poetry. My younger daughter... well, that's all so long ago..."

I did the stupidest thing I could do under the circumstances. I told Varya about my meeting with Bedrosyan and this, as I should have known, has made things worse, much worse. She's been crying and fighting with me every night since I told her. Thursday night was the worst. Sasha Cornilov showed up here in the afternoon with a warning for his favourite aunt and I heard about it from her. Oh, did I ever hear it.

I got the same warning from Cornilov, and more. I met him on the stairs—the elevator wasn't working again—as he was leaving. He dropped all pretences and acted and talked like the thug with secret power that he is. I asked him what they had against this pitiful, weak, lonely woman. Wasn't it enough they'd arrested her innocent husband and daughter?

He laughed at first, and then got close to me and whispered, "Innocent? Are you stupid, or just naïve? Nobody's innocent, Uncle, nobody. Sergey Efron is far from innocent. He was one of our agents in France—oh yes, an agent, a spy (the word he used was *razvedchik*). It's too bad you didn't know him. He could have told you stories, real spy stories, not the stupid ones you waste good paper on. Oleg Vinograd might have learned a trick or two from him. But he got corrupted, our innocent Sergey Iakovlevich Efron, lost his way. Re-corrupted would be the better word—after all, didn't he fight with the Whites? You know what we think? We think he was always corrupt—a spy for both the French and the English. This is just for your ears, because you're getting on my nerves and I need to set you straight in a hurry."

"Go away," I said.

He looked with pity at me. "To think that I talked to a few people on your behalf. You're lucky, very lucky, you're married to Aunt Varya."

"I don't need your favours, and neither does Varya."

"You don't?" He was shouting now. "You stupid shit. How do you think you got an apartment in this palace? Do you really think it's enough that someone spends a few hours reading your vomit?"

I got angry too and told him I didn't want to see him in our apartment again. Then he lost it. The look on his face and what he said—he had to bend down because of his height—shook me. He leaned his whole weight on me, crushing me against the wall, and whispered, his face so close to mine that I felt his breath, "You stupid man, you stinking shit, you have no idea what we can do to you and to your family. No idea. I'm of the mind to take you on a tour, an educational tour. I can spit on my boots and make you lick them. I can make you eat my shit. Don't make me do it. Don't abuse your privileges. I'll come to your apartment to talk to my aunt whenever I want. *I—do you get it?—I* don't want to see *your* face when I come to see her. Is that understood?"

He started down the stairs, but turned back after a few steps and hit me in the solar plexus. I must have lost consciousness for a few seconds, because when I recovered he was gone and I was sitting on the stairs, breathing with difficulty. And then, as I was gathering strength to get up, I understood the true meaning of Cornilov's words. I had an indirect hand in what happened to the Friedkins. Because I had complained—to Varya and anybody who cared to listen—for so long and so often about the narrow squalid space we shared with the Marchuks.

I didn't tell Varya anything about my encounter with her nephew. I had learned my lesson.

Varya turned to face me. Her left breast, heavy with milk, spilled out of her nightgown. The nipple seemed lifeless, a powerful expression of what she felt. She said, "I don't get it. Why us, why you? You hardly know her. You met her—what?—a couple of times, maybe three times. You hear she's out in the street and you rush to offer our apartment. Why? You're not even a friend. She has friends, doesn't she? Isn't Boris Leonidovich her friend? Why doesn't he help her?"

I didn't answer; I had no answer.

She went on. "The Pasternaks' apartment is larger than ours. He's got the dacha in Peredelkino as well, surely big enough that they could stay there if he'd rather not have them here. He often has guests at Peredelkino, sometimes more than just two people. And he's all by himself there nowadays."

She looked at me, waiting, but, again, I had nothing to say.

"Why us, Pasha, why us? Look at little Larissa, Pasha, look at her. Don't you want to see her grow up? What difference does your silly gesture make? Tsvetayeva is a marked woman, and you know it as well as I do."

"Varenka, it's only one more day. They're going the day after tomorrow."

"There's nobody in the Pasternaks' apartment right now . It's empty. I ran into Boris Leonidovich in front of our building this morning. He was waiting for a taxi, all loaded with parcels. He didn't seem happy to see me. I asked about Zinaida, and he said she had been away for almost a week, fetching the boys from Koktebel. He was on his way to Peredelkino. He came back only for the night, to check his mail and pick up a few things. I couldn't resist—the thought of his empty apartment made my blood boil—and I told him about our guests. He looked rather embarrassed. Sheepish. He tried to appear startled, but didn't quite manage it. I think he knew—I mean, what I told him was not news to him, although he acted as if it was. I told him that I was very upset, scared. And I asked him whether he wanted to see Tsvetayeva, his friend. Yes, I was hoping that he didn't know about Tsvetayeva's latest predicament and that he would drop everything at once in order to see her, and that he would then insist she move in with them, with the Pasternaks, in their larger and empty apartment. At the very least, I hoped he'd want to see her, talk to her, hold her hand, give her a hug. She was only a couple of floors below him."

Varya laughed bitterly. "Well, he wouldn't. How naive of me to even think of it. His face did turn red, though, which isn't easy under that tanned skin of his. All that work in the vegetable garden, you know. Oh, he did mention the garden, his beloved garden, which gives him so much strength. He said he regretted he couldn't see Tsvetayeva but he had to get back to Peredelkino immediately. He couldn't spare even half an hour. He has been working on something very important, something vital, crucial for his work, something more significant than anything else he's done before, and he just could not put it off. 'One of those moments, Varvara Prokofievna, one of those moments an artist must seize,' he said. 'You understand, don't you? I'm sure Pavel Nikolayevich has moments like this too, when everything else is put aside and the only thing that matters is the work.' Then he made it worse. He said that he had urgent work to do in the garden at the dacha. His potatoes and his cabbage, his carrots and onions—his winter provisions were rotting and he had to harvest them. On his next trip to Moscow he'd make sure to visit Tsvetayeva, but he just couldn't do it this morning. The taxi came, to his relief. He got halfway in, then he ran after me. Took my hand and kissed it. His gallant self, as usual. He said, 'You are a good woman, Varvara Prokofievna, a very good woman. And your husband is a brave man. Please tell him that. God bless you both.' And he ran away. What an exit! Your hero, Pasha, the greatest living Russian poet."

I switched off the light and whispered, "One more day, Varenka, and it'll all be over. We'll soon forget this, you'll see."

Little Larissa sighed in her sleep and then made a brief sucking noise. I leaned toward Varya and nibbled her ear. It was wet from her tears. I touched her full soft breasts. She whispered, "No, not now, Pasha," but I knew better and I spent some time over there, then I moved, slowly, down her belly, to her thighs, and I parted them gently, and soon she was biting my neck, and all this time I was thinking that Tsvetayeva and Georgy would leave the day after tomorrow, on Monday, and that, with a bit of luck, once again I wouldn't have to make a choice, a real hard choice, that is.

We've lost the ability to make hard choices and stand up. We are spineless. We are afraid to make even meek, passive gestures, gestures that require no real backbone, like my offer to have Tsvetayeva and her son in our apartment for a few days. We are prostrated, frightened, terrorized.

Was Varya right? Should I throw out these two pitiable souls tomorrow or, even better, right now, wake them up in the middle of the night and throw them out in the street, into the hands of almighty God? It would be our mustachioed God who would catch them.

Artyom Laukhin
The Art of Poetry
(*The Paris Review*, Draft 1.0, June 1985)

The interview with Artyom Laukhin was conducted over two
consecutive days in February 1985. The first day we met at the
poet's home in Lytton Park, a neighbourhood of what had once
been North Toronto but was now well within the city. "The ugli-
est house on the street," Laukhin claimed, and, despite the cold
weather, insisted on coming out with me when I left to point out
its worst architectural features. He was renting it for next to
nothing from an acquaintance, a developer, also a former Soviet
Union citizen.

Inside, the small house was functional and comfortable. A den
at the back, kitchen, dining-cum-living room on the ground
floor. There used to be three small bedrooms and a bathroom
upstairs, but the previous owner renovated it into one huge
bedroom and a spacious bathroom. The bedroom, Laukhin told
me, had a large table under the windows facing south, where he
worked. At first he had been taken aback by the setup, but eventually he got used to having a bed in his workroom. If during
the night he had a thought or two worth writing down, he was at
his table in no time.

Laukhin sported a discrete moustache which, according
to him, went through many transformations and sizes, from
Gorkyan to no moustache at all. Light eyes, slightly bulging,
a frowning vast forehead, a round face, upturned nose, and
thinning hair. Medium height and broad-shouldered. A scowling bulldog, arrogant and impatient. He filled in his clothes,
and gave an impression of energy and strength. During the

interview, he often stood up and paced, and he used his arms to make a point.

We settled in the den, a well-lit, wood-panelled room, one wall covered with built-in bookshelves. An L-shaped, battered, blue leather sofa, stained coffee table, and a very old and dusty television set. Soviet posters from the twenties or thirties on the wall—several of them, all simply framed—either quite valuable or later reproductions. A play at Moscow's Satirical Theater, a movie, Lieutenant Kije, with music by Prokofiev, a three quarters portrait of a stern Mayakovsky in the threatening stance of a bouncer. Laukhin wore jeans, a T-shirt, tasseled loafers, and an old smoking jacket that reminded me of Babel's portrait on the cover of one of the first American editions of his stories. He said it belonged to his father, and it was one of those articles of clothing to which one becomes ridiculously and unexplainably attached.

I heard movement above us while we talked. Laukhin said he had a houseguest for a few days, an academic friend of his. It was a female friend, because when he left the room to bring us some tea and sandwiches I heard him talking and a young woman's voice answering. The poet had a reputation as a ladies' man, but he seemed unwilling to explain who his guest was.

When I left, he stepped briefly out with me. After criticizing the house, he pointed to the end of the street and said, "Yonge Street, up there, is the longest street in the world." There was a childish pride to the way he said this, an indication that he was happily ensconced in Toronto.

The next day we met in his office at Alumni Hall, a three-storey stone building on the eastern edge of the sprawling University of Toronto downtown campus. He wore blue jeans again, and a Maple Leafs sweatshirt. When we went to lunch, a five-minute February cold, windy, eye-piercing walk, he wore a light winter jacket, and no hat or scarf.

Overall, I spent some eight hours with Art Laukhin. His English is very good, grammatically correct and heavily accented. We began speaking in English, with small forays into Russian. Toward the end, I'd ask questions in English and he'd respond in Russian. He spoke rather quickly, particularly in

Russian. If uninterested, the flow of words slowed down dramatically, and I knew it was time to switch topics. As a condition of the interview, he insisted we discuss his father's forthcoming journal and not his own poetry for which he is now famous. The first volume of the journal has been delayed and is now scheduled for publication in the early fall.

Erika Belov-Wang

INTERVIEWER
Is Mayakovsky one of your favourite poets?

ARTYOM LAUKHIN
It's the poster, isn't it? I found these posters here, in Toronto, somewhere on Queen Street West. I admire Mayakovsky's energy, versatility, even his willingness to end it all, but I can't say he is a favourite. He's too political, too intense. He hits you with a hammer when a wooden stick would be more effective. My father was very fond of his poetry. He met him a few times when he was young, and he often talked about him.

INTERVIEWER
Are there entries about him in your father's journal?

LAUKHIN
No. The journal begins in 1936. Mayakovsky died in 1930.

INTERVIEWER
Suicide or murder?

LAUKHIN
I don't know. Some of his close friends were convinced he was killed by the KGB—well, it was the OGPU at the time. His lover, Lily Brik, who was involved with him in an on-and-off ménage a trois, was an OGPU agent. Mayakovsky's communal apartment had a secret entrance and the killers may have used it to get in and out, unseen. We specialize in this in the Soviet Union, in artists whose deaths

we argue about endlessly. Was Gorky poisoned? Why did Tsvetayeva kill herself? How did Babel and Mandelstam die? For how long was Meyerhold tortured? Who killed his wife? When was Pilnyak shot?

INTERVIEWER

Why poetry? Why not fiction, like your father?

LAUKHIN

My father did write poetry. That's how he began, but he decided early on that he wasn't good enough and gave up. I think he judged himself too sternly. He had had the bad luck of being born at the turn of the century. As a result, he struggled to become a poet during a miraculous period in Russian poetry, the first quarter of this century. At no other time did Russian poetry reach such heights and inventiveness, and have so many eminent practitioners.

INTERVIEWER

True.

LAUKHIN

My father dismissed his poetry as weak, conventional, worth only lighting a fire with. In desperation, almost as a joke, he wrote the first Oleg Vinograd novel.

There was something else too—my father's friendship with Pasternak. It wasn't just friendship, it was awe. He could laugh at Pasternak's idiosyncrasies, at his colossal egotism, but he was in awe of him. To my father, being a poet was the acme of existence.

INTERVIEWER

Your poetry has been described as being diverse, in the sense that it's not primarily lyrical, or epic, or overtly political, or short or long. You seem to navigate all seas. There is both quality and accessibility in your poetry. Even humour. You have many admirers, and, unusually for a poet, you have many readers.

LAUKHIN

Poetry today is often obscure, and not only to readers. I hear poets say, "I'm not sure what I tried to say here, or what exactly I said there." It makes me want to throw up. I can accept that you can find it difficult to explain certain parts, that it's a feeling or a *frisson* that's impossible to paraphrase, but to say that you don't know or you forgot what you intended to say, that's too much. Can you imagine Pushkin saying, "Ooops, what's this all about?" Or Shakespeare scratching his head, "I know I wrote this, but it's beyond me."

INTERVIEWER

I heard somebody say that after you finish a poem and you're happy with it, you spend just as long making it simpler, more accessible. Is that true?

LAUKHIN

I'd rather talk about my father and his journal and not about my poetry.

INTERVIEWER

We will, of course. But you're a famous poet, and the heading for this *Paris Review* interview is *The Art of Poetry.*

LAUKHIN

Then change it to *The Art of Memoir* or, even better, *The Art of Journals.*

INTERVIEWER

We will have time for your father and his journal. As much as you want. Our readers want to know also what makes Art Laukhin the poet.

LAUKHIN

Okay. I do not spend time trying to *dumb down* my poems.

INTERVIEWER

I didn't say *dumb down.*

LAUKHIN

You didn't, but you meant it. I don't look for the lowest common denominator. I believe simpler is often better, because it lets the reader get to the core beauty or the core interest quicker. Good poetry is to the point, direct, no dallying about. Think of Tsvetayeva's—to me she's the best Russian poet of the century. Her poetry is like a simple dress on a beautiful woman. I don't think readers should spend too much time guessing meanings or allusions. I'm not against difficulties in a poem if they contribute to it, but I'm against deliberate obscurity and meaningless-ness, even if it's nicely shaped. I doubt people read poetry for the mental exercise, but if they do they should do puzzles or mathe-matics instead.

INTERVIEWER

My next question is about *Poets in Heaven*...

LAUKHIN

Oh, not again.

INTERVIEWER

So much has been said about *Poets in Heaven*, the only major poem you've written since you left the Soviet Union seven years ago. What were the origins of the poem and the circumstances of its publication?

LAUKHIN

Too much—some of it sheer speculation—has been said and written about this poem already. It's a bad poem.

INTERVIEWER

You can put the speculation to rest here and now. You call it a bad poem, but most people would strongly disagree. I'm one of them.

LAUKHIN

Fedya Malgunov visited me in Toronto about a year before his death, in 1983, sometime in April or early May. He stayed with me, and one night we drank a lot and got to talking about our lives in the West, our new lives—though it wasn't that new for him, he'd been in America since the late sixties—and we drank some more, and he told me how unhappy he was, especially since his wife left him. He said he had not written anything worthwhile in ages, he simply couldn't anymore, and then he began to cry, and said that he was at the end of his rope, that he had days when he seriously thought the life he had was not worth living. It wasn't easy to look at him or listen to him in such a state. To cheer him up, I took out a draft of *Poets in Heaven* and read it to him. I'm not sure why I did it. Perhaps because it is about difficulties émigré artists have, about second thoughts and feelings of insignificance, but it is not a funny poem, or uplifting. I just wanted to stop him crying, and he did, said he loved my poem, and asked if he could have a copy. I gave it to him, a mistake.

INTERVIEWER

He translated *Poets in Heaven*, didn't he?

LAUKHIN

It had no title at the time. He came up with the English title and, yes, he translated it. I didn't expect it—the poem wasn't finished. I'm not even sure it would not have ended in the wastebasket. It had, if you wish, a premature birth because of that night of too much drinking.

INTERVIEWER

Because he translated it.

LAUKHIN

Because he translated it and because he included it in the article he wrote about me.

INTERVIEWER

That's the long article about you that appeared a few months later in *Vanity Fair*.

LAUKHIN

Yes.

INTERVIEWER

And, from what I understood, Fedya Malgunov didn't have your consent to use it.

LAUKHIN

He had my consent to write an article about me, and, while he was here, I gave him a lot of material to chew on. Fedya wasn't doing well financially at the time, and *Vanity Fair* had promised him serious money for a long article on me. But he did not have my blessing to include what came to be called *Poets in Heaven*. As I said, the poem wasn't finished—far from it. To start with, it was too long, too verbose. There were other things wrong with it. I bought that copy of *Vanity Fair* and brought it home one afternoon, put on my slippers, poured myself a drink, and sat down—here, right here, in the den—to savour Fedya's piece about me, full of pleasant anticipation. And then I saw the poem and blew up. I rang Fedya and gave him a piece of my mind. He was surprised, claimed it was good publicity for me and for the forthcoming journal by my father. Shouting, I told him I'd sue him and *Vanity Fair* for publishing a poem of mine without my consent. He swore I gave my consent when I handed him the copy of the poem, but that I had been too pissed to remember. Well, I was drunk that night, true, but I'm quite aware whether a poem of mine is finished or not. And that poem wasn't finished, definitely not. It might have led some to think I had doubts about my decision to stay in the West because of silly lines like *There are no poets in Heaven, no good poets anyway*, and if there was one thing I never had doubts about, well, it was exactly that.

Some readers concluded that I regretted having left the Soviet Union, and there were many back in Moscow who pounced on it. I was furious. *Vanity Fair* said that Bart, my agent in New York, had given Fedya and the magazine the right to include in the article anything of mine that had already been published, in English or in Russian. I don't know how Fedya did what he did, he probably told them that *Poets in Heaven* had been published in Russian already and *Vanity Fair* believed him and didn't check. It was a mess but I calmed down after a while, and I felt sorry for Fedya. He was my friend. We went a long way back, all the way to the Gorki Literary Institute in Moscow. I told myself, well, to hell with the whole thing, he's my friend and he's desperate, let it go, drop it, it's just one more bad poem out there, and God knows there are plenty of those. I rang him a week later, and we had a couple of glasses, thousands of kilometers apart, of course, and we cried a bit, we Russians being very good at it, at crying together, and we made peace. A few months later, he killed himself.

INTERVIEWER
He was depressed.

LAUKHIN
He was. I learned from his former wife that a few days before he took his life he drove from Los Angeles to San Francisco—she had remarried and was living there—and asked her to come back to him. She sent him away, and so, one thing and then another, and Fedya Malgonov reached the end. Like Mayakovsky,

> *As they say,*
> *the incident is closed.*
> *Love boat smashed on convention.*
> *I don't owe life a thing...*

Enough. Enough about *Poets in Heaven*, enough about Fedya Malgunov.

INTERVIEWER
Pavel Laukhin kept a journal from the mid thirties to the late fifties. It was a dangerous thing to do, especially in the Stalinist era. Why did your father keep the journal?

LAUKHIN
My father had had the most wondrous piece of luck—Stalin liked his novels. Of course, since it was Stalin, I'm not sure, and neither was my father, whether the luck was wondrous or monstrous. It likely stemmed from the genre of fiction he wrote—Socialist Realism which was the least stifling on espionage fiction as long as the foreign spies and saboteurs were villainous enough, and were duly caught and punished. My father was told one day, quite unexpectedly, that Stalin liked his first two novels and couldn't wait to read Oleg Vinograd's next adventure. That had a huge effect on his life and literary career, and also on our family. The journal describes this brilliantly, his sudden elevation to the ranks of the select and privileged, and the moral

contortions that went with it. It also cornered my father, typecast him. It was easy and convenient for him to continue writing spy stories, and he was told to keep at it. The message came from the very top. The sleepless hours of the beloved chief puppeteer were made bearable by my father's novels. It was a duty, an order. In 1946, he began writing a war novel (everybody was writing one then), and he was about to sign a contract with one of the state publishing houses when he was told in no uncertain terms—word had come down from on high—either include Oleg Vinograd, or drop the whole thing. So Oleg duly appeared in my father's first book after the war, caught several spies and fascists, and Pavel Laukhin remained a dedicated scribbler of spy stories. And also, likely to compensate for this, a secret and meticulous witness of his literary times.

Oleg Vinograd's exploits had given my father and our family security and safety, thanks to the benevolent nod of the Kremlin Mountaineer. My father's books were very popular and had huge print runs. He had an immense income, a large apartment, a dacha. Yet he felt constrained, cast, shackled. That's why, over time, Oleg Vinograd was given a difficult marriage to a wife that he believed was unfaithful to him, and a sickly daughter. There was also a father with old-age dementia and a mother who couldn't cope with it. All this gave Pavel Laukhin the elbow room to be more creative, to probe the human soul. Yes, my father knew he had a good thing going with Oleg Vinograd, but he also felt unfulfilled, frustrated. That's why he wrote his journal—that's where he kept his thoughts and aspirations and wrote in a freer style. Much of what he wrote in the journal, the dialogues, and the descriptions of people and places, his observations and thoughts, are like sketches or drafts of short stories, or of chapters in a larger narrative piece.

INTERVIEWER
Seven years ago, in the spring of 1978, you defected from the Soviet Union with nine notebooks containing your father's journal. How did you do it and why then?

LAUKHIN
The decision to leave the Soviet Union was something I struggled with after my father's death. He told me about the journal

once he learned about his brain tumor—he was fifty eight when
he was diagnosed—and he asked me to make sure it was published. He made me promise. Nothing else mattered to him. It
was both a plea and a command and I had to obey. I had some
hope of seeing the journal published during the early sixties.
After all, Ehrenburg's memoirs were being serialized in *Novy
Mir*, although he said very little about the Soviet Union or about
the daily life of his fellow writers, or little was left—at best a few
Aesopian pages here and there—after the editors and *Glavlit* had
had their ways with his manuscript. I didn't tell anybody about
the journal, but I did a trial run. I picked out an excerpt, a mildly
controversial one about a meeting at the Writers' Union in the
spring of 1954. It had some drama in it, and some humour. It
was a year after Stalin's death, and most people still weren't sure
which way the wind was blowing. I pretended I'd found it among
my father's papers. I cut parts of it here and there, not much,
massaged it, deleted a couple of names, wrote a few paragraphs
to give it context, and I approached several literary journals
with it. They didn't say no immediately, but in the end they all
did. They simply didn't see the point of it. "Why wash our linen in
public?" was their main response, and I quickly realized that my
father's journal would never be published in the Soviet Union. It
wasn't only that my father's writing and views did not conform to
the required norms, but too many of those mentioned were still
around, wielding power and influence in the very places I wanted
the journal published.

INTERVIEWER
Was the rejected excerpt the origin of *Conversations with
My Father?*

LAUKHIN
Conversations with My Father came later. When I thought of
Conversations, in 1969, I had not published anything in a very
long time. My involvement with the dissident movement—only
a few years, cut short by my accident—had had me blacklisted.
Never mind the samizdat and tamizdat—I wanted to be published openly in my country. I had had no income in years, and

had spent much of the money my father left me. The *sanovniki* at the Writers' Union were making unsettling noises and I was told that many had eyes on my apartment on Lavrushinsky Lane. In a way, it was a decision taken out of desperation. I thought that maybe, just maybe, I had been blacklisted only as a poet. Perhaps if I wrote prose I might have a chance. That's how I began *Conversations*. I was still working on *Bolshevo Days*—altering it here and there, but it was by and large finished. *Conversations was a revelation*—I mean, writing prose was. I remember one night, a few years after the war, I must have been eleven or twelve, when my father came home from a reading Pasternak did for some close friends from the draft of his novel. Before he began, Pasternak had told the few friends around him that he viewed his poetry as a step toward prose writing, which he considered the superior, liberating form. I was nearby when my father told my mother about it and about how horrified he'd been hearing his poet idol say such a thing. The whole incident stayed in my mind because it was the first time I heard my father saying anything critical about his beloved Boris Leonidovich. I thought about it again when I began *Conversations*. Like Pasternak, I soon found writing prose liberating—I was born again and freer. It was as if, after being in a playpen with a few wooden blocks, I was now permitted the whole courtyard, with all the toys I wanted. I could be long or short, verbose or concise. I could still be poetic, if I felt that way. The only constraint was the story. I had to have a story to tell. And that was never a problem in our country where the most ordinary day in the most ordinary life is a story.

There was something else about writing prose—I slowly lost my dread of the censors. *The Glavlit* censors, of course, but also, and probably worse, the implicit censoring done by the editors at all the journals. You see, you can't make cuts and changes to a poem, or very few and not to a good poem, before it's destroyed. While in prose, in a narrative, you can always salvage something, at the very least some good writing.

I had a fine time writing *Conversations*, and it wasn't just the novelty of writing prose. What delighted me more than anything else was writing about my father. I felt he was writing with me.

INTERVIEWER
Writing *with* you?

LAUKHIN
It is a book about Pavel Laukhin's last years, as seen and told by
his son. My father fell ill in 1958, almost four years before he died.
I put all I witnessed in—first symptoms, the diagnosis, doctors,
weighing the pros and cons of surgery and radiation, the pain,
the long waits and long stays in hospitals, his rage and impotence,
the slow loss of his strength, of his ability to do anything, even to
speak. And through it all I wove conversations I had with my father
in which he recalled the important events of his life. Inevitably, of
his life as a writer. Now, there was a big lie in all that, a porky as
you say here.

INTERVIEWER
That's UK slang. Why do you say that?

LAUKHIN
I didn't have any long conversations with my father after he fell
sick. Later he couldn't, and early on we didn't, or not about what
appeared in *Conversations*. What I included there were filtered
excerpts from his journal, purified of anything provocative. Only
a few of them, very few, and selected from the least controversial
entries that I felt would still be of interest to readers. I transformed
them into a dialogue between us or into a monologue I listened to.
They were his experiences, but distilled through my writing, that's
why I said my father wrote with me.

INTERVIEWER
Is that what's happening now, with your father's journals?

LAUKHIN
No. Preparing the journals, *I* am the one that writes with my father,
not the other way around.

INTERVIEWER
Is there a difference?

LAUKHIN

Of course, a huge one. In the forthcoming journal, he's the main
writer. In *Conversations* I was the main writer.

A lot was left unsaid in *Conversations*, or hidden between the
lines and behind the Aesopian language we perfected in the Soviet
Union. I learned from Ehrenburg's *People, Life, Years* what would
go through and what would not, and it still wasn't easy. I made the
tour of literary magazines and publishing houses with it. It was a
lengthy process, almost two years, and I'll skip the endless discus-
sions and equivocations, and the questionings of my intentions. I
heard the usual cant—the book was too pessimistic, inimical to
our people and the revolution's aims. What riled them above all
was the pessimism. I argued it was a book about the last years of a
sick man. They asked why did I have to write about such things? I
said I wanted to write about my father. Didn't I have happier things
to write about him? Couldn't I remember him as a healthy man?
They objected to the detailed description of the long process of
getting a diagnosis, the many consultations, the depiction of the
treatment and of my father's slow decay. My father had had access
to the best that Soviet medicine had to offer, and I slowly realized
another wrinkle in the censors' hostility—an uneasiness about the
portrayal of this kind of medical care. Word of the manuscript got
out somehow and there was pressure from PEN, who kept asking
why Artyom Laukhin had not been published in years in his own
country. In the end, I went along with all the cuts and changes they
asked for. I capitulated.

INTERVIEWER

Conversations with My Father came out in 1972, and Soviet readers loved the book.

LAUKHIN

It was my first book since *Youthful Eminences* fourteen years earlier. Fourteen years! *Conversations* appeared initially in *Druzhba
Narodov*, in two installments: in the fall of 1972, and in the spring
of the following year. The following year it came out as a book. It
was well received and surprisingly popular, even with readers
not particularly interested in the literary life. It touched many

people. They could relate to it because many of them had aging or sick parents.

Conversations had several reprints, in rather large runs, which was one of the reasons I was accused of bootlicking. The large print runs were a surprise to me at first, but I know now why they happened; it was my gingerbread, my *pryanik*. You see, I was no longer an active dissident, and I had agreed to the changes and the cuts in *Conversations*. I was a reformed rebel who had seen the truth. As such, I had to be rewarded. The *knut*, the threat, had worked on me. The *knut i pryanik*—the whip and the gingerbread, like the stick and the carrot in English.

The difficulties I had with *Conversations* confirmed for me that my father's journal would never be published in the Soviet Union. It strengthened my decision to leave.

INTERVIEWER

Are you saying that your father's wish to have his journal published was the only reason you left?

LAUKHIN

I can *almost* say that. I don't have to tell you that writers or poets, particularly poets, are not eager to change countries and languages.

INTERVIEWER

Why in 1978? You were born in 1936, so you were, what, forty-two years old. Why not earlier?

LAUKHIN

My father had been a Soviet millionaire, one of the few legitimate ones, and all from his books. One talks about best-sellers here in the West, but it's nothing compared to what happens back home. Yefremov's *Andromeda* sold twenty million copies in one year. Twenty million in one year, in one country! My father's books sold in the millions. They weren't bad novels, you know—my father was a skillful writer in a popular genre—and even in the lean years after the war publishers would make sure there was enough paper for the books the *vozhd* liked. I was four or five years old when a large apartment—large by Soviet standards—in the rent-subsidized Writer's Union building on Lavrushinsky Lane became our home. I had a privileged childhood and youth. We had an all-seasons dacha in Peredelkino, which my father, later, had the good sense to buy. He made significant additions and improvements to it. My father literally didn't know what to do with his money. All of it was left to me and my sister, since our mother died a few years before my father did. After his death I went on living in our apartment on Lavrushinsky Lane. I had an easy, charmed life. True, they stopped publishing me in the sixties, but my samizdat poetry was on everybody's lips. I was admired, lionized, I was—how do you call it here?—a pop star. I read in front of large audiences, and people screamed my name. Poets in the Soviet Union are respected, as the doomed Mandelstam said. They have influence, traction. I was significant over there; I'm not here. I'm not complaining. It sounds odd, but I'm an ignored pauper here compared to what I was and had there. This house is not mine, and I don't own a dacha. This is not a complaint either—I'm only listing the reasons why it took me a while to leave.

I had to be certain too that there was no chance that my father's journal would be printed in the Soviet Union. That was what he had wanted, to be published in his country and read by his people. For many years I nurtured the hope, the delusion that maybe next year, past the next bend in the river, things would turn out for the better.

There was also the matter of getting the nine notebooks containing the journal out of the Soviet Union. That added a few years.

INTERVIEWER
How did you get them out?

LAUKHIN
I had help, of course. But I'd rather not say more than that.

INTERVIEWER
Why in the spring of 1978?

LAUKHIN

I was in New York in March 1978 at the invitation of the Mystery Writers of America. It was the first time in twenty years I was allowed abroad. The Second International Congress of Crime Writers was being held in Manhattan, and I was asked to be a keynote speaker and talk about Pavel Laukhin's novels. I talked to a crowded (and overheated) room because they had made a great deal about my father, in the typical American way of exaggerating everything—Pavel Laukhin, Stalin's favourite author. He'd never been, of course not, Stalin was far from a simpleton. Anyway, I gave the speech, and didn't return home. My father's notebooks were out of the Soviet Union by then.

INTERVIEWER

You were not allowed to travel outside the Soviet Union for twenty years?

LAUKHIN

That's right. I tried several times, and I was always refused a passport. I had invitations from fellow poets in the West to visit them, an invitation to teach at Columbia University for a semester, and several invitations to address PEN gatherings, the last one in Holland. Each of my applications was turned down.

INTERVIEWER

Why was it approved in 1978?

LAUKHIN

Various members of PEN had written many times to the Soviet Writers' Union about my inability to travel outside the Soviet Union. News of this was passed along, I'm sure, to those who make decisions on such matters, and these interventions on my behalf may have had a cumulative effect.

INTERVIEWER

You left your wife, pregnant at the time with your child, in Moscow. Could it be that the authorities believed it would be less likely you'd defect with a pregnant wife waiting for you at home?

LAUKHIN
It could be.

INTERVIEWER
Your wife divorced you and remarried soon afterward.

LAUKHIN
From what I hear she's quite happy.

INTERVIEWER
You've never seen your child.

LAUKHIN
I haven't, no.

INTERVIEWER
It's a boy, isn't it?

LAUKHIN
A boy, yes.

INTERVIEWER
Don't you want to see your child? He's, what, six years old now?

LAUKHIN
I thought the interview was about my father's journal.

INTERVIEWER
Okay. In 1978, you defected. You spent the first few months of your new life in New York, with friends. You were in France for a while, and then in Germany. You visited London for a couple of weeks. For a long time you gave no interviews, and Pavel Laukhin's journal was only a rumour. Your only public statement was that you had yet to make up your mind where to live, where to put down new roots. You visited Solzhenitsyn in Vermont, but avoided the press afterward. There were articles about you, of course, and eventually many interviews.

LAUKHIN
Some not that friendly.

INTERVIEWER
Some not that friendly. The gist of them seemed to be that you were one of the young rebels in the Soviet Union in the sixties, after the end of the thaw, and you often seemed only inches away from disaster. You charmed your way through, riding on your talent and wit, to a unique position that allowed you trips to the West and saw your poetry published in many languages. You managed to appeal to Western tastes without wholly displeasing your Kremlin masters. You were an enigma in the free world—how you managed to sit on the fence so well and for so long. You were clever, said some, surviving, making the best out of what you were dealt. It was suspicious, said others, who drew comparisons to Yevtushenko and Eherenburg years before. Last year, Yakov Zladsky called you an adroit bootlicker. Did that make you angry?

LAUKHIN
It did—the outright lies, the exaggerations. To give you an example, my only trip to the West before I defected was a week in Paris in 1958. I was sent there with a group of Soviet writers and poets, and was shown off as a young, new talent. I was never allowed abroad again except to communist Hungary later in the same year. That one trip to Paris became "*trips* to the West." And, in his interview, Zladsky said, "Artyom Laukhin should explain his *frequent* trips to the West." Now, in 1958, my first collection of poetry, *Youthful Eminences*, most of it a naive paean to space and rocketry, had just come out in the Soviet Union. It had very good reviews, and the print run was not small. I was a published and popular poet at the age of twenty-three. I read from *Youthful Eminences* in halls, in clubs, at official gatherings, in private apartments. A few poems, some with easy, rhyming stanzas, were put to music. I was young, and young people looked up to me. Such things go to one's head and you begin to believe that nothing can stand in your way. That's why my inability to publish *Sunless Seasons* a few years later came as such a shock. *Sunless Seasons* clearly lacked the optimism of *Youthful Eminences*, but it was mainly introspective

poetry with no political statements. I wrote the poems between 1958 and 1962, a rather difficult time for me. My mother died in 1957, my father in 1961. I learned about my father's journal during that period, and I read it for the first time. I was a witness to Pasternak's humiliation after he was awarded the Nobel. All these factors, and the slow realization that there was something very wrong with our country made *Sunless Seasons* sunless, grey, preoccupied with death, with personal panics in small cluttered rooms, with love that goes wrong or is misunderstood. For a year or so I did the rounds of the literary magazines and publishing houses. I found no takers. I was told it was too pessimistic, that, while not overtly political, it had a latent poisonous message. About half a dozen or so poems from it were published in various magazines and literary journals over the next two or three years, in a slow, irritating drip, but the bulk of *Sunless Seasons* became samizdat material. It was better poetry than *Youthful Eminences*, much better, and it was an underground success. I began to associate myself with "bad" people, the kind who were eventually called dissidents in the West. I stopped writing poetry for several years; what was the point if you couldn't publish it? I was there, in Pushkin Square, in December 1965, after Andrei Siniavsky and Yuli Daniel were arrested, demanding open trials and respect of the constitution. I demonstrated for their fair trial, and read in Mayakovsky Square. After they were convicted, a letter asking for their release was sent to the Twenty-third Congress of the CPSU. I signed it. I spent a few nights in Lubyanka for that and, later, when *Sunless Seasons* was published in the West, I was subjected to a psychiatric assessment.

I was lucky, though, on two counts. First, because I was a poet. Poetry never disturbed the authorities in the Soviet Union as much as prose, and for good reason: fewer readers, of course, and the metaphorical, compressed, indirect way messages are usually expressed in good poetry. Second, I was in a car accident in January 1967. There was a demonstration in Pushkin Square against the new laws on "anti-Soviet statements" and on what they termed "unauthorized declarations" that had been added to the criminal code. The protesters were arrested and the organizers eventually tried and punished. I was one of the leaders, and I would have been there but for the accident. It happened in the first hours of that year. There were three of us, driving back to the city after a spirited night. I mean, we weren't exactly sober. It was winter, slippery, and the little Moskvich rolled over several times through a ditch and crashed into a tree. It was bad. A friend, the driver, died. The third person in the car—somebody we were giving a ride back to Moscow and whom we hardly knew—was in the backseat. He was hurt too, but not as badly as I was. I was in a coma for a week. I had a broken leg in two places, broken ribs, internal bleeding, a broken arm and a broken collarbone. It took me a year and a half to fully recover.

INTERVIEWER
You call this luck?

LAUKHIN
I spent months and months in hospitals and rehabilitation centres, the last one a sanatorium in Bolshevo, not far from Moscow. I was able to walk by then, hobble around. I used to walk past the Bolshevo dacha Tsvetayeva lived in for four months in 1939. It's hard for a poet to be in Bolshevo and not think of Tsvetayeva. I wrote much of *Bolshevo Days* that spring of 1968. I was in pain, my leg still hurt, but I was happy. I was alive, to start with, and I was writing poetry again. I also knew that *Bolshevo Days* was a good poem, much better than anything I'd written before. And I realized that I could be a poet, or I could be dissident—a fighter for democracy and human rights in my country—but I could not be both. Others could do it, better people, but I couldn't. I also realized how fragile life was. A trite observation, of course, but I had to calm down if I was to go on as a poet and if I was to fulfill my father's wish and publish his journal. So I wrote poetry no one wanted to publish, began *Conversations*, and plotted my departure. I had to find a way of getting my father's notebooks to the West as well. They had to be sent abroad before I left—I couldn't risk carrying them with me. All this took me almost ten years. I wasn't in a hurry, I took my time. I knew that I'd write my best poetry while I was still relatively young and among Russian speakers.

The publication of my poetry in the West—first a trickle, then more after *Bolshevo Days*—made it easier to think of leaving the

Soviet Union. I knew I'd go at some point but, perhaps unconsciously, I procrastinated. Meanwhile, *Conversations* kept me busy.

I did a couple of movie scripts too, based on my father's novels. A friend of mine was a director at Mosfilm. I had a good time doing them. I presume the bootlicking label came from that, from being seen with actresses and directors and party big whales (who always liked movies and actresses). Yes, I was bootlicking, but, it should be noted, Zladsky is an envious little man. Yes, I drank and laughed with the powerful and the fat-necked, and I even read them my poetry, which they wouldn't publish. But I never stabbed any of my fellow poets or writers in the back. You can't say the same about little man Zladsky, who seems to enjoy doing it lately. I never signed any condemnation, and I never raised my voice in a meeting or forum to denounce or castigate a fellow artist.

INTERVIEWER
Bolshevo Days was the poem through which the West came to know you.

LAUKHIN
Both the critics' and the readers' reaction to *Bolshevo Days* were miracles. But the first poems that were published in the West were from *Sunless Seasons*. In the summer of 1964, a poem from it appeared in *Grani*. It happened without my consent or knowledge, but I wasn't upset—not at all. I quite liked the poem, a melancholy piece, somewhat angry, and quite long, the longest in *Sunless Seasons*. It was this poem that was always singled out as having a poisonous message and being typical of the entire collection. I was summoned to the Writers' Union and was told to disown it. They were furious. "How?" I asked. "How does one disown one's own poem? It's done, it's out there already, in *Grani*, you can't say it didn't happen. It's like the air we breathe out, you can't take it back." (I remember one of them telling me it was unbearably bad breath.) They asked me to write something to the effect that the poem wasn't by me, and they'd get the appropriate newspapers and magazines to print it. They already had something for me to sign. I refused. I was later called to the Tse-Ka's building in the Old Square—Tse-Ka is short for the Central Committee—where I met

with Dmitry Polikarpov, then the head of the Cultural Section. The chief cultural strangler, as Solzenitsyn called him in his memoirs. Polikarpov asked me the same thing—to disown my own poem, say it was stolen, condemn its publication. I refused. He made all kinds of threats, including being expelled from the Writers' Union. I stalled. I said I needed time to think. Polikarpov seemed edgy, hesitant, and that gave me some courage. There were rumours Khruschev was not happy with him. I thought time might be on my side. It was, but not the way I expected. Those were months when the *sanovniki*—the highest of them, the *bolshie kity,* the big whales—had little time for vermin like me, as one of Polikarpov's assistants told me. They were frantically dealing with the Cuban crisis. Soon afterward Khrushchev was dismissed and replaced, and not much later Polikarpov was replaced too. And, somehow, they either forgot about me, or they had bigger things to worry about. Well, you need a bit of luck in life. And then, a few years later, in early 1968, *Sunless Seasons*, the whole collection, was published by the YMCA Press in Paris. I was still recovering from my accident at the time.

INTERVIEWER
How did the publication of *Bolshevo Days* in the *New Yorker* come about?

LAUKHIN
In 1969, *Sunless Seasons* appeared in Germany, in the wonderful translation by Dieter Rotloff. I've been very lucky in that two such superb poets have translated my poetry—Dieter Rotloff and the American Philip Korn.

INTERVIEWER
Fedya Malgunov translated your poetry into English too.

LAUKHIN
Yes, Fedya as well. Dieter spent one year at the Gorky Literary Institute in the fifties—that's how we met—and his Russian is very good. More importantly, though, he's a fine poet, with an amazing ear for Russian nuances. It's a different story with Philip Korn.

Sometime in 1969 Philip happened to see Dieter's translation of one of my poems—*Faraway Lanterns* is its English title. Philip spoke no Russian at the time, or very little, but he knew enough German to want to read more of my poems. He wrote to Dieter. They had met a couple of times, but didn't really know each other. Dieter sent him a copy of *Sunless Seasons* in German, and Philip translated a couple of the poems. He told his agent, Bart, about me, and approached the *New Yorker* with his translations. And so, in late 1969, the *New Yorker* published the two poems from *Sunless Seasons* that Philip had translated. I was surprised by the magazine's interest in me, although Dieter told me during one of his frequent visits to Moscow that Bart and Philip were lobbying the weekly on my behalf. The outcome of their efforts was one of the June 1971 issues. I was on the cover. Well, it wasn't me exactly, but some cowboy cartoon of me[1]. One of my students found a copy of that issue recently on Queen Street, here in Toronto, in a used bookstore, and had me sign it. I used to have a copy in Moscow, Colson Emslie brought it for me on one of his visits, but I left it there. I'm on the lookout for another copy.

INTERVIEWER

Bolshevo Days was in that issue, wasn't it?

LAUKHIN

Yes, it was. Not in its entirety, it was a very long poem, but a large part of it. I had had great hopes for *Bolshevo Days*, thought I could publish it in the Soviet Union. There was an increased awareness of Tsvetayeva at the time. Her poems had been trickling back into the Soviet Union, and many were even published officially, but there was a reluctance to talk about what had happened to her, to her husband, Sergey Efron, and to their daughter, Alya. Or to Tsvetayeva's sister, Anastasya, for that matter. I remember one editor at LitGazeta...

INTERVIEWER

That's *Literaturnaya Gazeta*.

---

1 The cover of the June 1971 issue has a caricature of the younger and much thinner poet on the cover, his moustache, cowboy hat and boots, and loaded holster farcically oversized. The caption is "Artyom Laukhin Conquers the West." (E.B-W)

LAUKHIN

Yes. I remember the editor telling me that we should concentrate on the poetry, the magnificent poetry of Marina Tsvetayeva, and not on her fate or that of her family. He said they'd be glad to publish the stanzas dealing with her art and creative effort, but that even there he felt a few changes might be required.

I couldn't publish *Bolshevo Days* in the Soviet Union and could never understand why. It was fairly matter of fact, mainly events and personal emotions, with no political comments or interpretations. So, like *Sunless Seasons*, *Bolshevo Days* came out in samizdat, and for a while it was the talk of the town. And then the *New Yorker* published Philip Korn's translation, and there was an explosion, the miracle I mentioned earlier. Philip, Dieter, Fedya Malgunov, and Bart did interviews about me with anybody interested. Colson Emslie as well, my good friend and colleague here in Toronto.

INTERVIEWER

Bolshevo Days is your longest poem by far. I cried when I first read it. I must have been fifteen or sixteen. I was in tears from the very beginning, when Marina is talking to Alya at the railway station in Moscow and then on the train to Bolshevo, asking her about the family and receiving only half-answers or none at all. Why wasn't Seriozha in Moscow? Why in Bolshevo? Why was his last name Andreyev now, and not Efron anymore? Why hadn't her sister Anatasya met her at the train station when she arrived from Leningrad? Arrested? Anastasya was arrested? What for?

Did you write the prologue—*Questions on the Train*—first, or after you'd written the rest of the poem?

LAUKHIN

I wrote it toward the end. I already had three of the four main parts done when I decided to write the prologue.

INTERVIEWER

I read *Bolshevo Days* first in the *New Yorker*, and then I decided to get hold of the whole poem in Russian. I was in agony when Alya, pregnant at the time, was taken away from the house in Bolshevo, looking back and smiling at her helpless parents as she was walked away between her captors, the last time Marina saw her daughter. And I shared Marina's torment and anger as she slowly figured out what was going on around her and her young son, both of them newly arrived in the Soviet Union to reunite the family. I shared her shock when she realized that her Seriozha, and possibly Alya too, had been working for the NKVD for many years.

LAUKHIN

Philip's translation was masterful. It was Philip too who told Bart about *Bolshevo Days*. Bart got in touch with me and offered to be my agent. I thought he was mad—an agent for a poet? Especially one in the Soviet Union? It was a secret arrangement, of course. Bart came to Moscow in the spring of 1970 as part of an American delegation of publishers and editors, and he made sure he met me. He's not having an easy time of it now, poor Bart, with the many delays of the journal.

INTERVIEWER

Why did you choose Toronto and its largest university?

LAUKHIN

Why not? It's a beautiful campus, a very good university, with an interest and scholarship in Russian literature. It's in the heart of a big city and I like big cities. And there are real winters here. Russians need solid, long winters.

INTERVIEWER

From what I understand, you had many offers from other universities.

LAUKHIN

True, I had offers. But, first of all, I wanted to be in North America— farther away from the Soviet Union than Europe. Also, one of my conditions was that I wouldn't teach poetry writing or any kind of writing. That excluded many offers. I insisted on a light teaching load too. I needed time for my poetry and—more important to me at that time—to turn my father's journal into publishable shape. Toronto went a long way to meet my conditions, and the endowment was instrumental. And Colson Emslie was in Toronto, and he and I had become good friends.

INTERVIEWER
Who made the endowment?

LAUKHIN
The donor wishes to remain anonymous.

INTERVIEWER
Private money?

LAUKHIN
Ha! Yes, private, capitalist money. The university had agreed to co-fund a new chair for me in Soviet Russian literature. That's what I wanted to teach—good Soviet Russian literature. There is quite a substantial body of it: Mandelstam, Akhmatova, Pasternak, Babel, Solzhenitsyn, Bulgakov, Grossman, Pilnyak, Mayakovsky. Others too. And Tsvetayeva, of course, although the Soviet label doesn't apply to her. Newer writers and poets as well, like Yevtushenko, Akhmadulina, Vozhnezensky. Even little man Zladsky.

INTERVIEWER
And you?

LAUKHIN
And me, yes, why not? But I don't teach my own poetry. There are also those who, while they wrote within the constraints of socialist realism, were still superb artists, wordsmiths, and they deserve to be known and studied. Writers like Ivanov, Paustovsky, Kataev, others. It's worth studying them under a magnifying glass. Their works suffer terribly from being straitjacketed, but fragments of them have plenty of merit.

INTERVIEWER
You talk of a substantial body of good work in Soviet Russian litera-ture, yet you made some incendiary statements about the Western assessment of it.

LAUKHIN

What are you referring to?

INTERVIEWER

It was a reaction following the interview with Zladsky in which, toward the end, he said he was horrified by what he'd heard you were doing with your father's journal. He said, "I join cause with literary scholars and call it a crime. Since Artyom Laukhin defected to the West to find fame he has added only a self-pitying and confused lament to his meager poetic output, and is now destroying—like a modern painter applying new colours and shapes to the Lascaux murals—the unique and valuable journals his father left."

LAUKHIN

Ah, yes. Well, if fame in the West was what I was after, what better umbrella than Soviet Communism? Stalin could rise from his eternal slumber and easily make a case for it, an excellent case in fact, and those that followed him could do almost as well. Would Akhmatova, Mandelstam, or Pasternak—Zladsky too, of course—be famous today in the West were it not for the Communist persecutions? Would Pasternak have been awarded the Nobel Prize for literature? Isn't Mandelstam famous here mainly because of his wife's depiction of their suffering under Stalin? And that silly sixteen-line poem about the *Kremlyovskyi Gorets*—the Kremlin Mountaineer, as it was often translated here, not that accurately—wasn't that the only poem of his known over here? Wasn't Akhmatova's *Requiem*, probably her best poem, the direct result of Stalin's fine work too? He had ordered her son's imprisonment, and made sure that any parcel she brought for him required her to queue for a long time in the biting cold. He hired hundreds of walk-ons, other mothers and wives of prisoners, and they were there, queuing with her, each time she lined up. He was a superb stage director, Josef Stalin, patient, careful about the smallest details, all for the glory and fame of Soviet literature. Oh, he was very good at it, he could squeeze fame from his literary actors and actresses like toothpaste from a tube. He squeezed their life away too, sometimes, but that was the price they had to pay.

INTERVIEWER
That's very cynical.

LAUKHIN
Perhaps. But not very. Tsvetayeva, the best poet of them all, is less well known only because she left Russia soon after the revolution and, while abroad, suffered only from poverty. Poverty was never enough to catch the attention of literary critics or of the brave members of the Academy in Stockholm, but terror and political repression went a long way.

Yes, the persecution of writers was an admirable thing. How did Solzhenitsyn cannily put it—"not necessarily undesirable"? He'd know.

The laurels we receive in the West are both a blessing and a curse. We can never be entirely sure of our worth. There's always that nagging question: are we praised for our art or for of our persecution and suffering? I read recently in a biography of Solzhenitsyn that it is easier for a third-rate Russian writer to be translated into English, provided he provokes a political scandal at home, than a good French writer or an Italian one. Sad, but probably true.

INTERVIEWER
It applies to your poetry too.

LAUKHIN
Of course it does, although I was not involved in any major political furor. I would have been, but I was saved by my accident. My defection might have caused a bit of commotion, but by then the West knew about me because of *Bolshevo Days*. Indirectly, *Bolshevo Days*, my best work, no doubt, and the poem that made me famous, owes much to Stalin too. The tense household Tsvetayeva found in the Bolshevo dacha, the terrible revelations, the arrests of her daughter and then of her husband, the way Alya turned around and smiled at her mother for the last time, all these were delicate subplots and scene directions crafted by the chief puppeteer. Yes, he understood clearly—he had been a poet himself once—that the best poems are written in hell. Look, I have written nothing since I

left, nothing except *Poets in Heaven*. No worthwhile poetry, that is. I am the living proof of Stalin's subtle wisdom.

INTERVIEWER
When will Pavel Laukhin's memoirs be in bookstores?

LAUKHIN
Ah, the sore spot. I wouldn't use the word memoirs. Journal is the right term, an almost daily log of events, personal notes, and observations. Nine thick notebooks, seventeen hundred tightly handwritten pages—with often faded, hurried, abbreviated writing, difficult to make sense of—covering the literary scene of the late thirties, the forties, and most of the fifties. The first volume will be out in the fall. Yes, I know, I've made promises before, but this time I'm quite certain because the first volume is practically done.

INTERVIEWER
Which years are covered in the first volume?

LAUKHIN
The journal starts in the spring of 1936. The first volume ends at the end of 1940.

INTERVIEWER
How many volumes are you planning?

LAUKHIN
Four or five altogether. It ends in 1959. There aren't many entries in the final year, as my father was ill and depressed.

INTERVIEWER
Literature being one of the islands of society, will your father's journal do to Soviet literature what Solzhenitsyn's *Gulag Archipelago* did to the Soviet regime and society?

LAUKHIN
It's nicely put, but it's stretching the simile too far. My father's journal will be of greatest interest to historians of literature. It

will appeal to historians proper too, because it offers a personal view of almost twenty-five terrible years of Soviet life. It will captivate the lovers of literature, of course. I like to believe it will have other readers as well. They'll find juicy bits and lots of gossip, since my father loved stories about people. They'll find intrigue, literary infighting and skullduggery (often lethal, that's Russia for you), literary opinions and commentary, encounters, notes about his own work and reactions to it, his reactions to the reactions to his work, his dreams as a writer. The drudgery of day-to-day Soviet life. New facts about Stalin's terror. Mouthwatering, all of this, of course, but, I don't delude myself, mainly to specialists and lovers of literature. Solzhenitsyn's *Gulag*, a literary masterpiece, was and remains a scathing denunciation of a bankrupt and brutal regime. His best work by far.

INTERVIEWER

You are under immense pressure, but there are insinuations that you are delaying the publication of the journal on purpose. It's been almost seven years since you left the Soviet Union. Why is it taking you so long?

LAUKHIN

My father's entries are the notes of a man obsessed with putting everything down and at the same time worried that he'll be caught with them. There are rambling, detailed personal notes that, now and then, are of little interest; mystifying abbreviations; meticulous and yet hurried handwriting. Pavel Laukhin walked and talked the official line, while being a witness to Soviet literary life—the literary Gulag, if it makes you happy. My father's journal needed a lot of work, serious work, to separate the grain from the chaff, and to bake good, black Russian bread from it, solid, filling bread, smelling of the blood-soaked earth it came from. I knew it would take many years. True, I didn't quite expect it would take me seven to bring out the first volume. There are many reasons for it. I am the first to blame, of course, but there are other causes. Keep in mind that when each volume comes out, it will be published both in Russian and English. I'm trying to do both versions at the same time—well, almost at the same time—with the help of my students and collaborators, and it's not easy. I have to consider the needs of my students too.

INTERVIEWER
How do your students help you?

LAUKHIN
I first do the Russian version, of course. Each student then works on the translation of a segment, usually one related to his or her own studies. Once happy with the segment, the student returns it to me. Most times I send it back, asking for a rewrite. There are often several drafts. I am the one that puts them all together and work on the overall latest draft, and that sometimes results in further alterations. I try to make their output livelier, closer to the spirit of the Russian original, but I often add or—more rarely—remove material, because English language readers need context that Russian readers do not. Then back it goes to my students, mainly for grammar or awkward constructs. Whatever changes they make this time are again closely scrutinized by me. Then we work on another batch. In this way, many slices of the journal are moved along, each at different stages of completion.

INTERVIEWER
You're doing some heavy editing on your father's journal, including your own additions. Colson Emslie, your colleague here in Toronto, was asked in a recent interview about it. He said he had had a look at the manuscript of the first volume and compared parts of it to the original notebook entries. He commented that, let me quote him, "I have seen the difference between the raw material and the final product. Art Laukhin's narration has muscle, immediacy, a romping, jaunting quality, a unique effervescence. It's like being slapped constantly by the power, the forcefulness of his words. His father's language is factual, weaker, almost dull by comparison, and Laukhin often has to break into it." Most scholars, though, are saying that you're committing a crime by altering your father's entries. They are horrified. They say these are not Pavel Laukhin's daily entries anymore, but Art Laukhin's interpretation of them.

LAUKHIN

They are footnotes to literature, not scholars. They should all be sent to Kolyma, all of them. I adored my father. I feel I am writing with him when I weave my own words with his. I wouldn't do it any other way. I toyed for a while with the idea of using different typefaces to separate his writing from my own, but I soon gave up on it. It was too cluttered. A transcript and an unedited English translation will be available later to anyone interested, and my father's note-books will be gifted to the university. Believe me, it's the best way, especially for the English version of the journal. People and events need introductions, and places, customs and ceremonies must be described. It would be all footnotes, otherwise, and I abhor footnotes. Even the original Russian version will make sense to only a few, and these few are getting old.

INTERVIEWER

Where do you work?

LAUKHIN

I write poetry—write, that's an odd verb to use, since the writing is the least part—just about anywhere, as most of the time I'm putting it together it in my head. If you're asking about the work on the journal, both at home and at the university. I work with my students at the university, but when I have to concentrate, to really put my nose to the grindstone, as you people say, it's at home. I have a large room on the second floor of the house, quiet, with windows facing south. I like a lot of light.

INTERVIEWER

In 1978, you met Solzhenitsyn. What did you talk about?

LAUKHIN

What do you say to somebody like Solzhenitsyn? Soldier, *zek*, cancer survivor, math teacher, writer, polemicist, memoirist, Nobel-prize winner, bricklayer, phonetician, acoustician, husband and father, sage, reader of the nature and the essence of the Russian soul, in touch with God. Is there anything you can say that would be of the slightest interest to him?

It wasn't an easy visit, not at all. Not for me, or, I think, for him. He wanted to know what was going on back home, but how interested he really was I'm not certain. I had left the Soviet Union a month earlier and I got the impression he already had fresher reports. He said he was very much looking forward to reading my father's journal, that the journal was invaluable, and urged me to get it out as quickly as I could. He also said that when he was in the hospital ill with cancer he read one of my father's novels and that he had enjoyed it. He couldn't remember the title, though, or what it was about. He apologized for not being familiar with my poetry. He said he had very little time for reading.

INTERVIEWER
It sounds as if you don't have pleasant memories of the visit.

LAUKHIN
Interesting memories, but I can't say pleasant. It's not easy to have conversations with famous wise men. They are amenable to monologues, maybe, but not to conversations.

INTERVIEWER
You've been here, in North America, for seven years yet Britishisms pepper your speech—rang him, porky, tight, rather. Why is this?

LAUKHIN
The teachers I had in school taught us British English. I was not aware of it at the time, of course. And I had an English girlfriend in the early seventies. For a couple of years—oh, a bit more than that. She was a student in Moscow. Somehow, the English I learned from her is imprinted in my brain.

INTERVIEWER
Weren't you married at the time? Well, of course you were, since you were still married when you left.

LAUKHIN
I was married.

INTERVIEWER
What happened to the English girlfriend?

·LAUKHIN
She finished her studies and left. She got married not long after she returned to England.

INTERVIEWER
Have you seen her since you left the Soviet Union?

LAUKHIN
That's not what the interview is about.

INTERVIEWER
Another dead end. Besides Philip Korn's initial one, Fedya Malgunov did a translation of *Bolshevo Days* into English a few years later. Which one do you prefer?

LAUKHIN
Depends on my mood. Probably Philip's.

Monday, 6 April 1953

Before she left with Larissa in the morning Varya asked if Stalin's death would affect us. She leaned on me as I was sitting and doing some revisions, and I glanced up at her, unsure of what she meant. She looked pale and tired because she had slept poorly overnight, tossing and sighing, and long before daybreak she switched on her night-lamp and read.

"Yes, of course," I said, "it would affect everybody."

"I mean ... he liked your books."

That was what had kept her awake. She'd gone to see her sister the day before, and God only knew what she heard there.

"Did your sister offer counsel?"

She ignored the sarcasm. "She doesn't think Berya will be the one. He has revisionist ideas, very dangerous."

That was Sasha Cornilov's assessment, not her sister's. "Was your nephew there?"

"He left shortly after I arrived."

"What did he say?"

"Not much, kept to himself. He didn't seem particularly worried, but my sister is. She said you should be worried too."

Stalin had long ago lost interest in Oleg Vinograd. That was the gist of a friendly but convoluted message Fadeyev passed on to me when he became chair of the Writers' Union the second time, in forty-eight. He called me into his office and, after idle palaver and a few drinks, he adroitly mentioned the *vozhd* and his love of literature. It might have been more than a few drinks because, after I told him how Stalin had sent back to me several galley proofs marked by his own hand, I added, "I must have reached perfection in my craft under his guidance, because he hasn't done it for quite a while now." Foolish aside, of course, but Fadeyev was drunk too and, anyway, he wasn't the type to report asinine remarks. He laughed and, shaking his finger at me, said Stalin had not read any of my books for years. I asked, stupidly, how he knew. He said, "I know." I couldn't refrain from gasping. I didn't understand—then or later—why he found it opportune to let me know that my novels were not on Stalin's night table anymore. After he refilled my glass Fadeyev assured me the *vozhd* had been simply too busy, and there was nothing I should worry about. His bloodshot eyes tried to smile as he added, "Anyway, Pavel Nokolyevich, your novels are selling very well without any propping, and making up for many other doing rather poorly. We're not capitalists, but must be mindful of our rubles."

I had not told Varya then about Fadeyev's message, and I certainly didn't tell her now. Why worry her? Instead, I said what I repeated to myself often, that I was a good writer—in a minor genre, true, but a good writer none the less—that I had a large number of readers, and that my readers were utterly unaware that Stalin had been fond of my novels.

"You won't do anything foolish, would you?" Varya said.

"Foolish?"

She left the room without answering.

I had seen Fadeyev two days earlier, on Povarskaya Street, briefly, as I was coming in and he was leaving, and he didn't look well at all, pale and puffy. At lunch, later, I heard he'd been drinking more than ever. Another favourite of the now dead puppeteer, but, unlike me, he had lasted much longer and on much higher heights.

Was I right to dismiss Varya's worries? Could we go the Fredkin way if the new *vozhd*, whoever he turned up to be eventually, happened to like the work of a budding artist in need of a better place to live? It might take a while for the new leader to emerge and become secure, and he may not be as ruthless as Stalin was, but did we really know? Did anybody know anything?

Zinaida Nikolayevna came down to the door of our apartment just as I was about to leave. She was holding a small suitcase.

"I saw Varya as she went out," she said to me, "and she mentioned you'd be visiting my husband today. Don't know why you'd go, Pavel Nikolayevich, since he's coming home in a few days, but if you do, take this to him, please. " She pushed the suitcase towards me. "You'll save me a trip. Boots. A few other things too, but it's boots he's asking for, so he can go out for a walk now that the weather has turned."

Looking around her, she seemed ready to come in, but changed her mind and whispered, "Have you seen it in the newspaper?"

"I saw it."

"What do you think?"

"Would be a relief for Boris Leonidovich."

She looked at me with a smirk. "Well, only as it is for all of us. He's not a doctor, your friend Boris, and doesn't think he's a Jew either, with all the Saviour and Transfiguration and other unpublishable Christian piss he busies himself with."

Was she reading her husband verses, or she heard that somewhere? Was it a comment on the novel?

Zinaida seemed in a hurry and left. An odd woman, now probably rushing to gossip with her cronies, and yet supportive of Boris Leonidovich in her grumpy, abrupt, limited way.

The train was slow and crowded, and it was only after Mytishchi that I found an empty seat. After pointing out at the window and the beautiful day, the young man in the next seat wanted to know where I was heading to. He was well dressed, smiling, and smelling of vodka. I said Bolshevo, and he said he knew Bolshevo very well because his father had spent a few years there. When I asked if he'd lived there, he laughed and said, "In a way. Free of rent. He was an engineer, and got lucky when the war came. I'm speaking too much. It's a good thing I'm off here, *Chateau* Podlipki." He laughed again, stood up, and, after lighting a cigarette, went down the corridor.

Pasternak shook his head when he heard Zinaida wasn't coming, but was very glad of the boots. Opening the suitcase, he chuckled. "Ha, it's not just boots, it's a coat and pants and what not. I think Zinaida has used you as a mule. I'm leaving a day after tomorrow, and she wasn't keen on carrying all these. Was she having a game of cards?"

He wasn't interested in an answer, as he quickly became irritated. "These are not the right boots. I wear them working in the garden, in Peredelkino. Ha, she cleaned and shined them. What for?"

I asked him how he was feeling, and he calmed down. The last time I saw him was in January, on Lavrushinsky Lane, after being discharged from the Botkin hospital, and he had gained weight since, although not much. Pale, his white hair whiter and carefully combed, somewhat unsure on his feet as he stood up from a chair to greet me. He had a brown, worn out housecoat over his pajama, clearly not something recently bought in one of the stores of our workers' paradise. He was keen to put on his boots and go out for a walk. "We should take advantage of the nice day, Pavel Nikolayevich," he said. He had socks on already, and as he steered his feet into the boots Zinaida had sent, he said he was feeling fine, a bit frail, true, but delighted to go home, to Peredelkino, to his novel. Yes, the doctors had recommended rest, but he could not afford it. "The novel awaits me. It seems foolish to say such things, Pavel Nikolayevich, but in a way I'm grateful for what happened to me. God had wished this on me for a purpose, I have no doubt about it. Things are clearer now."

"Clearer?"

"I felt death's heavy breathing on my face, Pavel Nikolayevich, and I'm no longer afraid of her. I asked for a furlough, a few more years to finish my novel, and my request was granted." Tapping his forehead, he added, "I know now I'll have the strength and the time to finish it. What would be the point of this respite otherwise?"

He bent to lace his boots, but gave up with a groan and looked at me. "Just tie them up, for me Pavel Nikolayevich, never mind all the holes. It will be easier to get them off later."

I helped him put his coat on, and we went out. We found an empty bench after a couple of tours during which Boris Leonidovich received many greetings with dignified nods of head. It wasn't unseasonably warm, but the sun was lumen-strong, and the sky of a baby-crayon blue. As we sat down, I thought Bolshevo was an odd place to have a sanatorium, and I told Boris Leonidovich that I didn't expect Bolshevo to be so drab.

He nodded. "Drab, yes. I had the same impression when I came here just before the war. I saw Tsvetayeva in Bolshevo, in thirty-nine, not long after she arrived. The dacha they were confined to was a bit off, though, not exactly in the town."

"Tell me about it."

Boris Leonidovich waved his hand. "Another time. It's a longer story and I don't have the fortitude."

The patients were out in droves, walking and talking and gesticulating. Well, they had plenty to talk about. Two older men passed by our bench, one of them holding the day's *Pravda* under his arm. I warmed my face in the sun, eyes closed, and thanked the gods for my good health. We were quiet for a long time, or so I thought, when I heard him say, "I should go there, Pavel Nikolaevich, pay my respect."

He'd been talking before, no doubt, and I missed it. "Go where?"

"Yelabuga, of course."

It was unexpected, but I knew what he was on about—jolted by one of his occasional guilt trips into a trip to the faraway Urals.

He confirmed what I thought. "I lie in bed at night, unable to sleep because of the noises around or God only knows what, and, as I'm in Bolshevo, I often think of her. I need this pilgrimage, Pavel Nikolaevich, a way to reach some peace. Would you come with me?"

That was unexpected. "Why me?"

He didn't answer for a long time. At last he said, "You were generous with her. Generous and brave, yes, brave too, I know the pressure you were under, Kolya Klyuchev told me at the time. I think your wife complained to him—she's never liked me since. I felt so ashamed afterward."

Kolya Klyuchev. Poor Kolya, long gone, dead in the war, blown into a million pieces by an artillery shell that fell on his operating tent. Untangling the body parts of the patient, the surgeon, and the two nurses helping him proved impossible afterward.

"What would you do there?" I asked.

"I don't know. Kneel at her tomb and pray."

"They wouldn't like it," I said after a while.

"Times are changing. The amnesty, and now this thing in *Pravda* about the made-up 'doctors' plot'. You know who'd been arrested in this plot? Vovsi, the cardiologist who looked after me at Botkin in the fall."

"On Povarskaya I've heard people say you faked your illness."

"Fake a heart attack?"

I nodded. "You saw the nooks tightening around Jewish necks, and called in sick."

"But the doctors—"

"That's the thing, Boris Leonidovich—Jewish doctors. Vovsi is a Jew, isn't he? The Jewish doctors look after their own, including false diagnostics, while carrying on with their terrible deeds."

He swore—the first time I heard him use profanity—and then laughed softly. "Yevgeny kept me informed. I didn't want to know, but my son thought otherwise. He and Zinaida wanted me to be prepared, in case they came to me. Imagine it, Pavel Nikolyevich, force the Jews to sign an appeal to Stalin begging to be spared for the medical crimes their brethren committed, asking to be resettled far away in the East. Ha. The inquisition would have been proud of such an idea."

"Oistrakh signed it, and Grossman and Marshak. Landau, the physicist, too."

He shook his head.

"Would you have signed it?"

"The Lord saved me." And, because I looked puzzled, he added, "Everything has a reason, Pavel Nikolayevich, don't you see? This heart attack saved me from groveling. Somehow they didn't come to me with the appeal. I might have been in the emergency ward at that time, and they probably thought that was the limit. It also put me past the *vozhd*'s demise and all that mess."

When I said goodbye to him in front of the main building, he said, "Well, maybe I'll wait for Ariadna Efron's return."

I realized he was back on his planned journey to Yelabuga. "Sure, she'll want to see her mother's grave," I said.

"She'll be released soon, won't she?" he asked.

"One can only hope. I don't know how long her sentence is, but, as a woman…"

"Yes, the amnesty said the women would be released first. Especially those with light sentences."

He was probably thinking of Ivinskaya too, and, vaguely malicious, I asked, "Why not Zinaida Nikolayevna? Why don't you travel with her?"

He shrugged, but wasn't prepared to elaborate. Instead, he went back to his boots. "I may need a new pair of boots. This one…" Then, confirming what I just thought, he whispered, "Olga Vsevolodovna would be out soon too, wouldn't she, Pavel Nikolayevich?"

6

With a sigh, he picked up the draft Erika Belov-Wang had sent him. That's all he needed now, busy as he was. It had been Bart's insistence that got him into this. In her brief handwritten note, she warned him she needed his corrections "earlier than **ASAP!!!**" in order to meet the magazine's deadline.

She had left a few things out of the transcript. Insane Erika Belov-Wang might have inserted a paragraph or two about frolicking with the poet. Something like, "Just before lunch we had sex on the carpet behind Art Laukhin's desk. I had a bruise on the small of my back the next day and I'm sure his elbows and knees hurt for a while. In case the reader is wondering how this came about, I initiated it—although he did seem to stare at my legs and crotch throughout the interview— hoping to bring the reader more intimate information about the poet. And if you're interested in Art Laukhin's sexual flair or preferences..." It was probably her editor who chucked it, after he called her into his office and asked, pointing at the paragraph, "What's this?"

"It completes the portrait."

"Erika!"

Over lunch Laukhin had asked her, "Why did you do that?"

"Why did I do what?"

"You know—fuck me."

"It takes two."

"You're not answering me."

"To know you better. To gain insight and ask better questions."

"Do you always do this?"

"You mean, fuck my subjects?"

"Yes."

"Not always. And never women."

An odd name, Erika Belov-Wang, its parts incongruous. He should have asked her how she'd ended up with it. He meant to, at lunch, but after what transpired between them just before, he forgot. She went on with the interview later as if nothing had happened. She was right, nothing of consequence had happened (or not yet; perhaps whoever opened the door while they *were at it*, was simply waiting for the right moment to tell all), but he'd felt awkward afterward. It wasn't the generational difference, it was simply his age. Twenty years earlier, even ten, he'd not have used the word insane to describe Erika Belov-Wang. He would have said daring, full of life, curious, sparkling, at worst barmy—the words he'd once used to rationalize his delight in Joan Geraldine. The Joan Geraldine of ready laughter and mischief.

Joan Geraldine Huxley—now with a different last name—had come from London to study Russian language and literature in Moscow. She was fond of introducing herself as Joan Geraldine, and at first Laukhin thought that Geraldine was her last name. Later she explained she liked the sound of both her given names together, that she was offering people a choice. They first met in a restaurant on the south side of the river, likely one of the last times he and Tanya had been out together. His friend Kyril Vronkh arrived with one of his students, Irina, who soon afterward became his second wife. Irina brought along Joan Geraldine—a colleague, she said—who in turn had someone in tow, a second secretary from the British embassy. Later, Laukhin called her mostly Joan, and Geraldine now and then in bed. In the rare times she mentioned her, Tanya always called her Joan Geraldine, and always scornfully. She had her reasons, of course, although Joan Geraldine's blatant pass at him that evening was hardly the first Tanya had witnessed. Far from it. She'd seen it happen so often she was immune to women trying to seduce him, and, anyway, by then she was involved with a doctor at the hospital in Serpukhov where she worked as a respirologist. Or was she already with Vadim? Whichever, she had never been happy with him, Laukhin. Her medical studies had kept her very busy, and the long days in training and nights at hospitals, and later the weekly commute to and from Serpukhov had given him many opportunities. And he was rarely able to say no to an opportunity.

Afterward, Joan Geraldine claimed it had been obvious to her that first evening in Zamoskvorechye that Laukhin and Tanya were not together anymore. Perhaps. Joan Geraldine had made clear what she wanted the first time they slept together. He dutifully mentioned love, and she laughed and said, in English, "There is no need for porkies, Art." No one had called him Art before, and the word porky—he guessed its meaning—was also new to him. He'd hear it often afterward, because it was a favourite of hers, but the first time she used it she'd added, "I have a fiancé waiting for me in London. Your English will improve, and so will my Russian. And I'll learn how poems come together." Such frankness annoyed Laukhin, but she was delightfully mad, full of life. She had smooth white skin and breasts with large, pink nipples.

She wrote very short stories and brief poems—English haikus, she called them—but told Laukhin she knew she was not a writer. She wanted to be a translator of Russian literature, and that was why she'd decided to spend two years in Moscow. "I have creative spark," she said to him once, "but it's only a spark, short lived. I cannot concentrate for long. A translation keeps me on track, focused. I had dreams of being a writer once. No more. Life highlights one's limitations. I can see my future in a country house in Dorset or Hampshire. Three pink-faced children and a husband who commutes to work and fucks me on weekends. The house—it will be a big house, Art—the garden, the children and their schools, the family meals, the occasional dinner parties, all these will keep me busy. I'll do my translations, small pieces to start, more after the children are in school. Slow, finicky, unpressured work. But they'll be translations of the highest quality, and the praise I'll get will remind me of my early dreams."

Her Russian had been very good when he met her. She had studied it at Cambridge, and told him she'd had several Russian lovers already.

In England. Laukhin wasn't sure whether to believe her, since Joan Geraldine was given to exaggerations, as she was the first to admit.

* * *

Of course, Erika Belov-Wang had to raise topics she knew would be uncomfortable for him. She was paid to do that. Some of the things he had said in the heat of the interview might have to change. He wouldn't claim he hadn't said them, he'd simply cross them out. He could correct or delete anything he didn't really mean or want to have published. This was agreed to at the start, part and parcel of the way the *Paris Review* did its interviews, one of the reasons they were so readable.

He'd told a few porkies too, and they showed up in the transcript. He wasn't sure now whether he should fix them; it would only take more of his time.

The lie about *Poets in Heaven* had not been premeditated. It had been a surprise to him that Erika Belov-Wang wanted to talk about it. It had not seemed right to tell her that he was still working on the poem (although he hadn't touched it in more than a year), that it was troubling to him, a difficult poem which he just might not be able to finish, and that its premature publication had been much more than a passing irritation.

There was one porky he wouldn't be able to do much about, the one regarding his son. He had told it many times since his defection, and he really had no choice. The interview made it clear he had left Tanya, at the time pregnant with his son, in Moscow. It sounded awful, and the awkward way he'd ducked Erika's follow-on questions—"Don't you want to see your child? He's, what, six years old now?"—was even worse. Well, he could always ask her to delete that entire passage. Should he bother?

* * *

The sound of the lawnmower startled Laukhin. It was still light outside, but it wouldn't be for much longer. He thought it was Ivor Bendiksen, his neighbour to the east. Ivor was retired and obsessed with his lawn. Laukhin wouldn't be surprised to see him one day sprawled out on it, measuring each blade of grass with a ruler. But the noise came from his own backyard—one of Efim Apelbaum's underlings was cutting the grass to a civilized length. Laukhin had told Efim he'd mow the lawn himself, even buy a lawnmower, but the big man wouldn't think of it. "You're my guest, Tyoma," he'd said as he squeezed Laukhin's shoulder. "It's better that someone lives in the house, anyway." The only favour he had asked of Laukhin in return was to find out whether Bendiksen or any of the other neighbours was thinking of selling their houses.

In high school they called Efim "The House" because he was built like a house and was a head taller than anyone else in their class. He had not minded it. He'd been the one Jew in Laukhin's class—there were a handful—who struggled academically and only just squeezed through from one grade to the next. After high school Laukhin lost touch with him. They met again in the early eighties in Toronto, at a store in Finchurst Plaza that catered to Russian tastes. As he went in, Laukhin noticed the man towering above everybody else at the other end of the narrow store. It was Efim. This time they kept in touch. A year later, when Laukhin mentioned he was looking for a new place to live, Efim told him he had a small house that was empty. He had bought it as a tear-down and intended to build a larger house, but he was too busy with other projects to do it right then. Laukhin would be doing him a favour if he moved in. The location was fine—although the subway was a twenty-minute walk away—and so he agreed. The rent was ridiculously low. At first Efim said it would be rent free, but Laukhin balked. He said he'd pay the property tax. Efim wouldn't hear of it, and eventually they agreed on utilities and half of the tax.

* * *

Should he work on the transcript, or answer Kyril's odd letter? He felt like doing neither—he should work on the galley proofs. He wasn't even sure that Kyril expected an answer. Laukhin switched on the table lamp and picked up the letter. He'd read it several times and still couldn't be certain what his friend meant to say. He'd been away for too long and had lost the ability to read between the lines. Kyril had written to him before. The first letter had reached him via Colson, who brought letters back from Kyril and from his sister in Leningrad each time he travelled to the Soviet Union. The letters Kyril sent on his own arrived from everywhere. One seemed to have been written in a hotel in Budapest. One was posted from Krakow, another from Lyon, both likely taken abroad and mailed by visitors or travelling friends. Kyril had signed them all with a straight, unadorned K. Each letter had a postscript saying that there was no point in writing back because the demands of his work kept him constantly on the move. There was no return address on any of the envelopes.

He decided to have a drink before he re-read the letter. Still holding it, he made his way down to the kitchen. The bottle, kept in the freezer, was covered with minute ice crystals. He once heard a wit say Russians drank a lot of vodka because it was the only thing they had that didn't freeze during the winter. He poured the clear liquid over ice cubes, feeling as if he was watching a commercial with the sound off. Vodka on ice—most of his Russian friends would be puzzled. Kyril would be incensed. He was probably drinking when he wrote this last letter. It had also been posted in Krakow, but it was signed with the familiar curlicued Kyril, where the K was four or five times the size of the other letters. Kyril's Tverskoy Boulevard address was on the back of the envelope, a first, and the postscript telling Laukhin not to reply was missing.

What should he make of such openness? Why was Kyril being less careful? The part that baffled him most began on the second page.

I am too old or too cynical to write such things, but here I go. There's something happening here, something hard to define or pin hopes to. There is talk of a new thaw, and there are novel fancy words to define it. You'll say it happened before only for the freeze to return. True, and I'm as weary of false hope as anyone here, but people **are bolder** and they **talk louder** since the new vozhd took over. He's only four years older than we are, Tyoma, practically our generation. Maybe that's what's needed—new, less tainted blood, less affected minds.

I was summoned to Vorovsky Street the other day by the first secretary. Markov is still the big shot at the Writers' Union, but not for much longer. He told me he had neither the strength nor the stomach to carry on. "It's not my fight anymore," he said. An *odd statement from somebody like him. He didn't hide his dis-pleasure at the way things were evolving.*

The village hooligan—remember that old portrayal of him?—has mellowed, though. He's well over seventy now, probably seventy-five. Bent, lined face, second chin. Still a full head of hair.

*Here's the startling news, Tyoma—**they want you back.***

Did you just sit down? Have you decided you needed a drink before you read on?

Yes, they want you back in the Soviet Union. Not old Markov—he was only the tired messenger, at least that's what he kept saying. He let me understand that the call came from the highest levels. Not from the new vozhd, *not that high up (he wouldn't have time for this), but from high up nevertheless.*

I'll try to reconstruct the discussion I had with him word for word, because it's important you get it with as little retelling as possible.

Markov said, "It will be as if he, Laukhin, never left. He'll be received back in the union, of course. And if teaching literature is something he wants to go on doing, they'll see to it. He can't return to his old apartment, but he'll get an equivalent place—they'll see to that as well. And he'll be published—yes, all his poetry, includ-ing Bolshevo Days. *And—have another sip, Tyoma—Pavel Laukhin's journal will also be published." Now, as regards the journal, Markov added, "they (and they from what I understand, includes the union and our literary generals) might call for some minor adjustments, but they'd be kept to an absolute minimum."*

I asked, "Why?"

Markov reiterated he was only the messenger. He then said, "Why would Laukhin publish his father's journal abroad? Why give ammunition to our country's enemies? Surely, he wants to come back to his own country and people and language. Seven years, and Laukhin has not published anything except Poets in Heaven. *Those who've read it say it's full of nostalgia, of regrets, of the author's inability to write anything good where he now finds himself. Laukhin needs Russia, and Russia wants him back. He should not waste his talent and life over there." He stopped and frowned, the village hooligan at his thoughtful best. "There is the personal situation too," he added.*

I said, "Personal?"

Markov said, "Surely, Laukhin wishes to see his son. He has not remarried, and has no other children. His son is six years old, and if he wants to be at all close to him he should return to the Soviet Union as soon as possible."

I said, "I seem to have been chosen as the messenger to Laukhin. Why me?"

The village hooligan dismissed my query with a "not worthy of you" gesture. He said, "Kyril Innokentievich, we know you send letters to him now and then. It's fine, it's fine," he assured me, "there isn't much harm in that, it's how old friends are."

He left it up to me to write to you whichever way I saw fit. I was given carte blanche. He said, "Kyril Innokentievich, you know the best way to reach Laukhin's heart and mind."

I asked, "Am I allowed to talk about this?"

"You mean to friends?"

"Yes."

Markov shook his head and said, "It'd be better not to."

I said, "Send me there. Send me to Canada. I'll be a better messenger face to face."

Markov laughed. He said he'd relay my suggestion to those who decide such matters, but he didn't believe it would be approved.

When he dismissed me, he said it would be best to post my letter to you from outside the Soviet Union. He smiled and added, "Use one of your friends."

There was more. After his tête-à-tête with Markov, Kyril had lunch at the club. There was talk about publishing *Zhivago* in the Soviet Union. And, listening to friends and sipping his last drink, Kyril remembered that it was the village hooligan himself who had demanded Pasternak's ouster from the Writers' Union at the time of the *Zhivago* scandal.

Kyril had written a paragraph about himself too. He had not felt well in the last few months, but the doctors couldn't find anything wrong. Not yet—it was always like that. Maybe it was just not being young anymore. Young Irina, on the other hand, was fine. So were his children, whom he saw little of thanks to their mother.

And there was a postscript:

> *PS: The same infighting at the institute. I understand my stu-*
> *dents less and less. The lineups have not disappeared. We build*
> *whatever we build, although there's some confusion lately as to*
> *what exactly it is.*

Laukhin understood the PS—daily life in the Soviet Union had not changed much—but the rest of the letter was baffling.

Old Markov was an odd choice as a messenger. A reluctant messenger, most likely, as the first secretary couldn't be looking forward to the journal's depiction of his role in the Pasternak affair. Although his father had not felt well that day in October 1958—the first sign of the brain tumour?—he had insisted on attending the special extended meeting of the Presidium of the Writers' Union. Laukhin knew about the vile speech Markov made that day on Vorovsky Street because his father had been very upset afterward and talked of little else for several days. During Markov's speech, Ehrenburg leaned over to his father and whispered, "From village hooligan to union hooligan." His father left before the vote to expel Pasternak from the Writers' Union was taken; he was allowed to go only because he was clearly sick. He walked out, propped up by Ehrenburg and Tvardovsky, who were both glad to avoid voting too.

To think that Markov was still alive and about. Too many people were still alive and about.

What made them think he would return?

He thought again of Tsvetayeva's words, *"Here* I am unnecessary. *There* I am impossible."

Tsvetayeva wrote somewhere that emigration had made her a prose writer. She had exaggerated, because she wrote her best poetry while away from Russia. It had made him, Laukhin, a prose writer.

Could he really call himself an émigré? That was the consecrated, if now tarnished, term for Russian fugitives from the Soviet regime, but didn't emigration entail hardship, misery and grief? He experienced none, never had to struggle to keep "body and pen together," as Nabokov put it. What a difference three decades and a war made. They found a chair for him, gave him awards. There'd been nothing for Tsvetayeva. She'd had it hard as an émigré, fully deserved the title. She left Russia after losing a child to starvation during the civil war—in itself enough grief, and it never really got better for her. She wandered—Berlin, Paris, Prague, Paris again. No one was interested in her poems. A destitute life. Poverty, the kind that sticks to you like dirt. She had lousy affairs, another child, a husband who couldn't find a job or hold one. He *did* have a job, though, as an NKVD agent. He betrayed his comrades, and helped end the earthly days of a few sad men whom the motherland found undesirable. A job he kept secret from his wife.

What made them think he would return?

He knew of no happy returns to the Soviet Union. Tsvetayeva's had been tragic. Prokofiev had regretted going back. Even Gorky's return, despite all the honours and the flattery, the mansion with servants, and the special privileges, had not been happy. Stravinsky had been the clever one—he stayed put. He went back for a visit, but that was all. Lucky for him Stalin wasn't still around. The physicist Kapitsa returned for a visit while Stalin was alive and wasn't allowed to go back to Cambridge.

Well, maybe Aleksey Tolstoy, the Comrade Count. That scoundrel had been the only one who had not minded returning.

Fedya Malgunov thought long and hard about going back. Laukhin talked to him about it while Fedya visited him in Toronto. He had many problems, poor Fedya, not the least of which being his beastly wife who, after pushing him to flee the Soviet Union, left him for another man. Fedya told Laukhin he did not blame her. "She was tired, Tyoma, tired of counting pennies. It was fine to do that back home, everybody was doing it there, but here? The life she had with me, well, she couldn't hack it any longer. So she found Steve with his big house in Palo Alto."

What made them think he'd return?

They were certain of two things, the literary *sanovniky*. Unlike here in the West, poetry and poets remained significant in the Soviet Union. Poets there had always had—what was the word he had used with Erika Belov-Wang?—traction. To be listened to, even if it meant being reported, was not something to be sneered at. It was important to feel important.

Coupled to this was the privileged life poets led there—as long as they paid lip service to the Party's dictates or their poetry remained sufficiently obscure. What better example than Pasternak? They attacked him in forums and newspapers, and he ignored it all, enjoying his large, beautiful apartment in the heart of Moscow, a year-round dacha in Peredelkino, access to the best doctors, and enough money to have a comfortable life and to support another family besides his own—his son and first wife, after he divorced her and married Zinaida, and later his lover Ivitskaya and her family. While he, Laukhin, now lived in a house belonging to a friend, had a modest university salary—well, he was doing little teaching, just as he had wanted—and his only hope for financial security were earnings from his father's journal.

But he had no desire to return. He had made his bed and he'd sleep in it. Anyway, he was beginning to feel comfortable here. Almost. He might even consider writing in English. Not poetry, of course, but prose.

* * *

There was a second postscript in his friend's letter:

> *PPS: I finally dug out a few things about the Fredkins. He was shot in 1940, here in Moscow. His wife died in forty-nine or fifty shortly after her release from Ekibastuz. She tried to find out about the children from where she was, in exile, near Omsk, but she had little time left. I know all this from a second or third cousin of his, an older man I met accidentally in Kharkov and who has the same last name. When I heard it, I asked him if he was any relation to the Moscow Fredkins who were arrested at the end of 1939. Friedkin's wife had sent him a letter shortly after she was released, but he didn't answer it. 1949 had been a tense year and he'd simply been afraid. He didn't know about the children anyway, or not much, and had not been keen at the time to learn more. He heard the little ones had been with her sister for a while, but she had moved away from Kiev, and he didn't know where. They may have taken the names of the relatives they ended up with, if they were lucky enough.*

It was quiet now. Efim's lawn gendarmes had finished their noisy task. Laukhin had a vague recollection of seeing Efim's name in his father's last notebook. He walked upstairs, pulled the copy from the small bookshelf he kept near his worktable, and sat on his bed. It was the only notebook he kept a copy of at home, and it had been a long time since he had looked at it. He was beginning to doubt his memory because it took him a while to find it, yet there it was: his meticulous father had made a note of Efim's visit to Lavrushinsky Lane in February 1958, only a cursory mention in a larger entry. He read it in its entirety.

A giant young man, Efim Apelbaum, came here yesterday to congratulate Tyoma on his first book of poetry. Tyoma had not seen him since high school. He'd changed so much that Tyoma did not recognize him at first. Not a reader of poetry, Efim, by his own admission. Not a reader of anything. Amusing young man, though. He had lunch with us and told us countless stories from his three years of military service.

This morning a large package with printed copies of *Youthful Eminences* arrived at the apartment. Tyoma was out. I opened the package, took out a copy, and gazed at the slim volume for a long time. I had tears in my eyes, tears of pride and gratitude for having such a gifted son. A pity Varenka isn't with me anymore to share this joy.

I read Tyoma's poems for an hour, maybe longer, and then took a copy upstairs to the Pasternaks. Zinaida opened the door, wearing a red apron. There was a familiar smell drifting from the kitchen. I said, "Mmmm, boiled potatoes and cabbage, what else could a Russian soul desire."

"Your idol is in the bedroom," she said. "He's not feeling well. When he's well he's elsewhere. But *I* always have to look after him when he's not well."

I brandished the slim book. "Look, Zinaida Nikolayevna, Tyoma's first volume of poems. I brought you a copy."

She nodded, but did not take it for a closer look. Surly Zinaida, she had long exhausted the store of social graces she came into this world with. "Nice," she said. "Give it to the poet laureate. I've heard rumours he'll get the Nobel Prize. It will turn out handy in prison."

"Zinaida Nikolayevna, don't be so gloomy. No one would dare touch him if he gets the Nobel."

"We'll still have to eat, won't we?" She was in one of her moods.

I asked, "What's ailing him this time?"

"He can't pee."

"What?"

"You heard me. He can't pass water. An infection, probably, but the doctors can't make up their minds. Go in, he'll be glad to see you."

Boris Leonidovich looked feverish. He lay on his bed in crumpled pyjamas, the cover tossed aside. He said he was in pain, terrible pain. He described it to me at some length, and then, lowering his voice as if it were a secret, said, "They finally found a catheter. A doctor will come tonight. Imagine, Pavel Nikolayevich, putting a tube through it…"

He made a feeble gesture for me to come closer and went on whispering, "They want me to tell Gallimard to stop the French edition of *Zhivago*. I won't do it. I said I was too sick to do anything about it. They are not happy with me, Pavel Nikolayevich, not happy at all. Maybe that's why no one could find a catheter for me in the whole of Moscow." He tried to laugh.

I commiserated with him for a while, and then showed him Tyoma's slim volume. "For you," I said. "For you and Zinaida Nikolayevna."

He made a sound through his nose. "Zinaida, ha! Zinaida does not read *my* poetry!"

Theirs was a spent marriage, yet they carried on. They were too old, too tired, too set in their ways to separate.

He flipped through Tyoma's volume, and said, "The proud father bearing gifts. The first of many, I'm sure." He pushed it back to me. "Tell him to sign it. And I want a dedication, to Uncle Boris or something like that."

I said, "Keep it. I'll get Tyoma to sign another copy. He's got a whole package of them downstairs. It just arrived."

"No, no, take this one back. I won't be able to read it now, anyway. Bring me one of your books instead, Pavel Nikolayevich."

His father and Pasternak became close after the Laukhins moved into the Lavrushinsky Lane building. The Pasternaks' apartment was a makeshift, five-room, two-storey penthouse, with an internal staircase leading to the upper floor. As a child, Laukhin often perched on the staircase, gazing at the goings-on below him. The Pasternaks had taken over the room upstairs when the poet thought his parents would return to the Soviet Union. They didn't. Later, from the late forties onwards, the Laukhins and the Pasternaks also had Peredelkino in common.

They had been an odd pair, Pasternak and his father, but they had liked each other from the very beginning. Even at a literary level, although this was surprising. His father's novels had an irony that appealed to many readers, including Pasternak. He read them when he was ill or under stress—a backhanded compliment—and even said he had learned "a trick or two about structuring a novel from Pavel Nikolayevich." One of the little flattering lies that cemented a friendship, Laukhin was certain. Pasternak was also affected by the hero's surname, Vinograd. Yelena Vinograd had been the muse of Pasternak's breakthrough book of poems, *My Sister Life*. What's more, Oleg Vinograd's sister, also called Yelena, had an on-again off-again relationship with a poet. If providence had brought them together, Pasternak once declared while tipsy, he "would do all in his power to keep it that way."

* * *

Toward the end, the writing in his father's journal dried up. The extensive entries he'd written in the mid thirties slowed to a trickle by the late fifties. The same minute lettering, but harder on the eye because of the uncertain, shaky hand. He had completely given up his tight, economical line spacing, and a page often contained no more than a couple of brief, wavy lines. The trail of words dribbled downward after an initial, timid ascent.

During the two years before his death, he mainly noted down his observations on the tumour that would eventually kill him. There were bemused jottings at first, during the lengthy confirmation of the initial diagnosis, even humorous. "A brain tumour is encouraging news. Our doctors are wrong more often than not, so it could be something else, less threatening." Or, "Here is a real circus act, keeping the body in balance with no help from the brain." There were bitter and resentful notes later. At the very end the writing was resigned, then helpless, then confused. Brief sentences or single words. The last entry was one word—*seychas* (now). The next to last a scrawled blasphemy. Nothing in the last month of his life.

He had lost his balance and had fallen one morning as he got out of bed. Laukhin heard the thud from his room and rushed to the large bedroom. His father tried to get up on his own, but couldn't. He looked at Laukhin with a baffled smile, as if saying, "Look at the fine surprise your old man is pulling off." It was not much of a surprise, though, because his father had begun to complain of feeling weak the spring after his trip to Yelabuga with Pasternak. His wife's sudden death a couple of months after the trip had been a blow to him and Laukhin had put his father's weakness down to that loss. In hindsight, it was more likely that the tumour was already sapping his strength.

Laukhin remembered mentioning the trip to Yelabuga to Ben during one of their weekly meetings at the beginning of the year. He was already pushing Tsvetayeva on Ben, but hadn't yet thought of the poetess as the subject of the next bundle. "My father made detailed notes during that trip, thirty pages, maybe more. It's the last journal entry related to Tsvetayeva. And, in a way, the main entry about her too, although she had already been dead for fourteen years. It's worth your while, Ben, to have a thorough look at it."

It was in the second to last notebook, this long description of the trip his father and Pasternak took together in the fall of 1955 to Yelabuga, the small town on the Kama River where Tsvetayeva died in the early days of the Great Patriotic War. Reading it again and preparing it for the bundle, Laukhin noticed something he hadn't before—"Pasternak" was now mostly "Boris Leonidovich." He surmised that as his father's friendship and admiration for Pasternak grew, he found it more appropriate or more natural to use the first name and the patronymic of the poet. He might not even have been aware of the switch. Laukhin found the use of "Boris Leonidovich" fitting for the trip, and decided to keep it. The *New Yorker* editor had grumbled about it, but to Laukhin's mind the addressing form of the name expressed both the warmth and the irony his father felt about his famous friend during their last years.

Pasternak had called their trip a pilgrimage. He had to make it, had no choice if he was to have any peace of mind. He had not been able to do it earlier, but, with "the thaw" after Stalin's death, he felt he could postpone it no longer. His flapping heart was a signal too, a warning that he might not have many seasons left. He had asked Tsvetayeva's daughter to accompany him but, only recently freed, she was too weak and could not face the trip. She also feared she wouldn't be allowed to return to Moscow. Pasternak told Pavel Laukhin he was secretly relieved when Alya declined to go. She had changed after fifteen years in camps and exile, no longer the easy-going, smiling Alya he had once known. There was now something fiery, direct, intense about her that reminded him of her mother. She suggested he take Olga with him. She and Olga Ivinskaya had become fast friends since

Alya's return. There was no surprise there, as they had the work-camp experience in common, although Ivinskaya's time there had been much shorter and she had been among the first to be released after Stalin's death. Olga, to whom Alya had mentioned the trip before she made the suggestion to him, quickly began to make plans for the trip, but Pasternak demurred. Zinaida was already upset by his renewed interest in Ivinskaya and would have made his life miserable. His children would not have been pleased either.

And so it happened that Pasternak set out with Pavel Laukhin as his sole companion. Best companion too, all things considered, because Pavel Laukhin would also look after the more practical aspects of the trip, details that he, the cloud-dwelling poet, had no inclination or ability to deal with. He expected others to look after these things. He would travel but not without some minimal comforts, and he counted on his friend to cover any deficit if the expedition turned out to be too costly.

His father and Pasternak left on their trip to Yelabuga at the beginning of October 1955. At Pasternak's insistence, they travelled by riverboat, just as Tsvetayeva had done fourteen years earlier, in August 1941.

Wednesday, 5 October, 1955

We have not seen the sky since embarking. The river stretches endlessly in front of us, grey and brown in daylight, dark grey and gloomy at dusk. We stay on deck as much as we can, but after half an hour we return to our cabins shivering. It's too cold and damp. The forays we make from our cabins are short and energetic. Comical too. To warm up, we try to walk fast, but, for Boris Leonidovich, who's ten years older than I am, a venerable sixty-five, it's a struggle. He tells me again about his weak heart and his belief that it will soon kill him. Sometimes, I run ahead and do a quick lap on my own. I also jump and slap my sides and shoulders. Boris Leonidovich claims that I have an odd way of jumping, almost backwards. He fears that I'll end up sprawled on my back.

I did not expect such cold and I'm not suitably dressed. Boris Leonidovich has been more cautious—Zinaida packed warm clothes in the two large suitcases he brought onboard—and has loaned me one of his long-sleeve undershirts, frayed, yellowed, ancient. He jokes it might have belonged to his father. Boris Leonidovich's eyes are red from the cold and wind, and he has a nasty cough that keeps him, and me, from sleeping at night. I can hear his cough from my cabin, across the shared salon.

We've been told that starting tonight or tomorrow morning the temperature will be back to the seasonal average, even a bit warmer.

Every day Boris Leonidovich talks about Tsvetayeva. A duty, he says. In August 1941, two months after the war began, he went to the river station in Moscow to see Tsvetayeva and her son off on what turned out to be her last journey. She and Georgy were being evacuated, like so many others.

"Remember those days of panic, Pavel Nikolayevich, with the Fascists closing in on Moscow? We left too, a couple of weeks after her. Anyway, at the last minute I had to run and buy bread and sausages and cheese for the two travellers. Tsvetayeva had brought no provisions for the trip. It wasn't easy—the shelves were empty and I had to pay a fortune. Imagine, Pavel Nikolayevich. What did she think she was boarding, the Queen Mary?"

For Boris Leonidovich this trip is like a wake. It's also his reparation to Tsvetayeva. We must, he insists, reminisce and talk about her. I don't mind. The remorse gnaws at his heart. He's often frantic when he talks about her, almost incoherent, and I wonder how this can be—our foremost poet. But at other times, he is calmer, the pleasant, melodious stutter under control, his charm in full bloom, his words chosen with care and power, and I could listen to him forever. I am, as usual, in awe of him.

Here and there the river is so wide that you can't see its banks.

There is a dining room—quite large, and with an odd odor that I can't quite make out—where we are served our meals. We eat our lunches at long rectangular tables with fixed benches. First drinks are served before noon, so the room is often filled with smoke and shouts, and we eat quickly, without lingering. In the evening, a couple of round tables with cloths and chairs are brought out and set in a corner, near the captain's table, for the first class passengers.

The riverboat is called *Kirov*. We have the best living quarters on board, a suite—three cabins in a row—and Boris Leonidovich assures me that he got it as a special favour. Dovlatov's cousin works in the administration of the inner waters, and Dovlatov owes him a lot. He does not elaborate and I do not pry. (Favour or not, they were not cheap. I know, because I paid for them, Boris Leonidovich being hard up financially right now, with his dental work and repairs to the dacha. I don't mind, even if he never pays me back, which may very well be the case. After all, *The Ambassador's Ring* has sold almost a half a million copies, and there's word of re-issuing my first three novels.)

The sleeping cabins are small, and once the bed is unstowed, there isn't much space for anything else, but the cabin we share in the middle—the one we both call the salon, with an exaggerated French accent, and in which we spend most of our time—is large and well furnished. Plenty of light comes in during the day through the wide windows. There are two swivel chairs in front of them, and we often sit there reading, chatting, watching the river-world slide by. The windows cannot be opened, but a door leads to a small deck outside. A battered sofa and an oblong cherry-wood table with four chairs complete the furnishings of the salon. The table is exquisite, with an inlaid oval stripe, like a racetrack, in the middle.

The steward, Arkhip, late thirties, smelling of vodka, and sour-faced prior to a considerable tip I provided at Boris Leonidovich's insistence, told us that the boat has been on the river for more than twenty years. Boris Leonidovich wondered aloud whether Tsevtaeva and her son had travelled on it to Yelabuga. He shook his head annoyed; he should have remembered, having seen her off, but couldn't. He asked Arkhip whether he'd been with the boat from the very beginning. No, no, only after the war, he said. He'd been with the Murmansk fleet during the war, and an inch from losing his life. It turned out to be a long story, with the outcome that he was much happier floating on sweet river waters.

During our morning walks we pass through the second-class quarters. Mainly peasants on short trips, a few blue-collar workers and soldiers on furlough. The second-class comrades are quiet in the morning, their stares vacant. After lunch, and especially in the evening, they begin to drink steadily from their own supplies of homebrew and exchange words and nasty, callous laughter. After night falls, there are shouts and now and then fights. I'm fascinated by them, by their animal acceptance and attachment to this routine. Boris Leonidovich is, I feel, repelled by the sight of them—not that he does not enjoy a tipple now and then. He always walks faster as we pass through second class. They talk about us, I'm sure, and make jokes and laugh behind our backs.

"The river," Boris Leonidovich said on one of our morning walks, "is like the Russian soul. Now wide and generous, now narrow, furious, mean-spirited, cruel. But, most often, murky, grey, patient, load-bearing."

Wednesday–evening, 5 October, 1955

We dine each night at the captain's table. Korotkov is overwhelmed by our presence on the boat—undoubtedly by Boris Leonidovich's more than mine—and is all smiles and suggestions about how to make our trip more pleasant. He had a samovar sent to our room and he wondered whether we'd like to have breakfast or lunch there. "It can be arranged. Not dinner, though. No, I prefer to have the honour and pleasure of your company for dinner. Ah, Marietta will be delighted to meet you, Boris Leonidovich. She's the one in our family who keeps the literature torch brightly lit. I'm not smart enough for such things, but she is. Oh, yes, she is."

Marietta is Marietta Alexeyevna Korotkova, the captain's wife, and she will come aboard in Yaroslavl, where the Korotkovs live. He has telegraphed her, and she's dropping everything to join the trip. He, Korotkov, hopes that we don't mind his indiscretion. His plump face is all humble smiles and excuses. I suspect that behind the perpetual diffidence and modesty there is a man who knows his mind.

Korotkov's second in command is a fan of Oleg Vinograd and has endless questions about who feeds me the stories, which must, he's certain, be based on reality.

7

Laukhin called the gallery just before noon, after he'd tried Audrey's apartment the previous evening and early that morning without getting an answer. Lezzard picked up the phone. Audrey was in Owen Sound, meeting with a reclusive artist. "Come over later this afternoon," he said. "We'll find a tipple, somewhere. What's the point in pining alone? There is nothing a drink will not cure. Are you done with the second half of the galleys?"

"Please tell Audrey I called."

He went home and worked on the Tsvetayeva bundle, but made little progress. Still, he wasn't unhappy with what he had. Much of the material had been translated and massaged into reasonable shape. The initial four excerpts had become ten. He had added two new ones, a small dinner at the Laukhins, the first in their new apartment on Lavrushinsky Lane, and a visit his father made to an ailing Pasternak while the poet was recovering from his first heart attack, and divided the lengthy account of the journey to Yelabuga into five shorter excerpts. The Yelabuga entries were in decent shape, but there was still a fair amount of work to do on Brodelshchikova's story, and improving rough spots throughout. Not too much polish, though, because—Ben was of the same opinion—the raw entries were compelling.

The handwritten sheets he had were legible enough, although much erased and cut and pasted. Ben still needed to type in the word processor the last seven excerpts of the bundle and do a first rough translation of an entry Laukhin initially thought he'd leave out but was now thinking of including—Pasternak's story of his visit to Bolshevo. He had asked Ben for the first translation weeks ago, but had seen nothing yet. Everything was agonizingly slow with Ben these days because malicious Marion was playing games with him.

* * *

His father's description of the journey up the Kama River to Yelabuga was long-winded and often lyrical. He couldn't make up his mind whether to cut certain passages. Did they contribute to the appreciation of the trip and its drama? Add colour and texture? Perhaps, but it often seemed excessive. And then, there was the space limitation.

It was not clear to him what caused the stylistic change. Had it been the boat trip itself on the wide, solemn river? The sight of decrepit towns and villages and mournful woods past their peak fall colours? The melancholy of the riverboat, with its monotonous noise, its slow progress and routine? Had it been the overwhelming presence of the great poet, and Pasternak's guilt-laden recollections? Or the intimation that he, Pavel Laukhin, was approaching his last years?

He kept staring at his father's notes in a dreamy daze, unable or unwilling to decide. He imagined taking the same boat trip with Audrey, under Pavel Laukhin's approving guidance and Pasternak's lecherous eyes. He told himself he had rediscovered the masochistic pleasures of unrequited love, the unexpected and long-forgotten delights of a pining heart.

Audrey finally answered the phone around ten o'clock that night. She had just got back, and sounded tired and remote. The trip to Owen Sound had been a waste of time.

Laukhin begged for a date. "Surely I deserve it, Audrey, a proper date, a reward for being persistent."

"You mean dinner?" she asked after a long pause.

"Yes, dinner."

"All right. We'll go to Martha's favourite eatery."

"Let's not go to a restaurant, Audrey. I can cook, you know, and the result is usually edible. I'll do something Russian. This Saturday?"

More silence at the other end, but he knew he had finally won when she asked, "Authentic Russian?"

He could barely whisper, "Yes, of course." And he barely heard her say that she was flying to London for a few days—her father was not doing well—but the following weekend might work. "I'll call you as soon as I get back," she added. "Art, are you still there? Having second thoughts already?"

* * *

What exactly had happened to him in such a short time? And at his age? Not that forty-nine was old, not these days. Maybe a bit old compared to Audrey, fourteen years younger, if what he had put together about her was right. The time had not been that short either. It had been three months since he first went to the gallery. The one thing age brought to one's arsenal was patience.

He resolved to give serious thought to the dinner with Audrey. He'd lied, he was a lousy cook, but he might be able to get something from a Russian store, at least a soup. He could get take-out from Balalaika, if the restaurant was still around, and reheat it at home. Something simple that he could pass off as his own. Well, he might admit he'd bought the soup. He could also ask Efim's wife to make something for him.

Was his torment with Audrey near an end? She'd agreed to come to his home for dinner, and, without a doubt, that meant something. Without a doubt? He'd been in New York and then Boston, and had not seen Audrey in more than two weeks. The last time he had—he'd walked her from the gallery to Martha's apartment, not far at all, in an ugly highrise on Prince Arthur Avenue—she'd talked about moving back to London and about how much her father needed her. "I would have gone back earlier, but Josiane's recovery has been very slow. It's not that Father is not looked after, but he thinks I should move back to London. He says that the few months I lived with him after I left Nicholas have spoiled him."

"Nicholas wants me back too," she added when they were in front of her building.

"Do you want him back?"

She didn't answer immediately, then said, "The stars are just not aligned, Art."

What exactly did that mean? He must have looked downcast, because she kissed him on the cheek before running into her building.

* * *

He worked feverishly the entire weekend, finished the introduction— he would read it through in a few days, once he was distant enough to be critical—and went back to the galleys. On Friday, Ben had left another segment of the trip, a short one, and Laukhin worked on it too. He had expected a lot more from Ben, and decided to have a serious talk with him on Monday. Not that he knew what to say.

On Monday, though, Ben didn't show up for his weekly hour. Laukhin called the graduate residence. A man with a heavy Indian accent answered and went searching for Ben. He returned quickly and said he had knocked on Ben's door but there had been no answer. No, he had not seen Ben that morning. Laukhin asked to speak with Paul Karman, but Paul had just gone out. It made sense, Laukhin thought, Paul would have left for his tutorial, which followed Ben's. When Paul came into his office, some fifteen minutes later, Laukhin asked him if he had seen Ben recently.

"He went home for the weekend," Paul said.

"To Corby Falls? He has time for trips?"

"His cousin was in town on Friday and he drove up with her."

"He's behind with the work on the bundle. Way behind."

"He's in love."

Laukhin swore. "It's what you people call 'letting down the side.' No, it's more than that, it's treason. Article 58-1(a), death or ten years prison with confiscation of property. I'll take over his shack on Clara Lake." He threw up his hands and let them flop on his thighs. "On second thought, I won't do anything. Becoming a Russian scholar is punishment enough."

That night he had more bad news. Audrey called and insisted that they go out to a restaurant on Saturday.

"What's happened, Audrey? I did nothing this week but read cook books."

"A restaurant would be better."

"Why the change of mind?"

"Please don't push me," she said. "I just got back home and I'm too tired to argue. I'll make the reservation."

* * *

They walked from Martha's apartment, up Bedford Street at first, then along the stretch of Davenport that slowly curves north, and then up the quiet, winding Poplar Plains Road, the best part of the walk. His heart was apprehensive and heavy, and he hardly said anything as they made their way to the restaurant.

Sipping his double vodka, Laukhin asked how her trip went. She shrugged and said, "My father's not well, and my husband misses me—or so he claims."

"You saw him?"

"Yes, I saw Nicholas. He came up for a visit and stayed for dinner. He and Father get along well. Always have."

Audrey seemed to be elsewhere, wistful, pensive, as if fretting about an intractable problem. She began talking about her mother. How did Martha learn about this discretely located restaurant, with its unexpected view of Toronto's skyline? Did Dirk bring her here? One of her Toronto friends? The place she came after—or before—a romantic assignation? A pleasant restaurant, she had to give it to her. A classy, expensive French eatery, the kind Martha approved of, with discreet waiters, and a menu on which the English translations were afterthoughts in a small font size. Nicholas had taken her to a similar place in London on their first date, and she'd been impressed. Nicholas himself had impressed her too: the respectful manner in which the maitre d' had greeted him by name; the way he discussed—in accented but fluent French—*les choix du jour* with Carmelo, the old Columbian waiter who, according to Nicholas, had lived many years in France; the way he asked her permission to order for her. She fell for him—for his manners and looks, for being tall, svelte, suave. After Martha met him—she came to London for their engagement party—she said, "Audrey darling, he's a thinner and younger version of your father. He even speaks like him. I expected more imagination from you." And, after she delivered that little dart, she plunged in another, "I don't know, there's something fishy about him."

So that was what had been preoccupying Audrey—she had decided to talk about her husband and her marriage, and she had not known how to go about it.

Audrey went on. She was no fool, Martha, but she, Audrey, had never been inclined to pay attention to her. Nicholas's insistence that they get married as soon as possible might have raised Martha's suspicion. In time, too late, Audrey did find out what was fishy about Nicholas. He was confused as to the gender of those he liked to sleep with. He thought, when he married her, that he'd straighten out, and very likely believed he was in love with her. He knew, too, that having a wife would help his career.

They ordered and the waiter smiled and nodded several times, as if their choices were extremely wise. The waiters were all young, Laukhin thought—not Carmelo's age—and, in their buttoned-up, tight-fitting uniforms, they functioned like a competent and disciplined boat crew, an impression likely triggered by the odd layout of the place, with an upper deck as you walked into the restaurant, and stairs with heavy iron railings leading to a lower level. Their table was near the glass wall facing south onto the dark blue night and, far away, the lights of Toronto's skyscrapers and the red needle of the tower near the lake. Peering in the light strewn darkness he had the feeling he was in an underwater boat, a modern yet run-down Nautilus in which the captain—like Nemo did for Professor Aronnax—had parted the drapes of a gigantic porthole to make his evening more agreeable.

Audrey's voice reached him as if from afar. How naïve she'd been. It was laughable, now that she thought about it. She'd had had no idea. She had been in love with him, and impressed by his Cambridge degree, eminent family, promising career, amusing friends, good looks. When the penny finally dropped—well, more of a lengthy slide, since it took years—she moved out. Not immediately, because he told her he'd change. He didn't. He begged her to stay, and promised (again) to change. Even now he was asking her to reconsider and return, again promising to change.

She'd been quite down after she left Nicholas, and felt stupid for not seeing the obvious earlier, even more stupid for still hoping after she did. Hoping for almost three years.

When she left Nicholas last fall she went back to the flat near Covent Garden where she'd grown up. "Your room is waiting for you," her father said when she told him about her decision. He couldn't hide his delight at seeing her back. "With you here," he declared, "dark thoughts will be easier to contemplate." He wasn't too sorry she had left Nicholas, although he had always liked his son-in-law, nor was he interested in her reasons. He would have liked a grandchild, a granddaughter if he had his choice, but he'd get on without one a while longer because, as he said to her, rather mysteriously, "There'll be other opportunities."

Martha's comment, when Audrey rang her a few days later to let her know she had moved back with her father, had been equally calm. "You'll soon find solid ground again." She added that she was sure that Audrey could stay with her father for as long as she wanted.

The waiter brought their appetizers and the bottle of wine Audrey chose.

There had been another thing—she had wanted a child, badly. Always had. She thought that a child would make life easier for her, whether she left Nicholas or not. He was understanding, and tried his best during awkward, sweaty nights, but she didn't get pregnant. They went to doctors and were told to keep trying. It was mainly her, they were told. It would be hard, but not impossible. That brought her down, too.

After she left him, Nicholas rang her almost everyday to persuade her to come back. He loved her and needed her. What he proposed, although he never stated it clearly, was an open marriage held together by a strong friendship. She was torn and confused and felt inadequate, as would, she assumed, any wife whose husband preferred men. That's when Martha suggested she go to Toronto for a few months, to get some distance while considering her future. She had even found a job for her—so that she wouldn't have too much time to brood—at a fine art gallery. The owner, Jean Lezzard, was in need of temporary help. Martha and Dirk had been buying art from him for many years, and Audrey had met him once during a visit to Martha in Toronto. He had seemed, at the time, an interesting and knowledgeable man, although rather abrupt. She thought she could learn from him about the local art scene and about running a small gallery. The idea of opening her own gallery intrigued her, and Martha had been encouraging. She was willing to finance her.

She had followed Martha's advice but only after her father encouraged her to go. "Your mother has the right idea, Audrey," he said. "Don't worry about me. You'll be back soon, anyway."

Laukhin drank steadily throughout Audrey's long story. Not because he was fond of the wine—he had never enjoyed wine much— but because he didn't like where her speech was going. From time to time he stared past her, to the far wall where there were faded images of clowns, vaguely akin to some of Chemakoff's prints—an exhausted, feeble Chemakoff.

The waiter came with their main courses. Audrey said she felt somewhat guilty—Laukhin would have been much further ahead with his father's journal if he had spent less time with her at the gallery. Not that she ever minded his presence, she hastened to add.

"That was cruel," he said.

"It came out wrong."

She stared at her plate in the silence that followed. "Do you like Toronto?" she asked after a while.

"It kind of grows on you."

She nodded. "Are you keen on staying?"

"Staying?"

"Staying, living in Toronto."

"I have a good setup here for my work, and three very good students."

He had ordered duck, but after a few bites realized he wasn't hungry. She removed the backbone from her fish and he watched her handiwork with admiration.

"How did it happen, Art?" Audrey asked, looking at him. "I mean…leaving your wife?"

Oh God—again? "This is an abrupt change of subject," he said.

"I'd like to know."

"Things were not right between us. They'd been bad for some time."

"Some time?"

"Several years."

"But it wasn't only your wife, Art."

"Sorry?"

"She was pregnant. When you left, she was pregnant with your child. Things could not have been *that* bad."

It was what he had feared all along. "It's complicated," he said.

"You've said that before. It doesn't seem at all complicated to me."

He sighed. "One day you'll understand."

"What's there to understand? I bought the last issue of the *Paris Review* at Heathrow when I saw your name on it, and read your interview. You were just as evasive in the interview as you are now with me."

What an ass he'd been! He should have deleted that part of the interview. He had thought about it, but there was nothing new there, nothing that had not been thoroughly aired seven years earlier, so he'd left it in. What an ass!

When he didn't answer, she refused to let go. "Did you leave her or not?"

He fought the impulse to tell her the truth and said, "Yes."

"Pregnant?"

"Yes."

Audrey shook her head in dismay.

"One day you'll understand," he repeated.

"I'll understand you left your wife while she was pregnant with your child? Art, some things cannot be understood." He kept quiet and she went on. "All right, what? What will I understand? Help me to understand now."

"I can't."

"You can't? Why? You don't trust me? You say you love me, yet you don't trust me."

"It affects other people."

"It affects me too."

It was only after they ordered coffee that he gathered the courage to ask her what was happening.

"Nothing, Art. Nothing is happening."

"You changed your mind. You were all set to taste my cooking, and then, just like that..."

"I need to trust people, Art. I can't live with secrets. I don't want to do it anymore. You sound like my husband—it's complicated, one day I'll understand. 'Beyond my control' should be in there somewhere too as an excuse. That's what Nicholas kept telling me. Keeps telling me. I don't want complications anymore."

"You can trust me."

"But you don't trust me, not even with an explanation. What you did was terrible."

"I would tell you if I could. Please, trust me."

"Trust you? You didn't tell me you had a child in Moscow, a child you've never seen. I had to read about it in the *Paris Review*, Art. How can I trust you?"

She kept staring at him, but there was nothing else he could say.

"We need to talk, Art."

He burst out laughing. The couple at the next table glared at him. "Aren't we?" he asked after he recovered.

"A serious talk."

It was comic material. He'd write a poem about this dinner, he'd call it *A Serious Talk.* "There *isn't* much merriment around this table, Audrey," he said. "About?"

"About me. About what I want, or feel, right now. And, in a way, about you and me."

"This does not sound good at all."

She sighed. "Art, I like you. You are a poet, an extraordinary man. People in the know say you are a genius, and I'm sure they are right." She smiled. "Even Lezzard speaks highly of you. You are also nice. Very nice. Funny too, although not naturally inclined toward levity. I feel good when I'm with you. There is even an aura of mystery about you, but perhaps that's true of anybody who runs away from Communist Russia. But at this time…"

"Oh boy."

"At this time, I have other commitments."

He was tempted to say that he wasn't asking for a commitment. A flimsy relationship, insubstantial, he'd settle for that.

"Other commitments?"

"I'm married, Art. My husband says he loves me and wants me back. I won't be here much longer, in Toronto. Your life, at least for a few more years, is here—your teaching, your students, your father's journal. My life is in London, with or without Nicholas. I love London. My father is there too. He's not well, and he's alone. I don't think I did, but if I gave you the wrong impression, sent the wrong signals, I'm sorry."

"You mean, you'd rather have complications with your husband than with me."

"I'd rather have none at all."

He stared at his hands, not knowing where else to look. They were on the table, palms down, fingers slightly spread, as if his body needed additional support.

She touched one of his hands. "I like you, Art. Don't misunderstand me. In fact, I... No, it's better this way."

He desperately wanted to believe that this was all a misunderstanding. Even though he'd half-expected it, the truth was hard to hear. It constricted his breathing and he gulped for air.

"The stars are not aligned?" he asked.

She nodded, although, he was sure, she heard the sarcasm in his voice.

"What the hell does that mean? Oh, don't answer that. It's my wife, isn't it? I mean, my former wife. Leaving her in Moscow..."

"I wasn't making it up, Art. I'd miss London, and my father would miss me... But, yes, I can't get over the fact that you left your wife when she was pregnant with your son."

Why was she touching his hand? "I need another drink," he said. "Do you mind?"

"Of course not," Audrey said. "Don't be silly. I'll join you. Let's have some brandy."

What else was there to say? They ordered the drinks. The silence was heavy. He thought of Twain's seedy stagecoach passenger—the one with the crushed cork leg—gasping for brandy. Except that his pain was real.

"You're smiling," Audrey said, relieved to break the silence.

"I'm having my annual do with my students next Saturday," Laukhin said. "A combined dinner, my students and Colson Emslie's students, at the Emslies. It's always been there, a tradition since I joined the department. I provide the drinks, and Kate cooks. Russian fare, of course, for these occasions. Come with me. Dinner for my indentured, the ones slaving away on my father's notebooks. Kate calls it 'Colson's and Art's annual feeding of the serfs.'"

She seemed to be searching for a way to decline the invitation, and was saved momentarily by the arrival of the waiter bearing brandy snifters.

"I'm afraid I can't," she said. "I'm going to London on Friday night."

"Again?"

She nodded.

"How does Lezzard put up with you when you're always away?"

"Josiane is just about recovered. She's already coming for a few hours three days a week. Lezzard doesn't need two permanent staff, so it's time for me to leave. I'm going back to check on an opportunity. Martha's pushing me to open my own gallery."

She lowered her nose into the snifter, breathed in and began coughing. It took her a while to recover. The awkwardness returned. They drank quickly, with the silence hanging about them oppressively, like news of death, the death of their relationship, of their affair. What affair? It was over before it started.

She touched his hand again. "Remember *Strong Symmetries*, that small ink and watercolour Lezzard had in the small room? He took it home to make room for the large Chemakoff oil."

He remembered it, the mannequin birds. Bird mannequins? What a sad way to end the evening—to end the whole thing—with both of them desperately searching for things to talk about.

"It's not in the books either," Audrey went on. "I checked."

Laukhin nodded.

"I thought you'd be more interested," she said.

"Maybe he owns it."

"Wait. Then I checked the books for 1981. I looked for the early Chemakoff oil he tried to sell the Osterhoudts in the fall of 1981 in the deal that fell through when he asked for cash. Well, there was no entry for it in that whole year. I checked several years. The only Chemakoff oils listed in the books, not many, were new ones, painted after he left the Soviet Union."

He couldn't care less.

"I did something else," Audrey went on. "I asked Lezzard about the small ink and watercolour, where it was. He wondered why I was interested—did I have a customer in mind? I said, yes, myself. I might want to purchase it—a memento of my Toronto interlude. Was it still available? He said, it was, but only for cash. Cash again, Art."

He was only half-listening to Audrey's story.

"I asked him why he needed cash. He didn't like the question. He said that it was not his drawing, that it belonged to a dealer in France he'd known for a long time who wanted to lower his taxes. He had bought it with cash from Chemakoff many years before, and he wanted to keep it that way. As simple as that—beyond Lezzard's control."

He'd go home, drink, and write about a beautiful woman chattering away while her suitor's heart was sinking. The whole evening was deserving of a poem—the careless way she kept touching his hands, a gesture clashing with her indifference. Part two of *A Serious Talk*.

They left and walked for a while in silence.

"Mr. Gratch returned this morning," Audrey said.

She waited for his reaction, but he had nothing to say. He should leave, just say goodbye and leave. It would be a relief for both of them.

"It was busy," Audrey went on, "as Saturdays usually are, and Lezzard and I were closing on a sale with a client couple. They wanted smaller payments spread over a longer period. Lezzard is very good at this, knows how far he can push, and it was only a matter of time before we had an agreement. Then I noticed him staring past the couple and becoming red in the face. I turned and saw Mr. Gratch leaning on the wall near the door. Lezzard told me to take over and went—well, flew—to him. I had never seen Lezzard walk so fast. We, of course, were startled, and stared at the two of them as their voices quickly got louder. They spoke Russian, clearly having an argument. I tried to get the couple back to the interrupted deal, and eventually did, but all three of us kept throwing looks at the drama near the door. It ended with Lezzard opening the door and showing Mr. Gratch the way out. He kind of pushed him out, actually. It was comical, two short elderly men shouting at and shoving each other. Lezzard was upset and still red when he returned. The buying couple looked at each other, and the man made a joke of it. 'Late with your monthly dues, Mr. Lezzard?' Probably without thinking, Lezzard answered, 'Yes, funny, but it's money he was after.' He realized what he just said and rectified it somewhat with, 'Charity. They all think I'm rich,' and then, responding to our disapproving looks, added, 'Russian Jehovah's Witnesses, imagine that.' As soon as the couple left, he went into the small room and, after closing the door, made a long phone call. Just as he did the previous time he had an argument with Mr. Gratch."

"Will you come to my place?" he asked. "Let's end it all with a splash."

She stopped to look at him, either startled by, or considering his out of the blue proposition. "It wouldn't be a good idea," she said after a while.

"This is it, then?"

"I'll call you."

"Something tells me you won't."

"I'll call you."

He was grateful for her lie, for the few inches of air between the ceiling and the water level, the few inches into which he'd thrust his nose and open mouth.

In front of her mother's apartment she did something unexpected— she kissed him. It was an open-mouthed kiss, not rushed at all. He could still taste and smell the brandy, and felt her breasts against his chest, and the back of her neck under his uncertain fingers. She moved away slowly and said, "Let's not get carried away. Not tonight, anyway…"

He didn't get it, didn't get it at all. It was as if she was attached to a bungee cord, and every time she got close to him, the elastic force pulled her back, out of his reach.

It had turned cooler and windy. He walked to the Yonge subway. Once underground, he wished he'd taken a cab. The platform was dirty, the walls dull from years of grime. It must have been one of the requirements laid on the builder—make the stations unbearably gloomy. Coming from Moscow, it was one thing he couldn't get used to. It made him think it was the Toronto subway, not the Moscow metro, that was built by convicts. The train was almost empty. Now and then it screeched, much like his heart. On a seat across from him a young woman with a Blue Jays baseball cap was nodding off, oblivious to Laukhin's misery. At the near end of the car, a bookish looking man, thin, with a long grey beard and an umbrella from an earlier decade, was writing feverishly in a notebook and shaking his head. His lips were moving as he wrote, but, if he was talking out loud, his words were drowned out by the noise of the moving car. A great poem, Laukhin thought, or last instructions for tomorrow's brunch.

She had brought up the subject of Tanya, couldn't get over it— those were her words. Leaving his pregnant wife in Moscow was, in Audrey's eyes, a callous act which defined him. And so it would be in anybody's eyes. It was a barrier, an invisible fence that set alarm bells ringing every time she tried to walk through it.

* * *

Tanya had rung him that Sunday morning and said she needed to see him. It was, she added, rather urgent.

Laukhin said, "Come home. We'll have lunch together, like in the old days."

"There's none of your women skulking about? Joan Geraldine?"

He laughed. "You know very well Joan Geraldine went back to England long ago. She's married and bringing up twins now, and has little time for anything else. Come, Tanichka. The refrigerator is full. Old Fenya cooks for an army. You know that, she can't change. Bring Vadim along."

"Vadim is away for a few days."

Come home—that had slipped out, although the Lavrushinsky Lane address remained her home on paper, since she had not officially moved out. And she still kept many of her things in the small bedroom. She had a key to the apartment, and he believed she dropped in to pick up a thing or two of hers when she was certain he was not in. She still worked at the hospital in Serpukhov and would take the train back to Moscow on weekends. For the last three years, she spent any free day she had with Vadim in a cramped room in a communal apartment. It must have been hard on Tanya, after more than ten years on Lavrushinksy Lane, but Vadim had told her he was going out of his mind thinking she was still living in the same apartment as her estranged husband. "And you are too, with your wife and child," Tanya reminded him. At least that was what Tanya told Laukhin later, while she stored a few of her things in a suitcase. But Vadim was an insistent man, and in some way old-fashioned, and they moved in together in a small room vacated by a friend of his who had been transferred to Kiev.

Tanya arrived out of breath. "The elevator is being fixed," she explained. "That's what the sign said, but no one was working on it."

They ate in the kitchen. He didn't have to do nuch, just heat up the stuffed peppers prepared by old Fenya on Friday. She cooked the same amount she used to when his sister lived at home with him and his parents.

Tanya declined a glass, but Laukhin poured himself some vodka. He felt a wave of tenderness and regret. She looked good, Tanichka, although—her old battle—she had put on a few pounds. She seemed preoccupied, and wasn't even indignant when he proposed a trip to the bedroom.

He reached for the saltshaker. Old Fenya had stopped using seasonings altogether. "Well?" he said.

"I'm pregnant."

She had been pregnant once before, soon after they were married, but felt too young to be a mother, and he hadn't cared one way or another. She'd had an abortion, and, somehow, afterward, never got pregnant again.

"Are you sure?"

"Yes, of course."

He felt sad all of a sudden. "That's wonderful, Tanyusha."

"It was a bit of a surprise. I'm not that young anymore. Vadim took it well, considering."

He knew what she meant. Considering that Vadim already had a fifteen year old son, that both Vadim and herself were still married to other people (although Vadim was in the process of divorcing), that she and Vadim lived in one small room with a shared bathroom and kitchen. He got up, walked to the sink where he turned on the tap, then, moving his chair closer to hers, sat back down. He brought his face close to hers and whispered, "Are you happy about it?"

She was surprised by his precautions, but whispered back, "I think so."

"You *think* so?"

"Yes."

"But you're not entirely sure."

She sighed. "Tyoma, we can't go on living in that room, Vadim and I, and soon the baby."

He nodded.

"You have to help me," she went on. "You have to help us."

He waited for her to go on.

"What I mean, Tyoma... Let's exchange this apartment for two smaller ones. One for you, and one for Vadim and me, and the child."

"I don't think the Litfund will let me." He poured himself another vodka and took a mouthful, his face still close to hers. "My hold on this apartment is tenuous. I expect to be thrown out at anytime."

"You've been saying that for years."

"Let's go for a walk."

"Now?"

"It has stopped raining."

"Will you help us?"

"I can't think while I'm static. I need to move."

"Give us some money, then. We'll put a down payment on a cooperative apartment. You can do this with the money your father left you. We'll pay it back, of course. In time."

His father had left him millions, true. He also had left him his notebooks. His father's swollen face, eyes barely open, came back to him, as did the words he whispered whose meaning only he, Tyoma, understood. "Fuck Oleg, Tyomka, fuck Oleg Vinograd. For me, Tyomka, for me." Sixteen years, and all he'd done was get the notebooks out of the country with Joan Geraldine's help, or rather, with the help of one of her friends at the British Embassy. He had not done anything else in sixteen years.

They finished in silence and he washed the dishes.

She wore fairly high heels—it was one fashion she had always liked—and yet she climbed down almost noiselessly, her hips swaying. The large entrance hall was dark. A woman he had never seen before was wiping the marble floor with a wet rag.

There were several buses in front of the gallery, and a large crowd. They walked the other way and turned left on Tolmachovsky Lane. The pavement was still wet and there was a chill in the air.

"When did you find out?"

"Yesterday morning."

"Who else knows?" he asked.

"Why are you asking?"

"Well?"

"Vadim knows, of course. I called him yesterday."

"Nobody else?"

"What does it matter? I told my mother."

"Ah... That's not good."

A group of noisy children running by forced her a step or two in front of him. His wife—she was still his wife, officially—moved with the same grace as when they first met, despite the added pounds and years. She had never been a light woman, but it was the way she moved that had first attracted him to her. He took her arm and said, "Let's walk toward the river, like in the old days." They turned left on Bolshaya Ordinka. "Has Vadim told anybody?" he asked.

"I doubt it—he's away. Will you give us the money we need?"

"I'll do more than that," Laukhin said.

"More than that?"

"I'll leave you my apartment."

"You'll do *what?*"

He told her. It was a thought, well, a plan, that had come to him lately, and now that she was pregnant it made even more sense. She should come back to live with him and tell everybody about it. They'd be a couple again—just for appearance, of course. She should also announce that she was pregnant with his baby. Vadim would be the only one aware of the lie. Her mother too, Laukhin conceded, since she already knew who the baby's father was. He had been invited to a conference in the West in the spring, in America, and he might be allowed to go because he'd have a wife at home, a pregnant wife, and he'd be expected to return. But he wouldn't, and she'd be left with the apartment.

"They'll throw me out of it," Tanya said. "I'm not a member of the Writers' Union. I'm not even a writer."

"If you're here in the apartment, pregnant, and you marry Vadim as soon as possible, you may have a chance. You'll need to give a few gifts too."

"A few gifts?"

"Bribes. Sway the right people. How do you think I'm still on Lavrushinsky Lane?"

"I don't know who they are—*the right people.*"

"I do."

"With what money?"

"My father's money. I can't take it with me, so I'll leave it all for you."

She stopped. "They'll confiscate it," she said.

"Maybe. But until then nothing stops me from giving you money and some very expensive gifts before I leave. There won't be much left to confiscate."

"Tyoma, it won't work. They'll force me out of Lavrushinsky Lane once they're certain you won't return."

"You'll be here with Vadim, and very pregnant. At the very least they'll give you something else in exchange. Maybe something on Bezbozhny Lane, or farther away on Lenigradsky Prospect. My defection will create a stir, Tanya. You'll condemn me, you'll say how shocked and indignant you are. You'll wail about how heartless I was to leave you pregnant with my child. They won't just throw you two—or three by then—out of Lavrushinsky with nothing in exchange.

They're smarter than that. They'll want to show off how well they treat you, because, Tanya, there'll be western journalists swarming all around you by then, keen to hear your story."

She looked at him as if he had lost his mind.

"It's not crazy, Tanya. In the worst case, you'll be left with the dacha in Peredelkino. That's mine—well, father bought it years ago. I'll put it in your name. They won't be able to take that from you. It's like a house, Tanya, a house in Moscow's suburbs."

They walked for a while in silence. At the canal they turned left once more. He looked across the bridge at the dazzling shapes and colours of St. Basil, and then at the massive red wall along the river.

"You'll miss all this," she said.

"I know. Well, some of it."

"What will you do there, Tyoma?"

"I'll publish my father's journal. I promised him I'd do that."

"That's all?"

"What am I doing here? I write silly screenplays and drink and laugh with people I dislike."

"It's your country, your people, your language. It's your history and your parents' history. We just passed the Ardovs' house. You used to go there with your father and Boris Leonidovich. You saw Akhmatova there, talked to her. All this has a meaning to you, the smells are familiar."

"That's just it, Tanya, they're so familiar we're not aware of the stink."

"You're loved here. Loved and admired."

"I promised my father, Tanya."

"You have your friends, here, a good life, privileges. You won't have that there. Think of Fedya Malgunov."

"I haven't published anything of substance since *Youthful Eminences*."

"What about *Conversations with My Father*? It was a huge success."

"All lies, Tanya. All lies."

Porkies, as Joan Geraldine would say, and how well the word fit. Porkies for the pigs hiding behind the red wall across the river.

They took a few steps along the embankment.

"Where will you live?" she asked.

"I don't know. I don't have to decide now. Probably in America."

Thursday, 6 October, 1955

Korotkova is being a bit of a pest. A beautiful pest, I must admit. Useful too. She met us on the deck, on the morning of the third day, wrapped in a long red dress and a fur coat, looking as if she came straight from a glamorous soirée that pushed into morning. Boris Leonidovich whispered to me, "Just like a high-roller dame on the Mississippi." She walked with us for a while and then invited us to her cabin, the Captain's cabin.

A suite, not a cabin. A large, comfortable living room, with armchairs and a mahogany table. Unseen, a bedroom. This captain looks after himself. A bottle of Georgian champagne was waiting for us, and she ordered a few things to nibble on from a woman waiting there.

Korotkova's eyes shine when she talks to Boris Leonidovich. She hasn't said so, but I know she's dismissive of my books, of brave Oleg Vinograd. She has eyes only for the poet. He's flattered, and when Korotkova disappeared for a few moments he whispered to me to leave at the first opportunity. She has an attractive face, open, with daring eyes. Her lower lip has a slight deformation, almost as if a lover had bitten it recklessly and left a permanent, oddly appealing mark. Young too, early thirties. Her beauty became more apparent when she peeled off her fur coat. Once settled comfortably in a chair, with a glass in his hand, Boris Leonidovich's eyes measured Korotkova's curves. What happened to our wake for Tsvetayeva? Ah, how quickly we forget our duty and promises in the presence of beautiful women.

Not a stupid woman, it turns out. She's quite familiar with Pasternak's poetry and talked about it with a hurried fervour, as if eager to get to the end of a pitch, but also with feeling and passion, with the voice of a genuine lover of poetry.

She knows Tsvetayeva's work too, knows some of her early poems by heart, and she got all worked up when she found out that both of us had met her and that Boris Leonidovich had corresponded with her for many years. It was news to her that Tsvetayeva killed herself in Yelabuga and that she might have taken this boat there in the summer of 1941.

7–8 October, 1955

The boat is fairly big, with three passenger levels. Our suite is on the top one. Marietta Alexyevna says that *Kirov* holds up to two hundred people. It has been recently refurbished. It is, she claims, by far the best boat on the Volga-Kama route. Best for comfort, that is.

I like the boat, its routine, the luster of the polished wood and the bronze handles, the crystal chandelier hanging over the captain's table (acquired by Korotkova from a clandestine pawnbroker in Kazan, and anchored to the ceiling in several places; they had an awful time getting reimbursed, and there were dangerous insinuations of taste for a bygone era). I like the eerie quiet that descends at night when the boat is berthed, the vibrations of its giant hull each morning as the journey resumes.

......

The sun tried to get through today and it's much warmer. Now, at dusk, sky and water meet in a somber, blue-grey, darkening sameness. We spent the afternoon outside, on the small deck off our salon. The captain told us he'd keep the boat close to shore this afternoon as there was a very beautiful stretch ahead. He'd also keep the engines low—something he couldn't do often, but for us he'd do it as a special treat.

Around four o'clock Korotkova arrived with morsels of smoked fish, blini, caviar, fried aubergines, and, bless her thoughtful heart, a bottle of chilled vodka and another of wine. She also brought a book of Pasternak's poetry, which she asked him to sign. Boris Leonidovich was happy to oblige, and without any forethought wrote at length. Then he snapped it closed and said, "There you are. Don't read it now. Let's enjoy these treats. Marietta Alexeevna, you are an absolute treasure."

We didn't say much as we ate the *zakuski* and washed them down. Boris Leonidovich smacked his lips happily, and we sat back to enjoy the unhurried, drifting panorama of villages and little towns, the skeletal woods, now and then the steeple of an old church still standing. It was like a slow motion movie, almost silent except for the soothing sounds of the waves and muffled engines. Then Boris Leonidovich read one of Tsvetayeva's poems, an early one entitled, simply, *Song*, miraculously republished a few months before her death in a Moscow magazine. It had a haunting refrain, "My love, what was it I did to you?" and I ended up with tears in my eyes. Then he read a poem called *Homesickness* from a loose sheet with small neat handwriting. Did she give it to him? Did he copy it? We ate and drank some more, and we all had teary eyes, and then Korotkova produced the book of Boris Leonidovich's poetry he signed earlier and asked him to read from it.

......

I have brought a new notebook with me. I told myself that this trip would be worth recording in minute detail, and vowed to write everything down. I scribble often in my cabin, in bed. Tonight I'm writing in the salon, during the quiet time before dinner, sunk in one of the swivelling chairs. Earlier, Boris Leonidovich was in the other chair, looking at the grey waters and talking about Tsvetayeva. Random thoughts; he was not really concerned whether I was paying attention. Eventually, his voice began to tremble—"I apologize, Pavel Nikolayevich, this is silly, I'm not myself after the heart attack"—and he stood up and left the room.

He returned half an hour later, and watched for a while as I wrote. All writers are relentless scribblers, so I was surprised when he said, "I hope you're not keeping a diary, Pavel Nikolayevich. It's a dangerous habit."

I lied with what I trust was a straight face. "I'm not a reckless child, Boris Leonidovich. I'm thinking that Oleg Vinograd's next adventure could take place on a boat like this one, and I'm making notes."

He nodded and sat down. After a while (I was quite aware that he was watching me write) he said that he's also thinking of a story—about a journey not unlike ours, also on the Kama River. An elderly man, on the boat to Perm. The man has heard that somebody who had been dear to him before the war spent the last months of her life not far from there. She had been arrested and spent a decade in camps, and after she was freed was forced to live in a small town in the Urals. Her health had been ruined in the camps—a miracle she survived at all—and she must have died soon after her release. The elderly man hopes to find her grave, and to talk to people who knew her during her last days. He's sad, depressed; a tragic figure, ridden with guilt. In some way—Boris Leonidovich still needs to figure this out, although he has a couple of ideas—her arrest had saved him. He never sent her letters or parcels while she was in prison or in the camps, and didn't get in touch with her after her release—he had a wife and children to think of. He never talked to anyone about her, what she had meant to him, what she did for him. Now, after so many years, with the thaw, with him so old that he's been dismissed as irrelevant and senile, with his wife dead and his children estranged, he's taking this trip. In his own eyes, he's a coward, a man of no mettle. He's desperate to talk about her, to unburden himself, to find somebody to tell him that he's not such a terrible human being, that he did what he did simply to protect his family. He seeks forgiveness by making this journey to the place his former lover spent her last days, and also hopes to recall the couple of happy years he had with her. But he finds nobody, no kindred soul he can talk to about himself and about her. The people in Perm are either not interested, or do not remember her at all. He thinks of killing himself, although he realizes it's a meaningless act, given his old age. He drinks.

8

On the afternoon of the dinner at the Emslies it rained violently and for a long time. It stopped just before Laukhin left his house, and by the time he emerged from the Bloor subway, the sun was back out. The Emslies lived in the Kingsway neighbourhood. He had been to their place so often that he had several routes. This time he took the longest. Large puddles glistened on the road. The rain had brought renewed shine, and the grass, the flowers and the wet soil filled the air with a sweet, raunchy aroma. Audrey came into his mind, a mixture of lust, battered ego, and longing.

He would not think of Audrey. Not tonight—an act of will.

On the way to the Emslies he'd think only of them. He first met Colson in the summer of 1971. Had Kate tagged along during Colson's trip to Russia that year? Colson was thinking of a book on Akhmatova at the time, and had travelled overnight from Leningrad to Moscow to meet Lydia Chukovskaya, but the poet had cancelled on him at the last moment. A year earlier she had done the same thing, and now he realized she was avoiding him. The voice on the phone that morning sounded young and upset. He had said his name already, but Laukhin caught it only the second time—Colson Emslie, professor of Russian literature at the University of Toronto. He said he was in Moscow for two days, and somebody had told him that Artyom Laukhin had known Pasternak, had met Akhmatova a few times, and was a repository of stories and facts about them.

"Ask a poet about a poet," Colson added when Laukhin kept quiet at his end of the line. "That's what my thesis supervisor always said—almost the only words of his that I remember."

Laukhin said his father had been the real repository. "I've heard many of his stories several times, and some of them are still with me." He felt sorry for the young man, but his call came when he had plans for the day. He thought of hanging up, but he reconsidered and said, "I'm meeting somebody in Peredelkino later today. Come with me—it's the best I can do. We'll barge in on Chukovskaya, if she's there, although I doubt that she'll talk to you, and I think I know why. She's working on a book about Akhmatova too."

The sky was maddeningly blue now, and that made the pain of losing Audrey more intense. He could have walked to this dinner arm-in-arm with her. But "the stars were not aligned," and he'd lost her. After that horrible dinner with her, he'd sat down at his worktable and dashed off a few lines. Probably worthless, but he hadn't written any verse in a long time. Maybe it would lead to something—pain and loss were seeds of poetry. What if the director-general up there were to tell him to pick between Audrey's love or the end of his long dry spell? Which would he choose?

There he was—thinking of Audrey.

Yes, Kate had been with Colson on that trip, how could he forget? Fourteen years ago. Laukhin met them in front of Kievsky Station, and Kate wore a red coat that stood out. Laukhin's first words to her were that she looked "very October", a remark met by a blank stare. Colson was beginning to lose his hair already, but Kate seemed very young. Later, Laukhin learned that Kate was a child psychologist. She had an attractive face, somewhat Slavic in shape and colouring. She spoke little Russian, but said, now that she had married a Russian scholar, she'd learn it. She encouraged Laukhin and her husband to speak Russian in her presence, claiming she was learning by immersion, like a child. He remembered thinking that if he liked the Emslies he'd give them the full Peredelkino treatment, a guided walk that would end at his dacha with an improvised meal and a few drinks. He'd done it before with Dieter a few times, and Philip, and Bart and a couple of other foreigners. Bringing the Canadian professor and his wife along would also dispel the inevitable awkwardness of his first moments with Joan Geraldine, who he had agreed to meet with that day.

The blue sky was turning pink, as if the director-general was running a tutorial in pastel colours. On the curving road, a fox emerged from a hedge. A fox! Was this from brazen curiosity or to escape from a flooded den? There, his mind had turned away from the Emslies without turning to Audrey.

Colson was very tall, over one meter ninety. Lean and lithe was Joan Geraldine's pillow description of him later that night, when Laukhin asked her what she thought of him. She also said that he moved with unexpected grace for such a tall man. After he told Colson to meet him in front of the Kievsky Station, near the tower, Laukhin wondered aloud how he'd recognize him. "I'm tall," Colson said. "Look for a tall thin man with a not-so-tall not-so-thin woman. There can't be too many pairs like us around that tower. My wife is wearing a red coat."

The first story he'd told Colson—and he told many the day he met the Emslies—was about slipping money under Akhmatova's pillow. In the spring of 1947, the poet visited Moscow and stayed, as always, with the Ardovs, on Bolshaya Ordinka, a block or two from the Laukhins' apartment on Lavruhsinksy Lane. Pasternak gave a reading at the Ardovs from an early chapter of what would later become *Zhivago*. Pavel Laukhin went, of course, and dragged along his eleven-year old son. A year earlier Akhmatova had been ousted from the Writers' Union, which effectively—it was hard for a westerner to appreciate this—made her unable to earn a living. The story that made the rounds was that during that evening at the Ardovs, Pasternak surreptitiously gave her some money.

"But what that story ignores," Laukhin said, "is that the one tasked with the delicate sliding of the envelope of money under her pillow was me, eleven years old, and bored out of my mind. It also ignores that most of the money came from my father, who always had a wad of cash with him, as Pasternak knew only too well. Before he began reading he approached my father who was in a corner with me and whispered (I could hear him), 'Pavel Nikolayevich, I have only eighty-three rubles with me. Lend me some money for Anna Andreevna, say a couple of thousand. I'll pay you back as soon as I can.' He never did, by the way, but my father didn't care. Later, as everybody settled down for the reading, Father gave me an envelope and said I should slip it under Anna Andreevna's pillow once Pasternak started reading. He said to wait for his signal. It was something to do. I kept turning and glancing at my father for a sign, but it didn't come for a long time. Either he fell asleep, or was waiting for others to do so. Eventually, he squeezed my shoulder. I looked around at first. Akhmatova's eyes were closed, and she didn't seem even to be breathing, but I didn't think she was asleep. I had seen her once before, two years earlier, just before the war ended, when she and Pasternak gave a joint recital at the Writers Club, and my father took me along. She had enjoyed, then, a small respite in the euphoria of the imminent victory. She seemed heavier that evening at the Ardovs, and with a lot more grey hair.

"And I did it. I snuck away, found the small room, and slipped the envelope under her pillow. Later I learned that she had become used to such handouts, but she never learned that the money that time, and likely many other times, came from my father."

Laukhin told the story in Russian while they were still on the train. Colson was delighted by the tale, and he was beaming as he related it to his wife.

"I should have told the story in English," Laukhin said as they got off the train.

"I understood it," Kate Emslie said. "Well, parts of it. I knew it was about Akhmatova."

"You'll learn Russian in no time," Laukhin told her after he stopped laughing.

The middle-aged man with the child he'd seen near the Kievsky Station tower and then on the train got off too. Why on earth would they bother? Was there more to the pair of Canadians he just met? He'd never heard yet of a child being used to deflect suspicion. Maybe they weren't following them at all.

"He got on her nerves at the end. She got tired of Pasternak, of the charade, of the bumbling, naïve, pure soul."

"Akhmatova?" Colson Emslie asked.

"Yes."

Laukhin knew he was performing for them, but he was enjoying it; an actor doing his best to entertain his audience, and Colson's obvious pleasure only egged him on. The evening at the Ardovs was a long entry in his father's journal, and Laukhin had read it several times. As he described the Ardovs' apartment and the carefully selected participants at the reading, Laukhin wasn't sure whether it was his own recollection, his father's notes, or a combination of the two. Most likely the latter, but with a dab of additional colour, here and there, like an old painting restored. He had been, after all, an apprentice of the original artist. He felt a surge of enthusiasm. He'd tell them stories, the long-limbed Canadian professor and his attractive young wife, and they'd forget their—his—disappointment with Chukovskaya. It was then, passing by the small Transfiguration Church on their way to the village, that Laukhin decided that his father's journal would not be a simple rendition of what he had hurriedly noted down, but that he, Laukhin, would make it more vivid, livelier. He would write with his father and, in a way, be with him again.

* * *

Ben, Paul, and Helen were already at the Emslies when he arrived. Holding a glass filled mainly with ice cubes, Ron Martens, one of Colson's students, was describing something round and large to Paul, waving his free hand above his head in a wide arc. Ron's Ph.D. thesis, close to completion and said to be excellent, was on Leonid Dobychin, an obscure Leningrad writer who disappeared mysteriously in 1936. Ron had spent a long time on it, and Colson was keen to see him finish. Laukhin once heard Colson tell Ron, after a seminar on Sholokov's novel *Virgin Soil Upturned*, where the speaker, a robust women from the Moscow Literary Institute, spent much of her discourse listing the reasons for the lengthy gestation of the novel, "Good God, Ron, I hope it won't take you twenty-eight years too to finish your thesis."

Holding a glass, Colson came toward him saying that two of his students were not able to come, and that Helen was helping Kate in the kitchen. "Kate is making *okroshka* soup and *pelmeny*," he went on. "Very ambitious, especially the *pelmeny*. There was a bit of a crisis this morning—the dough, it seemed, was not elastic enough—but things have stabilized. You said you might bring somebody with you, Tyoma. Poor Kate, she counted on a dozen guests."

Colson was the only one among his non-Russian friends and acquaintances who sometimes called him Tyoma. From his damp face, Laukhin gathered that Colson had begun drinking long before his guests arrived.

"I failed," Laukhin said. "I should have let you know."

Ben approached, pointing an empty glass at the kitchen. "Things are looking good in there," he said, "but I'd chase Helen out, you know. She's a hazard. She always claims she's helping the hostess, but she invariably ends up destroying the dinner. It's still *vreditelstvo*, isn't it, even if the damage isn't deliberate? I need another drink." His student had had a head start too, Laukhin thought. Ben must have heard what Laukhin said to Colson because he added, "I also said—well hoped—I'd bring someone with me."

"Never mind, Ben," Colson said. "Kate invited a friend she'd like you to meet. Kate sees the world as a large set of couples and singles, with the joining of the singles into couples as the recipe for happiness. The truth is that Jennifer—that's her name—is not exactly Kate's friend, but the daughter of a distant relative of hers, in Toronto." He frowned. "I'm not sure, now. Perhaps Kate invited Jen on account of Paul."

Helen came out from the kitchen with Kate trailing her, and another young woman who wore a pearl-grey halter-top and black slacks. Kate gave Laukhin a warm hug. Helen carried her now visible pregnancy with an imperious waddling, "Mission accomplished" written all over her face. The young woman in black slacks introduced herself as Jennifer. She took a sip of iced vodka and made a face before telling Ben that Kate was trying to get her drunk. "She's not really my aunt, but I have no aunts and I have always wanted one and, as long as Auntie Kate doesn't mind, I'll continue to call her auntie."

Laukhin refilled his glass before sitting down for dinner. On Kate's instructions, Laukhin sat on her right, with Ben across the table from him, on Kate's left. Paul was separated from Ben by Jennifer, and Helen sat on Laukhin's left.

He listened to Ben telling Jennifer it might be a long boring evening for her because, inevitably, they ended up talking shop. Jennifer said that, although she was a law student, she wasn't allergic to books and literature. She had slender, graceful arms, and when she smiled at Ben her eyes were somewhat mocking but not telling him to keep away. When Paul asked her something, she turned away from Ben.

It was going to be a long grey dinner. Tanya used to say that, "grey time" or "a grey slow evening" whenever she had a dull or difficult time in the company of others. The image of Audrey sitting beside him floated briefly in his mind. Had she not stumbled at the airport on that last issue of the *Paris Review*, she would be sitting there, beside or across him, and the colours and the scents of the evening would have been different. He tried to listen to what Paul was telling Jennifer, a typical story of his, a version of one of the fights his parents regularly had with the city of Manchester. A Hungarian-Russian couple, the Karmans owned a corner store in a mixed neighborhood of that city, a store that seemed to be in a chronic state of near insolvency. It didn't stop them from sending Paul money every other month or so, but, if asked what his parents were doing back home in the UK, he was fond of saying that they were running a corner store into bankruptcy. Short, skinny, with slicked-back black hair carved by a part that began behind his left ear and ended nowhere, Paul was a chain smoker and unable to sit still for long. He liked beer and noisy pubs. A quick drunk, Paul would often start singing or get into an argument. He usually emerged unscathed, but one Monday he appeared at his weekly session with Laukhin with a black eye he could barely open. Ben told Laukhin he had once rescued a penniless Paul from a pub at closing time. He also complained he often ended up footing their pub bills because Paul had lost the little money he had betting on horses.

It was in his dealings with Paul that Laukhin felt most unsuitable in his position. He kept telling himself he was there to teach his students about literature, not how to navigate life. Drinking he understood, it was familiar to him, embedded in the Russian or Soviet fabric. Gambling, though, was not; it had disappeared or faded, or had never had the same hold, and betting on horses didn't even seem like gambling. He'd been stunned last fall when Paul asked him for a loan to bridge-fund his gambling debts. Paul had referred, more delicately, to his *wrong choices*. "What kind of wrong choices?" Laukhin asked. "At the races, Artyom Pavlovich, horse races. Bad luck has followed me for a month now. It's temporary, and I'll recover. Believe it or not, I'm quite good at it. Seven hundred dollars, for two weeks. I owe this amount to impatient people. You'll get your money in two weeks, I promise. My parents are sending me some, and then the stipend is due too. It all comes at the same time, you see." He wrote him a check, of course, but wasn't sure about it at all, and the next day he talked to Colson who launched into inane generalities about gambling as an addiction. Later, after asking if Paul had borrowed money from him before, his colleague had some common sense advice. "No? All right, you've had him as a student for what—two, three years? If he does it again, then you can think about it, but for now forget it. You're not running a nursery. Betting on horses, well, that's his choice, as long as he functions as a student. He's a good student—isn't he?—and you're happy with him."

Did he have a weakness for Paul, a tendency to turn a blind eye because he was the only one of his students who wrote poetry, or who admitted to it, although he dismissed his own efforts as amateurish. He told Laukhin he had come to it rather late, reading Russian literature at Cambridge. He had not had much of a life there, going through a melancholy period and having to be very careful with his bursaries and maintenance grants. He turned to writing verse, and met with some success. Studying with Art Laukhin, in Toronto, had seemed his next best step. Colson once asked Laukhin what he thought of Paul's poetry. "It's all right, now and then," Laukhin answered. "As he drinks, there's a narrow window of spot-on alcoholic content during which he wrings out a couple of good lines. He has to learn that such bursts are not enough. He'll mature late, as a poet, but he will, I'm sure."

* * *

Jennifer's hair was gathered in a ponytail at the back. Large hoop earrings emphasized the frailty of her neck. The skin on her bare shoulders seemed marble-smooth, and Laukhin wished he could touch it to confirm his visual impression. He pictured his lips sliding down her back, just under where the straps crossed, and then slowly journeying to even sweeter spots. He wondered about how he might remove her halter top, and what lay beneath, and about how much vodka and wine he had drunk. He imagined Jennifer telling him to go ahead and take it off, but without using his hands.

He was nothing but a lecherous old man. A lecherous tree. A few minutes earlier he thought of Audrey by his side, and now he was imagining removing a much younger woman's clothes with his teeth.

He turned and saw Kate looking at him and wondered whether she had guessed the lewd path of his thoughts.

"I read your interview," Kate said, "the one in the *Paris Review*. Colson was having a chuckle over it last night, and I read it this morning."

"A chuckle? There wasn't anything comic in it."

"Oh, I don't know. The way you talked about Solzhenitsyn—it was amusing how you tried to hide your dislike of the man. And Zladsky, sorry, little man Zladsky. You'll soon be very unpopular with your fellow Russian émigrés. Probably are already."

"Zladsky started it."

"Did you enjoy it?"

"Enjoy it?"

"The interview. Perhaps I should have said the interviewer. Colson saw her briefly with you, and said she was very attractive."

"He saw her? Where?"

"Oh, at Alumni Hall probably, I'm not sure."

"You're smiling. Why?"

"I shouldn't?"

"That's all that Colson said? Nothing else? Nothing titillating?"

"Should he have? Was there something else?"

It had been Colson, no doubt, and he told Kate about it. He could hear the pillow talk: "There was no one in the room that I could see, Kate, but I heard something. I took a few steps inside and saw the interviewer's skirt on the floor. Her panties were on Art's desk, on top of an old copy of *Ogoniok*. I saw a pair of long boots too. There was huffing and puffing coming from behind the desk, and I thought it best to retreat discreetly." At the other end of the table Colson was listening to Ron Martens.

Laukhin changed the subject and told Kate, who had met Kyril Vronkh during one of the Emslies visits to Moscow, that he had received an odd letter from his old friend.

"In what way odd?"

"He suggested I should return to the Soviet Union."

"What?"

Ben lifted his eyes and looked at him.

"He said he was only a messenger of the Writers' Union, but that they were promising me the moon and more."

"Like?" Kate asked.

"My poetry published, my father's journal published, an apartment and a dacha. Even a teaching position, if I was interested."

"Do you believe them? Are you tempted?"

"The oddest thing was the freedom with which Kyril wrote. Either, as he implied, he was a messenger and wrote with the full blessing of all concerned, or indeed something is happening under Gorbachev."

"You wouldn't go back, though, would you?"

"I wouldn't."

"Besides, you couldn't leave your students in the lurch," Helen said.

* * *

After dinner he cornered Colson. "In February, when the young woman from the *Paris Review* interviewed me, you were the one who opened the door to my office, weren't you?"

"Did I come in?"

"A step or two only. Took a peek, then shut the door and left."

"Without saying anything?"

"You made a sound—an exclamation."

"Why would I do that?"

"You know why."

"I do? Did I see something horrifying? Something untoward?"

"Aha!"

"Aha what? What were you doing with her?"

"At some point, close to noon, she took her clothes off and..."

"But you locked the door, didn't you?"

"I had lost my key."

"You were fucking the *Paris Review* interviewer in your unlocked office. Wow!"

"She fucked me. Before I knew it, she was almost naked."

"It's a fine point."

"Who was it then, Colson? If it wasn't you, who could have been?"

"Anybody."

"And not say a word about it?"

"A gentleman. Horrified, of course, but raising the matter would have been beneath his dignity. Or a gentlewoman."

"No one else would have resisted embarrassing me."

"Maybe it was one of your students. Or one of the cleaners."

"At noon?"

"I don't know."

"You smiled—I saw you smiling. It was you."

"It wasn't me."

"It was you, and you told Kate about it too. She sounded as if she knew about the whole episode."

"You've had too much to drink, Tyoma."

"That I certainly have."

On the subway ride back home, the more he thought about it, the more certain he was that it had been Colson. What a relief. It was his warped sense of humour to keep it from his friend, to let him stew without knowing for sure.

* * *

The next day he bought thirty-three red roses at a flower shop on Bloor Street. He told the florist to select the most beautiful roses she had. These turned out to be the most expensive as well, but she assured him that for that number of roses she'd give him a good price, and free delivery. He put a small note among the flowers:

> *I have many faults, Audrey, but callousness is not one of them. I can only repeat that one day you'll understand. I hope I'm not wrong in my hopes. I beg you, do not act rashly. Do not make a decision based on wrong premises.*
>
> *Art.*
>
> *PS: I'm lonely and wretched.*

A couple of days later he received a card from Audrey:

> *That was very sweet, Art. And foolish. The roses are wonderful and I can't take my eyes off them.*
>
> *Audrey.*

PS: Come Thursday night to the gallery. There is an opening soirée. Horrible stuff—art to break your heart, as Lezzard says—but also wine and sandwiches.

PPS: I do hope you'll come.

Sunday, 9 October, 1955

(Early Monday morning.) The night is slowly lifting. We spent the whole of yesterday in Kazan, marooned, waiting for a spare part to arrive. The boat is still moored, and there are shouts from the dock that amplify the overall stillness.

I hasten to record Boris Leonidovich's account of his visit to Bolshevo on the last day of June 1939, as I heard it from him only a few hours ago. Korotkova was away from the boat the entire day, but she made sure we were looked after, and in the late afternoon surly Arkhip brought us a tray of goodies. We overdid it last night, drinking and talking, and then Boris Leonidovich suddenly began telling me about his visit to Bolshevo. I write it now in his words:

Early that Friday morning, Marina's daughter, Alya Efron, phoned me from the weekly where she worked as an illustrator. I was busy with translations from Petofi, a task I had started with little enthusiasm, but to which I was slowly warming up. Anyway, I couldn't be too choosy since I desperately needed the money. I worked quickly from glosses and from German translations.

When Alya phoned, I already knew Tsvetayeva was in Bolshevo because Alya had called to tell me some ten days earlier, shortly after her mother returned to Russia. She phoned me often that spring, whenever I was in Moscow. And I was in Moscow most of the time, all by myself, because we were moving to another dacha, and Zinaida was in Peredelkino supervising the move. Alya was full of life, radiant, as only women in love can be. People didn't smile much in those days—nor do they now—but she did. She was always with Mulya Gurevich—do you remember him, Pavel Nikolayevich? She was a sweet girl—well, not a girl anymore, she was twenty-six or twenty-seven already—and I was very fond of her and her bright laughter. I first met her in Paris, in 1935. I met her father at the same time, and I liked him too.

Alya began by curtly asking me when I intended to visit her mother. It was unlike her. There was reproach in her tone, and dismay, even exasperation. I must have given a non-committal answer—I was quite busy with the translation and I had a deadline to meet, and I needed to take advantage of Zinaida's and the children's absence to concentrate. She cut me short, and said I must go to Bolshevo right away to see her mother, who was not doing well. Not well at all, Alya repeated when I kept silent. Her mother was very upset, angry with everybody, with her and with her father—especially her father. She was screaming at Georgy and had even slapped him. She was barely talking to the Klepinins, the large family with whom they shared the dacha in Bolshevo. No one understood what was happening with her mother, and no one knew what to do. Alya hoped that seeing me, a poet and a beloved old friend, would be good for her. "You must go, Boris Leonidovich, I beg you," Alya said. "You're the only one who might calm her down. We don't know what else to do." She added, in a whisper, that I should not tell anyone about the visit.

I couldn't say no, Pavel Nikolayevich, although I wasn't looking forward to seeing Tsvetayeva. I'm ashamed but it's true. I felt guilty then, and I'm ashamed now. I just didn't have the stomach for it. But I agreed in the end, and Alya told me how to find the dacha where Efron and now Marina and their son were living.

It was a hot day. I took the eleven o'clock commuter train and walked from the Bolshevo platform. By the time I found the dacha, beyond the village, I was tired and thirsty. There was a dusty, dark blue car parked in front of the house, with a man asleep in the driver's seat. Tall pine trees encroached on the large wooden bungalow from three sides. On a bench in the front yard, in a small clearing with a well to the left of the house, Tsvetayeva sat smoking. There was no one else around. I could hear a baby crying in the house. She didn't look up at me as I approached, or she glanced up without recognizing me. I had aged since I last saw her in Paris four years earlier, and so had she. Thin, a nondescript grey dress, hair cut short—grey too—sunken eyes. She looked terrible. She ignored me as I walked closer, and it was only when I said, "Marina Ivanovna, my dear, it's me, Boris," that she lifted her eyes. We embraced awkwardly and I sat down beside her. She asked how I was doing, how Zinaida was, the children, Yevgenya. She asked what I was working on. She did it all properly, politely, and she listened to my answers, but I'm not sure she heard them. She dropped her cigarette, crushed it, and lit another one. Her hands were trembling and she fought with the matches. She caught me looking at her efforts and said, "I never thought lighting a match would be so hard." I lit a cigarette myself and smoked with her. I asked about her husband. She said Efron had gone to Moscow that morning—a car had picked him up. She added that it happened now and then, although her husband was not a well man. She repeated the last sentence about Efron's state several times, softly, as if to let me know that there were several ways to interpret what she said. She then added, although I didn't ask, "Nina Nikolayevna has taken the children on a little excursion to give me some peace and quiet, to let me recover. I had ... I had another meltdown this morning. I'm not doing very well—but then, why would I?"

"Nina Nikolayevna?"

Klepinin's wife, she answered. They had known the Klepinins in Paris, and the two families were something between acquaintances and friends. The Klepinins had returned from France with their brood, six or seven of them, at about the same time as her husband. A remarkable couple in their own way, Tsvetayeva said, members in Paris of the Eurasian Movement and active in the Russian Orthodox Church. Klepinina had been a well-known scientist. She liked poetry, and tried her best to make Tsvetayeva's new life bearable. Nikolai Klepinin, her husband, had been an officer in Denikin's army, and he might have met Efron while they were fighting together, although Tsvetayeva wasn't sure. He later studied at Boston University, wrote for newspapers, published two books. Like Efron, who went by the name Andreyev since his return to Russia, the Klepinins now went by a different last name.

I was very thirsty from the long walk from the station, and I told Marina Ivanovna that I'd go into the house to fetch some water. I insisted she remain seated, that I could easily do it myself. Two people were drinking in the sitting room when I entered. One was, I gathered, Nikolai Klepinin. Like Efron, he would be shot two years later. The other man, somewhat younger than Klepinin, and much better dressed, seemed upset by my sudden appearance in the house. He stood up and asked me in an imperious voice, "Who are you? What are you doing here?" I told them my name, that I was an old friend of Tsvetayeva, and had come to visit her. I added I wanted a glass of water. "Who told you she was in Bolshevo?" the man asked in the same curt voice. I said her daughter was worried about her mother's health and she thought my presence would do her good.

Klepinin stood up with some difficulty and shook my hand, saying it was a delight to meet such a famous poet. He seemed genuinely pleased to meet me. He disappeared for a moment and came back with a carafe of cold water and a glass. "Take it outside with you," he said. "Marina Ivanovna may be thirsty as well." He smelled of alcohol.

I asked for the place of use—*mesta pol'zovaniia* —the wonderful euphemism we have in our language for the toilet. Klepinin smiled and pointed his finger to the door and said the outhouse was behind the house.

"Or the woods," the other man said.

Tsvetayeva was smoking again when I rejoined her. I asked who the other man in the house was. She didn't know. She said he visited quite often and talked in a whisper with Klepinin or her husband. "A horrible man, I think," she added with a shudder.

I offered Tsvetayeva a glass of water and we sat there in the silent shade of the pine trees, the summer buzz of insects around us. I hoped that in time she'd begin to talk, and she did. But what I'm telling you now, Pavel Nikolayevich, is not just her story, as she opened up to me that day under the Bolshevo pines, but also the additions and clarifications Alya Efron has made since her return to Moscow after sixteen years of camps and exile. She's not the young, laughing Alya anymore, as you can imagine.

Alya and her boyfriend, Mulya Gurevich, met Tsvetayeva and Georgy at the Leningradsky station when they first arrived back in Moscow. After she embraced her daughter, Marina looked around her and, not seeing Efron, asked why he had not come to the station too. Alya said her father was not feeling well and was waiting for them in Bolshevo. He had not been in good health since he returned to the Soviet Union. Marina's next question was why hadn't her younger sister, Anastasya, come to the station to see her after so many years? Alya looked at Mulya Gurevich who shrugged and said they should hurry to the Yaroslavsky station to catch the train to Bolshevo. He told the porter who was wait- ing for them to lead them through the square so that Tsvetayeva could get a quick whiff of her beloved Moscow. Excited, Georgy was running around his older sister. Outside the station, Tsvetayeva stopped and took a long look around her. She told Georgy to calm down or he'd get separated from them. She then explained to him that there were three railway stations in Kalamchyovskaya Square, and that was why people called it the Three Stations Square. Alya said the square was now called Komsomolskaya. Tsvetayeva looked at her daughter without comprehension. She was overwhelmed by the swarming multitudes, and by her own memories.

The train was crowded, but Mulya managed to get two seats in one compartment. He and Georgy stood in the corridor, their backs against the compartment's glass door. Tsvetayeva looked around her. An old woman and a young boy, probably her grandchild, were talking to each other, but the others were quiet. Unsmiling faces, shabby clothes. Tsvetayeva asked Alya again about Anastasya. Alya said she'd tell her another time. Another time? Why another time? But Alya looked around the compartment and didn't answer.

Many people got off at Mitishchi, and there were only few left standing in the corridor. Alya told her mother that Mulya made her very happy. She went out and leaned against him in the corridor. Tsvetayeva followed after a while and asked Alya again about Anastasya. Alya looked around her and whispered that Anastasya was in prison. What? Yes, she'd been arrested. When? Why? In 1937, in September. She was in Tarusa when they came for her. Why, in God's name? Alya shook her head and said she didn't know. Why didn't you tell me, write to me, about this? Alya said she couldn't. Marina got very upset. Couldn't? What do you mean, *couldn't*?

Mulya said, softly, "I know it's upsetting, Marina Ivanovna, but Alya doesn't know—nobody knows anything."

Tsvetayeva asked about Andrey, her nephew—what was he saying, how was he coping? Alya whispered that they took him too, at the same time they took his mother. They arrested Andryusha as well? Yes. What for? Alya shook her head—she didn't know. Had anybody else in the family been imprisoned? Alya looked at Mulya and said with a sigh, "Father's brother-in-law, Vera's husband."

Her head spinning, Tsvetayeva had more questions. Whispered questions—she understood that many things were not talked about loudly in the country she had just returned to. How long had Sergey been in Bolshevo? Since he arrived. She, Alya, had lived in Bolshevo until recently too. Why Bolshevo and not Moscow? That's where they had told him to stay for a while. They? Who were they? His employers. Who? Who pays his salary? Alya looked at Mulya, and Mulya told Tsvetayeva that it would be better if her husband explained all this to her.

Where did Alya work? For the weekly journal *Revue de Moscou*, published in French. Alya then added, laughing, "Mom, try to smile. I've never been happier. We are together again, and Mulya is very good to me. It's going to be all right, you'll see."

Tsvetayeva had looked forward to seeing Efron for almost two years, but the terrible news about her sister and her nephew and her sister-in-law's husband, and Alya's whispers and reluctance to talk, petrified her. Later she tried her best to put on a cheerful face, but she found it very hard. The lack of privacy made it even harder for her, with ten people living in the same house and constant noise around her. She didn't think she had done much since she had arrived in Bolshevo except wash dishes and cover her ears. She was cracking up, she was certain. Everybody got on her nerves, her family, the Klepinins, the friends and relatives and other visitors who came to the dacha now and then. She was fearful too, a fear that was new to her, a fear whose source or cause was difficult to define, even harder to acknowledge. She'd wake up at night, shivering. Sometimes—well, he'd noticed—she'd have trouble even lighting a match. She was dismayed, but she didn't know how to hide her worries, her fear, her despair. It took time to acquire that ability.

Sitting with her on the wooden bench under the pines, I told Tsvetayeva that everybody in the country felt that fear. "In our building in Lavrushinsky Lane," I said, "the residents want to switch off the elevator at night. It keeps them awake wondering where it will stop and who'll be the next one taken away." It was true—but I meant to lighten things up. And I added in the same vein that there was a sign in the elevator saying it was prohibited to flush books down the toilet. Seeing the way she looked at me, I gave up and told her she should try to write. "That's what keeps us going," I said. "Write your wonderful poems. I beg you, Marina Ivanovna, do not give up." A stupid thing to say, but I was at a loss.

She said, "Write? Write? Look at my hands, look at my fingers. I wash dishes and I smoke—that's what I do all day long."

"We need your poems, Marina Ivanovna."

"No one needs my poems, Boris Leonidovich. Anyway, to write you require peace of mind and a place of your own, however small. Where should I write? In the forest?"

She told me she had demanded explanations from her husband. And in time, alone in their bedroom, she had learned a few things. Not as much as she had hoped, because Efron himself had no answer to many questions.

Like Alya, he didn't know why Anastasya and her son had been arrested. It had been a mistake, of course, and they'd be released, he assured her. He, Efron, had sent letters in support of them. He had asked questions about them too, but had not received any answers. Not yet.

One mystery was quickly solved. The Bolshevo dacha they were all living in belonged to the NKVD. She asked her husband the reason why. Was he being paid by the NKVD? Had he been working for the NKVD in France as well? She begged him, "Seryozha, Seryozhenka, tell me it's not true, please. Tell me the police in France were not right to say, when they interviewed me, that you had been involved in kidnappings and assassinations. Tell me that my friends in Paris were wrong to accuse you and shun me. I swore to them you weren't an NKVD agent."

Efron's answers were slow in coming, but they came eventually, and she understood the terrible truth. Her Seryozha had worked for the NKVD for a long time. He had lied to her for years. She accused him of betraying his friends and comrades. Was there anything worse that that? Was there anything that could justify that?

He replied that he had had to find meaning in his life, and a way to return home. He had felt for a long time that he could no longer live abroad. It had been the only way. And he believed in the new Russia.

She thought she'd go crazy. Her Seryozha, a former White officer, was hiding under a different name in an NKVD dacha in Bolshevo, all expenses paid. When they snatched him in France, with the French police closing in on him, the NKVD had a simple message for him: We'll take care of you, just keep mum, change your name and stay put until we tell you otherwise.

He believed in the new Russia? Was the price not too high? What kind of people were they, the builders of the new Russia, if they required such deeds as the price of admission?

Later she asked why he hadn't warned her, hadn't written to her about Anastasya and her son. He said the letters would not have gotten through. She said he could have found a way to tell her to delay her return until matters cleared. He could have, for example, written to her to stay in Paris for a while and look after her sister while she was so sick. Anything to alert her. There were people who travelled from the Soviet Union to France—why not send word with one of them? He had not trusted them? Not one of them? He asked what would she have lived on in France, she and Georgy? Here, in the Soviet Union they would not starve and be humiliated, and Georgy would get a good education. Anyway, he had not been able to do it—neither he, nor Alya. "In God's name, why not?" It had been the only way to be all together. All of them, the whole family. "Together?" Yes, both he and Alya had agreed on that. "Together? Together in prison, Seriozhenka? Or in the grave?" Marina, don't talk like that, please.

She was trapped, she told me under the Bolshevo pines. Trapped with no escape. She was empty, unable to feel anything. The only thing that kept her going was Georgy. She couldn't abandon him.

The man who had been talking to Klepinin came out of the house and walked toward us. Klepinin staggered after him. The man stopped a few feet in front of the bench and, pointing a finger at me, said, "You have not been here, you don't know this place, you have not met any of us. You must forget everything about this visit. It's a terrible breach of security, and I'll have to report it."

With that, he turned around and left.

That was the story of his visit to Bolshevo to see Tsvetayeva. Boris Leonidovich remained quiet for a while and then said, "We should turn in."

But he didn't move. Instead, he went on, "Two months later, in August, Alya was arrested in Bolshevo. They took her away right under her mother's eyes. And in October they took Efron away. Tsvetayeva witnessed that too. She never saw them again."

It began to rain, a light rain, and a wind seemed to rise from the water. I closed the doors to the deck.

"Can you imagine, Pavel Nikolayevich, what her Bolshevo days must have been like?"

I couldn't answer that.

Later, I asked, "I heard Mulya Gurevich was working for the secret police too. What happened to him?"

Boris Leonidovich shrugged. "They all worked for the secret police, all the expats who returned to the Soviet Union and had contact with foreigners. Mulya was no exception. He was shot in fifty-two. He survived unscathed for many years only to be taken away and executed shortly before Stalin's death. Alya told me this not that long ago. She was pregnant with Mulya's child when she was taken to Lubyanka. She miscarried in prison."

He stood up and sighed. "Bolshevo! I spent two months in the sanatorium there, at the beginning of 1953, after my heart attack. Well, you know that. A blissful misfortune, my heart attack, in many ways. Unlike Tsvetayeva's, my Bolshevo days were peaceful and quiet, a time of reconsiderations, of gathering thoughts and forces. I knew little about the storm outside the sanatorium, about the Doctors' Plot and the mad plan to relocate Jews, and I wasn't forced to sign troglodyte appeals for clemency. Stalin died while I was there, and none too soon." He smiled. "The same day Prokofiev died. I heard there were no flowers left for his funeral."

187

9

That Thursday Laukhin lost his temper. "For God's sake," he shouted at Ben in his office, "slap yourself together. What do you want me to tell them? Ben Paskow is in love? No, this time I'll keep my word—the Tsvetayeva-bundle goes out on Monday. You're twenty-seven years old, Ben. No more lovesick pining, no more nursing your heart's wounds. Love and scholarship do not mix—like lox and kerosene, kaboooom!" He mimed an explosion with catastrophic consequences for Ben.

The image of lox and kerosene was from one of his first poems, a paean to rocketry. The slim 1958 chapbook *Youthful Eminences*, its sheets already yellow and brittle, was somewhere in the bookshelves, among other books and magazines in which his poetry had appeared. The round grey illustration on the cover showed the stray dog Laika, wires and all, probably only hours before she was fried. He remembered hesitating before lending the collection to Helen. "My ex-wife sent it to me. Either she thought it would embarrass me or she wished to be rid of anything of mine."

"I'll be all right," Ben said.

Laukhin rolled his eyes. His best student was like a helpless animal, a puppy that couldn't hold it in and did it in the house. He walked to the window and stood there with his back to Ben.

"I need you all right *now*," he said. "You just told me you couldn't do anything this week. You haven't done much in weeks and the deadline is October, only two months from now. There can be no more delays. I had another call this morning from the *New Yorker*, not a happy one. We've got to finish the bundle this weekend. You've done the entry of the morning at the hotel, haven't you?"

"I've started it."

"It's not a long entry. Finish it and then do the train trip back to Moscow, quite short too. I'll be here, in my office, tomorrow at noon, to pick up your work. I'll spend the weekend at home and do nothing else but revise and correct the whole bundle."

"The last seven excerpts need to be typed in."

"A secretary will type them on Monday and we'll review everything."

Ben mumbled his consent. Still facing the window Laukhin took a deep, noisy breath and then turned and changed tack—after all, fools needed a gentle touch.

"Ben, Benya, Benchik, you are the only one who can convey the drama, the pall of daily misery, trivia and terror, the need to weigh every word, even among friends, and yet the need to talk, to find a kindred soul, to gossip. I can't figure out how and why, but you get it. It must be the air in Corby Falls. Or compensation for your atrocious accent. Helen is preoccupied with the coming baby. And Paul, well, Paul could help, but he's often careless, or drunk, and we'd have to go over his work. It's too late now, anyway, for anyone else."

He walked back to his desk. "You can do it, Ben. *We* can do it. They're mad, threatening to sue—as if art can be done to deadline. One last heroic exertion, Ben, and then I'll return to that blasted introduction. If I don't send it with the proofs, it will be included only in the second edition, if there is a second edition. Ben, are you listening?"

Chastised, Ben nodded and walked slowly out of his office.

The interview in Tuesday's *Globe and Mail* (it had appeared simultaneously in the *New York Times*) had added to the pressure he felt. Bart had insisted on it. It was good publicity, no doubt, but it also tightened the vice one more turn. Laukhin told the interviewer that by late October or early November the first volume of the journals would be in bookstores, in time for Christmas sales. He said he was certain this time. He had the galley proofs and was working day and night on the final corrections. It had been promised long before now, he agreed, but this time it would be out. He couldn't help it, he was a perfectionist. Poets are uncompromising, it's their nature, but he was confident that the readers of his father's journal would think it well worth the wait and painstaking effort—his and his students'. Yes, the journal was wonderful, and readers would get another early taste of it when excerpts, all related to the Russian poet Marina Tsvetayeva, appeared in the *New Yorker* in October. *Globe* readers would see the Tsvetayeva bundle as well, in several Saturday issues. The excerpts contained his father's recollections about Tsvetayeva, about how terribly she was treated upon her return to the Soviet Union, including by many of her fellow writers and poets. Yes, there would be a few surprises, especially about the end of her life, in Yelabuga. Nothing earth-shattering, of course, after all Tsvetayeva was only a poet, not a movie star or a politician, but they would shock some people. And fascinate others.

* * *

He'd go home and chain himself to his desk for the next three days. He had to be back at Alumni Hall on Friday, briefly, to pick up Ben's final translations, but that was it, he had no other commitments. It would be a long working weekend, with a lot of coffee and minimal food.

No, it wouldn't be that bad. A secretary would type in the remaining excerpts—both his and Ben's handwriting was legible—and he'd borrow Bill MacNaughton's secretary for a few hours as well; the chair of the department was supposed to help too, not just administer.

He'd have time to catch a glimpse of Audrey at the gallery later on that day, have a word or two with her. "I do hope you will come," that's what she wrote in her note, thanking him for the flowers. She made a special point of inviting him. He'd go late, toward the end of the vernissage, after some serious, solid, sustained work on the bundle.

What had he said to Ben—love and scholarship do not mix? What a *bolshoe* porky! Such hypocrisy from someone who had subjected the sleepy Department of Slavic Languages and Literatures to not one but several romantic upheavals. While negotiating with the university, he had gone to meetings with Lydia, who never said much, just smiled and smoked, and now and then applied a new layer of lipstick. He claimed he needed her there because he was unused to Western ways. In time, everybody got used to her harmless and vague ways, and she became the object of mild admiration for putting up with him and for her effective handling of him when he got drunk and obstreperous. And then, a few years later, he dumped Lydia, and Ewa Kucharsky, a student in their department, moved in with him. At least Ewa was not *his* student. She was twenty-eight, married, and close to finishing her Ph.D. in Polish Literature. Her husband, also a scholar, had returned to Poland unable to find a job in Canada. Laukhin's affair with Ewa lasted six months—it started in November 1981, and the department got wind of it sometime in April the following year. The scholar had returned and wanted his wife back. When Ewa demurred, he threw a brick through Laukhin's windows two nights in a row. The third night, Laukhin and Efim took turns guarding the house, but nothing happened. The real storm broke the next day when Ewa's husband went to Alumni Hall and complained to chair Bill MacNaughton. It was a surprise, as Laukhin and Ewa had managed to keep their affair secret, but there was more and worse. Her husband claimed that Laukhin was helping Ewa—writing entire chapters of her thesis. Because her thesis was about contemporary Polish poetry, the complaint was heard and there were awkward moments for the department. Olga Tamanova raised the issue at a department meeting—the propriety of an affair with a graduate student. Either academic impropriety or an abuse of power (or both) were happening right under their noses. Laukhin turned red and loud. He punched the table, shouting that he'd never discussed Ewa's thesis with her (a lie, he had). He claimed passion, the primacy of love, and that he, for one, was not going to live without it. There were embarrassed looks around the table, then Colson Emslie cleared his throat, said that they needed to be pragmatic about the whole thing. He made several points: that Ewa Kucharsky was an exceptional student who needed no help from Laukhin; that Laukhin had never taught Ewa Kucharsky or ever interfered in her favour; that, finally, all they needed to do was to ensure that neither Laukhin nor any of his close friends, and Colson included himself, would be among those examining Ewa Kucharsky's thesis. There were several dissenting voices, and arguments broke out again, but after surveying the scene for several minutes and trying to introduce some order, MacNaughton moved adroitly to postpone the discussion. He coughed and hemmed and said that he would review the guidelines—if there were any—for such an unusual and delicate situation. In the corridor afterward, after Laukhin left, still furious, his colleagues shrugged their shoulders and mumbled, "Well, he's a poet. A Russian poet. Of course." They didn't say as much, but they all thought that poets could be forgiven such bursts of passion, such blindness, such disregard for the rules. That's what Colson told Laukhin the next day. In the end, Laukhin was too important for the department and for the university, and pragmatism prevailed. Because a co-supervisor of her thesis was at the time at the University of Illinois, Chicago, Ewa moved there in the summer of 1982 and completed her doctorate in early 1983. She was offered a position there and she accepted it.

He had not seen Ewa since February. Her visit then had been a melancholy, vaguely tender goodbye. She'd been there when Erika Belov-Wang came to the house for the first day of the interview. When he got home the following day—the day young Erika fucked him in his office—Ewa had asked how the second day of the interview had gone. After he mumbled it had been all right but he needed to see the transcripts, she told him she was pregnant.

"Mine?" Laukhin asked.

She laughed. "Now, that's silly."

There was something familiar in all this, and he recalled Tanya—Ewa called her "wife number one," as if there had been others since—telling him she was pregnant with Vadim's child.

"Are you keeping the child?"

She nodded. "I'll probably get married."

"You divorced only last year."

"It took a long time."

"Aren't you rushing?"

"I'm thirty-two. No more quick trips to Toronto, Art."

"You have somebody lined up?"

"The father."

He knew that Ewa was seeing somebody in Chicago, a colleague of hers who taught Polish and Russian history, and yet for a second, hearing she was pregnant, he thought the child might be his. Of course, it couldn't have been. It had been five months since he last saw her.

* * *

He gathered all of the Tsvetayeva material in a green folder, switched off the desk lamp, and ran down the stairs with fake energy. The bright light outside blinded him. He was in a bad mood, and thought a walk might help. He rounded Queen's Park, turned west and walked slowly along Hoskin Avenue, turned north on Devonshire and then east on Bloor. On the stairs of the crumbling Royal Conservatory a shameless pair were all over each other.

The Yonge subway was crowded, and he got out at Eglinton, although the Lawrence station was closer to his house. Walking slowly from the subway station, he thought of Audrey.

Ivor Bendikson was back at his battle against growth. That was what retired people did on this continent—mowed their lawns, and when they couldn't do it anymore, they lay down and died. At least, his next two days would be quiet. Ivor stopped the engine. "A couple of people were looking at your house this morning," he said.

"Oh?"

"They were in a car across the street."

As always, Ivor made Laukhin pry the vital information from him.

"And?"

"They looked Russian."

"Really."

Ivor nodded.

It had been a long day, and this was its first amusing moment. "In what way?"

"Well, you know…"

"How many Russians have you met, Ivor, beside me? In your entire life? Movies don't count."

"Many."

"Oh. Where? When?"

"In 1945—"

"None since?"

"What? I met you, of course. Yes, in 1945 I was twenty-two years old, and in a US Army uniform. There was an improvised get together in a German village, a day or two after the end of the war, and, I remember it well, a lot of drinking. The officers on both sides were uneasy, and very few could speak the others' language. There were two Russian women, one young and pretty. She had huge boots."

"Huge boots," Laukhin said after a while.

"Yes."

"Is there more?"

"I didn't like their faces."

"Whose faces?"

"Those two, across the street."

"Russian faces."

"Yes. One of them got out of the car and walked up and down the street a couple of times."

"Was one of them big?"

"Big?"

"Yes, big and tall. Very tall."

"I don't know. Maybe the one that didn't get out of the car. The one who did wasn't particularly tall."

"It's all right, Ivor, I know what it was all about."

Efim had called a few weeks ago to warn him that he was planning to tear down the house and build a new one. "You don't have to move yet," Efim shouted on the phone. "Not before the new year. It'll be a fancy house, because that is a fancy area. I have a fancy architect, of course. I hate fancy architects, Tyoma. I said, OK, where are the drawings? No, the fancy architect first has to see the place. I said, I know the dimensions, I'll tell you the dimensions of the lot. No, the fancy architect has to see the street. I said, OK, drive there, look for a while, drive back, what's the big deal? No, he has to take pictures, then look at them, let the whole thing sink in. Sink in, I liked that. Every day of 'sink-in' costs me money. It's an entire process, Tyoma, a process which can't be rushed. Ha!"

"Did they take pictures?" Laukhin asked Ivor.

"I don't know. I stopped watching them after a while."

Among the junk mail he found a couple of bills and a letter from his sister. Larissa rarely wrote to him, once a year perhaps, and her letters were short and said little. But this time the envelope seemed to have more heft. He took the letter upstairs. The bed was a mess, the way he had left it in his morning rush. An image of Audrey and himself all over each other near the unmade bed surged in his mind. They blundered about trying to dispose of their clothes, she as awkward as he, an amused and sly smile on her lips.

He pushed the books and other papers to a corner of the worktable to make room for the folder with the Tsvetayeva bundle. There, ready to be opened and worked on after he had a shower, likely the first of many that weekend. He undressed, wrapped himself in a fresh towel, and sauntered across the landing to the bathroom. He had got used to the size of his bedroom-study, but the vastness of the bathroom still made him uncomfortable.

Back in the bedroom, he sat down to read his sister's letter. She had separated from her husband and would be divorcing him. (There was a hint, at the beginning of the letter, of a new man in her life, but nothing else about him). Laukhin was surprised. Larissa was forty-five, and her marriage had seemed solid. But what did he know? She had married and moved to Leningrad, and they'd grown apart. The distance hadn't helped, and he never got along with his brother-in-law. In Toronto, Laukhin had blamed him for his sister's letters being so short and impersonal. Maybe his troubles with Tanya had contributed to his estrangement from Larissa, because the two of them had always been close.

She wrote that she was staying with Tanya in Peredelkino for a couple of weeks, a needed change of scenery and people. It had been years since she'd been in the Laukhins' old dacha, and she felt melancholy that Moscow was encroaching on the village. That was what struck her most after so many years.

> ...I'm writing just after lunch. I like my room, my old room— remember it? It seems much smaller now, but it has all I need. I have pushed the table to the window, and I spend much of my time writing letters and looking out the window. The summer light cheers my heart. I have the best view in the world, especially if I lean over the table a bit. This morning I took a long walk. I ended up in Izmalkovo and sat staring at the lake for an hour or so.
>
> I saw Tanya and Vadim and little Mitya, when I arrived. They left yesterday, but Tanya and Mitya will be back next week. They are all fine. Mitya is tall for a seven year old boy. He looks very much like Tanya, but I can see some of his father in him. Oh, Tyoma, Tyoma...
>
> Tanya is beside herself about my decision, but she'll get used to it. Vadim laughs. Why now, you'll ask. Because I'm done with him. I said the same thing to Tanya, who replied, "Is that your answer, 'I'm done with him'?"

Well, there is no changing my mind about it. I've never been happier. Contented, finally at ease with myself.
I'm learning English. Perhaps, one day, I'll visit you ...

He sighed. Clearly, Larissa still believed that Mitya was her nephew. Amazing strength from Tanya to hide the truth from her friend for so long. Mitya certainly grew up never doubting Vadim was his father. His parents probably told everybody to hide "the truth" from him. A necessary lie everybody gravely agreed to, for the good of the young boy. But not a lie.

* * *

The call was from Viktor Zhelenin, the publisher and editor of *Sintesy*. He looked at his watch—it would be 10:30 p.m. in Paris.

Sintesy had published a few of his poems in the past, and, like a fool, Laukhin had promised Zhelenin to send some of his new poetry to him. It didn't pay much, but none of the Russian journals in the West did. Laukhin had not known at the time that he'd almost stop writing poetry. He had made this rash promise during a visit to the *Sintesy* office—in a former garage in the Paris suburb of Fontenay-aux-Roses—shortly after his defection, when he was still wondering where to settle down. Soon after that Zhelenin began demanding the promised poems and wouldn't believe it when Laukhin told him he had nothing to offer. In letters and, lately, phone calls, Zhelenin ranted about broken promises and ingratitude, although Laukhin never understood where ingratitude came in, unless it was for the delicious meal at a local restaurant Zhelenin paid for the day Laukhin visited.

Laukhin remembered the dinner well. Zhelenin's wife, Miriam Emmanuilovna, had been there too, a short, vivacious woman, with a good appetite. Andrey Aksakov was visiting with a writers' delegation from Moscow, and—a last minute arrangement—had travelled from Paris to see Laukhin. There had been a lot of eating and drinking that evening, especially by Aksakov, who was returning to Moscow the following day. When Laukhin mentioned that Aksakov might join them, Zhelenin had said, in his booming voice, "Of course, bring your friend along. I think Miriam met him many years ago," but later that evening, he noticed an exchange of glances between the Zhelenins when Aksakov ordered his fourth or fifth cognac.

It had been very warm in the restaurant. Zhelenin held forth throughout the evening, both amused and unhappy. "They loved us when we got here, all of them, the entire émigré community. We were invited everywhere and barely had an evening to ourselves. We were a novelty as so few left the Soviet Union in the fifties, and hardly anyone who'd been in a forced-labour camp. One old man even said to me that they were all very fond of us, both of us, even though Miriam Emmanuilovna was Jewish. You remember Trebukhin, don't you Miriam? Old man, short, no hair, always wore a green corduroy jacket. Yes, he said that. But they didn't like *Sintesy*. Not much at the beginning, and not at all later. They called me confused at first, ill-advised, then naïve and stubborn. When I argued that a humane socialism was not impossible, they called me an unwitting supporter of Communism, then a dodgy imbecile, a traitor to Russia, a Judas. We don't exist for them anymore, Miriam and I. *Veche* published an article claiming I was seven-eighths Jewish. Between us, I'm one-eighth only, not that it matters. *Russkaya Misl* was classier. Their research showed that I was only half-Jewish, but that the other half was mostly Polish. My ethnic make-up, they added generously, didn't make me a bad person, only incapable of understanding Russia's mystic soul and destiny. The new boys, Maximov and his cohort at *Kontinent*, are too clever for this. They simply dismiss me as a *popu-chik*—a fellow traveller."

Aksakov couldn't take his eyes off Zhelenin's wife. The *canard* was delicious, and a thin trail of the flavourful pink sauce found a way under her lower lip. Zhelenin bent toward her, and with his napkin delicately blotted it. Miriam smiled happily at her husband, and pushed aside a lock of hair pasted to her damp forehead.

On the last train to Paris that night, Aksakov said, "They seemed very happy together, the Zhelenins. Did you see how he looked after her? Oh, Tyoma, she was such a beauty thirty years ago. Do you remember her? No? I do. I was sixteen or seventeen, and in love with Miriam Emmanuilovna, a young, shivering, unspoken love. It was her great uncle who got the family out. He made a large donation to the French Communist Party, Maurice Thorez made a few phone calls, and in a couple of weeks they were gone." Laukhin asked his friend where he had heard the story, but Aksakov was unwilling to say or unable to remember. More likely the latter—he could hardly walk by the time they got to his hotel. He asked about his friend Fedya Malgunov whom he'd not seen in years, but didn't wait for an answer. He said he and Fedya had been in high school together, and that Fedya had been in love with Miriam Emmanuilovna too.

"We have nothing from you, Artyom Pavlovich, not a single line," Zhelenin said. His baritone voice sounded as if he was across the street.

"I sent you something about my father a month ago, Viktor Efremovich, after your last phone call."

"Our readers want your poetry."

"I'm not writing poetry these days—well, these years. Haven't in a long time."

A pause at the other end of the line. "There's *Poets in Heaven*, isn't there?"

"There isn't."

"Sorry? What's the title in Russian?"

"There's no title."

"Oh." Another long pause at the other end. "Well, we'd very much like to publish *Poets in Heaven*."

"It's not possible."

"Have you promised it to *Kontinent*? Those bastards gobble up everything. They had a long Zladsky poem in their last issue. Have you promised it to them? Somewhere else?"

"No."

"Some of our readers saw the English translation, and many more want to read it in the original Russian. Well, everybody, in fact."

"It doesn't exist."

"It doesn't... Forgive me, Artyom Pavlovich, what doesn't exist?"

"The original Russian version."

"What do you mean? It wasn't written in English, I know that. The long article in Vanity Fair—I have it in front of me—says that the author, Fedya Malgunov, translated the poem."

"It's not ready for publication. It may never be. It's a poem that's unfinished and, even worse, unsatisfactory to me."

"The English translation was satisfactory?"

Ah, the irony. "No, of course not," Laukhin said trying to stay calm. "Both the translation and its publication happened without my consent." As he heard himself say this, it dawned on Laukhin that he had said the same thing at the Writers Union when *Sunless Seasons* appeared in Germany.

There was a chuckle at the other end. "These kinds of words, Artyom Pavlovich, they don't make much sense out here."

"It's the truth."

Another long pause. "How could that happen? Why didn't you protest?"

He should have stayed at his worktable, not run downstairs to pick up the phone. "Viktor Efremovich, it's a long story, and rather silly. I told it all in a *Paris Review* interview. Buy the latest issue."

Long silence. Then, "You promised it to that shit, Maksimov."

Laukhin saw no point in continuing the argument. People heard what they wanted to hear. He said, wearily, "Viktor Efremovich, please."

"Well, it doesn't matter, we have the original Russian."

"What? You can't possibly have it."

"We do."

"If you have a copy of what Fedya Malgunov used for his translation, it's an illegally obtained copy."

"It's not illegal—we bought it." He spoke quickly, his voice raised, which was unlike Zhelenin. Clearly it bothered him that his integrity was being questioned.

"Who did you buy it from?"

"I'd rather not say."

"It's illegal because you didn't buy it from me or from my agent."

Zhelenin paused, and his next words were calm. "Illegal is a big word, Artyom Pavlovich. You can't use it if you keep giving copies to all your friends."

"I did no such thing."

"You should check your memory."

"My agent will sue *Sintesy*."

He heard another chuckle at the other end, this time a very satisfied one.

"He won't."

"Why not?"

"*Sintesy* has nothing of value. Ha!" Zhelenin was enjoying this.

"We'll sue you, Viktor Efremovich."

"You'll get a pair of jeans out of it. Used."

A distant click, and Paris was in his ears no more. Where on earth had Zhelenin gotten a copy of what he gave Fedya Malgunov? He was certain it was the version of *Poets in Heaven* he'd given Fedya, or a copy of it. It could not have been anyone else, despite what Zhelenin said. Why did he say that? The only explanation was that Fedya gave his copy, or a copy of his copy, to a friend of theirs who had, in turn, given it—no, sold it—to *Sintesy*. The only friends he could think of were Dieter and Andrey Aksakov. He'd call both of them and check. But first he'd have to call Bart and ask him to send a stern letter to *Sintesy*.

So much heartache for a failed poem. He should have burned all copies and versions of it long ago. Why keep at it for so long? Was it an unwillingness to accept that he could no longer write verse? When Erika Belov-Wang asked him if he was writing poetry these days, he'd said that he did and he didn't. Meaning? Verses, or images, or even a few words whose sound he liked still came to him, but all he did now was jot them down in a notebook. That was all? Just about. Well, he was still tinkering with *Poets in Heaven*, but he didn't tell her that. Anyway, it happened less and less lately, and he had not touched the poem in almost a year. Odd that this exchange with Erika Belov-Wang was not in the transcript of the interview. He didn't recall telling her to leave it out. Maybe it happened over lunch, when her tape recorder was off, and she forgot all about it.

Ewa Kucharsky told him he took so long on his father's journal because he couldn't imagine what he'd do afterward. "You fear you'd only be repeating yourself," she said. He had dismissed the idea. In fact, he got angry with her. "How would you know? How would you know better than I do?" But Ewa knew him quite well, and there might have been something in what she said—otherwise why did he get so upset? Seven years spent on one volume? He could have found a way to work more quickly, but, subconsciously, had not wanted to or had feared to. Ewa was probably right in saying he had no idea what he would do next. Well, he might indeed be finished as a poet—not such a tragedy, he had already written the best of what he had in him.

Could Zladsky have given the Russian version of *Poets in Heaven* to Zhelenin? Fedya had known Zladsky. No, it was unlikely. Zhelenin said it had been a friend and he knew that he and Zladsky were far from being friends. Zladsky's comments about Laukhin in the interview had been the gossip of Russian literati everywhere. Little, callous

Zladsky. He could feel the venom in Zladsky's words, imagine saliva gathering in the corners of his mouth as he let go, eyes bulging at the flabbergasted interviewer. "Laukhin grew up with a *gostinaya*—a living room. Do you know what that means in the Soviet Union, to have a *gostinaya*? Do you have any idea? My parents and I had one room. One room! Just one!"

This was a long festering hatred, far beyond the natural competitive urge or the envy writers or poets felt toward each other, beyond the struggle to make a living abroad, where hardly anybody read one's work. It was a desire to harm, as if they had carried their worst customs with them abroad—their delight in intrigue and backstabbing. Where did it come from? He barely knew Zladsky. They met once in Leningrad, in somebody's kitchen, where they spoke briefly. They met again a few years later, in Moscow, in front of the *Yunost* office. Laukhin and his wife just happened to be walking by, and Zladsky and Aksakov were coming out of a meeting which, judging from their faces, had not gone well. Aksakov was gloomy, and Laukhin understood from the few words he said that it had been an attempt to have one of Zladsky's poems accepted by the editorial board. Zladsky had taken the overnight train from Leningrad for the meeting. They exchanged a few words that time too, lies about how much they admired each other's poems, the few they could get their hands on. Aksakov thought Laukhin was going in and, puffing from his cigarette, allowed himself a joke. "Two beggars in one day," he said, "one after another." Laukhin said they were just passing by. Aksakov hugged Tanya and introduced her to Zladsky, then put his arms around the shoulders of the two poets and said, "If it were up to me I'd publish no one else but the two of you. But... I won't give up the fight, no, I won't." The third and last time he met Zladsky was in New York, a dozen years later, at a private gathering again, but this time in an apartment large enough for them to stare at each other from a distance, nod and half-smile, and then ignore each other.

What was beyond unpardonable, though, was what little man Zladsky did to Aksakov, somebody he had known well for years, a friend. Aksakov's new novel, the one that was eventually translated into English as *The Slackening*, had been considered by Faber Lemaire for translation into English and publication in 1980, just as Aksakov was settling in the US. The book, already translated and published in The Netherlands, had been highly recommended to Faber Lemaire, but they decided to get Zladsky's opinion as well on the book's original manuscript. And the opinion was such that they passed on the book. Laukhin heard the story from Aksakov three years later, in a crowded pub in London. At Bart's request, Laukhin had flown there to calm down his London publisher. Aksakov happened to be there as well "to check on a few opportunities," as he said rather mysteriously. He was taking the train to Paris the following day, and from there to Frankfurt. "It's probably nothing," he said when Laukhin wanted to know more. "At least I'm not paying out of my own pocket."

"I never learned what he wrote in his reader's opinion," Aksakov told Laukhin. "I didn't even know he'd been approached by Faber Lemaire for an opinion—my good friend Zladsky didn't bother to let me know. I was surprised by the rejection, especially after all the good things I'd heard about my novel. I don't recall exactly what crap Faber Lemaire wrote to me—the usual vague and polite words. Last fall I taught a course in New York, and I heard a rumour that Zladsky had been telling people that my book was shit. I heard it at first from a few Russians, and so I told myself, typical émigré intrigue, pay no attention to it. Then I heard the same thing from Olga. She wasn't Russian—I'm not even sure her real name was Olga—but she was going at the time through a Russian period. A bit eccentric. Married, lovely woman, smelled of wildflower honey. She was a part-time reader for Faber Lemaire, and we had a brief thing together. She dumped me rather quickly, unfortunately. Couldn't look at my bad Soviet teeth, but I'm sure there were other reasons. I asked Olga why Faber Lemaire rejected my book. She didn't know, but said she'd try to find out. And she did. She told me Zladsky had given it a thumbs down. She couldn't get her hands on his report, but talked to somebody who had read it at the time. I confronted my pal Zladsky this spring. I said, 'Yasha, dear friend, why didn't you tell me you read my novel for Faber Lemaire?' 'Who told you?' 'Never mind who told me.' 'I was warned not to talk about it.' 'Ah. And what did you say in your report?' He hesitated. 'It wasn't … wasn't my cup of tea.' 'Not your cup of tea. Oh, Yasha, what would we do without cliches.' 'Look, Andrey, they wanted my opinion. I had to give it to them, the truth. Literature … it's all we have, it's a sacred trust. I don't have to like everything you write.' I couldn't breathe for a long time, Tyoma. But eventually I managed to tell him what I thought. 'Listen, you little shit,' I said, 'don't tell me about sacred trust. I have a hard time making a living here, a foreigner who can barely speak English teaching young morons how to write like geniuses. You know damn well an English-language publication with a major American house is the ticket, the only one. The largest market, friend Yasha. It triggers translations in other countries. Have you thought of that? Sacred trust? What's more sacred than a friend in need? Couldn't you say you had no time to read the damned book? I mean, if you were so repelled by the novel. Fuck you, Yasha Zladsky. To think of the arguments and fights I had at *Yunost* for your stupid poems. At the end Polevoi barred me from his office. He told his secretary he'd fire her if he ever saw my face again. I did it because I had some influence there, and because you were my friend. Not because I loved your shitty *chastushki*.' I should have punched him, Tyoma. I should have broken his knees."

Laukhin nodded understandingly and expressed outrage, but he kept a skeptical view of the whole thing. Was Aksakov exaggerating to improve the story? Was there something in their past to explain Zladsky's cruelty?

Zladsky's attack on him, Laukhin, came a few months later. Aksakov rang him the following day from Philadelphia. "Hello, *gastinaya*-man. Yes, yes, I read it this morning. Ha! Had the time of my life. A *gastinaya* growing up, and a seasoned globetrotter. No, not a globetrotter. What did he call you—a *frequent traveller*? Not bad, not bad at all. It's too much, Tyoma, too much. I'm only calling to say that our ways are parting from now on."

"It's not funny, Andrey."

"Oh, Tyoma, it's funny, hysterically funny. He's a genius, our little man, the best. He's unbeatable at bludgeoning friends, and he has a vicious disregard for the truth. That's what he brought with him from the old country."

Yes, they were very good at it, his countrymen, that was what defined them. It had made the Soviet Union possible, all that cruelty and hatred and brutal personal attacks and *schadenfreude*. A German word, but the Germans were bungling amateurs compared to Russians. He thought of Zhelenin's conflict with Maksimov, and of his fights with the publishers of *Veche* and *Russkaya Misl*, and God only knew with who else or what else.

He heard Aksakov telling him he was moving to London. He'd teach at Queen Mary College for a year, then he'd see. Andre Deutsch had agreed to publish *The Slackening*, and that was the main reason he was moving. The publisher wanted him nearby, and he wanted to be nearby too. "At the very least to keep things moving. And I don't want another Faber Lemaire disaster—another friend's help without my knowledge. It's my big chance, Tyoma, and I can't have another fuckup. The Germans are interested too, and I hear encouraging noises from Paris. I'll be close enough to remind them all of my existence. I'll send Yasha Zladsky a copy of *The Slackening* in English. No, five copies, each with the same handwritten dedication, 'A shitty book to a shitty friend.'"

* * *

When he finally opened the green folder, it was almost five o'clock. He intended to work late into the evening. Audrey was still in his head, dancing on his cortex, but the walk, the shower, Larissa's letter, and the call from Zhelenin had slowed her to a lighter step—a quiet, ironic minuet.

Monday, 10 October 1955

Another day of remorse. The whole day. Boris Leonidovich has never been in worse shape. I have to give it to him—he takes remorse to heroic heights.

"How could I, Pavel Nikolayevich? How could I not tell Marina Ivanovna, scream at her, not to come back? What blindness overtook me? Wasn't it obvious already ours was a monstrous regime? Did I still have illusions?" He paused, as if considering the question for the first time. "Must have— after all, I was pleading with my own parents to come back as late as 1939."

He told the story of meeting with Tsvetayeva during his last trip to Paris. It was 1935, June or July. He had been literally dragged out of his sickbed to join the already large Soviet delegation attending the Congress of Writers in Defence of Culture. It was all because of Malraux who, disappointed by not seeing him and Babel among the Soviet writers who had already arrived, insisted to the head of the Soviet delegation that they attend. The congress was held in a small theatre, *Salle de la Mutualité*, not far from Notre-Dame. Tsvetayeva was living in Paris at the time, and she came to meet him.

She didn't look good. She had never been a beautiful woman, but there had been a boyish prettiness about her. He had fallen in love with her earlier, not for her looks but for her genius and her passionate, indomitable, direct nature. But when she came to his hotel in Paris—she sought him out, not the other way around—she looked terrible. He was not sure whether she was ill or just showing the years of poverty and unhappiness. The clothes she had on didn't help—a black dress, now greyish from too much wear and washing, clearly too warm for the summer weather.

At the time, he hadn't seen the obvious. He had been too wrapped up in his own unhappiness, and he carried on about his illness, how he'd been forced to come to the Congress at the very last moment, how, just before his departure, he'd been taken to a store in Moscow, given two shirts, a hat, and an ill-fitting suit, and then driven to the railway station. How he'd feared to refuse. How Poskrebishev himself told him, when he complained about his health, that they were at war and that he should consider himself called to serve.

"That's how men are, Pavel Nikolayevich, selfish, thinking only of themselves. Our sense of ourselves, our importance, is like a huge sphere always in front of our eyes, blocking out everything else. What she expected to hear from me, of course, was quite the opposite: That I'd come in spite of my illness; that I'd left no stone unturned to be allowed to come to Paris and to see her; that I'd done all I could in order to have this meeting, a meeting of poets and, yes, lovers."

He went to her house and met her husband and her children. Alya was already twenty-three, a beautiful young woman with a winning smile. It was impossible not to like her. He liked Tsvetayeva's husband too. They came to his hotel one day, Sergey and Alya, without Marina and—he realized immediately—without her knowledge. They asked him to talk her into going back to Russia. The two of them had already made up their minds to return.

It might have been their request that stopped him from telling her the truth about the Soviet Union. But if that was the case, it did not diminish his betrayal.

Tsvetayeva asked him about the prospects for her family in the Soviet Union, about her prospects as a poet. And he, the illustrious poet, the herald of the truth, fully aware of the terrible reality of life there, hid behind inane remarks. Instead of shaking her frail shoulders and shouting at her not to even think about returning, he told her that he couldn't advise her. He couldn't forgive himself now, knowing what happened to her and her family afterward.

"It was 1935, Pavel Nikolayevich. It was after Kirov's assassination and long after I saw with my own eyes what happened in the countryside in the early thirties. And after they shoved socialist-realism down everybody's throat. I was already forty-five, not an easily duped, empty-headed youth. But long whiskers do not take the place of brains."

They went to a restaurant one day, the two of them, away from the Congress. He paid, of course—she had no money. It was not a special place, more of a bistro, but the food was plentiful and the price was right. He had enough money to take her to a nicer place, but he was saving it in order to buy a few dresses for Zinaida. Yes, foremost in his mind was that his wife's wardrobe needed additions from Paris. He persuaded himself that Tsvetayeva would feel out of place in a nicer restaurant because of her clothes. She was famished. For some reason the waiter had to take back his first course, to replace or re-heat it, he didn't remember anymore. After a couple of minutes, at his prodding she gave up on the civility of waiting and dug into her own meal.

"We were all alone for three hours, and I could have told her the truth. But I kept my mouth shut, Pavel Nikolayevich. How many cuts are needed to see that we bleed? What was wrong with me that evening, what colossal folly froze my lips? Oh reason, what fools walk your paths!"

Boris Leonidovich's voice was trembling. He began to cough, an old man's cough, with no cause or end.

I told Boris Leonidovich not to get so worked up. An artist, I found myself saying, especially a poet, is rootless abroad, lacks nourishment, has less and less to write about, and, in time, withers and dies. Tsvetayeva had felt that way and that's why she had returned.

"Oh, what poppycock, Pasha," he said between coughs, wiping his face with a huge handkerchief. "What drivel, romantic nonsense that works well in novels and suits poets. I know, because I often make use of this notion of the unhappiness of the exiled myself. It's simply not always true. Didn't she write her best poems abroad? More to the point, did she write anything after her return? Two years is a long time for a poet. But she wrote nothing after she got back to the Motherland, not one line of verse. She couldn't find sustenance abroad, you say? Couldn't live? Well, after two years back here, immersed in her language, surrounded by her own people, she chose death."

Boris Leonidovich fell silent, and I didn't say anything for a while. It was the first time he had ever called me Pasha. Stopping a child from spurting twaddle.

And there was more, much more self-flagellation. Tsvetayeva was harsh with him after the Congress. He must have disappointed, exasperated her. He behaved terribly toward his old parents during the trip. He avoided meeting them, pretending that he was too tired or too busy. Unthinking, or thinking too much about himself. (He never saw his parents again.) He must have felt guilty afterward, because he told Tsvetayeva he had avoided his parents. He doesn't know if she used it as a pretext, or whether, as a mother, she found his behaviour incomprehensible, even monstrous. She let her feelings pour out in a letter she sent him a few months after the

Congress. She wrote that she had found him indecisive, fickle, and selfish, as most males are. Women are less egotistical—it is their nature. If she appeared hard, she wrote, it was because it takes being hard to be unselfish. Selfish, weak people run away from everything, including their duties to parents and friends.

"And later, when she returned, I failed her again. Soft, self-centred Boris Leonidovich ran away again. Oh, I saw her, talked and listened to her, smiled with her and hugged her. I appealed to Fadeyev and others to find work for her, and a place to live. I helped her. But I was half-hearted about it, fearful, scared. She had good reason to be disappointed in me."

We were outside, on the small deck off our salon. I liked looking at the river, at the solid, tranquil immensity of the water. It calmed me down, soothed me, soothed all of us, and Boris Leonidovich needed soothing at that moment. He told me the other day that people living near large bodies of water were calmer, more serene. He said that's what Moscow needs, a large body of water, like Leningrad, as less evil would then emanate from it.

"I shudder, Pavel Nikolayevich, I shudder when I think back. I saw her a few times, but not enough. I did everything to avoid her after her return. Everything, that is, that still allowed me to sleep at night. What masters we are, Pavel Nikolayevich, at rationalizing our weaknesses, our fears and cowardice. What masters we are at avoiding the truth about ourselves. Meyerhold's arrest, worries about my parents, Zinaida, my work on *Hamlet*, the translations from Petofi, the move—I couldn't and wouldn't think beyond them. I kept telling myself that she chose a very inopportune time to return."

Tsvetayeva came to Moscow to see him once. She rarely came to Moscow during that period, before her daughter's arrest. She was almost a prisoner in Bolshevo. She came to see him and he couldn't wait for her to leave. She was a woman whose poetry he admired more than anyone's else, and yet he wanted her visit to end. He was afraid of her, of her demands and criticism. He knew she saw through him. Yes, she liked his poetry, but she saw behind the façade the weak, vacillating man, hiding his flaws and his terrors. She couldn't see the need to compromise, to hide or snivel, in order to survive.

"Maybe afraid is the wrong word. I was overwhelmed by her, tired of her. She was too stern, too severe, too direct. And too pathetic. She came to see if I could help her find some work—translations or anything related to literature, however lightly. She read a few of her poems, and I read a few of mine. We talked about our families—I talked more, much more than she did. And all the time she stared at me with her sad, condemning eyes, expecting something more, something I was incapable of offering. In the end, I claimed I had an important meeting to attend to make her leave."

"Don't do this, Boris Leonidovich. You're being too hard on yourself."

"Stalin was right when he said to me, 'You don't know how to stand up for a comrade!' I didn't do much for Mandelstam either."

His head was down and he was looking at his feet, not addressing me anymore, but someone inside of him, someone who would understand and offer solace better than I could. Perhaps he was rehearsing for the final judgment.

He had another story, and he told it in a tone both resigned and sarcastic. *Literaturnaya Moskva* recently approached him for recommendations for a few of Tsvetayeva's poems to be collected in a thin volume. They came to him a month ago—Kazakevich and Paustovsky—and asked him to choose her best poetry for a collection of some fifty to sixty pages. They said he'd been her friend, and knew her poetry best. No one could choose better than him. They hastened to add, of course, that he should choose carefully, although everybody agreed that her poetry was not political.

"Oh, how happy I was, how grateful I was to them. And for what? They were happy too, mind you, the two them, and convinced of their immense importance, of their daring. What a bunch of clowns we are. No, not clowns, starving dogs. Throw us any bone and we lick our chops and wag our tails, grateful for the flimsiest morsels that the thick-necked masters offer us."

We were floating past a small town. The riverbank was too far away for us to see much except grey buildings and a couple of industrial chimneys belching whitish smoke.

Boris Leonidovich's thoughts switched back to Tsvetayeva. "How right she was about her poetry, Pavel Nikolayevich, how prophetic she was when she wrote, 'Scattered in bookstores, greyed by dust and time / Unseen, unsought, unopened and unsold / My poems will be savoured as are rarest wines / When they are old.' She wrote that in 1913, when she was twenty-one."

10

Laukhin spent Thursday evening reviewing the entire Tsvetayeva bundle, fixing bits here and there in the first four excerpts, and then marking paragraphs that still needed work in the largest part, the trip to Yelabuga. Reading and thinking for hours about Tsvetayeva's life felt like being hooked to a poisonous intravenous drip—a slow infusion of pain and nausea, unseen claws squeezing his chest. He was tempted to throw it all away. He looked out the window, got up and paced the room, then went downstairs for a glass of water; poured himself vodka too and took it back upstairs with him. He laughed loudly at himself—as a native Russian and someone who had spent most of his life in the Soviet Union, he should be immunized against such tales. It wasn't as if he didn't know Tsvetayeva's story, but it was the first time he had read the excerpts in sequence and in one go. Even in English, the intensity of the story stunned him. The need to concentrate on technicalities—resolving translation and selection problems—had not lessened its effect on him.

When the telephone rang, he ran downstairs relieved by the interruption. It was Bill MacNaughton, who apologized for disturbing him at home, but wanted to make sure he wouldn't forget they were getting together the next day. They'd have a late breakfast or an early lunch.

"I'll be in my office all morning, looking at numbers," Bill said. "By numbers I mean budgets and funding, and that's where the dean believes you could do more for us. For the entire faculty, not just our department. And he's not alone in thinking that. Your name, you know—there're rumours of the Nobel Prize. The dean wants you to spread your wings, cover others with the shade of your fame."

"That's quite dreadful, Bill."

"I know. What was I saying? Yes, help other departments as well. I know it's not the best time now, you being so busy with the first volume, but…you see, I promised the dean I'd talk to you."

Laukhin told Bill he'd pass by his office the next day. "Noonish," he added. "I have to pick up something from my office." He expected Bill to hang up, but he didn't. He cleared his throat. "There's something else, Art."

"Yes?"

"I'm not sure how to say it. It's not good, Art, not good at all, to attack people so fiercely. Words spread like an oil slick, and you never know who'll be contaminated and develop a grudge. And then, when you ask for support…It's not wise, Art."

"What are you talking about, Bill?"

"Your attack on Zladsky."

"What?"

"I read your interview in the *Paris Review*."

"Ah."

"Zladsky has many admirers and friends."

"You're not asking me to scrounge money from south of the border, are you?"

"We do receive, of course, endowments from Canadians living there. And, well, yes, even Americans, some who have studied here."

"Fuck Zladsky, Bill."

"Sorry?"

"You heard me."

"And Solzhenitsyn, now—"

"I didn't attack Solzhenitsyn—don't invent things."

"Not directly."

"Not even indirectly."

"The people who gave him the Nobel Prize are still alive and influential. They might even still be on the committee that awards the prize for literature. Why antagonize them? You're not help-ing yourself."

"My words about Solzhenitsyn were respectful and restrained."

"We'll talk about it tomorrow."

"Not if you want me there."

"Well, I'll see you tomorrow, then. Try to be sensible."

Sensible. He was as sensible as he could be. He'd been cautious about Solzhenitsyn, even guarded, in the interview. The Emslies had got the same impression as Bill MacNaughton, though. This sensi-tivity about Solzhenitsyn likely started with Colson, who had read the sarcasm and dislike in what he'd said to Erika Belov-Wang. And Colson would have mentioned his impressions to Bill—collegial amusement over a cup of tea.

* * *

His visit to Vermont had only confirmed what he had always felt about Solzhenitsyn. He had met him a few times in Moscow—the first time at the Sovremennik Theatre a month after the publication of *Ivan Denisovich*. He couldn't remember how he and Tanya ended up celebrat-ing that New Year with the actors and actresses of the theatre, nor if Reshetovskaya, Solzhenitsyn's first wife, had been there with the sud-denly famous author. But he recalled how Solzhenitsyn had ogled the lightly clad actresses with both disapproval and want. He ogled Tanya too. The Laukhins arrived late—was it already 1963?—and there were too many people, and too much cheer and noise and energetic shaking for proper introductions. They found Kyril there, inebriated and loud, and he invited Tanya to dance with him when he saw them, helping her out of her winter coat and handing it to Laukhin, and then drag-ging her away. Afterward some young actor butted in and danced with Tanya, and when they were done Tanya came back to where Laukhin was chatting with Kyril and whispered, "That old man couldn't take his eyes off my boobs. I don't mind, but why the sour face?" They fol-lowed Tanya's gaze, and Kyril said, "That's Solzhenitsyn."

He remembered how irritated he came away from his trip to Vermont with Fedya. Did he really expect advice on where and how best to settle? Fedya Malgunov told Laukhin that Solzhenitsyn and Svetlova had thoroughly researched that topic in a cross-continent trek three years earlier, during the summer of 1975. It was Fedya who talked him into the trip to Vermont.

At the car rental agency, soon after they landed, Fedya handed him a map and began rattling off numbers and exotic names. "It's the 93 from Boston, and the 89 shortly before Concord. After Lebanon we drive back south on the 91 for a short distance, and then it's the 131 all the way, or almost. The 131 is not a freeway, but there won't be too much traffic. It's not complicated, Tyoma. Trickier after Cavendish, as the house—well, the estate—is a few miles past it. I think I remember the way, though."

"I can't read maps, Fedya."

"Start learning."

On the drive from the airport, Laukhin asked Fedya how well he knew Solzhenitsyn.

"I did a few things for him. And with him. Still do."

"Like what?"

"I love driving these big American boats. Superb capitalist excesses. What did I do? I played tennis with him at Stanford, among other things. He loves tennis, and he's awful at it."

"What else?"

"A bit of research now and then. I drop in at the Hoover Library or at some other California institution for him. No point in having him fly so far for some minor details or double-checking. You can't talk about this, Tyoma."

"About you helping Solzhenitsyn?"

"About this visit."

"Why not?"

"I'm not sure—perhaps to avoid setting a precedent. Aleksander Isayevich seldom agrees to visits." He chuckled, and shook his head. "Well, he won't be happy."

"What?"

"It's too early. He sees most people in the evening, after he's finished work for the day." ·

"Oh, fuck it, Fedya. Let's turn around."

"No, no, Tyoma, humour me. I need the money, need it badly."

He had agreed to the visit for Fedya's sake, couldn't say no to him. His friend had had an assignment from a magazine, an article on Solzhenitsyn provided he could find something new, or, at least, a new angle. Laukhin's arrival on the continent offered him the chance of a fresh visit with the Vermont recluse. A fresh perspective too, witnessing two artists' first meeting and their intercourse. "Two giants of literature, Tyoma," he had said to him grinning in the airplane, "you, the younger one, the poet, and Solzhnitsyn, the older one, the great narrator, the sage. Who knows, there may even be a clash. After all, Tyoma, he could hold a dim view of your rather privileged life. I'll just sit there, listen, and make notes, mental notes, of course."

The morning was grey. Laukhin kept the map on his lap, and, for a while, as they drove through the nondescript suburbs with innumerable billboards, gas-stations, and shops, he tried to make sense of the numbers Fedya had recited earlier and the yellow highlight marking the route on the map. It wasn't a short drive. He dozed off, exhausted by nights with little sleep, the stress of so many new things, the curiosity and harassment of the press. In his half-sleep it dawned on him that he had agreed to visit Solzhenitsyn because he hoped to get some respite from the incessant demands on his time and opinions. When he looked about him again, they were driving on a winding road. There were mountains or hills not far away, their flanks wooded. The snow on the sides of the road were thick for long stretches. Fedya was wearing sunglasses. Laukhin realized he'd slept for quite a while because he felt invigorated, but it could have been the shining sun and unexpectedly clear sky. When Fedya stopped the car on the side of the road to relieve himself, Laukhin climbed out too and filled his lungs with fresh air and the smell of spring.

The estate was on the unpaved and delightfully named Windy Hill Road, a few miles from the village of Cavendish. The chain-link fence around it was an eyesore. After waiting at the tall gates for a couple of minutes, Fedya exchanged a few words with a female voice and a TV camera, and the gates opened. A winding lane led to a two-storey house which had, or so it seemed to Laukhin, recent additions on both sides. Svetlova appeared—an attractive woman whose dark hair held a hint of grey—and directed them inside, into a large room the height of the house. She said her husband had not expected them until much later that day. Fedya said they'd been unable to arrange a later visit. They sat down while Svetlova left to fetch her husband.

It took almost fifteen minutes for Solzhenitsyn to appear. They could hear the sound of a typewriter from somewhere upstairs, but except for a blond boy who briefly appeared and said hello both in Russian and English, there were no other noises. Laukhin walked over to the window for a view of the mountains. He heard steps coming from the door the child had disappeared through, and a woman's voice saying, "No, no, you can't do that."

Solzhenitsyn looked shorter than Laukhin remembered, and plumper, and his long beard reminded him of a retired and less wicked Chernomor. The writer repeated what his wife told them, that he had expected them much later. It was not often, he added, that he'd interrupt his work for a visit, but he'd make an exception this time. He had not read his guest's poetry (here he inclined his head toward Laukhin in a old-fashioned, almost military gesture that Laukhin presumed was meant to remove any guilt), he had time for few other things besides his work, but he had heard others praise it. Fedya said it was entirely his fault they had showed up early. Solzhenitsyn said Fedya Malgunov would have to play tennis with him as a payback, and Laukhin thought that there was a thin smile on his lips, a hint of a smile.

They had a light, improvised lunch in the large kitchen. It was Svetlova who led the conversation at first, wanting to hear news from Russia. Solzhenitsyn seemed uninterested, and hardly touched anything that was put in front of him. He then slowly took over. He expressed a brief curiosity in Pavel Laukhin's journal, wanting to know how it was smuggled out and the state it was in. He expected short replies and showed irritation at details. The subject of where Laukhin should settle was quickly dismissed too. "I'll assume," he said without seeking confirmation, "that like most Russians you don't like warm climates. It means the north-eastern part of the United States, say from Philadelphia up. The west and the central part of America are full of happy philistines. Don't bother. Canada has the right climate, of course, but..." He ended the sentence with a shrug that Laukhin could not interpret. That was it, subject exhausted. The rest of the time he talked about his struggles, his monumental *Red Wheel*, the huge amount of detailed history he had to master for each of its four knots, the little time he had left to finish it. He missed Russia and hoped to return one day. He hoped God would hear his wish, for his sake, for his family's sake, and for the sake of all Russians. Svetlova smiled and said what her husband meant is that his return to Russia would simply mean that the current monstrous regime would not be there anymore. Solzhenitsyn blinked a couple of times and added that he was getting old—he was sixty already—and he'd accept his fate, whatever it was. Again, the most important thing for him was the cycle of his historical novels.

It was a long and rather impressive discourse, undoubtedly already repeated many times. At the end, he looked at his watch and excused himself because he had to go back to work, although he added, magnanimously, "Please stay as long as you want." Then, looking at his young wife, "You'll look after our guests, won't you, my dear."

No, he, Laukhin, had never cared for the man or the novelist, but it was Solzhenitsyn's refusal to sign a letter of support for Sinyavsky and Daniel that had appalled him. Sinyavsky's wife had approached Solzhenitsyn and he declined because—an irate Rozanova told Laukhin the story the next day—he didn't approve of writers who sought fame abroad. Imagine. The hypocrisy of that statement had left Laukhin speechless. It was even more shocking thinking about it now, knowing what happened later. Clearly Solzhenitsyn couldn't stand others to be in the limelight, even in front of prison gates. He was jealous whenever attention was not focused solely on him. There was no other possible explanation. More than sixty Moscow writers had signed the letter.

* * *

Laukhin left his house at nine o'clock. It was warm and windy outside and he smelled dust and imminent rain. On Yonge Street he hailed a cab and got to the gallery in twenty minutes. Inside, the event was at its end. There were empty glasses and dirty plates everywhere. Two or three small groups of people were still hanging in. Audrey and her mother were talking with an older man who looked as if he had just returned from an elegant canoe trip. Laukhin waved a discreet hello in that direction. Audrey smiled back and nodded slightly. Martha Osterhoudt, taller than her daughter, looked at and through him. Jean Lezzard was in another small group. A giant Bouvier lay half-asleep near the folding doors to the smaller room, as if guarding Lezzard's prized Chemakoffs.

Flyers introducing the artist were everywhere. He picked up one and also a glass of wine before beginning his tour. He learned that

Marga Lear had turned to sculpture in her forties. She'd been a writer in the past, and continued to be, and the two artistic expressions were still battling it out for her soul. She found sculpting a more direct art, also a more complete and fulfilling one. She was quoted as saying that "like barrels left outside in the rain and steadily filling up, artists accumulate a mysterious energy, peculiar to each art, which has to be released, that is, expressed. Working with clay, I feel that my fingers are direct conduits of this energy. It's almost as if all I have to do is plunge my hands into the wet clay and, miraculously, it will shape itself into that something that I have only vaguely known, but obsessively pursued."

Marga Lear discharged her energy on two-dimensional shapes as well, black or dark red blotches on large sheets of paper. Laukhin glimpsed, in one of them, old bearded men, with round backs and pointed hats, and then he admonished himself for seeking a banal resemblance.

He finished his tour undisturbed near the giant dog. The Bouvier lay on his belly, its head between its paws. Laukhin bent down, patted the dog, and looked around. The Bouvier gathered enough strength to lick one of his shoes. Jean Lezzard walked by and Laukhin said hello. Lezzard stopped grudgingly. "That's all we need here," he said. "Don't bother Audrey, she has work to do."

"Cheer up, Jean, it's a vernissage. Have a drink."

"I've had too many already."

The giant dog switched its wet attention to Lezzard's shoes. "He licks everybody's shoes," Laukhin said. "A sensitive dog. Doesn't want to hurt anybody's feelings."

"This bloody beast ate all the sandwiches," Lezzard grumbled glancing down. "You'd think that the only reason people came to this opening was to feed the dog. For all I know he had a few glasses of wine too." Unfazed, the dog went on with his licking. Lezzard moved his foot and the Bouvier looked up at him with reproachful eyes. "Come, I'll introduce you to the artist. Be of some use—don't let me say anything that I'll regret later. I've already had a shouting match with the husband. Perhaps he's also had too much wine. We almost came to blows. *Quel imbecile.* Wealth, professor, like fame, is a licence to say stupid things." He picked up a half-full glass of wine and drained it, closing his watery blue eyes.

They joined the small group that Lezzard had left moments earlier. The artist was a small, frail, intense woman with dyed black hair. She had a faint accent and spoke in a halting way, choosing her words carefully. She was telling a man, who turned out to be her husband, that the dog looked lethargic. Turning to Laukhin, she said, "Mugs is usually in his element surrounded by art. I don't know what's wrong with him. He's going to fail the field trials tomorrow."

"Mr. Laukhin, here," Lezzard said nodding toward him, "loves your work, Marga. Marga Lear, the artist. Her husband, Howard Lear. You should feel flattered Marga—Art Laukhin is an artist too, a famous poet. In Russian, unfortunately. I mean, unfortunately for those who do not understand Russian."

"I'm one of them. What exactly do you like in my work, Mr. Laukhin?" Marga Lear's challenge was direct. She must have had a whole evening of empty words.

"Tell her, tell Marga word for word what you just told me moments ago near the dog," Lezzard said nodding at him.

Lezzard would pay for this. "The energy," Laukhin said. "One feels there is an excess of it at first, and yet it is creatively restrained."

The artist stared at him, disappointed.

"It sounded better in Russian," Lezzard said.

"Oh, I know now," Marga Lear said looking at Laukhin. "There was an interview with you in the *Globe* the other day. Taking a very long time with some family memoirs, or something like that."

"Jean thinks the dog has had one drink too many," Laukhin said.

The feeble joke drew a hostile stare from the husband. Howard Lear, short and intense too, but wide, looked like a bulldog ready for a fight. Laukhin was saved by a young man in a bright red shirt who was hovering around the group. He held glasses in both hands and was at the precise stage of intoxication when delight comes from keeping the body straight and the words rolling. "Athletes go to bed early," he said, and for some reason he winked at Laukhin. "Early curfew, not parties, is what Mugs needs."

Howard Lear's eyes drifted to the young man and back to Laukhin, unsure yet whom to tear up first.

"Marga is from Belgium, originally," said Lezzard in the tone of one expecting that, with such a remark, the conversation would fork out into unexpected and intelligent vistas. He pointed to the two-dimensional shapes that had attracted Laukhin's attention earlier and added, "She does these things strictly with her thumbs."

"Really," Laukhin said. He failed to see what the country of her birth had to do with it.

"To be truthful—" Marga Lear said.

"Marga is very talented," Howard Lear interrupted. "She could use her knuckles and the results would be just as striking."

"Don't say such silly things, Howard," said Marga Lear. "Especially when Jean is around. He is a wicked raconteur. Anyway, we should get going. It's late and it has been a full day. Do you think you can get Mugs on his feet? He seems to have had a breakdown of some sort. We may need a tow-truck. Good night to you all. Good night, Jean. Not the vernissage I had hoped for. A rather motley opening crowd, on the shy and penurious side, wouldn't you agree?"

They nodded to the rest of them and left, the dog the only one of the three reluctant to go.

Lezzard saw them to the door. Laukhin turned to the young man and asked, "Which one did you reserve?"

The young man took a while to comprehend Laukhin's question. "Good heavens, have you had a good look at them? The only thing I reserved was a bottle of wine. And now, I'm afraid, I have to return it. I feel sick." He ran off, muttering to himself.

"The young man in the red shirt is being sick in the toilet," Laukhin told Lezzard.

"Who cares?"

Lezzard was in a foul mood. With her mother in tow, Audrey approached them holding two umbrellas. She was wearing a black dress—not too elaborate, but with a low neckline. Martha was glamorous, and Laukhin saw hardly any evidence of fading due to age. Audrey made the introductions. Lezzard repeated his remark about Laukhin and his poetry, and Audrey mentioned the long awaited journal. Martha made Lezzard look puny. Laukhin thought that, as much in love as he was with Audrey, the daughter was a muted copy of what Martha must have been. She was leaving, Martha announced, acknowledging Laukhin's presence with a simple nod. She was staying in Toronto for a few more days, at the flat, before going away. "Probably to Montreal at first. Dirks isn't sure where to spend the rest of the summer. I talked to him this afternoon, and he had this whole story about his sister being quite sick, and that we'd stop in The Netherlands for a while to look in on her, and, while there, spend a few days in Nordwijk with Dirks' friend—another impossible Dutch name—who always invites us, to my despair, because it's a dingy resort, with sand blown in your eyes and terrible food, and staid Dutch who, nevertheless eat a lot and laugh loudly. We had a bit of an argument and we still don't know whether it's Austria or..."

Laukhin didn't immediately realize that Dirks was Martha's third husband, Diederik Osterhoudt. Audrey had once told him that Martha often referred to Dirks as The Unpronounceable. She said that things happened around Dirks, but he always seemed at a considerable distance, and, although she had met him in the past, she was now beginning to think that Martha had stashed him away under the floorboards of one of their many residences.

Audrey turned to Laukhin and said, "I was afraid you wouldn't come. Don't leave. I'll walk Martha home and be back in a few minutes. It's raining, but a walk will do me good, clear my head."

By now there were very few people left in the gallery; a mirthful group of four or five, and two stragglers who still managed to look interested. Lezzard glanced at his watch. "Good God, it's almost midnight. I better get these revelers out." Mesmerized, Laukhin watched Lezzard's hoarding technique. First, he led the stragglers to the larger group. He then proceeded with perfunctory introductions and said something that created some merriment. The rounding up phase was complete. Next, he pointed to an exhibit close to the exit door and the enlarged group travelled there together. It was kept compact by Lezzard's outstretched arms. With his willed bonhomie, Lezzard had the pose of an avuncular bird of prey. One or two more minutes passed in amiable chatter; then Lezzard looked openly at his watch. He pointed toward Laukhin and said something. The group poured out into the night. Lezzard left the door ajar. Laukhin joined him to breathe in the fresh air. It was raining, but not hard.

"What did you tell them?" he asked. "They took off in a hurry."

"I said you'd offered to help clean up the mess in here and asked for other volunteers. Are you waiting for Audrey?"

Laukhin nodded.

They went back inside. Lezzard found a bottle of wine and an empty glass and dropped exhausted into an armchair. He poured, drank, waved the bottle at Laukhin to see if he was interested, and then poured and drank again. *"Quel métier, mon dieu,"* he said. "I soothe, I cajole, I laugh at bad jokes, I listen to the most inane comments and nod in approval. I praise what should not be praised, sell what should never be sold."

Audrey came back. Her clothes and hair were wet, drops on her collarbone threatened to slide downward.

She looked around with a discouraged air. Paper plates were piled on top of each other, slanted by plastic cutlery and leftover crudités. A plate with potato salad was on the floor, near where the dog had lain. A solitary olive glistened in the middle of it, like a bull's eye. Clear plastic glasses, some printed with lipstick, were everywhere, along with paper napkins, water bottles, and flyers about Marga Lear. Lezzard mumbled something about opening another bottle of wine, but without conviction, and Audrey shook her head at Laukhin to ignore the request.

"Cleaners are coming in the morning," Audrey said. "I have to be back here by eight to let them in, but I hate to leave all these dirty plates and leftovers overnight."

Laukhin volunteered to help clean up the mess.

Lezzard emptied the bottle into the glass, took a sip, and then raised the drink in a mock toast. "Hang on to him, Audrey. He's the reliable, helpful type. It must be a first for a famous poet—a professor as well—to clean up after a party."

"I had a row with Martha," Audrey said looking at Laukhin. "It was only a short walk, and we still managed to quarrel. To think that I have to go back."

Lezzard made a valiant effort to get up, without success. "Order a cab for me, *chère* Audrey," he said, waving his hand at a phone beyond his reach.

Audrey ordered the cab, and she and Laukhin began to throw everything in garbage bags. Lezzard made no attempt to help. He held the emptied plastic glass in his hand, his eyes shut, a lonely, bitter old man peddling art to Philistines.

The cab arrived and Audrey helped Lezzard up from his chair, down the stairs, and out. "He's had a lot to drink," she said when she came back. They had filled two garbage bags and Laukhin took them outside and left them near the curb. A large paper plate of yellow cheese slices was almost untouched. She wrapped the cheese, placed it in a bag with a bottle of wine and gave it to Laukhin. "Your pay for the help. I hope you like cheese."

"I'll walk you to your place," he offered.

She locked the gallery. It had stopped raining, and the wet smell of the night engulfed them. A garbage truck came out of nowhere and halted noisily nearby. Silent and efficient men in neon-orange vests fed the compacting monster. It was as if an invading alien team was feeding itself with the city's detritus. One of the men had a short conversation on a two-way radio. He climbed into the truck, while the others jumped onto invisible running boards, and drove off. The mother ship had radioed that there was better nourishment on Bloor Street.

Carrying the bag of food nonchalantly over his shoulder, Laukhin felt like a seasoned traveller, unafraid of life's tough spots. When Audrey hesitated to go into her building, he heard himself say, "You don't want to disturb your mother, and you don't want another argument. That's how old people are—cranky and unpredictable. Best to avoid them. Wake her up now, and you'll get no sleep. Come to my place, Audrey. It's a fifteen-minute ride by cab. Come see the poet's home. We have wine and cheese. I'll sleep on the floor, of course."

"It's a thought."

He didn't expect her to agree, and her noncommittal answer confused him. It was only moments later, when she asked, softly, "Shouldn't we get going?" that he realized what was happening.

It was well past midnight. They hailed a cab and sat side by side during the ride without speaking, without touching. He was paralyzed by the fear of saying or doing something that would make her change her mind. He consoled himself with the thought that it was hard to be both in love and witty. All he could think of was that in half an hour they'd be naked and holding each other. That very day he had told Ben to slap himself together. An odd expression, he'd realized the moment it came out of his mouth, but that's exactly what he needed to do right now.

In the kitchen, Laukhin put his recompense in the fridge. He had enough cheese for the rest of his stay on earth.

"Jean Lezzard was in a foul mood tonight," he told Audrey. "I think he was ready to strangle the artist, or the husband. Especially the husband. The dog got on his nerves too. Why did he do it, if it distressed him so much?"

"Oh, it wasn't the show, or not only the show. Howard Lear is paying through his nose, believe me. No, it's something else that has been bugging him for a couple of days."

She told Laukhin that Lezzard had been in a foul mood since reading the interview with Laukhin in the *Globe*. He read it on Tuesday morning, just before she arrived at the gallery to help organize the new show. He'd mentioned it to her, cursing as he did, but she thought he'd just been venting his frustration about the upcoming vernissage. When he got up to welcome Marga Lear, who had dropped in to inspect the installation, Audrey picked up the newspaper from his desk and read the interview. She read it carefully, twice, because she knew from Laukhin that he was preparing the material on Tsvetayeva. He had included the right hooks to interest readers: "An early taste of Pavel Laukhin's memoirs for the readers... Famous and tragic Russian poet... Compelling recollections about Marina Tsvetayeva... The surprising and shocking end of her life, in Yelabuga, a small sleepy town on the Kama River..."

It was Yelabuga that stuck in her mind. Despite Laukhin's ominous words about the town in the interview, she thought the name enchanting, a reminder, although she didn't understand why, of bearded sorcerers, talking heads, and witches.

They were still in the kitchen, and Laukhin wasn't sure what to do next. He had the age and wisdom of trees, but felt clumsy and awkward. He opened the bottle of wine and took two glasses from the cupboard. He handed her the glasses and stared at her speechless, both because he couldn't keep his eyes off her, and because it is in moments of impasse that goddesses spring to help.

"Shouldn't we go upstairs?" Audrey said. "We can't spend the night in the kitchen."

They went upstairs, Laukhin carrying the bottle of wine.

She was surprised by the size of the bedroom. "I thought only Martha had such a large bedroom."

"It's where I work too," Laukhin said, pointing at his worktable. "The last owner was probably a playboy. He needed only a bedroom and bathroom. There used to be a mirror on the ceiling, according to Efim."

"Efim?"

"The current owner, an old friend. I rent the house from him. Rent is the wrong word, since I hardly pay any. "

He excused himself and went into the bathroom. Looking in the mirror, he realized he still had the bottle of wine with him. He picked up a towel from the floor and hung it on a hook. There was a strand of his hair in the sink, and he flushed it down. He should have a cleaning woman more often. He washed his hands and went back.

Audrey had put the glasses on the night table. He placed the bottle of wine on the floor nearby. She said, "I don't think we'll need it."

When he touched her—her shoulders, rather clumsily—she was shivering. "It's been a while, you know," she murmured.

"That's my line. Anyway, it's like bicycling. "

She chuckled. "Oh, I hope it isn't. Switch off the light, Art."

"I want to see you."

"You'll feel me."

He could barely breathe as he switched off the light. Her lips were soft and cool, and her tongue moved slowly, tantalizingly slowly. She stopped and whispered, "There is enough street light to see our way through."

She was quicker than him, because—and he sensed it more with his hands that with his eyes—she had dropped her skirt and squeezed out of her blouse while he only managed to kick off his shoes. He sat down on his bed and, without letting go of her, he bent and buried his face in her soft skin, whispering mute words of thanks. She must have freed her breasts because he felt them on his forehead, and he moved his face and, straightening up a bit, began to kiss them gently, and feel them and nuzzle them with his nose and his mouth and his lips and his tongue, one and then the other. He felt her hands caressing his head and neck. He must have forgotten himself, because he heard her say, softly, "Art?"

"Yes?"

"This is very nice, but there is more of me, you know."

"Sorry."

"And, Art?"

"Yes?"

"Is it hard for you to undress in the dark?"

"It's just..."

She bent towards him and whispered in his ear, "You need help?"

Wed, 12 October 1955

I'm up as usual before dawn and, as I do most days, writing in my note-book. I wonder again whether I'd have taken to keeping a journal if I were able to sleep in the early hours of the morning. I'm addicted now, like a smoker who lights a cigarette when his eyes first open on a new day.

We were up late last night again, talking and emptying the bottle of cognac Korotkov sent in the afternoon. Arkhip brought it to us, but by the way he looked at Boris Leonidovich, I wondered whether Korotkova and not the Captain had arranged its delivery. Neither of them was at din-ner last evening. We were told that Korotkova was not feeling well, while the Captain was detained by some minor emergency in the engine room, nothing we need worry about. (Can an emergency be minor?)

Toward midnight, while talking about Tsvetayeva's first days back in the country, and the shock Bolshevo must have been to her, Boris Leonidovich mentioned Efron.

I said, "Poor Sergey Efron. He returns to Russia, thinking his duty to the Motherland is done, and then, two years later, slam-bam, in the dungeon and gone."

Boris Leonidovich became agitated. "It's terrible, of course, the way he disappeared, and particularly terrible for his family, but he was not an innocent victim, unlike so many others. He became an agent for the NKVD while he was in the West, in Paris. It was Efron who recruited the Klepinins for the NKVD, and he probably recruited others. From the late twenties—for almost ten years, Pavel Nikolayevich—he was a secret agent, a *razvedchik*. Ten years of duplicity and betrayal! He was involved in the death of oppo-nents of the Soviet state living in the West. The French police were on his trail after the last operation he was involved in, the killing of the commu-nist defector Ignace Reiss in Switzerland. The NKVD smuggled Efron out of France and into the Soviet Union in October 1937, afraid the French police were getting close to him. They had no choice but to get Efron away. But they didn't want the West to learn of it, hence the hideaway at Bolshevo, and all the secrecy, and the new name they gave him."

He stared at me and, as I didn't say anything, he added, "To make matters worse for Tsvetayeva, their daughter, Alya, had already returned to the Soviet Union in the spring."

"Why did they do it, Boris Leonidovich? Why did they arrest him two years after he was taken back to Russia and then shoot him?"

"I don't know. Nobody knows and we'll probably never know. Those were insane, barbarous times. To ensure his silence? Was he seen as a liability and a potential embarrassment if his existence in Russia under another name was discovered? Probably, but will we ever know for sure?" He paused and then added, "Sometimes I think it was the punishment God prepared for him, for all he'd done. But it can't be, because his wife and his daughter were punished too."

He stood up and began to pace. He went on talking about Sergey Efron, hardly pausing for breath, and it was obvious that he had thought many times about what he was telling me. He didn't know, and likely would never know, whether Efron directly participated in actual killings, or just in their organization and logistics. It didn't matter, though. Efron had spied on his friends and betrayed them to the NKVD. He betrayed his former White Russian comrades, refugees like him, barely tolerated and barely surviving in foreign lands. Forgotten, wasting, useless people, hungry most of the time, who would write now and then an article in the émigré press, which nobody read, and in which the Soviet Union was taken to task. Wretched, uprooted souls who talked disapprovingly about the sorry fate of Russia in smoky cafés, drinking cheap wine and weak tea. He betrayed them, his friends, his comrades in exile and in penury. He, Boris Leonidovich, could understand changing one's mind and falling in love with the Communist regime. But he could not understand spying on and betraying your friends. He couldn't think of anything more despicable.

"But then our entire regime is based on this, Pavel Nikolayevich. It's a disease in our country, an epidemic, this ability of ours to betray our friends and neighbours." With a sneer he added, "Relatives too, even our immediate families. And Efron was a willing carrier of the disease."

I remembered Sasha Cornilov's words on the stairs of our building, while his huge body pinned me against the wall. I said, "Cornilov told me something like this at the time Tsvetayeva stayed in our apartment for a few days. I didn't believe him. I thought it was his way of getting at me, of showing me how stupid and naïve I was. He almost pushed me down the stairs, that's how mad he was about what I was making Varya do."

And, after a while, he whispered, "Alya worked for them too..."

"Alya Efron? She worked for the NKVD?"

"She did. I'm not sure what she did for them, probably not much, but she did."

"Good God. Did you learn this from her mother as well?"

"No. I don't think she ever knew or even suspected it. I know this from Alya herself. Today she speaks highly of her father and of his activities, in which she might have been involved. She didn't confess it openly, but I understood it from the stories she told after her return from camp and exile. She adored her father."

I opened the door to our small deck and stepped out in the cold air. There were a few pale lights to the west, slowly dimming. Boris Leonidovich followed me. He said Tsvetayeva had been the only innocent one in her family. She and her young son, of course. I said, "I'm sure it was a relief to the authorities that Tsvetayeva killed herself. One less person in the know about murders abroad on behalf of the Soviet regime."

It was getting late. I lit a cigarette. For some reason—related to the minor emergency?—the engines had stopped and we were drifting, slowly. The river was very wide in this spot. There were clouds above us because I could see only a few stars. We were like a ghost ship, a few lights gliding silently on the dark waters. A ship bearing the ghosts of Tsvetayeva, and Efron, and so many others.

It was cold and I thought of going back to our salon and then to my cabin. Reading my mind, Boris Leonidovich said, "Don't go in yet, please. Keep me company for a few more minutes. I wish I could smoke again. I wish I could cry too, but there are no more tears. And it's not just me. The whole country has no tears left. Monstrous mutations have happened to us, in a couple of generations. Plugged tear-ducts. The survival of the scoundrels. In our country, the scoundrels have become the fittest. Compassion has been selected out of our genes."

I didn't say anything for a long time. I had no answer. Then I muttered, "*We* survived, Boris Leonidovich. What does this say about us?"

He snorted. "Exactly."

I said, "Let's go in and try to get some sleep."

"She heard nothing from or about her husband. Not one letter, not one official word. He was shot at the end of '41, after her death. The first news from Alya arrived in the spring of '41. A letter from a camp in Komi. A year and a half without news from your child, a child taken away while you watched. When she killed herself, everybody who mattered to her, except for her son, was in prison—her daughter, her sister, her husband. What kind of country is this, Pavel Nikolayevich? What other countries do you know where things like this happen? No sister, no daughter, no husband— and no friends either, because they were all afraid to help her, frightened that they'd end up like her family. I was frightened."

II

When Laukhin woke up in the morning, Audrey, already dressed, was sitting at the table by the window reading the Tsvetayeva material he had been working on. He propped himself on his elbow and watched her for a while. She sensed he was awake because she lifted her hand and, without turning, wiggled her fingers—a silent greeting.

"How long have you been up?" he asked.

She half-turned to him. "Two hours or so. I couldn't sleep, my mind was racing. Too many things happened yesterday. I sat down at your desk, and here, in the poet's own chair, I had a moment of madness and thought of writing a poem. But then I saw this," she waved the papers she held in her hand, "and sanity returned."

"What do you think of it?"

"Heartbreaking. Such terrible times, yet I'm gripped, mesmerized. Poor woman."

"I mean, is it a good read? Would you buy Pavel Laukhin's journals after reading that much?"

"It's more than a good read—I can't put it down. This is my second time reading it. But I'm biased. I've heard a lot about Pavel Laukhin's journal and about Tsvetayeva the last three or four months. And I was reminded of Tsvetayeva only the other day by your interview in the *Globe and Mail*."

"So it worked. I was pushed into doing the interview by my agent, and you're the proof it worked."

"Are these the soon-to-be-famous Tsvetayeva excerpts?

"Yes. There's more work to be done, but it's all there, in the green folder. I'm revising the last part, the trip to Yelabuga. That's what I'll be doing this weekend, chained to my desk. Monday morning I'll do a final review of the entire bundle, and have a secretary type it. It's got to go out by Monday evening. Buy the first October issue of the *New Yorker*, Audrey. It will all be in there."

She went back to reading the excerpts. He looked at his watch—a few minutes past seven. He was disappointed he hadn't woken up with her, naked beside him in his bed. He'd have liked to watch her sleep. He asked her why she was already dressed, but she didn't hear him, and she seemed startled when he repeated his question in a louder voice. She told him she had to leave soon—to get back to the gallery and let the cleaning crew in—and wondered whether he could make her a cup of tea. Of course, tea—one thing that the English and the Russians had in common.

He got dressed and shuffled to the bathroom. Downstairs in the kitchen, he rummaged through a cupboard, finding Japanese green tea, celestial offerings from Bengal, a tisane (some French herb), exquisite dark Darjeeling, a tea with a smoky whiff and unpronounce-able Chinese name, a box of tea bags—all Ewa's purchases.

When he returned, Audrey was still there, at the table, holding the green folder on her lap, and looking out the window. He listed for her all the choices she had.

She nodded, absently, "Black tea, please. With milk."

"So English."

He boiled water and made the tea. He went back up, removed the green folder from Audrey's lap, gently helped her up, and steered her, as if she were blind, out of the room.

In the kitchen, sitting down at the small table, Audrey smiled and said, "I'm at my worst in the morning."

"Have you slept at all?"

"A couple of hours. I watched you for a while, but then you turned the other way."

Her hair was tussled in places, although attempts had been made towards a perfunctory order. There were minor traces of last night's makeup on her face.

"I saw that older Russian man again, Mr. Gratch," she said. "He was walking back and forth in front of the gallery Wednesday afternoon."

"Did he go in? Did he have another fight with Lezzard?"

"I don't know. I was sent on an errand by Lezzard, and he was there, pacing, as if he was waiting for somebody. He didn't recognize me, or didn't see me. He wasn't there when I got back an hour later. Maybe he did go in while I was away, but Lezzard didn't seem disturbed when I came back."

"Well, the painting which troubled him is not there anymore."

"I took pictures, you know."

"You did what?"

"The day the two Russians came in July, I closed the gallery, went out and bought a Polaroid camera, went back and took pictures of the large Chemakoff oil. Of the room too—I took pictures of the room with the painting in it."

"What on earth possessed you to do that? What did you have in mind?"

"I don't know ... I thought it might come in handy."

"Handy for what?"

"No idea. Maybe we should tell the police that Lezzard is trafficking in confiscated art."

"You didn't tell me you took pictures."

"I didn't want you to laugh at me."

"I don't think it's a good idea to tell the police."

"Ah, the Russians' fear of the police."

"Yes, it's that, but it's more than that. Say we tell the police, and they grab Lezzard. I doubt they'll be able to prove anything, even with your photographs, but assume they do. The gallery closes as a result and Josiane loses her job. And other artists have one less gallery to sell their work. Besides, whoever is behind this in the Soviet Union will find another Lezzard. Toronto is only a minor outlet among many. I have another argument, Audrey. Is it better that Chemakoff's paintings—and others' too, I'm sure there are others—is it better that they remain hidden in some vault in the Lubyanka or God knows where else? Isn't it better that they are getting to the West and being shown?

True, it enriches Lezzard and scoundrels like him in the Soviet Union, but it's still better than the alternative."

"I'm certain there's a flaw in your reasoning, a moral one at the very least, but it's too early in the morning to argue. What am I drinking here?"

In spite of her lack of sleep, her face was flushed.

"Something called Red Rose," he said. "Your face is rosy—lovely and rosy. I can't fathom this investigation of yours."

"I'm almost sorry it's my last day with Lezzard. He's beginning to obsess me. I had this strange dream about him last night. I think I was still a student, because I was worried about an exam, but somehow I knew everything about the Kerguelen-Lezzard Gallery, and about Jean Lezzard and his dispute with Dorbao. In the dream, I went to the gallery. Nicholas was with me."

"Your husband? After spending the night with me you dream about your husband?"

She smiled and touched his hand. "I didn't dream about him, he was in the dream. Anyway, in the dream Lezzard was being slowly killed by a painting sent to him by Dorbao."

"A painting that kills?"

"Yes."

"Very medieval. How did you know it was the painting that was killing him?"

"You just know these things in dreams."

Laukhin took their mugs to the sink and washed them. "I'm full of admiration," he said. "Most of my dreams are much simpler. Trees fall on me, I try to get away, my feet won't move, I wake up. I'm doing better lately, though. I've had this recurring dream in the last couple of months. I have a speeding ticket, I tell the judge I have no car, the judge tells me I can't publish my father's journal. I tell him I am there, in front of him, for an absurd traffic ticket, he laughs, tells me I'm a fool, and orders me to jail. That's the most complicated dream I ever had, and it's always the same, and over very quickly."

He was drying the cups with a tea towel—another gift from Ewa—when he sensed her behind him. She hugged him, and he felt her breasts on his back, the hard nipples, and the warmth of her abdomen and thighs. "You're very sweet, Art Laukhin. Men who do the dishes turn me on."

He gripped her wrists and tightened her hold of him. They remained together for a while, and he thought himself the luckiest man in the world.

"Let's go back up," he said, without daring to move.

"No, I must go home and change before I run to the gallery. Brush my teeth, have a shower. Martha's going to give me one long look."

"I don't understand any of this," he said softly. "I don't dare hope this will last, Audrey. Are you ... are still going back to London?"

Still hugging him, she said she had postponed buying a ticket because she didn't know what to do about him. She had thoughts of returning to London to see how she felt about him from afar, whether he faded away or not. For a long time she had hoped to avoid a romantic entanglement with him, and yet little by little she had become very fond of him. It was like a drug that worked slowly, but the cumulative effect was an attraction harder and harder to deny. It may have partly been the healing flow of time, but she knew that his insistent presence in her life was another reason she could now think about Nicholas without feeling wretched.

"I kept telling myself that the timing was awkward, that my father needed me, that I couldn't possibly live in Toronto. I just didn't see myself doing it, and I wasn't going to suggest you move to London. It would have implied a commitment on my part that I wasn't ready for."

He sensed her smile behind him as she went on. "I had some rather shameless thoughts, though. I wondered what it would be like to ... take a tumble together, you and I. The roses you sent me had a definite effect, helped focus my thinking. I told myself that, well, if you showed up on Thursday evening at the vernissage, and if I still felt warm toward you—the hormonal itch, as Martha calls it—then, why not, after all."

"I had no idea you were thinking this way. I was in despair."

"I'm a guarded person when it comes to love. I do not easily share beds with men—not often, or lightly. And yet I wanted to sleep with you before returning to England. I wanted to do it because of the physical attraction, of course, but also because some voice told me that, sometime in the future, I might not mind spending a week or two back in Toronto. And the same voice asked why not have a dress rehearsal before my leaving for London? An undress rehearsal? I thought it would help me later on, while deciding about my future."

Audrey let go of him and picked up her purse.

"When will I see you again?" he asked, turning.

"I'll call you. Sunday evening?"

"Why not tonight?"

"Shouldn't you work? Anyway, tonight I'm dining with Martha. She insisted."

"Tomorrow, then."

"I'll call you on Sunday. Sunday evening, provided you've done all you have to do."

"Why not tomorrow? Just come around, Audrey, however late. Undress and slide into bed, and slowly wake me up."

"You'll be tired and unable to work the next day."

"We'll just cuddle, then."

"Cuddle?" She kissed him. "I'll call you on Sunday."

She walked out quickly, and he followed her to the door. Afterward he thought about going back to bed. The smell of her might still be there.

* * *

"What on earth are you doing here? Shouldn't you be chained to your worktable?"

She looked lovely, tall, slender, in a white cotton blouse with a long, ruffled V-neck and a faint empire waist. Capri pants, and espadrille wedges with leg straps that made her as tall as he.

"I had to see you again, if only for a few minutes. Sunday seemed so far away."

He hugged her and buried his face in the pit of her neck. "It's your scent that does it—the same you, yet subtly different every time. It's witchcraft, Audrey. You are a tall witch."

"You're tickling me—stop talking nonsense."

She sought his mouth, and pressed her groin against his. "You fool," she whispered on his lips, "it's *Dawn Mitsuko*."

"Ah, Japanese witchcraft."

She pushed him away and looked around. "Well, if nuzzling is called for, let's go inside, away from the curious. Maybe the cleaners will be late."

They climbed up the steps clumsily entangled. To Audrey's surprise the door was unlocked. Inside, they found Lezzard, at his desk, reading a newspaper clipping, and looking pasty and shrunk. He threw a jaundiced eye at them. He must have been surprised to see him there, so early, with Audrey.

"Couldn't sleep last night," Lezzard said. "I thought I might as well come in."

Audrey said, "You could have let me know."

Lezzard growled and stared at Laukhin. "Why are *you* here, at this time?"

"Oh, just a short visit. A word with Audrey, rather urgent."

The art dealer fluttered the newspaper clipping at him and Laukhin realized it was his interview in the *Globe*. Lezzard's eyes were blood-shot. "I thought you were a busy man."

"I am."

"Can I have the second half of the first volume? Have you finished correcting the proofs?"

"Not yet. I've had other things to do. "

Lezzard held his head with both hands, remaining motionless and, it seemed, breathless, for several seconds. "Three Tylenols," he said. "Three!"

"You should go home and rest, Jean," Audrey said. "You don't look well."

Lifting his head slowly, Lezzard said, "Never mind how I look." He waved the newspaper cutting again. "Why don't you stick to it? If you're so busy, why waste time on crap like this?"

He wasn't sure what Lezzard was on about and resented his being at the gallery. It felt invasive. This was his morning after with Audrey.

"What crap?" he asked.

"This woman poet—Tsvetayeva, or whatever her name is. What makes you think the readers of the *Globe*, or that fancy magazine in New York, would be interested in this old stuff?"

"It's not that old—less than fifty years."

"It's fascinating, Jean," Audrey said.

"Fascinating," Lezzard repeated. "Listen to her, fascinating."

Laukhin was in too good a mood to do it, but the thought of punching Lezzard crossed his mind.

Probably sensing trouble ahead, Audrey said, "It is. I read it this morning and I couldn't put it down. Horrible, of course—what happened to Tsvetayeva."

A middle-aged woman in faded blue overalls poked her head in the door.

"I'll do the large room first, then," she said.

Audrey said, "Yes, please start there, very good."

Lezzard was looking puzzled at Audrey, then at Laukhin, then back to Audrey. "You read ... What did you read this morning?"

"The whole thing, all the Tsvetayeva excerpts from Pavel Laukhin's journals. The excerpts to be published next month, you know, ahead of the first volume."

"Where did you read them?"

Audrey hesitated a moment then braved Lezzard's glare with a casual, unflustered, "Art has them at his home."

"Does he now," Lezzard said.

She blushed and was quick to add, "Art is under the gun to finish the story about Tsvetayeva this weekend, and took everything home with him to have a last go through. Another day to type it into the computer on Monday, and then off to the *New Yorker*. And the *Globe*. It's all there, mostly handwritten pages, but quite legible."

"Ah, he let you read it. He doesn't usually do this, you know, let other people read his work before it's published. I've tried many times. But I assume you were nice to him. Probably very nice."

Laukhin heard voices in the next room and then the loud drone of a vacuum cleaner. He bent over Lezzard's desk and, his face close to the old man's, whispered, "Why don't you mind your own fucking business, Jean."

Judging by the noise, the vacuum cleaner was coming their way.

Lezzard nodded pensively and got up, a move that, although slow, made him grimace. "I need to disappear for a couple of hours, Audrey," he said. "You'll be here for a while, won't you? Josiane said she'd drop by too, but don't leave before I get back." He walked out, treading gingerly.

"A horrible man," Laukhin said looking after Lezzard. "To think I used to get drunk with him."

"Oh, he's not that bad. He has a venomous tongue. Art, you should get back to your bundle."

She came close to him, another kiss, and morning Mitsuko threw one more loop around his ankles.

"I'm shackled, I can't move."

"Bye, darling."

"Only English women say that properly—darling. I love the word. It's better than a hundred 'I-love-yous.' You'll call, won't you?"

"Yes."

"Darling."

"I'll call you, darling."

He floated to Alumni Hall to see Bill MacNaughton. They went to the Bloor Street Diner. Laukhin liked Bill, but he fidgeted throughout the meal, impatient to get back to his work. Impatient too to be alone and think about Audrey. He walked Bill back to St. Joseph Street. As they parted, Bill said, "You're impossibly agreeable this morning. What's wrong with you? Or is it what's right?" Laukhin laughed and said, "I followed your advice—I'm being more sensible." Before he went home he dropped by his office and picked up Ben's draft translations of the last two excerpts.

He spent the rest of the day going over them. Ben's first drafts were very good.

* * *

On Saturday Laukhin worked on Brodelshchikova's story, touching it up here and there. It was the most important excerpt of the entire bundle, and he went over it several times to make sure the old woman's story was in the best possible shape. He felt confident and buoyant, and he worked fast and well. On Sunday he'd work on whatever he had skipped earlier. He was certain there was enough material to put together something coherent and compelling by Monday.

Audrey phoned around seven, just as he was eating a sandwich in the kitchen. "Art," Audrey said, almost whispering, "this is a bit on short notice, and, yes, I told you I'd ring on Sunday, but could I sleep at your place again tonight? I know you're busy, but you still have to sleep."

"Why, yes, of course."

"I promise I'll leave early in the morning."

"I could come to your place."

"No, no, it's better I come there. That way, you'll be ready to sit down and work right away in the morning."

"Is your mother still there?"

"Yes. She has an early flight tomorrow morning. She said she'd leave today, but changed her mind."

"Are you all right? You sound, I don't know, tense, stressed."

She inhaled deeply and sighed. "She has that effect on me." She added that she'd bring something to eat and be at his place in less than an hour.

He rushed to have a shower and a shave.

Audrey arrived with a bottle of white wine and sushi. She said she had not known what to do with herself on Saturday afternoon, and she rued her promise to ring him only on Sunday night because he had so much work to do. Her mother had gone out, but had said she'd be back in the evening, and she feared more difficult hours and words with Martha. The dinner with her on Friday had not been easy. She made the mistake of telling her she'd hang around for a while longer. Martha didn't understand Audrey's decision to delay her return to London, and, when she learned Laukhin caused it, called him too old for her. "She called you scruffy looking too," Audrey went on. "I told her I liked your looks. The rest of the evening was rather awkward, and I had a lot of wine. To avoid Martha, who's catching an early morning flight to Montreal, I thought of spending the night in a hotel. But then I convinced myself to end this headmistress act of mine—after all, you have to sleep tonight anyway, and you might as well sleep with me."

"You've made the happiest man in the world happier," Laukhin said. "I'm beginning to like your mother."

The wine was fine, some miracle from Burgundy, and he was the only one drinking it. He ate most of the sushi too, as Audrey barely touched it. She seemed stressed or with something else in her mind, the way she'd sounded earlier on the phone.

"You're still thinking of Martha," he said.

She shook her head and sighed. "Did you see the paper today?" she asked.

"No. I don't often read newspapers, and this weekend..."

"Mr. Gratch is dead."

"The elderly Russian? I know one person who won't mourn him—Lezzard."

"He may have had something to do with it, Art. Gratch was killed."

"What?"

She went to her purse and returned with a newspaper clipping. "I was watching television this afternoon, just to avoid thinking of Martha. It was a news item, a murder in an apartment building in the north of the city. I paid little attention, and I didn't catch the victim's name, or only a bit of it that sounded like Gratch, but I couldn't be sure. And then they said it was a building with many former Russians. So I watched the next news, and I heard the name, Yakov Gratch. I run out and bought all the newspapers. The *Toronto Star* had the longest write-up. I think it's our Gratch, Art." She handed him the clipping.

It was a fairly long article. Yakov Gratch, sixty-seven years old, was the twenty-first homicide in Toronto that year. He was found dead by his niece, a school teacher who had lunch with her uncle every Friday. He never missed a lunch. He waited for her outside his apartment building, and she picked him up and drove to some neighbourhood restaurant, lately south on Bathurst, to Moe Pancer's Deli, which he'd taken a liking for, although the food there was not particularly Russian. But this Friday her uncle wasn't there waiting for her. She parked the car and went up to his apartment. She rang and knocked—no answer. She became worried that something had happened to him, as he wasn't in the greatest of health. She was about to go and look for the janitor when, without thinking, she tried the door handle and the door, unlocked, opened. She walked in and found her uncle dead. She could barely walk out, so shaken was she by what she saw.

Ilya Talashkin, a floor-neighbour, described Yakov Gratch as a somewhat bitter man, often impatient with people. Talashkin had been away much of Thursday—babysitting his grandchildren—but on Friday it was his door that a shocked Mrs. Trauberg had banged on. He called the police and then went into Gratch's apartment. Gratch was tied up on a stool, likely with a bullet in the back of his head or neck, but Talashkin didn't look too closely. Gratch's head was slumped over onto his chest. His face seemed to have been worked over with a knife. Maybe it was an impression, because of the blood from the bullet-exit wound. There was a lot of blood. Clothes and drawers were thrown on the floor in Gratch's bedroom, as if a search for something had taken place.

According to Talashkin, Yakov Gratch arrived in Toronto in the mid seventies. He'd been wounded and decorated in the Second World War. He was an engineer by training, but at his age found no job in his profession in Canada. He worked as a draftsman for a while, was laid off, held a succession of poorly paid jobs. He wasn't doing great lately, his main income being the Old Age Security, and that wasn't much. He had been trying to get into one of the much cheaper assisted housing apartments.

Detective Sergeant Dempsey said Gratch died sometime on Thursday, and that it was murder, no doubt about it. The neighbours had not heard or seen anything suspicious, although the police were still talking to them. Dempsey surmised that a silencer had been used in the execution. That was all he was prepared to say for now.

The last paragraph was more specific. "As we were ready for print, we heard from a source that the police found a small package of crack cocaine in Mr. Gratch's apartment. We called the police, but they had no further comment to make, refusing to either conform or deny it, although Detective Sergeant Dempsey agreed that crack-cocaine was becoming a problem in the city. We phoned Mr. Talashkin too, and asked him whether Mr. Gratch might have dealt in drugs. Mr. Talashkin had a good laugh."

"We should go to the police, Art," Audrey said.

He had another sip of wine before he answered. "We should. We will, but not now."

"When, then?"

"Let me finish this, Audrey, get the first volume off my hands, and then we'll do it. I promise. A few more weeks, at most a month."

"It may be too late."

"It's not as if Lezzard is closing shop, is it? Besides, we don't really know, do we, that Gratch's death is connected with him. They found crack cocaine in Gratch's apartment, after all."

"Mr. Gratch didn't look like a drug dealer to me. He seemed more like a desperate blackmailer. He discovers what he believes to be— and we do too—trafficking in confiscated Soviet art. An old man, with hardly any income, he's not doing well. He thinks of a way out."

Laukhin shrugged.

"I called the Jehovah's Witnesses, Art. There is a Russian branch here, in Toronto, and I phoned them. I said someone approached me for a charitable donation, and I wanted to make sure I wasn't swindled. They don't have a Mr. Gratch. Never had a Gratch among their members."

* * *

Later that night, holding Audrey in his arms, he felt her shiver. "Are you cold?"

"No. Yes. Maybe I'm coming down with something. I'm not feeling that well, Art. Let's sleep. I'm tired."

"Move in with me, Audrey."

She sighed. "Let's not talk about it now—let's try to sleep." After a while she added, "I can't think about such things at night. You smell nice, darling. Very nice, in fact, for an old Russian."

"Marry me, Audrey."

"What? Why?"

"I smell nice."

"That's all?"

"I'll write long poems about you."

"Long poems I won't understand."

"I'll translate them."

"Does it ever work?"

"You'll become immortal."

Her fingers slid lightly down his cheek, and then onto his lips. "You've had too much wine."

"I haven't."

"Let's sleep. I'm getting up early tomorrow."

"Again? Why?"

"I must let you work, remember. Martha will be gone by then. Promise me you won't get up with me."

"Not get up with you? That's the best part—well, not the very best, but right up there..."

"It becomes, you know, a dragged-on thing. I'm often sappy in the morning. You have a lot of work, Art, and you've already lost several hours tonight."

"When will I see you again? Tomorrow night?"

"If you're done, only if you're done. I'll call you. Let's sleep."

She turned her back to him and fitted her buttocks against his crotch, her long legs zigzagged against his. Her neck smelled faintly of perfume and salt. He told himself to stay awake through the night. He had a premonition that he wouldn't share a bed with Audrey that often and he wanted to savour every second of it. He remained awake for a long time, but it was a losing fight.

Thursday, 13 October, 1955

We berthed in Yelabuga this morning. Korotkova was keen to join us. Boris Leonidovich was hesitant about it at first, because he had already sent word that he'd arrive with only one other person. Two might be a problem, but in the end he agreed. Korotkova had been a great help to us. She'd been a good companion too, intelligent, generous, practical. How wrong first impressions can be. She'd wait in Yelabuga for two days for the boat's return trip. Boris Leonidovich and I would take the train back to Moscow a day earlier, although, after his first glimpse of the town today, he muttered that we may want to stay another night before boarding the train. "We shouldn't leave Marietta Alexeyevna by herself in this desolate place."

Can I insist we leave as planned? Can I deny him a night in Marietta's arms? Am I a bit jealous?

We were met at the pier by a teacher named Rozhanov. Mid forties, wearing a brown suit and a blue shirt without a tie. He was driving an old GAZ that might have seen the war—school property, he said—and it took a while to fit everybody and the luggage in. Luckily, Korotkova brought very little with her. Rozhanov drove us to the hotel—old and dusty—on the main street. Karl Marx Street. We dropped our luggage, and then Rozhanov took us to the Brodelshchikovs' house, on Voroshilov Street. Everyone seemed preoccupied, and we drove in silence. The streets were empty. The GAZ emitted noxious fumes and made ominous sounds at each gear shift.

The Brodelshchikovs live in a small log house, the kind of house a child would draw, a flat rectangle with a gable roof and three windows. The courtyard is fairly large. An apple tree with sparse yellow leaves. Chickens. A black pig, leashed like a dog, watches our small cortege.

The door opens directly into the main room—living room, dining room, kitchen, all in one space. An impressively large stove. A pine table, relatively new, with four chairs that don't match. A small samovar and glasses on the table. A wooden bench near the door. A radio on a stool in a corner, a decrepit armchair in another. Our hostess, Anastasia Ivanovna Brodelshchikova, is a tiny woman, withered by age and life. Backswept hair and round wire-frame glasses. Squinting eyes. Thin lips. A blouse that may have once belonged to a much larger woman. A long skirt with large front buttons. Thick brown socks. She moves with some difficulty. Her lean husband towers over her.

It seemed that Rozhanov had already explained to the Brodelshchikovs who we were. After exchanging a few words with them he disappeared, because he had classes to teach. He was courteous and efficient, but edgy and not overly pleased to see us. Rozhanov was reserved for a lover of literature and an admirer of Pasternak's poetry, which Boris Leonidovich told me he was when I asked. Where did he find this willing and discreet guide to open the Brodelshchikovs' door for us?

We sat at the table. Brodelshchikova talked about Tsvetayeva without being prodded, as if she had said it all before, several times. She, Tsvetayeva, never did anything but smoke and shout at her son. They often fought in some language of their own, a foreigner's language. She never swept her room, never cooked. She had a few provisions—some dried beans and somebody sent her a small bag of flour. She rarely talked to her or to her husband. Anybody else would have sat down, had tea, something to eat, would have talked - if only to make time pass faster. But no, not the White émigré woman, not her. It was hard, unpleasant for the Brodelshchikovs. Tsvetayeva was worried, constantly worried. Frightened. But she wouldn't sit down to have a drink or two and forget her troubles for a few hours. She never drank, never laughed. A few laughs would have chased away many griefs, but she never even smiled. Brodelshchikova paused for a while watching us, and her husband said something, and, nodding, she went on. Her husband had caught a huge fish, a pike. They couldn't finish it themselves, it was too big. Brodelshchikova cooked it and invited the newcomers to share it. It was a long evening. Brodelshchikova did all the talking, so much that her mouth hurt. Her husband never talked much unless he had had several drinks, and then he'd rather sing. But she, the White émigré woman, barely said anything all evening. She thanked them, and then she said that she was very tired. The boy talked more than his mother did.

Brodelshchikova's voice was neutral, disinterested. Clearly, she was repeating a story she told many times.

"No, it wasn't good for us," she went on. "The rent, well, let's not talk about it, and, on top of it, they didn't have ration cards. I don't know why. Frankly, we didn't want them here, with us. I felt sorry for her afterward—not before, mind you, but afterward. Of course I did, who wouldn't?"

There was nothing surprising in what she said. Even the fact that she referred to Tsvetayeva a couple of times as "the White émigré woman" didn't surprise me. The power of official labels. For Tsvetayeva, they must have been just one more couple that didn't want anything to do with her. She must have been used to it by the time she got to Yelabuga.

"I didn't want to see you," Brodelshchikova said looking at Boris Leonidovich. These words came unexpectedly, and we, the visistors, looked startled at each other. She went on. "What for? What's in it for us? There have been a few others like you who have come here asking about her, and it's been hard to get rid of them."

"We are grateful," Boris Leonidovich said.

"It's my husband. He wants me to tell you ..."

We looked at him. Tall and bent, thinning white hair and moustache. A rumpled collared shirt under a rumpled suit. He'd put his suit on for this visit, a suit that had not been pressed in a while.

"Yes, he's pushing me to tell you what happened. He's a fool, an old fool. I keep telling him I couldn't see anything, but he won't let the matter go. I keep telling him it would be only trouble for us. He says we're not getting younger and we'll soon die. Ah, men are stubborn. He says we know who you are. He says it's now or never, that I must talk now."

I looked, puzzled, at Boris Leonidovich, and he at me.

Pointing a finger at Boris Leonidovich, Brodelshchikova went on. "Rozhanov told us you are a poet, like her. He said you are a good man, Tsvetayeva's best friend. Were you her best friend?"

"I was a friend of hers, of course," Boris Leonidovich said.

"I'm going to tell you something, something I haven't told anybody."

Both Boris Leonidovich and I nodded encouragingly, but she had eyes only for him.

The husband suddenly spoke. "The teacher," and he pointed to the door through which Rozhanov left, "also said that her daughter is alive and that you are in touch with her." He asked, without looking at Korotkova, "Who's she? Is she the daughter?"

Boris Leonidovich introduced Korotkova. Reintroduced her, because he had already mentioned her name to them. "A friend. A friend of ours, a friend of poetry as well. And an admirer of Tsvetayeva." He looked embarrassed at me, sheepish, and shrugged and rolled his eyes, as if to say, "I know it's pompous, but I don't know how else to describe her."

Brodelshchikova was not happy. "I thought there would be just two of you. Rozhanov said that there would be two of you, two men, older men."

I laughed, trying to lighten the mood, "Well now, easy with 'old,' please. Not that old. Mature, ripe, full-grown, yes."

The couple looked at each other, and he shook his head.

"We don't want her here," Brodelschikova said curtly.

Boris Leonidovich was surprised and tried to rise to her defence, saying, "Look, we may want to—"

Korotkova smiled and said, "I'll go for a walk in the town. Will an hour be enough? I don't mind, Boris Leonidovich, I really don't mind. I understand."

She walked out, and I was grateful to Korotkova for quickly settling the matter.

Brodelshchikova was still unhappy. "I don't know if I remember. I don't know what's in it for us. My husband, he's just pushing me. It's been fourteen years already. And things like this, one is better off forgetting. But he won't let me. What does he know? He didn't go through it—*I* did. It's hell to go through it again. He's not allowing me to forget. And we, I don't know what's in it for us. What do we get in return? Only trouble, for sure. I really don't know."

I had a sudden idea. "Where is she buried?"

She hesitated, uncertain. "The poetess?"

"Yes."

"In the town graveyard."

The husband said, "An unmarked grave."

I took all the money I had in my pocket, and I carried a fair amount, for emergencies and Boris Leonidovich's whims, and placed the treasure on the table. "We'd like to put a sign there, a stone or a cross, a monument of some sort, something to remind people of her."

Boris Leonidovich seemed about to say something, but no words came out.

The husband said, "We don't know where she was buried. I told you, it's an unmarked grave."

Brodelshchikova jumped in, "Oh, we'll find out. I think I remember where. And I know other people who do too."

I said, quickly, "Since we're so far away, we'll leave the money with you. We trust you'll make sure it's done. We'll send more money later, of course."

In the silence that followed Boris Leonidovich said, "We've brought you something, Anastasia Ivanovna. Small tokens, for putting up with us."

I took out, from a small bag I brought along from the hotel, a box of fine chocolates, a bottle of expensive Georgian brandy, a collection of Boris Leonidovich's poetry inscribed by the author "To the last friends of Marina Ivanovna Tsvetayeva," and a copy of my *Undertakers' Feast*, which I had signed.

Brodelshchikova pushed the money aside to make space for our offerings then poured us some tea. It was weak and had the faint scent of apples. She sipped from her glass and looked at her husband who prompted her with a gesture, and she began her story.

"That Sunday everybody went out of the town. Volunteer work. They were building a road for airplanes, you know what I mean, and we were all told to go out there and help. I went with Georgy, her son. Everybody who turned up would be given a loaf of bread. My husband, well, my husband had gone fishing early in the morning, so I went for both of us. She, Tsvetayeva, was the only one left at home. It was a scorching day and it was hard work. I'm not a big or a strong woman, as you can see, and I began to feel faint. So I left after a couple of hours."

Brodelshchikova spoke softly, and it was not easy to follow her. She didn't tell anybody she was leaving, she just took off, thinking she'd return later, because she still wanted her loaf of bread. She walked home slowly, feeling rotten, and entered the yard from the back lane. Hot and exhausted, she had only one thought in her mind: to get to the cellar and sleep. She sometimes slept there in the summer, when the heat became unbearable. Her husband had built a pine shelf in the cellar, to the left of the ladder. The shelf was small, a few planks, too narrow and short for her husband, but fine for her, and all she could think of as she walked home was lying down on the old coat she kept there and catching her breath. She had slept there the previous day too, on Saturday at noon, because it had been a sweltering day and she could hardly breathe.

She looked at her husband, who nodded encouragingly at her. He had a kind wrinkled face. Although he remained quiet, he seemed to have some control over her.

There was a door to the cellar from the yard. In the summer, you couldn't see it because of a nearby bush planted by her husband years ago. She didn't know what got into him, for where could one run, if that was what made him do it? She went down into the cellar and lay down and slowly recovered some strength. Now and then she could hear Tsvetayeva moving above her, faintly most of the time, but louder if she stepped near the trapdoor even though the only rug in the house was over it.

She didn't know at first who they were and what they were after. Quite confused, she didn't even know where she was. She must have fallen asleep in the cool cellar, and their voices and heavy steps above her head woke her up. At first she thought they were trying to have their way with her, with Tsvetayeva. Fools, she thought. Skinny as a branch, lifeless, ashen-faced, and not young anymore. Tsvetayeva was protesting, no, no, no. Don't force me, please don't do it—or don't make me do it. She couldn't hear that well, and that's why she thought they were going to rape her. But then she understood that was not what was happening above her.

Brodelshchikova halted her story and drank some tea. It took a while, because she was swallowing with difficulty. Her face was white.

She realized that they were the secret police—not immediately, but after some time—from the way there were talking to Tsvetayeva, threatening, yelling, but also laughing. Sure of themselves, not in a hurry. There were three of them, two of them older, in their fifties, one quite young. She saw them later, that's how she knew what they looked like. The oldest one, who seemed to be in charge, had a thick voice and might have been the only one who felt sorry for Tsvetayeva. He spoke to her for a long time. He said it would be better for everybody, and especially for her children. He said they had talked to her son, who'd told him he thought he'd be better off if she were somewhere else and he could live as he wanted to live. He felt chained to her, condemned to be forever associated with her and her name. She should think about her daughter as well, not just her son. Her daughter's sentence would be lighter if she disappeared. Because, in due time, they'd arrest her and interrogate her, and she'd end up incriminating her daughter. She, Tsvetayeva must have said something, because he said to her, "Believe me, you would. Your husband did." He said something else about her husband, but she, Brodelshchikova, couldn't hear or couldn't remember what he said.

I was having a rough time, listening to Brodelshchikova's story. Boris Leonidovich's was biting his lower lip, his head lowered. He was holding his right hand over his chest, in a protective or comforting way.

Tsvetayeva said something that Brodelschikova again couldn't hear. The oldest man, the one in charge, went on, impatiently, with an edge in his voice. He repeated that she, Tsvetayeva, would end up telling them all they wanted to know about her daughter. Nobody held out, nobody. He told her it was a simple choice: do this for her children or be arrested and endure the worst things she could imagine, and end up the same way, dead. The only difference was that her death would be long and painful, and her children would be much worse off. If she let them help her ...

"Help her ..." Boris Leonidovich whispered.

That's what they kept telling her, or something like that. Brodelshchikova, scared as she was, couldn't understand everything even when she heard the words. Tsvetayeva's voice had been soft throughout, but then she screamed, not loudly, but a scream all the same, like a wounded animal without strength. The other two said things too, but Brodelshchikova couldn't make out what they were saying. Maybe they were farther from the trapdoor.

"I didn't see them, then. How could I? But I saw them later, and I knew who they were from their voices. I'll never forget those voices. Perhaps they've stayed with me because I couldn't see them while I was in the cellar. Like a blind man with sharp hearing, I don't know. They didn't leave the town afterward; they stayed around to make sure that their traces were covered, and that it was all written down as suicide. I don't know why they bothered. Yes, they were there later, around the house and in the house, talking and mingling with the local police."

She took a noisy slurp of tea, tears in her eyes. She stood up, walked over to the stove, and brought back a small paper bag from which she took out a few yellow cookies and laid them on a plate. They were hard but I ate one, softened with tea.

The other older man - she thought at first he was young because of his voice, a rather high voice for such a big man, and his laughter was foul and grating - had white hair, and was very big, huge, with huge hands too, and thick, greasy lips. He looked as if he had just got up from feasting on a fat goose and forgot to wipe his mouth. He was always laughing, and she never knew why. She didn't think he was all there, something wrong with his head. And the way they talked to him, the other two, and ordered him around, he didn't seem to understand much about what was going on. When she saw them later, in the yard, he was waiting there for the other two, and was talking to himself, laughing, jerking his head up and letting it slowly back down.

The younger one, also big and tall, had a long scar on the left side of his face. He'd smile at you suddenly and for no reason, and you didn't know whether to return the smile or to ignore it and run away. Tsvetayeva knew him—from the past. She had met him before.

I asked, "She knew him? Are you sure?"

Brodelshchikova nodded. Yes, Tsvetayeva knew him. She asked him—she begged him, "I've met you before, in Moscow, haven't I? Yes, it was soon after my husband was taken away, and I went to Moscow. You write poetry too, like me, yes, somebody told me that. What's your name? Help me please. Help me. I'm not ready, not yet, I need a few more days. I need to make sure that my son is looked after. And ... It's not much of a life, granted, and I've thought often of ending it all, but ... It's so sudden. I'm not ready. Give me a few more days and I'll do it, yes, I will. Please, give me a few more days."

It was then that the older one—the one in command—asked, "Do you know her?" The one with the scar must have nodded, because the old one said, "Well, I'll be damned. That's why you were sent here. Couldn't figure it out."

I glanced at Boris Leonidovich, who looked back at me with raised eyebrows.

She, Brodelshchikova, thought of leaving her hiding place, of sneaking out noiselessly, but she was paralyzed with fear. She had no strength at all, and didn't know whether there were other agents or policemen in the yard.

Tsvetayeva kept pleading with them, but in a voice that grew weak and uncertain, almost as if she was agreeing to what they said, as if she saw the logic of it. She asked again, but without conviction, for a few more days, so she could go to Chistopol and talk to a few people—she mentioned some names, three or four names. She said, "I must make sure they're looking after my son. I don't want him to end up in an orphanage. I had a daughter who died in an orphanage." The man with the scar, said something, but she didn't catch it. The one in charge said, 'Don't worry, we'll take care of him. You say you have friends in Chistopol who'll look after him? Write a letter entrusting your son to them."

The huge one laughed, and kept laughing until the one with the scar told him to shut up and get out. He left the house and stayed in the yard, and she gave up any thought of creeping out of the cellar while they were still there.

"She must have agreed—or she realized she had no choice. The older man told her to write something, confirming her suicide, something to her son. I think she did it, and not just one letter, but several of them. One to her son, and others, I'm sure. My husband saw three letters on the table, when he returned home and found her."

It took Tsvetayeva a long time to write the letters, more than an hour, or so it seemed to her. The men didn't talk to each other while Tsvetayeva was writing. They just kept going in and out of the house, and she heard the big one talking outside, in the yard, with somebody. She didn't know who.

"And then I think they did it. I'm not sure how, maybe they just smothered her, there was so little life left in her. I didn't hear her voice, just some muffled moans. But there were things going on up there, above me, and I heard grunts and quick steps and somebody pushing a chair, and brief sentences like, 'No, no, not there, here,' and also, and this I remember very well, 'She's not heavy, not heavy at all.' It was the older one speaking, mostly."

She had been very scared. If they found her there, in the cellar, only God knew what they'd do to her, so she stayed put, didn't move, hardly dared to breathe. She hadn't been so scared in her life, and was not proud of herself.

"I just couldn't do anything, you understand, not anything."

Tears were running down her cheeks. She wiped them with the sleeves of her blouse. Boris Leonidovich had slid down in his chair, and he was not looking good. His mouth was open and his large lower lip was trembling. There were tears in his eyes too. I knew what he was thinking: that Brodelshchikova was just the last in the long line of people who couldn't do anything for Tsvetayeva.

Varya's words came back to me, "She's tragedy, Pasha." As in classic tragedies, there was nothing that Brodelshchikova could have done. She played by the proper rules, she was fated. She was the unseen witness, who suddenly appears for the edification of the spectators. A modern *deus ex machina*.

Boris Leonidovich said, "Her friends couldn't do anything for her either, her so-called friends. So don't scold yourself, Anastasia Ivanovna."

Brodelshchikova looked at Boris Leonidovich, trying to figure out the meaning of his words. After a while she continued her story. "They stayed for another half-hour. I heard them walking above me, but I wasn't exactly sure what they were doing because they weren't saying much to each other."

She heard them walking in and out of the small bedrooms, and she heard them go up the ladder to look into the attic, but there is hardly any space up there, only enough to hang salted fish to dry, and she was more afraid than ever that they'd discover the trap door and find her, but they didn't, and then they left. She waited another half-hour, maybe longer, she didn't know, and then she left too. She stole back along the route she'd taken earlier, through yards and gardens and hidden lanes, all the way back to where she had been working in the morning, although she was still very tired. She was asked where she had been for so long, and she told them that she was sick and that she had been sleeping in the shade. They shook their heads, but the way she looked convinced them.

The husband poured more tea. He smiled at her. An approving, toothless smile.

We drank the tea quietly, without saying anything.

"When my husband found her, later that afternoon, she had a hemp rope around her neck. It was attached to a nail too low to properly hang oneself, if you know what I mean."

The husband nodded.

"I told no one about it," Brodelshchikova said, "except my husband. And I only told him weeks later, after they were all gone, and the boy was taken somewhere else. What happened to him?"

"He died in the war," Boris Leonidovich said. "He had always wanted to join. He was too young, of course, only sixteen in '41, but he was a big boy and they let him join. He died in the summer of '44."

She shook her head. "Well, he didn't seem to suffer much. I mean, he didn't seem to care that his mother was dead. He didn't even go to her funeral. I think his mother's death was a relief for him. Odd boy. They didn't get along."

The husband said, "Children, what do you expect? They suck your strength, and then they dance on your grave."

I wondered if they had children. Was something gnawing at him?

The husband reached over the table and grabbed the box of chocolates. It took him a while to open it. The variety of chocolates inside seemed to stun him, but eventually he chose one of them. He timidly offered the box around, but no one else was interested. In the silence that had fallen around the table, he ate several more chocolates in quick succession. Then he put the cover back on, as if to say enough for today. His rough hand kept moving over the lid, in a possessive, almost sensual gesture.

Brodelshchikova was staring at the money on the table. "My husband forbade me to repeat what I just told you. He made me swear. And I didn't. But now he has changed his mind. He says maybe things are not as bad as they used to be. He says I shouldn't die without letting others know what happened to her. He says it's not easy to keep it bottled inside you for so many years. He says things like this eat at you from the inside. He knows better than I do what's good for me. Men, they always know better ..."

The husband interrupted her. "You say she has a daughter that has been ... there, you know, for many years, and has just returned. You ought to tell her the story." He leaned forward, staring at Boris Leonidovich, who was sitting across from him, and went on in a raspy voice, "I don't know what's best, what's the right thing to do. My wife is upset with me for pushing her to tell the story, but it's not right that the woman's end should remain hidden. You should write about it, but not now—years from now, after I'm gone. You hear me? Only after we're dead, both dead. You're smart, you'll know what to do."

I looked at Boris Leonidovich and he looked at me, but he said nothing.

We left soon afterward. Korotkova was already there, waiting in the yard, staring at the leashed pig. She waved.

Boris Leonidovich turned to me and said, "Sasha Cornilov, he's your cousin, isn't he?"

I sighed, "First cousin."

Korotkova joined us and said, "You two look as if you've been to a wake."

12

Audrey was shaking his shoulder in the dark. "Art, Art, get up, the phone's ringing."

He felt her breath on his face. "Let it ring."

"It's been ringing on and off for ten minutes."

The phone was in the kitchen, and it wasn't that loud. He found his shorts and somehow climbed into them, then stepped out onto the dark landing. He switched on the light in the downstairs hall. He was somewhat alert by the time he got to the kitchen and picked up the handset from its wall cradle. It was Paul Karman. He was at the Black Bull, a pub on Queen Street West, and needed him to come right away with some money because he couldn't pay his bill, and the people holding him were being difficult.

"Difficult?"

"They're insisting I have to pay."

"That's not outrageous."

"I don't have the money."

"*Govnyuk.*"

"I'm so sorry, Artyom Pavlovich."

"How much?"

"A hundred and ninety-six. Without tip."

"A hundred and ninety-six! In a pub?"

"It took a while."

"You're drunk."

"I ate too."

"Caviar?"

"I had company."

"Oh, good. Who? Is Ben there with you? Let me talk to him, you're drunk."

"Ben's not here."

"Who then?"

"Friends."

"Can't they help you?"

"No."

"Why not?"

"They seem to have disappeared. I thought they'd pay."

What an idiot. "What time is it?"

"Close to two—they're closing at two."

"Paul, I can't come right now."

"There's no one else…"

"I'm not alone, Paul."

"I'm so sorry. I'll pay you back, of course."

"Call Ben."

"I did. You're not the first person I called."

"And?"

"He's away. He said something about Jennifer earlier."

"Write a cheque."

"No cheques. Cash or credit card."

"Credit card, then."

"Mine doesn't work anymore."

"Fuck."

"I called Helen too."

"And?"

"It was her husband who answered. He threatened me."

"Did you speak to Helen?"

"He wouldn't wake her up."

"Did you explain your situation to him?"

"He hung up."

"You have other friends, surely—the students in your residence."

"Gone for the weekend. All gone. Even Srinivasa, the mathematician. He went to Burlington. He has a cousin or an aunt there."

"I don't have that much cash on me, Paul."

"They take credit cards."

"Paul, I'm with someone."

"I'm sorry."

"Fuck it, Paul, any other night …"

"I'm sorry."

Paul didn't sound good. "Are you all right?" Laukhin asked after a long pause.

"Kind of."

"All right. I'll be there."

Back upstairs in his bedroom, Laukhin switched on the table lamp and began to get dressed. Audrey leaned on her elbow and asked what was happening. He told her and she laughed. She got up and took money from her wallet. "Take a cab. I want you back here quickly."

"I have enough for a cab."

"Just in case. Your student will need money for a cab too. Let's not argue."

She opened her bag, retrieved a nightgown and slipped it on. It didn't cover much.

It took some time for the cab to arrive. The driver wore a Sikh turban, a *dastar* Colson had told him, and was listening to soft Indian music. He seemed half asleep. That's what being an émigré is all about, Laukhin thought, driving a cab in the wee hours of the morning in an unfamiliar city. Doing odd, rough, menial jobs just to keep afloat. He should try it, drive a cab for a while, like some of the early Russian émigrés between the two world wars.

He told the driver to wait in front of the pub while he went in. There were hardly any customers. Paul was hunched over a corner table, head resting on crossed forearms. The right side of Paul's face was battered red and blue, and there was dried blood under his eye. Two men were watching from a nearby table, and from their size and faces Laukhin deduced they were the source of Paul's injury. A middle-aged man was at the counter, doing the accounts or whatever bartenders do at closing time. When Laukhin handed him his credit card, the man looked up and said, "You should have a talk with your son."

In the cab, Laukhin said, "Shouldn't we drop you at a hospital?"

Paul shook his head.

They searched for an open drugstore to get disinfectant and bandages.

"Did you try to sneak out?" Laukhin asked.

Paul batted the question away.

"What happened? Who did this to you, Paul?"

"Not now," Paul whispered after a long silence.

Laukhin dropped him in front of the student residence, and gave the driver his address. When he got home it was past three o'clock. The front door was unlocked, and he thought that, pressed and upset as he'd been when he left, he forgot to lock it. But when he saw that the landing light was on, he sensed something was wrong. He knew he had not switched it on before he left. The door to his bedroom was ajar, and he felt momentarily dismayed by the thought that Audrey had left.

There was enough light from the landing for Laukhin to see that Audrey was not in his bed. He switched the lights on. She was on the floor, lying on her back near his worktable, her eyes closed, legs straight, one arm by her body, the other bending away from it. For a split second he thought she had decided to sleep on the floor. But her nightie was bunched up around her waist, and, as he kneeled down, he realized she was alive, but not with him. He called her name several times, at first softly, then louder, but she didn't respond. It was then that he saw the blood in her hair, its source seemingly from somewhere above her right temple.

He could only think that she had got up, tripped in the dark, hit her head on the table and lost consciousness. He wondered whether he should move her back to the bed, but decided against it. He ran down the stairs and called 911. When he explained that his girlfriend had hurt her head and was unconscious, the dispatcher's voice hardened. Where was the hurt woman? Upstairs, in his bedroom, on the floor. They'd send an ambulance at once. The lights inside the house must be on, and outside too, if there were any. He shouldn't touch or move her.

Laukhin gathered Audrey's clothes and packed them into her bag. He put the bag near the open door, then sat on the floor next to her. He thought he had heard her murmur. He touched her hand and her face, but there was no still response. While he waited for the ambulance, sitting there on the floor near Audrey, frantic with worry, holding her hand, he wondered why the door to the bedroom had been ajar. He remembered switching off the lamp on his worktable as he left, and he was certain he had closed the bedroom door behind him. He didn't think he had left the landing light on, but wasn't entirely sure. Maybe Audrey went to the bathroom, switching on the hallway light first, and had stumbled and fell after she returned. The worktable, though, was some distance from the bed. Why would she stumble and hit the table when there was enough light in the room from the hallway?

* * *

Two policemen arrived a few minutes before the ambulance. Almost pushing Laukhin aside, they rushed upstairs. They asked him what happened, and, as he began to explain, the paramedics showed up.

In the ambulance, as he sat holding her hand, she came around. She looked about her, or tried to, confused. Then she saw Laukhin at her side, and she focused on him, with some effort, as if telling herself, "Well, he seems a familiar face, I'll keep staring at him until I figure out what's going on." After a while she whispered his name. She seemed startled by her feat. When he told her that he had found her on the floor in his bedroom, and that she had fallen and had knocked herself out, she looked puzzled. Laukhin thought he heard a very soft "Yes" from her, but wasn't entirely sure. She was pale. He asked whether he should call her mother in Montreal and let her know, but she didn't answer. She looked puzzled again, or, maybe, just undecided. The paramedic sitting with them said that talking would be tiring for her and that it would be better if he said nothing. He was an older man, short and bald, and he didn't say it with much conviction.

After a while, she whispered, "You found me on the floor?"
"Yes."
"In your bedroom?"
"Yes."
"I don't remember getting up. My head hurts."
"You have a concussion."

"What happened?"

"You fell. You got up, probably to get a drink, or to go to the washroom, and you fell. Stumbled and fell. I found you near my worktable. I think you hurt your head as you fell."

"I don't remember a thing."

"You don't remember anything from last night?"

The paramedic looked disapprovingly at Laukhin. "I don't think she should talk now."

"I'm fine," Audrey said, trying to smile. "I don't remember anything from last night."

"Nothing?"

"Nothing."

"I proposed to you."

She looked at him baffled, "You what?"

"I proposed to you."

She considered this for a while. "What did I say?"

"That I'd had too much wine."

"Ah."

The paramedic shook his head and chuckled.

"You said you found me. Where were you?"

"I went out to get Paul."

"Paul?"

"Paul Karman, my student. He was stuck in a pub."

They arrived at the hospital. The paramedic said, "She's going to be in intensive care for a while, under observation. Not for long, if she's fine, and I think she'll be fine. You can't go in with her, sir."

Laukhin said to Audrey, "I'll stay while they're doing the papers. I'll be back by midday. Give me a call if you leave intensive care earlier."

"She'll likely be sedated," the paramedic said as the ambulance doors opened. "I wouldn't come back before two this afternoon."

* * *

He stood on the sidewalk outside the Toronto General Hospital, dazed, unable to think of what to do next.

It was almost dawn. He crossed College, and then walked along the crescent to Bloor. The subway was not running yet, so he took a cab home. He wondered whether he should try to do some work, but dismissed the thought. He went upstairs, took his shoes off and fell onto his bed. It had been quite a scare. The image of Audrey lying on the floor, her head under the table, came back to him, an Audrey almost naked, seemingly at peace.

Eventually he fell asleep, but was awakened a few hours later by Ivor's lawnmower. He glanced at his watch, and the events of the night returned to him. Nine o'clock—he had slept more than four hours. He got up, brushed his teeth and went downstairs. He was filling the kettle with water when Paul called. He wanted to explain what happened, but Laukhin cut him short. "Not now, Paul. Tell me later. I've had an emergency here, and I can't talk now. Yes, I'm fine."

He put the kettle on. He had no desire to sit down at his desk and work, but he had to. He had lost half of the morning. He wished it took longer to bring water to a boil.

The phone rang again as he was about to climb back upstiars. It was Ben. Paul had told him what happened last night and they concluded that their professor was not fine.

Laukhin sighed. "I'm all right, Ben. Thanks. Audrey spent last night here—¬"

"Audrey? Lezzard's assistant?"

"Yes, Ben, who else?"

"Sorry."

"When I got back home last night, after I rescued Paul, I found her unconscious, on the floor. They took her to the hospital. It was quite a scare, but she'll be fine. She came to in the ambulance. She's still at the hospital, and I'll go back there this afternoon. They'll keep her under observation for a while."

"Did you talk to a doctor?"

"No, not yet. The paramedic told me they'd keep her in intensive care probably until two this afternoon."

He stayed under the shower for a long time. For some reason his shoulders hurt. He towelled, dressed and went to the kitchen to make himself another cup of tea. The telephone rang again. It was Helen, who had heard from Ben what happened. She said she'd given her husband hell for not waking her up, and that he, Laukhin, should talk to a doctor at the hospital. He took a long deep breath and told Helen that Audrey was all right. Why was he was irritated by his students' concern?

Audrey would be all right, he repeated to himself after he hang up. She had regained consciousness in the ambulance. A concussion, nothing more.

He went back upstairs, made the bed, tidied the room, opened the window, and stood there wondering what exactly had happened to Audrey and what his future with her would be. Despite last night, things were definitely looking up. He could not have asked for a better weekend—Audrey had spent two nights with him. Two nights in three days. The story of her dinner with Martha filled him with hope. "I may hang around here for a while," she'd told Martha. Also, "I like the look of him." And yet, as far as he knew, she still planned to go back to London. Shouldn't this weekend have changed her plans? Shouldn't she have said to him she was reconsidering her return to London, and not just for a while? Why hadn't she left a small note on his worktable? "Art, darling, maybe I should give Toronto a longer try, much longer," or something like that. One of those short, gravity-defying *billets-doux* only women can write.

Maybe she had wanted to tell him this, once they woke up, but then she had this accident and...

He knew he should eat something, but he wasn't hungry. He went back downstairs, aware that he was looking for any excuse to avoid working. In the kitchen he opened a can of sprats, squirted some lemon juice over them, and cut a slice of bread. It wasn't hearty, flavourful black bread, but that wasn't that easy to find.

Climbing back upstairs, he wondered whether he should go to the hospital before sitting down to work, but it was too early. Audrey was probably still sedated, and he wanted to talk to her too, not just with the doctor. What would the doctor tell him anyway—except that she had a concussion?

It was while he was picturing himself entering Audrey's hospital room with a bouquet of flowers that he realized that the green folder with the Tsvetayeva bundle in it was not on his worktable. He took a cursory glance around without seeing it. Audrey must have taken the folder to read the bundle again while he was away—that would explain why she'd been near the table when she tripped. But where was it? Would Audrey have hidden the folder, as some sort of a joke? He couldn't see her doing that. He searched the bedroom again, this time slowly, methodically. No folder. Maybe Audrey had gone downstairs, taking the green folder with her to read in the den, and left it there. That would explain the light being on in the landing. He broke into a cold sweat as he went downstairs.

He spent half an hour looking for the green folder. It was nowhere in the house.

* * *

He went back to the hospital at two o'clock. Audrey had been moved out of intensive care into a private room. At the nurses station near her room, he talked to a doctor who told him that head injuries were difficult to predict, but concussions, which were mild head injuries, end up all right fairly quickly. Most of them.

"That's what she has, a concussion?"

"She has a bit of a dent on her skull. A minor skull fracture. I understand she fell and hit a table. Well, she must have hit the edge or a corner of it. It's a small fracture, but it complicates things. We're not sure it's just a mild head injury. That's why we'd like to keep her here for a while. A neurosurgeon will see her tomorrow morning. If she starts to bleed inside her skull it could put pressure on her brain. But we think she's progressing quite well."

"She doesn't know what happened to her."

"Post-traumatic amnesia is common. It usually doesn't last long."

"You mean, she'll remember what happened to her?"

"Probably."

"When?"

The doctor raised his narrow shoulders.

"When are you likely to release her?"

"She still has a headache, but that's fairly common too. More worrisome is that the sizes of her pupils are unequal and her speech is still a bit slurred. We'd like to keep her under observation a while longer. Another day or two. It should all clear up by then."

Audrey was happy to see him, but she was pale and said she had a bad headache. She had talked to Martha—she had to call her because she had no health-care insurance. Martha had insisted on a private room.

They played the what-does-Audrey-remember game.

"Do you remember Thursday?"

"The opening party? Yes, I do."

"Do you remember spending Thursday night with me?"

She smiled, "Of course."

"Do you remember the following morning?"

"I do. I bumped into you in front of the gallery. We went in together and found Lezzard there, in a foul mood."

"Earlier than that. What did you do Friday morning when you got up?"

"When I got up?"

"Yes. You left my bed and...?"

"I went back to Martha's apartment."

"Before that. You sat at my worktable and...?"

"I did?"

"You read something—for a couple of hours."

"Yes, of course, I read about Tsvetayeva."

"What else do you remember?"

"Oh...I remember having a fight with Martha."

"When was that?"

"Yesterday? I'm not sure. What day is it?"

"Sunday. Do you remember calling me on Saturday evening—yesterday—asking to come over?"

"I...I think so."

"What else do you remember?"

"I had dinner with Martha."

"When?"

Audrey thought for a while. "Friday?"

"Do you remember where it was? What you ate? What you talked about?"

"Yes."

"Good, good. What do you remember of Saturday?"

She frowned. "I took a cab to your house. In the evening."

"And?"

"We had dinner and went to bed."

"Go on."

"And then?"

She shook her head.

"Do you remember how you fell?"

She sighed. "I don't."

"Don't worry. The doctor is sure it will all come back to you. Do you remember anything you did after I left."

"After you left?"

"Yes. Anything at all."

She shook her head and sighed again. "No."

"You don't remember picking up the green folder, the one with Tsvetayeva's story in it, the folder you read on Friday morning?"

"No."

"You're sure?"

"I'm not sure of anything."

She covered her mouth.

"What's wrong?" Laukhin asked.

"I think I might throw up?"

"It's my fault," he said. "I should let you rest."

"I want to remember what happened. I think if I go through what happened earlier on, it will help bring back what happened last night."

She covered her mouth again.

"Would you like some water?"

He stayed with her until he was chased away by a nurse who said Audrey needed to rest. As he got up to leave, Audrey said, "I had hoped Martha wouldn't come to Toronto, you know. When she called on Tuesday to tell me she was coming, I reminded her that I was planning to travel to Montreal to see her before flying back to the UK. But she said she had other things to do in Toronto, and that she was coming anyway on Wednesday. A day before the vernissage—what timing! It ruled out any chance of a romantic night with you."

Laukhin took her hand.

She went on. "I knew I was not brave or modern enough to invite myself to your place, and I was afraid you'd given up on me after I'd turned you down so many times. I'm glad you haven't."

* * *

"It takes me a while to get moving these days," Helen said pointing to her belly, as they all sat down. in the small den at the back of the house.

As soon as he got home, he had a sip from a vodka bottle and phoned his students to say he needed to see them urgently at his house that evening. He couldn't reach Paul, but Helen picked up Ben at his residence and drove him to Laukhin's house.

"Where is Paul?" he asked.

"Haven't seen him since noon," Ben said. "He'll show up sooner or later. Why this urgent summon?"

Laukhin told them briefly what had happened the night before. At the end, after he said that Audrey was still under observation in the hospital, but fine, and that he had seen and talked to her that afternoon, he added, "Late this morning I found out something—well, didn't find, actually." He stopped.

"Well?" Helen said.

"I can't find the folder with the Tsvetayeva bundle."

His students stared at him, uncertain of what to make of what he'd just said.

"It's lost, gone."

"What do you mean?" Ben asked.

"I brought the folder with the entire Tsvetayeva-bundle in it home on Thursday afternoon and worked on it over the weekend. I was on schedule to have everything ready by Monday morning. But now I can't find it."

"I still don't understand," Ben said.

"It disappeared. I had the whole bundle on my worktable, in a green folder, and this morning... well, this morning it wasn't there anymore."

Followed by a perplexed silence, he went into the kitchen and picked up three glasses and the bottle he had a sip from earlier. He retureued to the den, poured himself a drink, and signaled the other two to do the same. Helen declined with indignation.

"How long have you been involved with her... with Audrey?" she asked.

"A few days."

"That's all?"

"I mean, I've been sort of seeing her for some time. Since May, when Ben discovered she was working for Lezzard. About three months, but without, you know... without much success. She was friendly, but..."

"And then she fell for you all of a sudden?" Helen said.

He frowned. "It only appears that way. We were to have dinner here, my cooking, a month or so ago, but she began to have doubts. There were things she'd read about me."

"Yet she dismissed her doubts. When did that happen?"

"Thursday evening. There was an opening night at Lezzard's gallery."

"And she was very nice to you Thursday evening."

"Yes."

"Thursday night the two of you slept together for the first time."

"What are you driving at?"

"Was Thursday night the first time the two of you slept together?"

"Yes."

"And she saw the Tsvetayeva bundle, there, on your worktable."

"Yes. I found her the next morning reading it. She found it fascinating, couldn't put it down."

"And two days later she comes and spends the night with you again."

"Yes."

"And the green folder disappears."

"Yes."

"How well do you know her?" Helen asked.

"What do you mean?"

"Is she what she claims to be?"

"Oh, come on, of course she is. She's English. You can't fake that accent—not between the sheets anyway. An English woman, from London, with marital problems, a sick father, and a rich mother here in Canada. Her parents divorced many years ago, and her father brought her up."

"When exactly did the folder disappear?" Ben asked.

"I don't know. I wasn't aware it was not there until around eleven this morning. The last time I worked on the excerpts was yesterday evening, just before Audrey arrived. They were spread all over the worktable in the bedroom, and I gathered them and put them all back in the green folder."

"And afterward you never glanced at your table at all—for, what, twelve, thirteen hours?"

"Well, I was busy, had other things on my mind. Audrey came over and then, in the middle of the night there was the call from Paul, and when I got back, it was awful, with Audrey on the floor, unconscious, barely breathing. I went to the hospital with her. I was tired afterward and slept. Yes, only this morning, around eleven."

Laukhin got up and began to pace. Helen's legs were swollen. She was wearing a loose sleeveless dress with faintly coloured sunflowers, and was sprawled across the blue leather sofa, under the threatening Mayakovsky. The face of the stern poet asked Laukhin where his proletarian vigilance had been.

"She has them, then," Helen said.

"That's silly. She doesn't."

"How do you know?"

"She left in an ambulance, on a stretcher. All she had on her was a thin nightgown. I stuffed all her things in her night bag and took it in the ambulance too. There was no folder in there, I'm quite sure."

"She hid it somewhere."

"Why would she do that? Anyway, I checked everywhere."

"She hid it somewhere outside the house."

"Where? What you're saying is that she went outside, hid the folder God knows where, came back in, climbed upstairs and then knocked herself unconscious so that she wouldn't be suspected of theft."

"Maybe she had accomplices," Ben said, "and she gave the folder to them while you were away."

He looked at his students in disbelief. "And after she handed over the excerpts, mission carried out, Audrey hurled herself head first against my worktable."

"Who else knew you had the bundle here?" Helen asked.

"Besides me? Audrey. Ben, did I mention when we met on Thursday afternoon that I'd work at home on the Tsvetayeva bundle over the weekend?"

"You did."

"Did you tell anyone else about it, Ben?" Helen asked.

"No, of course not. I mean, who, on earth..."

Laukhin shook his head. "Come on, it happened on Thursday night."

They looked at him puzzled.

"She fell for me, as you put it," Laukhin went on, "Thursday night, before she knew I had the folder in the house. Never mind that, before she knew about the folder period."

Helen laughed. "Then Ben did it. He snuck in while you took Audrey to the hospital and pinched the folder. He wanted to do last-minute corrections, didn't you Ben?"

Laukhin poured himself another drink. "There's a bit I didn't tell you. When I came home last night there were a few things wrong. The front door was unlocked, the landing light was on, the bedroom door was ajar. I'm now certain I locked the front door—I remember checking I had the key. I'm not entirely sure about the light outside the bedroom, but I think I switched it off. As for the bedroom door, I'm sure I closed it behind me, but Audrey may have gone to the bathroom while I was away. It's the unlocked front door that troubles me."

"Are you saying that somebody got in while you were away?" Ben asked.

'It seems that way," Laukhin said.

"And this person or persons took the green folder away."

"Likely."

"And Audrey got hurt while they were at it."

Laukhin nodded.

"Who?"

"That's the question," Laukhin said. Who? Who'd be interested in the bundle? The KGB, if we allow ourselves some wild guessing here, wants the whole journal, not just these excerpts about Tsvetayeva. Anyway, I think the KGB has other things to keep them busy right now, not my father's journal. Five, ten years ago maybe, but nowadays they have much bigger fish to worry about. They don't like the noises Comrade Gorbachev is making."

"Artyom Pavlovich, surely the KGB's not happy with your father's journal being published, and we shouldn't dismiss—"

Laukhin waved his glass. "Yes, well, never mind the mystery and the detective work for now. Let's assess the damage."

"The damage?"

"How long will it take to get the Tsvetayeva bundle ready given this new... situation? Ben, how long would it take you to prepare new translation drafts."

Ben said that the trip to Yelabuga was not in the computer, and neither was Pasternak's visit to Bolshevo. It meant all those entries, six or seven of them, would have to be reconstructed. He sighed. "It shouldn't take that long. After all, I've already done it once. Two weeks if I do nothing else. The morning at the hotel in Yelabuga and the train trip back—well, luckily, these should still be in your office. I slid the draft translations under your door Friday morning."

Laukhin sighed. "It's gone too. I picked it up on Friday. I had it in the green folder."

"Well, they are short journal entries," Ben said.

"What if Paul and Helen helped?" Laukhin asked.

"I don't know," Ben said. "I don't think we'd gain much. For them it's new material, a new translation. And, of course, there'll be less unity of style."

"I'll worry about the unity of style when I go over the first draft," Laukhin said. "Two weeks for the first draft and at most a week for me. Less, three or four days."

"Will the *New Yorker* go along with a three week delay?"

"I don't know, Ben," Laukhin said. He was back at the window. He thought he saw a cat in the falling darkness, near the shed, or a small raccoon. "We'll see."

Helen said, "Shouldn't you call the police, Artyom Pavlovich?"

Laukhin turned and gazed at Helen, and then shook his head. "What for?"

"Tell the police you had papers stolen from your room."

Laukhin laughed. "Yes, I can see myself explaining this. 'Well, sergeant, it was a green folder, about this big, with some thirty or forty sheets containing the story of a dead poet. The value of the stolen object? Let's see, now…'"

"Tell them that they hurt Audrey."

He moved away from the window. "If I call the police, they'll want to talk. Endless talk and endless details, the minutia about everything since I met Audrey. They'll consider the possibility of an intruder coming in and surreptitiously removing the folder either at night, when I left to rescue Paul, or early in the morning, when I went to the hospital with Audrey. They'll want an exact description of all my movements last night and this morning. And they'll also wonder whether I hit Audrey on the head myself, or caused her fall, and whether I invented the story about the green folder to cover myself. I don't have the time for it. They'd ask questions of Paul too, of course."

Helen's eyes bulged. "You mean you'll let it go? Just like that?"

"Some burglary," Ben said. "A stolen green folder."

"Ben," Laukhin said, "listen, all the work must be done at Alumni Hall and entered into the word processor every day. Sleep there, if need be. You must—daily, you hear me, daily—make sure everything is saved in the computer. Either you enter it, or you give it to one of the secretaries to do it, whichever is faster."

Laukhin sat down with a heavy grunt, a signal that the important decisions had been made and there was nothing further to debate.

Helen straightened herself up. "You're taking it very well, Artyom Pavlovich."

"It can't be helped, can it?"

Ben said, "It would be wonderful publicity, though, wouldn't it? I mean, in addition to the excerpts, think about the possible headline—'Excerpts of Forthcoming Memoirs Stolen'. Or 'Thieves Break into Famous Poet's House' and 'Experts Convinced of Soviet Secret Service Involvement: What Was It That so Troubled Them?' Afterward, of course."

"Afterward?" Helen asked.

"After the excerpts and the first volume are published. Surely we could talk about it then, and give interviews. It'd spur sales and lead to great anticipation for the second volume." Ben raised his hands. "It's a thought, just a thought."

Laukhin saw them to the door. "I'll see you both tomorrow morning. Eight o'clock sharp in my office. Ben, try to find Paul. Oh, God, I have to call Bart. And that soulless pedant at the *New Yorker*. I need another drink."

Friday and Saturday, 14–15 October 1955

I slept poorly, if at all, tossing and turning. I dreamed of Cornilov and the other two henchmen. They were having dinner in our apartment on Lavrushinsky Lane, and I didn't understand how they had ended up there. I was sweating and asking Varya who had invited them. Sasha Cornilov wouldn't let his aunt answer. He shouted, "But it was you, Pavel Nikolayevich, it was you who told me to come, and to bring my friends with me." I kept looking at Varya for an answer, but she seemed unable to hear me.

I switched the bedside lamp on and picked up my notebook. My watch showed three o'clock. By the time I finished writing Brodelshchikova's story it was quarter to six. I decided to go out for a walk. A walk would do me good, I thought. Passing by Boris Leonidovich's room I wondered if Korotkova was still in there. She'd been there around eleven o'clock last night. I heard their voices when I snuck into the corridor to confirm my suspicion. Well, it would not have been hard—Marietta was given a room right beside the poet's.

A uniformed policeman and a hotel clerk were whispering inside the front door. They seemed reluctant to move and let me pass, but eventually they did. It was still dark, and far-apart streetlamps cast dim cones of yellow light. The weather had turned cold and windy, and a thin rain was just beginning. I realized that my walk was not going to last long—maybe as far as the second light. I walked quickly but carefully because of the darkness and the uneven road. As I approached the second light, I noticed a couple. They had either been there all along or, more likely, had been walking like me and stopped within the hazy light. I thought at first they were lovers reluctant to part after a night together, and I slowed down. I was just about to turn around when I realized that they were not lovers, that they were involved in a heated discussion, and that I knew the woman—Korotkova. She was wearing her short fur coat, but I would have recognized her anyway. She was doing most of the talking. I didn't know who the man was. For a second I thought it was Boris Leonidovich, and that the two of them had gone for an early walk, but the man was much younger than the poet. He was also taller and broader. It crossed my mind that he looked like Sasha Cornilov, but I dismissed the thought. I had not seen Varya's nephew in years. My mind was still overwhelmed by the story I heard yesterday, and dreaming of him had somehow conjured his likeness here.

I turned around and went back to the hotel. I doubted they saw me. I wasn't sure what I saw, but just as a precaution, I said to the two men who were still there, at the door, that it was too cold and dark for a walk. And I added that it was getting wet too.

Korotkova took a midday train to Yaroslavl.

In the afternoon, as we boarded the train back to Moscow, Boris Leonidovich was unusually quiet, although he mumbled that, all things considered, he was glad Korotkova had been urgently called home.

A few comments sprang to mind, but I didn't say anything.

Later, much later, after dinner, in our pyjamas and lying on our couchettes with the lights off, Boris Leonidovich said he loved sleeping on trains. It was one place he felt at ease and safe. It was the rhythmic sound of the wheels over the tracks and the slight rocking motion of the coach. Likely, an unconscious recall of being an infant, lulled to sleep in a cradle; or of being in the womb, the thuds of the wheels imitating his mother's heartbeat. He had heard a doctor once talk about such associations.

I couldn't hold back anymore and I asked him why Korotkova had to go home all of a sudden. He seemed startled by my question—he wasn't used to trite interruptions while his mind was in poetic ascent. Maybe he was embarrassed too. Why was I asking? I lied—nothing, simple curiosity. He said that one of her children was sick, and that she had seemed troubled when she told him that she couldn't wait for her husband in Yelabuga after all. I asked him what time that was. He paused and asked whether I wanted to know what time she'd learned about her daughter's sickness or what time she'd told him about it. I said both. I also asked how she found out about her daughter's sickness. He didn't understand my curiosity (and sounded annoyed), but he answered. Her parents had called her around ten thirty, just before she knocked on his door to tell him. She'd said the line had been poor, and she had not understood exactly what was wrong with her daughter. From what she gathered, her daughter had returned home with a high fever, after only one hour of school, but that was all she knew.

I probably slept for a while but woke when Boris Leonidovich switched the bedside light on and complained of chest pains. He looked white. It might have been indigestion because the few morsels of meat in the stew at dinner had tasted a bit off. On the other hand, who knew what exertions beguiling Marietta had required of him. I gave him some water, told him a good night's sleep would help, and that he'd feel better in the morning. I wanted to ask him how long Korotkova had stayed in his room, but I didn't. He'd ask me why I wanted to know, and I wasn't sure what to say.

Boris Leonidovich switched his light off and said he'd try but he doubted he'd be able to sleep. After a while, he added, "That thing with the money and the sign to mark Tsvetayeva's tomb, that was brilliant, Pavel Nikolayevich. Thanks."

I said Brodelshchikova would have probably told us the story anyway. Her husband would have made her.

He said he wasn't sure about that.

He moans in his sleep. Moans and snores, and now and then a combination. This is the first time I've been in such close quarters with him. I have switched my light on and picked up my notebook again. It's close to three o'clock in the morning.

Listening to his sounds, and to the rhythmic thuds of the wheels on the rails, I think of Korotkova and the odd scene I witnessed early the day before. There is only one explanation, if I discard the unlikely possibility of Korotkova leaving Boris Leonidovich's room sometime in the middle of the night to slide into another man's bed. There is only one logical explanation. And it is terrible, although, in our world, not unexpected.

I wonder how much Boris Leonidovich told Korotkova. He promised the Brodelshchikovs to keep mum for a while, but once you share a pillow...

Should I ask him tomorrow morning? Should I tell him what I saw yesterday? What good will it do? It will make the old man's heart palpitate, undoubtedly, but otherwise? The damage has been done already.

Maybe I should tell him, though. What if she visits him in Moscow in the future?

Who is she, Korotkova? She seemed to be a genuine lover of poetry and literature. Passionate about it, knowledgeable too. Is her real name Korotkova? Is she really the captain's wife? The crew of the boat seemed to know her. Does she double as an informer for the police, without her husband's knowledge? The captain did not seem concerned by his wife's libertine ways with the famous, old poet.

No, she's more than just a common, run-of-the-mill informer. She's a trained agent, who superbly play-acted her way into the old poet's heart and bed.

13

Monday morning he was in his office on St. Joseph Street before six. He needed to ponder the awkward talk he'd have later with Bart. He'd slept poorly, berating himself for not thinking only of Audrey in her distress at the hospital. Helen's wary questions repeatedly came back to him: "And then she fell for you all of a sudden?" and "How well do you know her?" Poisoned questions. He recalled too his father's last line in the Tsvetaeva bundle, an affected last sentence he had read just before Audrey's phone call on Saturday. "She's a trained agent, who superbly play-acted her way into the old poet's heart and bed."

He was in love with Audrey, yet he allowed such dark thoughts. He didn't deserve her. Such stupidity. He wasn't old, or not a sixty-five doddering old like Pasternak had been in 1955. And Audrey hadn't play-acted her way into his heart and bed. She had not encouraged him at all, in fact. Anyway, an agent for whom? She'd been much keener than him to dig into Lezzard's illicit trade in confiscated art, and he felt certain that behind Lezzard there were people connected with the very organization she'd be an agent for. Furthermore, why would they bump her off just as she had successfully carried out her task?

* * *

Audrey called his office just after his students left and he was about to dial Bart's number.

"What are you doing right now?" she asked. Her voice was weak.

"I was going to ring my agent in New York. I'm dreading this call. How are you feeling?"

"So-so. I had a sleepless night. Come to see me, Art."

"I will. Not right now, later. I'm in deep shit, Audrey, an ocean of it. Something bad, something terrible has happened. The entire Tsvetayeva bundle is gone. It just disappeared. Gone, I can't find it."

"I know."

"You know?"

"I know what happened, Art. I know what happened to me Saturday night."

"You stumbled and fell. You hurt your head."

"I didn't stumble. I'm not clumsy. Never was, even as a child."

"What happened, then?"

"I'll tell you. Come here and I'll tell you. I can't do it over the phone. I know how the green folder disappeared."

"You know where the green folder is?"

"I didn't say that."

"Oh." Most likely, he reasoned, she had dreamed something, and now her tired mind thought it had actually happened. "I'll be there."

He bought flowers before he went up. Audrey thanked him for them, and said that Russian poets were famous for their manners around invalids. She smiled, but looked pale and tired. Her voice was weak, and she still had a headache. "Maybe it's because I didn't sleep at all last night," she said. "Couldn't. My mind kept returning to the night before, like somebody who had lost an important object and revisits obsessively images of the time and place she last still had it."

A nurse came into the room, and Laukhin thought she looked disapprovingly at him. Taking Audrey's pulse, she said, "The neurosurgeon will see you at ten thirty." She gave her some water and a couple of pills, raised the upper part of the bed, and left shaking her head.

Audrey glanced after her and then turned to Laukhin and smiled. "I remembered. I remembered what happened to me Saturday night. What a relief." There was tired satisfaction in her voice.

Laukhin took her left hand in his own. It was moist and limp. He sat on a chair near her bed. She talked mainly looking at Laukhin, but sometimes at the ceiling, as if she was still trying to recall details of what had happened.

She remembered taking a cab to Laukhin's house on Saturday night, and sitting with him in the kitchen, eating the sushi and drinking the wine she had brought with her, and then being in bed upstairs, together with him. She didn't remember his proposal to her—and now believed he'd invented it to make her feel better—but she did remember Laukhin asking her to move in with him, and his promise to write poems about her.

But then she hit a wall, remembered nothing further, save for waking up in the ambulance, and finding Laukhin next to her. She had a bird's eye view of what she remembered, and could move forward and backward along all the images associated with the memories she had recovered. She could see them clearly lined up along a time axis, but whenever she attempted to inch forward, past the image of being in bed with him, she hit that wall. It was not exactly a wall, more like a giant box of smoky glass hiding several hours of Saturday night.

Around five in the morning she got out of bed and left her room for a walk. She hoped the exercise would calm her so that she could sleep afterward. She was shuffling past the nurses' station for the second time when a telephone rang there. Not a loud ring, somewhat mute, but it reminded her of the telephone ring she had been awakened by while being in bed with Laukhin. On her bird's eye view of the events of Saturday night, the ring came from inside the box with the glass walls. And, slowly, very slowly, as she stood there frozen with anticipation, the smoky walls of the box began to clear.

She remembered shaking Laukhin awake, and his getting up and going downstairs into the kitchen where the phone was. She heard him talk on the phone for some time, and then he returned to the bedroom. He said he had to go and rescue his idiot student Paul Karman from a pub. He said he was terribly sorry and upset about it, and that he'd be back in an hour.

She remembered jumping out of bed, searching her purse and giving Laukhin some money. She also fetched a nightgown from her overnight bag and slipped it on.

Afterward she couldn't sleep. She remembered lying there, in Laukhin's bed, in the dark—well, it wasn't that dark, because there was enough light coming through the large windows and past the drawn curtains—and thinking that her life had significantly changed in a few days, and that she couldn't quite explain how or why.

And then the door to the bedroom opened slowly. It couldn't have been more than ten or fifteen minutes after Laukhin left, and she remembered thinking how quickly he had returned, and how considerate he was tiptoeing through the house because she had not heard the front door open, or any steps on the stairs or on the landing. She also thought that maybe she had fallen asleep, and it had been more than ten or fifteen minutes since Laukhin left.

It wasn't Laukhin. First one man stepped cautiously into the room. He had a flashlight. He quickly spotted her, and then the flashlight blinded her, but not before she saw another man coming in, also with a flashlight. She was too afraid to scream or move. They saw her, and one of the men came closer with his blinding flashlight, and she hid her face under her elbow. Then the light left her face and she felt the man sit on the bed. Somebody moved her arm away from her face, and then a gloved hand covered her mouth. He talked to her. He said that they hadn't expected to find her there, but that she had no reason to be frightened. They were looking for something, and no harm would come to her if she kept quiet. That was all she needed to do, very simple: keep quiet. He asked her if she understood. She nodded. He asked her where her boyfriend was. From his voice he was a middle-aged man. She said Laukhin had been called away—an emergency with one of his students. He asked her the time her boyfriend had left. She said, perhaps ten, fifteen minutes earlier, she wasn't sure. He asked her when she expected him to return. She didn't know whether it was better to say shortly or in a long while, not knowing what they were after. So she told them the truth, or her guess at the truth—in about half or three-quarters of an hour. He nodded and patted her shoulder. He said, "Good girl. You see, it's easy, and nobody gets hurt."

She had been very afraid, trembling uncontrollably, and she had peed herself, not much, a trickle. She couldn't think properly, but told herself to do as they said, whatever, unless they tried to harm her, in which case she would scream as loud as she could.

There was a third man with them, waiting in the upstairs hallway. They had switched on the light there when they came in, and she saw him at the doorstep, a large dark silhouette against the light.

They found whatever they were looking for quickly, something on Laukhin's worktable. It was the second man who had entered the room who found it. He spoke in an accent when he said, "I think this is it. Come and see," and she realized the one who had sat on her bed and talked to her did not have one. He also said something to the third man—she assumed it was in Russian, but wasn't sure—the man she had seen on the doorstep. He came in and said, "Light, the light," and they switched on the room light. He was older, in his late sixties or early seventies, but in good shape. A large man, tall, with sparse white hair. Unlike the other two, he was not wearing a bala-clava. He had a green corduroy jacket on that had seen better days, and a grey fedora. She was struck by how huge his shoes were. He barely looked at her. He took whatever the other man had found and sat down at Laukhin's worktable. She remembered the chair cracking under his weight. He sat with his back to her, reading or looking at whatever had been handed to him. She heard paper being shuffled. He didn't seem to be in any hurry. After a few minutes, probably no more than five, he said, "Yes. Good." He stood up and turned to leave. He was holding Laukhin's green folder. Without thinking, she said, well, it was probably more of a whisper, "You can't take that. That's Laukhin's work." The older man stopped and glanced at her—he probably didn't understand what she had said. When he took another step, she jumped out of bed, ran to him, and grabbed his arm, shouting, "You can't take this." She had no idea how she had the strength or the courage to do that, since minutes earlier she'd been so frightened she peed herself. She was convinced she looked ridiculous, a barmy figure clad in a nightgown that covered little. But she had annoyed the older man, because she was clinging to his left arm, the arm with the green folder, trying to halt him, and he said something to her, first in Russian, and then in English, ordering her away, back to the bed. But she didn't let go of him, and so, angry or merely irritated, he swung his arm.

He must have done it with a lot of force, because she lost her balance. That's when she probably hit her head on the table. Or maybe somebody hit her on the head, possibly with a flashlight. The last thing she remembered, though, was his face, the face of the older man. She saw the scar on the left side of his face, a highly visible scar that began on his forehead, went past his left eye, and ended in the middle of his cheek. And she immediately knew who he was. She had read about him on Friday morning, sitting in the same chair he had just got up from. Tall, big, the scar on the left side of his face. The age was right too. Cornilov, still alive.

* * *

Laukhin would have stayed longer with Audrey, but the same nurse who had frowned at him earlier chased him out. "The neurosurgeon will be here any moment now," she said. "He wants to do more tests and we have to prepare Ms. Millay."

Outside Audrey's room, Laukhin told the nurse that he wanted to talk to the surgeon.

"Are you a relative?"

"No."

"He won't talk to you."

He walked back to Alumni Hall weighed down by what Audrey had told him. Ben passed by his office just as he was opening the door. Laukhin asked him in and told him what Audrey had remembered.

Ben seemed bewildered. "You mean Cornilov came here, to Toronto, to get the Tsvetayeva excerpts?"

"It seems so."

Frowning, Ben lowered himself into a chair near Laukhin's desk. They sat there in silence, looking at each other.

"I should ring Bart," Laukhin said at last. "I dread this call."

"Maybe Helen is right," Ben said, "and we should call the police."

Laukhin didn't answer.

"They broke in and stole things," Ben went on. "They hurt Audrey."

"They won't catch them. It's been more than twenty-four hours. Cornilov is long gone out of the country."

"I don't know, Artyom Pavlovich..."

"Let me think about it, Ben. That's all we need at this time, the police."

Ben got up. "I better get back to my desk." He turned around at the door and asked, "Why, though? Why would they risk that much?"

"Who are *they*, Ben?" Laukhin asked looking at his student.

"Well, the Soviets, the KGB."

Laukhin was doubtful. "Maybe."

"Breaking into your house could have easily been a disaster for them. If you had been there, and scared enough or mad enough to begin screaming or making a commotion that your neighbours could hear… It could have turned nasty for them."

"Maybe it wasn't the Soviets, as you put it," Laukhin said. "Maybe it wasn't the KGB."

"What?"

"Ben, Ben, this is not the thirties or the fifties. Yes, the Soviets would like to stop the publication of Pavel Laukhin's journals, or at least discredit them, but how much effort would they put on such a thing? Not much, in my view. It's 1985. The journal is all about things that happened thirty, forty years ago, and few in the politburo or the central committee would get heartburn over some Stalin-bashing literary memoir. Many such memoirs have already been published. What else is there to fear? And the Soviets themselves have already decided—many of them, anyway—that Stalin was a monster."

"What are you saying?"

"You're right about the risks they took. You're right that the whole enterprise seems risky, hit-and-miss, not at all the usual *modus operandi* of the deadly Soviet secret service. And they are deadly, Ben, believe me, they are very good at what they do. But the Soviet secret service might not have been behind this."

"Are you saying that it was Cornilov acting on his own?"

He shrugged.

"I'm not following you."

"I don't know, Ben. I don't know what to think, especially now when I have the excerpts to reconstruct—*we* have the excerpts to reconstruct—and the galleys to go through, and the introduction to finish." Looking at his watch, he added, "And now another song and dance from famous poet Artyom Laukhin—the talk with Bart. To be followed, of course, by the conference call that Bart will insist on with all the affected publishers. Bart likes conference calls."

Ben was still on the subject of Cornilov. "What was worrying Cornilov to such an extent? Why would he do it? Even if the truth about Tsvetayeva's execution came to light, all he had to say was that he was following orders. He could always defend himself that way— he would not be the first or the last. What did he have to fear?"

"A wife."

"A wife?"

"I'm not sure, Ben. Yes, a wife, his second, much younger. He adored her—from what I heard before I left the Soviet Union—and probably still does. She gave him the illusion that his old deeds were forgiven and forgotten. Forgotten, anyway. Perhaps he feared his wife's horror, her revulsion, shock. He feared the scorn and contempt of others, too. Tsvetayeva is far from unknown in the Soviet Union these days. She has slowly become celebrated there. Her most famous poem, *The Rat Catcher*, was published in 1956, and a selection was published in the sixties. Shostakovich set six of her poems to music. They even named a newly discovered asteroid after her— 3511 Tsvetayeva. When the bundle is published everybody will learn that the poet Cornilov was one of Tsvetayeva's murderers. I mean, everybody who matters to him—his family, his friends, the literati, those in artistic circles. News and copies of the story will travel, and Moscow will be abuzz with it."

* * *

He called the nursing station around four o'clock and was told not to come because Ms. Millay was tired after the surgery.

"Surgery?"

"Yes. The neurosurgeon was not happy with what he saw this morning. He ordered more tests and then decided to operate immediately. There were complications."

"Complications? What does it mean?"

"It usually means there has been some bleeding that has put pressure on the brain. The surgeon will know the details."

"Is she worse? This morning she seemed to be doing all right."

"These things take time."

A guarded response, not reassuring at all. "Why wasn't I called?"

"Whom am I talking to, please?"

"My name is Laukhin. Art Laukhin"

"Are you related to Ms. Millay, Mr. Laukhin?"

"Yes," he lied.

"Let me look." After a while he heard somebody say, "No, not there," and after another long pause the same women's voice came back on the line and said, "I don't see your name here. We called her mother in Montreal, and her father in the United Kingdom. Who did you say you were?"

"Her fiancée."

"It's best to talk to the surgeon."

By six o'clock Laukhin couldn't stand it anymore and walked to the hospital. The nursing station was crowded, and the staff seemed tense. A nurse he had not seen before told him he could only glance in at Audrey and then he'd have to leave. "Don't talk to her. Maybe tomorrow."

The nurse did not tell him that somebody was already with Audrey. When he looked in through the open door, he saw Martha sitting on a chair pulled closed to Audrey's bed. Audrey's eyes were closed, but somehow she felt his presence, because she half-opened them and wiggled her fingers weakly at him. Martha turned toward the door and stared at him. She frowned, looked at Audrey who had closed her eyes again, and then back at him, and said, "Now, we don't want to tire the patient, do we? I was told there'd be no one else today."

She had a travel bag with her, and he gathered she must have come directly from the airport. Not a good sign.

After saying something to Audrey that he didn't catch, Martha came over to him and gestured him out. She came with him and said, "What happened? I can't get the real story from her. She fell? Somebody hit her? Somebody pushed her? I can't tell if she's just too tired to explain or the injury has made her incoherent. The information on her chart is that she fell. Did she fall?"

"Yes. Kind of."

"Kind of?"

"She might have been hit."

"Might have? Did it happen in your house? Audrey said it did, but she wasn't making much sense."

"In my house, yes."

"You must know more then."

He sighed. "I wasn't there, Mrs. Osterhoudt."

"You weren't there?"

"I was out."

"You were out." She paused, as if to take stock of what he just said. "Brilliant. Where were you?"

"I was called away. One of my students needed help. An ... emergency."

"What kind of an emergency?"

"He was detained somewhere."

"Where?"

"In a pub. Look—"

"And you rescued him. Bravo."

"How is Audrey doing?"

"Not well. When was this—when did it happen?"

"Saturday night. Well, Sunday morning."

"What time?"

"Between two and three."

"And you weren't there."

"No."

"You have Audrey in your house—in your bedroom, I gather—and you went out between two and three in the morning?"

"It's a long story, Mrs. Osterhoudt. I'm sure Audrey will tell you the moment she feels better."

"For God's sake, can't you see what's happening? Audrey may not be able to tell me. Ever." Martha barely moved her lips, yet he felt the impact of *ever* like a blow. "The doctors are not very encouraging. What happened while you were away?"

"What are you saying?" He must have misheard her, or it came out wrong because of Martha's obvious dislike of him. "She was all right this morning."

Martha shook her head, exasperated. "What happened while you were away, Mr. Laukhin?"

She had remembered his name. "Some people broke into the house to steal something, and she objected, and, I don't know, was pushed or hit."

"Hit on the head?"

"Maybe. Audrey doesn't remember exactly."

"Did you tell the police?"

"No."

"Why not?"

"It didn't seem ... I didn't have the time."

"No time? What did they steal?"

"Some papers." He was well aware how ridiculous his story sounded. The police would have a great time with it, if they ever got involved.

"Papers? What kind of papers?"

"About a poet, a woman poet, Russian. About the circumstances of her death."

"Papers about a dead poet," Martha echoed him. "My daughter is between life and death, Mr. Laukhin, and you're mocking me?"

"No, look, I know what I'm saying sounds odd, but if you knew the whole story, it would make perfect sense. I love your daughter, Mrs. Osterhoudt—"

"Yet you left her alone at night in your house because one of your students was detained in a pub."

"How could I know—"

"Yes, Mr. Laukhin, how could you possibly know that some nasty people would turn up to look for some papers about a dead poet. When did she die, by the way?"

Relentless Martha. No wonder Audrey was always fighting with her. He'd have snarled at anyone else, but relentless Martha was a grieving mother. Feeling like a fool, he whispered, "In 1941."

"Indeed. How could you possibly know that some nasty people would turn up to look for some papers about the death of a Russian woman poet more than forty years ago." She turned away, but then stopped and stared back at him. "Well, my lawyers or the police will have a field day with what you're saying. Let's hope it's my lawyers, Mr. Laukhin. Pray to God it's them and not the police. But you'll pay for this, one way or another."

She went back into her daughter's room.

Laukhin found a doctor at the nursing station who was able to talk about Audrey. Young enough to be an intern, he went into a long explanation, using medical terms that meant nothing to Laukhin. Listening to him, Laukhin was overwhelmed by the feeling that whatever he did or asked made no difference. He heard the doctor say they were doing all they could, but in cases like Ms. Millay's, with complications from an unexpected hemorrhage, only time would tell. *Only time would tell.* Ominous, hammer-blow words, the secular equivalent of *it's in God's hands now.*

"Please call me if anything happens," Laukhin told the doctor. He asked one of the nurses for a piece of paper and wrote down his name and his home and office phone numbers.

The doctor looked at the paper and said, "Are you family?"

"I'm Ms. Millay's friend. It was in my house, in my bedroom that she got hurt."

"You're not family."

"I love her, doctor. You can't get more family than that."

* * *

At home he drank until his mind was numb. Clogged brain gulleys—Kyril's expression. Kyril would arrive on Lavrushinsky Lane and say, "Let's clog the gulleys," and then produce a bottle of vodka from under his coat.

He called the nursing station at eleven that night and was told that Audrey's condition had not changed.

"What condition is that?" he asked.

"Are you family?"

"Yes."

"Who?"

"Her husband."

"Ms. Millay's mother left instructions to communicate exclusively either with her or with Ms. Millay's father, if he called from overseas."

"You communicated with me already."

"I did?"

"You told me her condition had not changed."

There was silence at the other end of the line.

"I'm her father."

"You're not."

"I'm coming to see her."

"The doctors are with her now—the neurosurgeon and other consulting specialists. Anyway, visiting hours are over."

"What are the specialists doing? Did you say consulting? Consulting each other?"

The nurse hung up on him.

At one in the morning he went out for a walk. He couldn't keep a straight line, and found it difficult to breathe. It was humid, and the late hour had brought little relief from the heat. Yonge Street was dismal and lifeless—only the occasional cab. *At night the city was exhausted, like the breasts of a middle-aged woman.* He was very drunk, no doubt, but Babel would have been proud of that sentence. He should tell it to Ben, ha, the Babel devotee. He'd likely say, mockly reproachful but proud of his memory, "Oh, no, Artyom Pavlovich, this is straight out of... whatever." Well, he wouldn't remember it tomorrow anyway. He cursed, remembering the intern's baffled face when he said *only time would tell*. They were all marionettes, with strings of time pulled by an indifferent puppeteer. Not indifferent—cruel.

Images came to him of Audrey looking distressed, half sentences, words fitting well together. He saw Martha too, Gorgon-like, angry and vengeful, and his first cousin Sasha Cornilov sneering dismissively. It had been a while since he'd had such clear images, unbidden, a very long while, but he felt none of the elation he once had in such moments. To think he had promised Audrey he'd write poems about her, and that it was now... Oh, he was drunk, very drunk, and tomorrow everything would sound false or trite.

He heard the phone ringing as he unlocked the door, but didn't rush to answer it. There was no point—any call at this time would be bad news. He undressed slowly and got into the unmade bed. He told himself that he could still smell Audrey—the smell of a good woman, his good woman for two nights—but he knew he was deluding himself. He heard the phone ring again and, as before, he didn't answer it.

In the end, exhausted, he must have fallen asleep, because he was awakened by the phone again. It was light outside. He looked at his watch—past eight thirty. He avoided his clothes strewn on the floor and went downstairs hoping the ringing would stop.

It was the police, a Detective Albano. He was in his car, close by, and wanted to come in for a talk.

"Now?" Laukhin asked.

"Yes, now."

"It's not a good time."

"It never is."

"Is it about Ms. Millay?"

"Yes."

"She's dead, isn't she?"

A slight pause. "Yes, she is. Didn't the hospital call you?"

"They did."

"She told an odd story to her mother before she died. Odd and confusing. Mrs. Osterhoudt is beside herself." Detective Albano's voice got louder, and Laukhin detected both sarcasm and an accusation in what he said next. "She thinks her daughter was murdered, and that you know who did it."

14

The late November snow was melting as it hit the ground. With only a windbreaker over his T-shirt, Laukhin was cold. Another sign of aging, he thought. It had been damp and cold since he got back to Toronto two days earlier.

He had returned from Australia in a savage mood. He had left in a savage mood too, but had hoped the trip would calm him down. It didn't. In Sidney he got into a fight, after signing books for two hours. He had not had much to eat, but needed a drink more than anything else, and he pushed Bart and the Random House publicist (who didn't need much pushing) into a bar. After a few drinks he lost it. Bart kept pulling at his elbow, saying, "Enough, Art, let's get something to eat." Laukhin, leaning on the counter, waved him off several times, "One last drink, Bart." A man near him, a big man with a beard and thin scarf tied around his neck, turned around and said, "Art and Bart, how cute. Come on, Art, listen to your sweetheart." Laukhin looked around, put his drink down, smiled and nodded at the big man, and then punched him in the gut. It was the smile that made the blow effective—a tip from Efim—but his opponent was big. He dropped his glass on the floor but quickly recovered and hit back, a blow to Laukhin's chest that left him unable to breathe. Somehow the Random House man put himself in front of Laukhin and managed to smooth things over. Bart put cash on the counter to cover their bill and they left. Laukhin threw up on the sidewalk.

For several days after Audrey's death he was too shocked to do anything. Her death had been too sudden, too unexpected, as if a landmine had exploded under her feet while they were holding hands. One day she'd been in his bed, naked and warm in his arms, and then she was dead. It made him wonder if this was why most deaths followed illnesses, to prepare the survivors. Even Detective Albano kept away from him after their first meeting, something he probably regretted when he learned that, despite his warning not to leave Toronto, Laukhin had gone to London for Audrey's funeral.

Audrey's father had taken her body back and her mother had flown with him. The day of the funeral a fine rain followed Laukhin on his way to Covent Garden. As it should be, he thought—clear blue skies would be indecent. The church wasn't large, yet the façade across the market was one grand colonnaded portico. Audrey's parents were there, of course, although he only guessed that the elderly, bent man who walked with difficulty, and sat in the front row was Audrey's father. He guessed too that the younger man who helped him reach his seat and look solicitously after him was Audrey's husband. The woman sitting near Martha, with another man and two children were, likely, Audrey's half-sister and her family. It was a large gathering. He assumed there were other relatives, many friends, former colleagues from some museum or gallery. He was surprised not to see Lezzard there.

Nobody paid any attention to him at the funeral service. Audrey had told no one about him except her mother, and Martha hardly knew him, mainly from the brief encounter they had at the hospital a few hours before Audrey died, the very unpleasant one during which she accused and threatened him. He kept apart anyway, and Martha either didn't see him or couldn't bring herself to talk to him. She seemed devastated, and it surprised Laukhin again. He had thought of her as a reluctant, indifferent mother. A generous one, true, but it was easy to be generous when you had a lot of money. Maybe her daughter's death had done something to Martha. Or, perhaps, Audrey's stories about her were exaggerated. Of course, Martha would go on holding him responsible for what happened to her daughter, and he couldn't blame her.

He sat on one of the back rows. Everybody was very polite—the Brits were polite people—and no one asked him directly what he was doing there. Only one older man, who sat near him and felt like talking while they were waiting for the service to start, asked him about his connection with the deceased. Unable to say he'd been her lover for three days, Laukhin lied he'd been a friend. The older man confessed he was there merely because it was his parish church, and, long retired and with little to do, he attended many services. He said he found funeral services soothing. He looked at Laukhin to see his reaction and then shook his head as if to deny what he'd just said. "I fear death and I come here hoping it will help me face it, small step by small step."

The three brief speeches meant little to him, as they were about an Audrey he had not known. It was the singing that did the damage. Listening to the hymns, the significance of which he knew nothing about, with strange and mostly incomprehensible words, he felt tears in his eyes and then, embarrassingly down his cheeks. Rivers. What he felt were regrets of colossal weight, what might have been, what he lost. He wiped his face under the curious stare of the old parishioner, and mumbled that hymns had that effect on him. He was clearly romanticizing his brief love affair with Audrey. Brief indeed. After all, their involvement began only three days before the accident. Three days. Two nights together, well, one and a half, and also the morning following the first night, the only time in which he had had an inkling of the delightful intimacy of early days, the buds of an *amour partagee*. Undoubtedly he made it all much worse for himself by imagining what his life with Audrey could have been. All rosy-perfect, of course. He even saw children in his delusions.

He left London drained. For days after his return he drank heavily, ate hardly at all, saw no one. He knew he had to bootstrap himself out of that dark despair, but he had neither the strength nor the desire. He thought of his father's long depression after his wife's unexpected death, and recalled Pasternak's worried words to his friend. Laukhin had taken his father upstairs to have dinner with the Pasternaks. "You need to be more miserly with your sorrow, Pavel Nikolayevich," Pasternak had said. Stingy, tight-fisted. We have only so much suffering in us. When we run out of it we croak. We're apportioned a cup, no more. You must save it like a shipwreck survivor rations the fresh water in his ocean-lost life boat." In the kitchen, washing the dishes with Zinaida after a mostly silent dinner, Laukhin had been doubtful Pasternak believed what he preached, but had been grateful for his efforts.

In some way, it was Pasternak's words that slowly towed him out of his despair.

To give himself a sense of purpose, at least for a while, Laukhin focused on publishing the first volume. He wanted to forgo the events surrounding the book's publication, but Bart warned him he couldn't do that, whatever the circumstances. Bart, long-suffering Bart, usually so reasonable and always on his side, had been spitting mad. He shouted down the phone line that Laukhin had a contractual obligation, and he'd sue him himself, never mind the publishers. When Laukhin said he doubted his agent would sue him just as he was ready to cash in on him, Bart said he certainly would because the publicity—and he'd make sure there'd be publicity—would only add to the sales.

As he drank and brooded beside Bart in the long flight to Sydney, it dawned on him that he had nothing from Audrey, nothing to remind him of her, save the few hours he'd been close to her. The few hours they made love and slept close to each other. That was all he had from her for the rest of his life. Would they last, would they always be with him? The permanence of hours. A good title for a poem, but a delusion, because there was no lastingness in a few hours. They'd be with him for a while, her smell, her initial awkwardness (his too), her soft skin on his face, her breasts on his lips, and her sigh as he touched her, her fingers as she clumsily guided him in, her buttocks as she turned away from him afterwards and fitted them against his crotch, and her smell as he tried not to fall asleep and breathed in the mixture of perfume and sweat of her neck. Her beautiful face too, her smile and gentle irony, they'd last for a while too, perhaps a bit longer. And then everything would fade away, and he'd be left with nothing.

* * *

He felt the knife casing in his pocket. That's what the sales clerk that morning had called the flat orange handle enclosing the blade. He'd demonstrated the retractable blade, easily sliding it in and out, and pointed out its ergonomic design. All that enthusiasm for a knife that cost $2.90.

"What do you need it for?" the young man had asked when he said he was looking for a knife.

He'd been tempted to say he needed it for a Russian bastard, an old Russian bastard—a *staryi ublyudok*. "Cardboard," he said.

"Cardboard boxes?"

"In a way."

"A Stanley knife," the young man said. "They are the best for that."

If only he could sleep. At night his heart raced to keep up with his mind. Before flying to Sydney he went to see a cardiologist and complained of heart palpitations. The initial diagnosis was arrhythmia, irregular heartbeat. Had he had such symptoms before? Maybe. If he had, he'd paid no attention to them. Well, the doctor said, very likely that was what he had. They'd have to do tests when he got back.

French, German, and Italian translations were being rushed to press. The Europeans were upset that the final draft of the first volume was not sent to them earlier. They claimed, with some merit, that their readers were much more interested in matters Russian than the parochial Americans. Bart had planned a December tour of Europe for interviews in advance of the spring book launches there, and warned Laukhin that they'd have to return in the spring.

Laukhin attended the Toronto and New York book launches on two consecutive evenings, and then he and Bart caught the last flight from New York. He arrived in London at noon the following day. The book launch was in the evening, and the next morning he flew back to New York for ten days of touring in the US. "Your largest market, don't forget," Bart told him when he grumbled. Then back to Toronto, with more readings and signings in several bookstores. Then the long trip to Sydney, with a stopover in Vancouver on the way back.

It was in Vancouver that it finally clicked and he understood what had happened. How thick he'd been. It was so obvious. Ben had figured it out much earlier, or so it seemed from what he told him at the book launch.

* * *

He had been surprised to see Ben with Jennifer at the launch in Toronto. It was held at the Bakers' large house, and he felt miserable during the event, as it was there that he first met Audrey. There were speeches by Bart and his Toronto publisher. Laukhin said a few words too, and then signed books for more than an hour. He took several breaks—quick drinks that his students had ready for him. Helen, a few weeks after giving birth, particularly enjoyed the event. It was her first outing, she confessed, in a long while. Pointing to her midriff, she said, "It's such a joy to wear these clothes again. Last weekend I burned all my maternity outfits and danced around the fire." Looking at Jennifer and Ben, she added, "You two look so lovely together."

Ben had not seemed very happy to Laukhin. He guessed Ben's state of mind and whispered to him, "Cheer up, Ben. Grin, show some teeth. You're better off without Marion. Jennifer looks stunning."

At the door, Laukhin's students were given copies of both the Canadian and American editions. The books had the same jacket, and the British and Australian editions used it too. To Laukhin's disappointment, copies of the Russian edition had not yet arrived from the German publisher. The Canadian books had come too late for him to sign any, but in the American ones Laukhin had written, over the leaping borzoi, a few words to each of his students. Their names were also mentioned in acknowledgements, where he credited Ben Paskow as his "main collaborator in this first volume because of his interest in the Soviet Russian literature of the thirties."

Ben thanked him for the books and for the kind words in the acknowledgements.

"Nothing to thank me for. You deserve it."

"I don't know. I let you down. The Tsvetayeva bundle was not published because of me."

"It doesn't matter, Ben. The staffers at the *New Yorker* lost interest. They suffer from ADD. Bart said they may still publish it ahead of the second volume. Anyway, I'm told there's enormous interest in this one. And I hear that there are good early reviews coming out."

"I should have had it all typed in much earlier."

"We all have our ups and downs."

"Maybe it would not have happened."

"What are you talking about? What would not have happened?"

"You know … Audrey's death."

"Now, that's silly. Jennifer looks splendid."

Ben nodded. "Your friend is not here," he said. "At least I've not seen him."

"Who?"

"Jean Lezzard."

"Oh. I hadn't noticed."

"It's curious. He's been so keen to read the journal. And now, when he can finally get his hand on the first volume, he doesn't show up."

"Maybe he's already bought the book and left."

"Wouldn't he have wanted it signed?"

"He's not a fool. And he doesn't have the patience to line up. Anyway, he can get it in a bookstore."

Ben seemed unconvinced. Colson Emslie joined them and told Laukhin he loved the dust jacket. Laukhin was pleased with it too. It showed something that looked like a roulette wheel, or a sector of it, with pictures of people instead of numbers, old black and white photos: Babel, Pasternak, Tsvetayeva, Mandelstam, Mayakovsky, Fadeev, Alexey Tolstoy, Bulgakov, Sholokhov, Pavel Laukhin. Victims, survivors, bootlickers. Solzhenitsyn too, the only one still alive. The roulette ball was slightly elongated and pointed at one end, like a bullet. In the centre was a photograph of Iosif Vissarionovich at his most avuncular. All of this on a faded background of Moscow's Kremlin, massive, mysterious, fearsome.

The Emslies were flying with him and Bart to New York. "I'll see a few friends and colleagues at the book launch, and we'll stay for a couple of days afterwards," Colson explained. Near them, Kate and Jennifer were in animated discussion. Later, after Kate joined them, Laukhin asked what it had been about.

"Oh, nothing, women talk. We'll be whisked from La Guardia directly to the reception. I won't have time to change and I worry about how my dress will hold up."

"Ah."

"Jen suggested I take off the dress once aboard."

"That's a thought, fly naked."

"Not fully naked, Art. I have a few little nothings underneath." Kate laughed and added, "I asked Jen if there was something wrong with Ben. He seemed so miserable."

"What did she say?"

"Nothing wrong."

* * *

Mrs. Grunwald was leaving—Lezzard should be alone now. Laukhin dropped his cigarette butt on the ground, walked across the street, and climbed the stairs. It looked as if Lezzard was preparing to call it a day too because his coat was lying on his desk. He seemed neither surprised nor happy to see Laukhin. There were a few awkward minutes during which they remarked on the snow and the cold weather that had settled on the city. Lezzard looked at his watch.

Laukhin said, "I didn't see you in London."

"London?"

"At Audrey's funeral."

"No…"

"Too busy?"

"It was a busy summer. And Josiane had still not fully recovered."

"Have you kept in touch with her mother?"

Lezzard hesitated. "Haven't heard from her since, you know…"

Laukhin looked around. He was surprised to see the large Chemakoff oil back on the wall of the smaller room. Hadn't Lezzard told Audrey he had sold it to an old client from New York? He walked over to it, and there they were—the welder, the zek, the SS officer, the miner, the knife-grinder. An unexpected gift. He walked slowly around the small room, clearly annoying Lezzard. There was another Chemakoff oil, undoubtedly painted in Paris fairly late, plus several prints that had been there before. The ink and watercolour that he had liked so much was gone, and he remarked on it.

Lezzard looked surprised. "Audrey bought it."

"Audrey? I wanted to buy it."

"You did? That's odd. She said it was a goodbye present for you."

He felt his heart rate pick up. The bastard was mocking him. He pointed to the large painting, and said, "I've seen this Chemakoff oil before, haven't I?"

Lezzard shrugged.

"Audrey said you'd sold it to an old client from New York."

"He returned it," Lezzard said.

"Didn't like it?"

"It doesn't matter. They can return it within a couple of months. It probably clashed with his furniture."

"It's a remarkable painting. An old Chemakoff from his Moscow days. I heard a couple of Russians carry on about it—here, in this room, as a matter of fact—how surprised they were to see it here given that Chemakoff had left that painting in Russia. They can't be easy to get, these old ones from his Moscow days."

"No, they are not easy to get."

"How do you get them, Jean?"

Lezzard looked sharply at him. "What the hell do you mean?"

"Do you know Mr. Gratch, Jean? Yakov Gratch. Rather, *did* you know him, because he's dead now."

Lezzard shook his head impatiently. "What exactly brings you here, professor?"

"Yes, you knew him. Audrey told me you had a few chats with him this summer. More arguments, than chats, according to her. Mr. Gratch said—I heard him myself, right here—that this painting you have on your wall was confiscated by the police in Chemakoff's apartment in Moscow many years ago. He knew that because he'd been an accidental witness to the KGB raid. So the question is, Jean, how did *you* get it?"

Lezzard took his time, but eventually said, "From another dealer, a connection I have in France."

"How did he get it?"

"I didn't ask. I'm not a curious person." He sneered, "You shouldn't be either."

"Mr. Gratch's death was rather convenient, wasn't it?"

"It's your story, professor. The KGB raid and the seizure of Chemakoff's paintings—who'd believe it? Early Chemakoffs have been in the market for many years."

"Mr. Gratch was killed, Jean. Murdered."

"Was he?"

"You didn't know?"

"I didn't."

"It was in all the newspapers."

"I must have forgotten. I have many things on my mind."

"Do you know when he was killed?"

"No idea."

"A few days before Audrey died."

Lezzard raised his arms. "I'm terribly sorry about Audrey, professor, but I'm not following you. Anyway, I'm closing the shop for tonight."

The sight of the old Chemakoff had cheered up Laukhin. "Do you have anything to drink?" he asked.

"No. Not at this time. Another time."

He took a pack of cigarettes out of his pocket, and a lighter.

"I thought you'd quit," Lezzard said.

He lit a cigarette. "I've had a few difficult months."

"You can't smoke in here," Lezzard said. "I can't stand the smell."

"You're leaving aren't you? It'll be gone by tomorrow. Have a drink with me, Jean."

"It's late, I'm tired," Lezzard said. He pointed to a coffee mug lying on the smaller desk. "There, use that."

"Come on, you've never been too tired for a drink."

"I am now."

Arrogant bastard. They watched each other in silence. After a while, Lezzard asked, "When is that part about the Russian woman poet—Tsvetayeva?—when is it coming out? You know, the one in that New York magazine? Or was it the *Globe*. Both?"

"It's not coming out."

"Oh?"

"It's been cancelled."

"Cancelled? Just like that?"

Laukhin shrugged. "It wasn't meant to be. The gods. The gods and a countryman of yours."

"A Frenchman?"

Clearly Lezzard was mocking him. "A Russian. Well, a Soviet citizen. He stole it from me, Jean. He stole the only copy in English I had. That's why nothing was published in the *New Yorker*. I had to redo it, and couldn't make the deadline."

"What do you mean, stole it?"

Laukhin wondered how much Lezzard knew of what had exactly happened that night. He told him, briefly, but he didn't mention Cornilov by name.

Lezzard played the stunned listener with aplomb. "You mean, it wasn't an accident?" he asked at the end.

"It wasn't."

"Did you tell the police?"

"Eventually."

"Terrible. It's terrible what happened. I liked Audrey very much."

He probably did—so what?

Lezzard looked again at his watch and said, "Well, you can publish it later."

"Maybe. Something was very odd, Jean, about that whole thing. I mean, how did they know?"

"Know what?"

"That they'd find the excerpts about Tsvetayeva in my house."

"You're sure that's what they were after? Sounds silly—a few sheets of paper."

"Oh, that was what they were after, no doubt about it. They didn't take anything else. You don't know how they knew, do you?"

"What? How would I?"

"Think about it. Think who else knew."

"Goodbye, professor. Drop in some other time. Earlier."

He had not thought of Lezzard as being involved at all. It still staggered him that he had been blind for so long. How could he not realize that Lezzard was at the centre of it all? Lezzard had been there that morning, at the gallery, nursing a hangover and unable to sleep. And he and Audrey had stumbled on him after their first night together, and they'd talked as if they've just been absolved from a vow of silence. They told him everything he needed to know.

God, it took him a long time. How could he not have seen what had been behind Lezzard's eagerness to read the manuscript or get a copy of it ahead of everybody else? It seemed so obvious to him now. How could he not think of Lezzard? It was Ben's words at the book launch that began the slow process of putting two and two together.

He dropped his cigarette butt in the coffee mug. "I didn't see you at the launch," he said.

"What? What launch?"

"The book launch, for the first volume. I looked forward to seeing you there. I made sure you got an invitation."

"Oh. I truly did want to go, but I had to be somewhere else, more pressing."

"I wanted to talk to you about the letters. Did you find more of them? I mean the letters of interest to us academics. Did you have another look at your mother's correspondence?"

"No... I told you, I've been very busy. Anyway, I doubt I'll find anything else." He looked at his watch again, and tapped it. "I have to go, Art. Go back to your poems. Go back to Babel's letters."

Where should he hit him? "I gave them to an expert," he said.

"An expert? What for?"

"To check the handwriting, the age of the paper. It's standard procedure. It took him a long time to get back to me because he sent them to a colleague in France for some sort of crosschecking—they know better there, it seems—and the letters got lost for a while. There was a bit of controversy too—there always is with experts. And when I pressed him for the results he pretended he hadn't known I was in a hurry."

Lezzard made a dismissive gesture with his hands.

"The thing is, Jean, the expert is not happy. He's still doing some tests, but he has reason to believe the letters are not genuine."

Lezzard sneered. "He's no expert."

"He's an expert all right. And he worked with other experts too. A team of experts—these were letters from Isaak Babel, after all. Interesting things came out, Jean. The paper on which the letters were written is, indeed, old, but not old enough. Mid to late fifties at the earliest. Definitely not the thirties or earlier. Yes, a bit of a problem there. Some twenty-five or thirty years difference."

"They don't know about Russian paper."

"Oh, they do. They know about all kinds of paper, Russian and otherwise. It shouldn't be Russian paper, though, should it? Babel wrote those letters while in Paris, didn't he?"

"Look, I really must go."

"What do you think of the first volume?"

It took Lezzard a while to follow him. "I haven't had time to read it yet."

"But you read half of it, didn't you? I gave you the first half of it, didn't I?"

"Yes. I read that."

"And?"

"I liked it."

"Did you buy the first volume?"

"Sorry? Yes, I did buy it. Too busy, you know. But I'll read it—finish it."

"You seemed so keen once."

"I have to go, I'm already late."

"I don't get it, Jean. You once promised my student Ben Paskow money, good money, for a copy of the draft. And now you can't be bothered to open the book?"

Lezzard stared at him and then said, "I've got to go. I'm meeting somebody."

"How long have you known him, Jean? How long have you known Cornilov?"

"Who?"

"Cornilov. Was he—is he—in this art-racket?"

"In where? What racket?"

"Selling confiscated art, Jean. Was Cornilov in on it, or did others let him know about you? Just curious, not that it matters. Something else too, also sheer curiosity: was he tasked to get rid of Mr. Gratch as a condition for his trip here? Or was that simply a favour Cornilov did in answer to an idle aside like, 'Since you are already there, Alexandr Petrovich, you might as well...' Oh, it makes no difference."

"I don't know what you are talking about. I don't know any Cornilov."

"He's the one who killed Audrey, Jean. With your help. He's my first cousin—did you know that? He didn't tell you?"

"All right, enough. I'm out of time, here. Go piss somewhere else."

That's when he did it. He slugged Lezzard as he reached to pick up his coat. Sucker-punched him. The punch didn't land well, but he felt good about it, as good as he felt when he thumped the big man in the Sydney pub. The effect was different, though, because Lezzard crumpled to the floor. His glasses, by a miracle unbroken, landed near his head. A trickle of blood gathered on Lezzard's lower lip. He bent down and made sure Lezzard was breathing. Did the miracle extend to Lezzard himelf—was he unbroken like his glasses? What if he didn't recover? Well, fuck him.

He stood there, shaking a bit, looking at Lezzard. The old man moaned and moved a bit. His eyes focused on Laukhin, and he asked, "What happened?"

Laukhin lifted him up and dragged him to the chair nearby. "Anything broken?"

Lezzard said nothing for a while, touching and massaging the left side of his face and mouth. There was more blood on his swollen lips now. He whispered, "Fuck you." He touched his mouth and looked astonished at the red spots on the cuff of his shirt. "Fuck you," he said again. He was breathing with difficulty. "Get out or I'll kill you." He could hardly keep his head straight as he spoke.

Laukhin took the knife out of his pocket and slid the blade out. Good old Stanley, whoever he'd been. He was delighted by sound the knife made. It attracted Lezzard's attention. Laukhin approached the large Chemakoff oil painting and without hurrying, slashed it, once in one diagonal, and then again in the other. The second diagonal took more effort. He turned to Lezzard. He was watching Laukhin with horror, his mouth opening and closing, unable to make a sound. Laukhin bent over him, and with the knife close to Lezzard's face, whispered, "I should have used this on you. But I'm a coward."

He heard Lezzard rasp, "You're a dead man. You're a dead man walking. You'll end up like Gratch. You have no idea who..."

Slowly, without hurrying, Laukhin took the Babel letters out of one pocket and his lighter from another, and lit the letters, watching them burn for a while in his hand, and then dropping them on the floor. For a few seconds, he had the insane idea of setting the place on fire.

How childish, how imbecilic. That was all he could come up with— slash an oil painting. It was pitiful, contemptible.

He left the gallery, and walked down the stairs gingerly. He took a few more steps and then stopped to look up and down the street. Heads down, a couple was hurrying toward Yorkville Avenue. It was windier now and colder, and the snow was beginning to stick together in small white islands. No one took notice of anything or anybody under the wet November snow.

* * *

There was a flat parcel leaning against the front door when he got home. He took it inside and placed it on one of the boxes. The living room was all islands of boxes, some piled up like cardboard stalagmites. He'd begun packing before his trip to Australia because his free housing was coming to an end. Efim would be wrecking the house early in the new year, and Laukhin had already looked at a couple of apartments near the university. They weren't large, but he'd see. The sales of the first volume had significantly picked up, and he might be able to afford a bigger apartment, even buy a house, although buying an apartment might suit him better. A condo, as they said here. No lawn to mow.

His boots had left wet traces on the wooden floor. There was neither an address nor a sender's name on the parcel, but a white envelope was clumsily attached to it. He carried the envelope into the kitchen, dropped it on the small round table, poured himself a drink, sat down, and opened the envelope. He read the letter, emptied his glass, poured himself another drink, and picked up the letter again. He sat there, drinking and re-reading the letter. After a while he began skipping the first half and read only the final paragraphs.

> *It took me a long time to convince myself to send this to you, but she was my daughter, and I must do as she wished. She told me about it the last time I talked to her, at the hospital, the evening you also came to see her and were unable or unwilling to explain to me what had happened to Audrey in your own house. She said that in our apartment on Prince Arthur there was a small Chemakoff, an ink and watercolour that you very much liked. She had bought it from Jean Lezzard as a gift for you. She knew that things were going from bad to worse for her, and wanted me to send it or give it to you, from her, in case she couldn't do it herself.*
>
> *I will always hold you responsible for her death, but I cannot not do it.*

> *Martha Osterhoudt*

He poured himself another drink and began to unwrap the parcel, the mannequin birds.

List of Russian Characters

The names of real people appear in italics.

Akhmatova, Anna Andreevna **(1889-1966):** Soviet/Russian poet.

Aksakov, Andrey: Soviet/Russian writer living in the West. Friend of Art Laukhin from Moscow.

Apelbaum, Efim: Friend of Art Laukhin in Toronto. High school colleague of Art Laukhin in Moscow.

Ardov, Viktor Efimovich **(1990-76):** Soviet/Russian writer. Friend of Akhmatova and Pasternak and many other writers and poets.

Arkhip: Steward on riverboat *Kirov*.

Babel, Isaak Emmanuilovich **(1894-1940):** Soviet/Russian writer. Shot in 1940.

Bedrosyan, Anastas Koryunovich: Official in the Writers' Union.

Brodelshchikova, Anastasia Ivanovna: Landlady to Marina Tsvetaeva and her son, Georgy, in Yelabuga in 1941.

Brodelshchikov, Mikhail Ivanovich: Husband of Anastasia Ivanovna.

Chemakoff: Soviet painter.

Chukovskaya, Lydia (1907-1996): Soviet/Russian writer and poet.

Cornilov, Alexander (Sasha): Art Laukhin's first cousin, on his mother's side.

Efron, Sergey Yakovlevich, 1893-1941: Tsvetayeva's husband, also called *Seryozha*. Fought with the White Army, then left for the West. Became a spy for the NKVD while an émigré in Paris. Fled back to Russia in 1937, where he was shot in 1941. Went by the last name Andreyev after returning to Russia.

Efron, Georgy **(1925-43):** Tsvetayeva's and Sergy Efron's son. After his mother's death he volunteered for the front in the Great Patriotic War (1941-45). Died from battle injuries in 1943.

Efron, Alya (Ariadna Sergeevna) **(1912-75):** Tsvetayeva's and Sergey Efron's daughter. Lived in exile in Paris between 1922-37. Imprisoned in labour camps and exile between 1939-55.

Fadeyev, Alexander **(1901-56):** Soviet writer. General Secretary of the Soviet Writers' Union 1938-44 and 1946-54.

Gurevich, Mulya **(1904-52):** Alya Efron's lover. Shot in 1952.

Ivinskaya, Olga **(1912-95):** Pasternak's mistress. Imprisoned in labour camps 1949-53 and prison 1960-64.

Klepinin, Nikolai Andreevich **(1899-1941):** Russian intellectual. Fought in the White Army then moved to the West. Became a spy for the NKVD and returned to Russia in 1937. Shot in 1941.

Klepinina, Antonina (Nina) Nikolaevna **(1894-1941):** Klepinin's wife. Shot in 1941.

Korotkov: Captain of the riverboat *Kirov*.

Korotkova, Marietta Alexeyevna: Korotkov's wife.

Klyuchev, Kolya: Pavel Laukhin's cousin.

Laukhin, Art (Artyom Pavlovich): Soviet/Russian poet living in Toronto. Art, to his friends in North America. Tyomka, to his parents and as a child. Tyoma to his Russian friends.

Laukhin, Larissa: Art Laukhin's sister.

Laukhin, Pavel Nikolayevich: Art Laukhin's father. Writer of espionage novels and of the journal. Pasha or Pashenka to his wife.

Laukhin, Tatyana: Art Laukhin's former wife. Also called Tanya.

Laukhin, Varya (Varvara Prokofievna): Pavel Laukhin's wife. Varya to her husband.

Lezzard, Jean: Art dealer in Toronto. His parents were Russian refugees after the revolution, settled in Paris.

Lyutov, Maxim: Anna Lyutova's father and Natalya's first husband.

Lyutova, Natalya: Cornilov's second wife.

Lyutova, Anna: Natalya Lyutova's daughter and Cornilov's step-daughter.

Malgunov, Fedya: Soviet/Russian writer who had defected to the USA in the sixties. Former friend of Art Laukhin. Dead in the early eighties.

Markov, Georgy **(1911-91):** Soviet writer. First Secretary of the Soviet Writer's Union 1977-86.

Pasternak, Boris Leonidovich **(1890-1960):** Soviet poet, novelist, and literary translator.

Pasternak, Zinaida Nikolaevna: Pasternak's second wife.

Pavliuk: Friend of Pavel Laukhin.

Shnaideman: Friend of Pavel Laukhin.

Solzhenitsyn **(1918-2008):** Soviet/Russian writer. Lived in USA between 1974-94.

Tsvetayeva, Marina Ivanovna: Russian poet (1892-1941). Went into exile in 1922 and returned to the Soviet Union in 1939.

Tvardovsky, Aleksandr Trifonovich: Soviet/Russian poet (1910-1971). Chief editor of *Novy Mir* literary magazine from 1950 to 1954 and 1958 to 1970.

Tsiriteli, Davit: Soviet/Georgian writer. Friend of Art Laukhin. Lives in the Soviet Union.

Vronkh, Kyril Innokentyevich: Friend of Art Laukhin. Lives in the Soviet Union.

Volkova, Yevgenya: Acquaintance and love interest of Pavel Laukhin.

Yevtushenko, Yevgeny (b. 1933): Soviet/Russian poet.

Yefremov, Ivan (1908-72): Soviet/Russian writer of popular science fiction and historical novels.

Zhelenin, Victor Efremovich: Former Soviet literary critic, now living in Paris and publisher of émigré magazine *Sintesy*.

Zhelenin, Miriam Emmanuilovna: Wife of Victor Zhelenin.

Zladsky, Yakov: Soviet/Russian poet living in the USA.

Glossary of Russian Words

bolshie kity: big whales. Russian equivalent of "fat cats" or "big fish"

chastushka: doggerel

chekist: Name generally used for anybody working for the secret police. The Cheka was a secret political police force established in 1917 to combat counter-revolutionaries. In 1922, it became a branch of the NKVD (see below).

Glavlit: Name (abbreviated) of the official state censorship. From Glavnoe Upravlenie po Delam Literatury i Izdatelstv, the Main Directorate for Literary and Publishing Affairs

gostinaya: living room

govnyuk: shithead

literaturnye sanovniki: literary dignitaries (see also sanovnik, below)

mesta polzovaniia: place of use (literally), toilet

Militsya: Short for the Workers' and Peasants' Militsiya. The public police force.

NKVD: The People's Commissariat for Internal Affairs, the secret police force during the Soviet era. Had many other different names/abbreviations among which GPU, OGPU and KGB.

poklonitsa: groupie

razvedchik: intelligence agent, spy

sanovnik: dignitary

stolovaya: dinning room

vozhd: leader. Stalin was often referred to as the vozhd

vreditelstvo: wrecking

zakliuchonnyi: inmate

zakuski: Russian hors d'ouevres or canapés

zek: A prisoner, especially an inmate of a forced-labour camp. An abbreviation of zakliuchonnyi (see above).

Robert Carr was born in Bucharest, Romania and fled from the Communist regime at the age of twenty-four. He moved from France to Israel and then settled in Canada. After working as an engineer in the aerospace industry for many years, Carr transitioned to being a full time writer. His first novel, *Continuums* was published by Mosaic Press in 2008.